Hill Wickham

Journals and Correspondence of Thomas Sedgewick Whalley

Vol. I

SALZWASSER VERLAG

Hill Wickham

Journals and Correspondence of Thomas Sedgewick Whalley

Vol. I

Reprint of the original, first published in 1863.

1st Edition 2022 | ISBN: 978-3-37500-097-4

Verlag (Publisher): Salzwasser Verlag GmbH, Zeilweg 44, 60439 Frankfurt, Deutschland
Vertretungsberechtigt (Authorized to represent): E. Roepke, Zeilweg 44, 60439 Frankfurt, Deutschland
Druck (Print): Books on Demand GmbH, In de Tarpen 42, 22848 Norderstedt, Deutschland

JOURNALS

AND CORRESPONDENCE

OF

THOMAS SEDGEWICK WHALLEY, D.D.

OF MENDIP LODGE, SOMERSET

EDITED, WITH A MEMOIR AND ILLUSTRATIVE NOTES, BY THE

REV. HILL WICKHAM, M.A.

RECTOR OF HORSINGTON

'Tibi gratulor: mihi gaudeo: te amo: tua tueor. A te amari, et quid agas, quidque agatur, certior fieri volo' – CICERO, *Epist. ad Basilum*

IN TWO VOLUMES

VOL. I.

LONDON

1863

PREFACE.

French literature was formerly considered rich in memoir and poor in history, whilst England, possessing her historians, had few annals. Whether posterity will judge that Messrs. Thierry, Guizot, Thiers, &c., on the one side, and the numerous recent British biographies on the other, have fully supplied these defects, remains to be proved. Certainly the popularity of each class of writings is manifestly on the increase on either side of the Channel.

The events in the history of the subject of the present Memoir, were not so marked from the usual scenes on the stage of life,

> Secretum iter, et fallentis semita vitæ,

as to call for a biography, and the silence which has continued for so many years would have remained unbroken, but for the contemporary letters of some persons of note, which he left behind him. The Editor hopes that interest will be found in these, and they appear to call for some mention of the individual to whom they were addressed. The publication of the diaries, representing, in foreign travel, incidents so different from what are at present found, and written in so natural and lively a style, requires no apology.

Our sentimental neighbours in France and Germany are fond of saying, that we apathetic English, though possessed of strong feelings, and remarkable for the fidelity of our conjugal vows, have no power of forming affectionate and lasting friendships. Attached and true as husbands, kind and considerate as parents, we are incapable, they say, of that ardent regard of a friend 'which sticketh closer than a brother.' If such a defect be a national characteristic, the subject of this Memoir forms a memorable exception. In the correspondence which this work presents to the public, we find acquaintance, commenced at a period of life when the judgment was matured, ripening into true regard with increasing years, and terminating only (and in some cases after a very lengthened period) in that bourn of earthly existence where all human affections must cease.

HORSINGTON:
February 10, 1863.

MEMOIRS,

JOURNALS, AND CORRESPONDENCE

OF

DR. WHALLEY.

MEMOIR.

THE REV. THOMAS SEDGWICK WHALLEY, D.D., was born in Cambridge in the year 1746. He was the third son of the Rev. John Whalley, Master of St. Peter's College, in that University, who succeeded Dr. Bentley, as Regius Professor of Divinity, in 1742, and was one of the King's Chaplains in Ordinary. The family claimed to be descended from Wyamarus Whalley, the companion of the Norman Conqueror, and his standard-bearer at the battle of Hastings. From this stock were derived the two Whalleys, the Major-General and Judge Advocate, conspicuous in the civil wars, and first cousins to the 'Protector.' But the pedigree of Dr. John Whalley, as enrolled in the Heralds' College, is only traced back through four generations to John Whalley, who was presented to the rectory of Cosgrave, county of Northampton, in the year 1601. The master of 'Peter-house' died suddenly, in the college garden,* when Dr.

* He was a man of much ability and learning, but singularly absent; in illustration of which peculiarity the following anecdotes are preserved:—He was advised to take horse exercise, and was met on a hot day toiling up a hill

Whalley was only two years old, after which event his widow (the only child of the Rev. Francis Squire, Canon and Chancellor of Wells) removed her young family of seven children to that city. It was a serious charge for a widowed mother to bring up such a family; but Mrs. Whalley was endowed with a superior and cultivated understanding, which enabled her to perform her task well, and to introduce her children into society with advantages which tended to secure their subsequent prosperity. They were favoured by nature with many personal attractions. The sons were tall and handsome, and all the daughters were beautiful—one pre-eminently so. For her eldest son John, a young man of great promise, she procured a commission in the regiment of Welsh Fusiliers; but he died young, in his homeward passage from India. Her second son, Francis, settled at Winscombe Court, on a leasehold property which he purchased of the Chapter of Wells, and where she died in the year 1803, at the advanced age of ninety-six years. Francis Whalley was long honourably known in Somersetshire as colonel of the 2nd Militia in that county, and commissioner under several Acts of Parliament for enclosing the common lands. The youngest son was Richard Whalley, of whom a memoir has been written by the present Mr. Harford, of Blaise Castle, and who was so much admired by Mrs. Hannah More, that she used to say in reference to him, 'she had known many persons who appeared to live *near* heaven, but only Mr. Whalley who seemed to live *in* heaven.'

near Cambridge, trailing a horse's bridle behind him. On being accosted, he said that, being tired of riding, he had dismounted, and he was quite unconscious that his horse had slipped his bridle and was gone. On another occasion, when Dr. Warburton was visiting him, a violent thunderstorm came on as they were seated at table after dinner, engrossed in a theological argument. Mrs. Whalley entered the room to ascertain whether the casement window, which opened to the ground, was closed, and found the room completely flooded, and the two Rev. Doctors of Divinity unconsciously up to their ankles in water.

Dr. Whalley was probably sent as a boy to the Charterhouse, where his brother Richard was educated, and he afterwards graduated at the University of Cambridge. The scholarship which he there acquired, he retained to his latest days; and it was his custom every morning, to the time of his death, to read a portion of Scripture either in the Septuagint version or in the Greek Testament, and a part of the Book of Common Prayer in the old Greek edition. He was well acquainted with both the French and Italian languages, speaking and writing them with great fluency and correctness of idiom, but pronouncing the former with a strong English accent. He maintained a regular correspondence in French with several foreign friends for nearly half a century, which enabled him to keep up his familiarity with that language. A few months before his death he passed an evening with his old friends the Count and Countess de Lagondie, at Le Mans, and the Count afterwards expressed his surprise at the perfect facility and idiomatic propriety with which Dr. Whalley expressed himself in French. When he took holy orders, his father's memory was still cherished by several men of eminence and position, and among them by the Bishop of Ely, who shortly afterwards presented him to the rectory of Hagworthingham, in Lincolnshire, with this singular proviso, that he was not to reside on it, as the air of the fens was fatal to any but a native. He continued to hold this preferment for more than half a century, performing its duties by a curate. Two or three years before his death, wishing to confer some lasting benefit on the parish, he erected, at his own expense, a new and commodious parsonage house. Shortly after he obtained this preferment, Mr. Whalley married, January 1774, Elizabeth, the widow of John Sherwood, and only child of John Jones, Esq., of Langford, a gentleman of ancient Welsh extraction. This union was one of great happiness, and continued for nearly thirty years. The expression of his attachment, in some verses presented to his wife on the first anniversary of their wedding-day, is given in the sequel. By this marriage he became possessed of a considerable fortune, and the estate of Langford Court, near Wrington, in Somersetshire, where he resided for many years, exercising large hospitality. One party was long remembered by all present. A company of neighbours came to dinner on a winter's evening in 1776, and during their stay, which in those days was protracted far beyond the limits of modern fashion, the snow fell so fast, that when the carriages were ordered, it was impossible to leave, and some of the more distant neighbours were detained, not unwilling prisoners, for several days. For animal cheer, the sheepfold, close at hand, supplied good mutton in abundance; and the cellar, famous since the days of an old Somersetshire toast, 'A bumper, Squire Jones,' was well calculated to keep the blood in active circulation. To prevent ennui a play was written and performed, and various pieces of poetry composed and recited. One poem, descriptive of the company, will be found in the sequel.

Within a year or two of his marriage, Mr. Whalley purchased the centre house in the Crescent at Bath. This elegant structure, which was then just completed, has for more than eighty years maintained its pre-eminence in beauty and fashion, in spite of the great additions which have since been made to the city. Bath was then in the zenith of its popularity. Royalty visited it for the sake of its medicinal waters; statesmen, forgetting the Roman adage, 'Post equitem sedet atra cura,' endeavoured to find an escape from the toils of office in its mild climate; and Mrs. Siddons collected the admirers of the drama in overflowing numbers to its theatre. Though no longer subject to the tomfooleries of Beau Nash, it was not raised in delicacy of feeling above the common taste of society, which still read Fielding's novels, as evidenced by the great popularity of Anstey's New Bath Guide. One of the leading fashionables of the day was Lady Miller, who lived at Bath Easton, and had a reception every Thursday, at which, during a certain season of the year, there was a contest for poetical superiority. A vase stood in the garden, into which original poetical compositions were deposited; these were drawn out and read aloud, and a prize awarded to the piece which was adjudged the best. Miss Burney, with her usual conceit, so opposed to the deferential manner of Her Majesty's tirewoman,* thus describes Lady Miller in the year 1780: 'She is a round, plump, coarse-looking dame of about forty, and while all her aim is to appear an elegant woman of fashion, all her success is to appear an ordinary woman in very common life, with fine clothes on. Her manners are bustling, her air is mock-important, and her manners very inelegant.'

The portrait Miss Burney draws of Dr. Whalley in the same year, is but little more favourable in reference to the morale, though she cannot deny some tribute of praise to the physique. Among the company assembled at Mrs. Lambert's,† she mentions Mr. Whalley as 'a young man who has a house on the Crescent, and is one of the best supporters of Lady Miller's vase at Bath Easton. He is immensely tall, thin and handsome, but affected; delicate and sentimentally pathetic; and his conversation about his own "feelings," about amiable motives, and about the wind, which at the Crescent, he said, in a tone of dying horror, "blew in a manner really frightful," diverted me the whole evening.'

Some of these Bath Easton prize poems by Dr. Whalley are given, and, whatever opinion may be formed of their

* See notes by Lady Llanover in last volume of Mrs. Delany's Letters.

† Mrs. Lambert was the widow of General Lambert, and sister of Sir Philip Jennings.

poetical merit, it must be allowed that they are written in much better taste than many of the pieces in the Bath Guide.

The year of 1778 brought a heavy bereavement to Mr. Whalley, in the death of his favourite sister, Mrs. Sage, whose memory he continued to cherish, with fond affection, to the extreme period of his own existence, half a century later. She was possessed of remarkable personal attractions, a sweet and affectionate disposition, and a cultivated understanding. The painting from which the engraving is taken, as Dr. Whalley often repeated, was very far from doing her justice, though it certainly represents a very lovely woman. She was married, in 1768, to Isaac Sage, Esq., who had been Paymaster-General to Lord Clive's army, and was afterwards Governor of Patna. In 1774 he purchased a house in Dorsetshire, built by Sir James Thornhill, and called by his name, finely situated in the centre of a handsome domain. But as Mr. Sage had scarcely arrived at middle age, and held a valuable appointment in India, he returned again to that country, leaving his wife and one daughter at home. As she was ardently attached to her husband, she could not bear the separation; and, in January 1776, embarked at Portsmouth to join him. This step was very imprudent in a woman of her delicate constitution, and only ended in disappointment, for her health soon gave way, and Mr. Sage was obliged to relinquish his honourable and lucrative post, and bring her home to expire, in Bath, at the early age of thirty-three. Though he survived her forty years, he never married again. Mr. Whalley's fondness for his sister was transferred, after her death, to her only surviving child, and was, through much disappointment, continued to her, till she finally closed his eyes at La Flèche.

His residence in Bath brought him the acquaintance of Mrs. Siddons and Mrs. Thrale-Piozzi. The former was then acquiring that self-command on the stage, and developing those dramatic powers, which were soon to recall her to the metropolis, and cause her to rank as the greatest mistress of the Tragic Muse that history has recorded. She was married to Mr. Siddons at eighteen years of age; and in December 1775, when she was only twenty, she was introduced by Garrick, in the character of Portia, to a London audience, but did not succeed. Upon this failure, she tried the Bath stage, where her theatrical talents soon attracted overflowing houses; whilst the strict propriety of her conduct, and her amiable disposition, conciliated general esteem. It was, therefore, with no small surprise that the inhabitants heard, at the close of 1781, that it was her intention to leave them, and to return again to the larger field from which she had once retired. She promised to satisfy her friends and admirers, on the occasion of her public farewell, as to the motives which induced her to take this step. 'Her reasons,' she said, 'were three,' which she should not reveal till that night. Dr. Whalley was in the secret; but was not the less charmed when she led forward on the stage her three children, most becomingly dressed, and repeated:—

> These are the moles that heave me from your side,
> Where I was rooted, where I could have died;
> Perhaps your hearts, when years have glided by,
> And past emotions wake a feeling sigh,
> May think on *her* whose lips have poured so long
> The charmèd sorrows of your Shakespeare's song.
> On her who, parting to return no more,
> Is now the mourner she but seemed before;
> Herself subdu'd resigns the melting spell,
> And breathes, with swelling heart, her long, her last farewell!

The following letters show what complete success attended her return to London. They also allude to the persecution she endured, which arose from an outcry, raised principally by envious persons, that she was parsimonious, and wanting in generosity. In reference to the last charge, her letter of

December 24, 1802, from Dublin, will refute it; for though the object is not mentioned, it was evidently one of charity, for which, at Dr. Whalley's instance, she promises the sum of 80*l.* As to her parsimony, she appears to have increased her style of living as the means of her expenditure increased. The *château en Espagne* which she originally built was certainly of no great magnificence for her talents to aspire after—viz. a cottage at Langford, near her dear friends, Dr. and Mrs. Whalley, and 10,000*l.* Doubtless the old Roman proverb, 'Crescit amor nummi,' &c., was felt by her when she could realise in a single night's performance (her benefit, March 1783) the sum of 650*l.*; still this feeling did not induce her to appear before the public when her powers began to fail.

The voice of friendship which she received—unlike that addressed by Gil Blas to the Archbishop of Granada, respecting his homilies—urged her, not to retire from the public, but to leave her seclusion, that she might revive its renewed plaudits; and this she occasionally did with great effect—as when she appeared, for the last time (June 8, 1816), at the express desire of the Princess Charlotte, in the character of Lady Macbeth. Six years after she left Bath, the greater part of which time Mr. Whalley had spent on the Continent, she asked him whether he thought her acting had improved in the interval. He replied in the affirmative; but added, that he regretted to observe that she had acquired a stage trick of pausing after certain sentences, to receive the expected applause of the audience. There was never any interruption or drawback in the warm regard of these two friends. When Mrs. Siddons was obliged, by ill health, to discontinue the correspondence, her daughter Cecilia, and her son, Mr. George Siddons (a civil servant of the East India Company), continued it. Endorsed on the letter dated October 8, 1787, are the words, 'My dearest friend Mrs.

Siddons's letters, too many of which are mislaid or destroyed.' Perhaps the last time they met was in May 1824, when the Editor went with Dr. Whalley to her house in Upper Baker Street. Dr. Whalley alone was admitted, and the visit was a long one.

Mrs. Piozzi, whose acquaintance Dr. Whalley appears to have made on her first arrival at Bath, after the death of Mr. Thrale, was formed in a very different mould from his other female friend whom we have just mentioned. The latter possessed genius in one particular branch—the former, general talent. The one was the child of nature, ardent in her attachments, and incapable of being spoilt by popularity; the other, though independent in her actions, was yet more the woman of the world, loving society, of which she was herself so great an ornament. A beauteous person, and natural grace, added much to the public reputation of the one; a highly-cultivated understanding developed the naturally strong mind of the other, and made her conversation, as Miss Seward expresses it, 'that bright wine of the intellect which has no lees.' Sir William Pepys said, in 1825, that he had never met any human being who possessed the talent of conversation to such a degree. Mrs. Siddons was born in an inferior station, and was required to build up her own fortune and position in society; while Mrs. Piozzi appeared to come into the world, armed *cap-à-pié*, like the goddess Minerva, with the combined advantages of station, wit, and friends, which were soon to procure for her wealth. Sufficient will appear in the following fragmentary correspondence, preserved more by chance than design, of these two ladies, to justify these remarks. The most important quality of the mind, common sense, was, however, but feebly developed in Mrs. Thrale-Piozzi's brain; and hence she was in constant difficulties during the greater part of her life. Though, at the death of Mr. Thrale, she was left mistress of Streatham Park, with an annual income of 2,000*l.*, yet, after contending with pecuniary cares for many years, she at length suffered the mortification, in extreme old age, of the seizure of her household goods, for the payment of a debt, for which she had no security to offer. Mrs. Siddons, on the contrary, when her bodily strength could no longer aid her natural genius, retired with dignity from public life; and in the bosom of her family, and in the regard of a select circle of friends, received every alleviation to her bodily sufferings which affection and ease of mind could afford. It was not, perhaps, Mrs. Piozzi's fault, that her declining years were not cheered by those affectionate attentions, which a mother may reasonably expect at the hands of her daughters. After the perusal of these letters, it is impossible to suppose that the kindly relations natural to the relative positions of mother and daughter were maintained. The estrangement commenced upon Mrs. Piozzi's second marriage; and time, so often a panacea, even after her husband's death had removed the cause, never healed it.* Dr. Whalley used to speak of Dr. Johnson's conduct in this matter as both unwarrantable and ungrateful. Though the great lexicographer, after his too commonly rude manner, spoke of Piozzi as 'not only an ugly dog, but an old one,' others mention him as prepossessing in appearance, with considerable talent in his profession, and irreproachable in his conduct. Still the great moralist, then in all the splendour of his setting sun, by the notoriety of his disapprobation of the connexion, so roused the public attention that the lady's conduct began to be felt as a national disgrace; and a *mésalliance* which might have been easily overlooked gave rise to newspaper attacks, pasquinades, and

* Piozzi died of gout, from which he had long suffered, at Brymbella, March 1809.

life-long family estrangement. The following verses are a specimen of the epigrams which the occasion called forth:—

> Rome once her famed Antonius saw
>   Forget a Roman's duty;
> And fail to keep the world in awe,
>   Seduced by Egypt's beauty.
>
> To prove this maxim cannot fail,
>   Another name I'll quote ye:
> Ah! who could equal Mrs. Thrale,
>   Or sink below Piozzi?

The feeling of prejudice on the part of her daughters, doubtless occasioned the adoption of a nephew of her husband, as the heir of her own family property—her children being handsomely provided for in Mr. Thrale's will. His brewery fetched 135,000*l.* This transfer, if undeserved, of maternal affection, to one who was a stranger by blood, might be supposed the most painful circumstance connected with this adoption of John (afterwards, by knighthood, *Sir* John) Piozzi Salusbury. No one can read these letters without coming to the conclusion that such a transfer of affection had taken place, and not only must have been painful to the 'ladies,' as she styles her daughters, themselves, but also very injurious to herself, as it removed a check to those extravagances in fortune and conduct, which cast a shadow over the last years of so much wit and force of character. Her giving a public ball at Bath to between 700 and 800 persons, to celebrate her eightieth birthday, was, when we regard the affair in its moral point of view, treating the entry upon so solemn a climacteric of life with a levity which reminds us of some of the famous grotesque pictures of the Dance of Death; while her regard for, and especially her letters (if genuine) to Mr. Conway, the actor, are little creditable to her as an aged matron. When we come to the closing scene, which occurred at Clifton, May 1821, we are, however, pleased to see three of her daughters by her bedside, and to find that she received every attention the trying occasion required from her old friend, Mrs. Pennington, so often mentioned by Dr. Whalley and his correspondents as Miss Weston.

She retained her beautiful handwriting, always regarded as a pattern of caligraphy, to the last. The Editor remembers, when as a boy he was on a visit at Bath, Dr. Whalley handed him a note he had received from her, probably within a year of her death, and called his attention to the beauty of the writing. Her appearance at that time, according to his recollection, was not prepossessing—her features being too *prononcés*, and her manners wanting in feminine gentleness. Old age did not become her. She had lost grace, without gaining dignity. . . . .

In 1779, Dr. Whalley published anonymously his poem 'Edwy and Edilda,' called a tale in five parts, which procured him the acquaintance of Miss Seward, soon to ripen into a life-long friendship. This lady appears to have regarded herself as the patron of the Poetic Muse, and assiduously sought the acquaintance of every rising genius. The public estimation of her merits has much fallen since her own times, though respectable names are still not wanting to uphold her credit. Her father was a minor canon of Lichfield Cathedral, and Mrs. Delany mentions having met him at Ragley, the seat of Lord Hertford, and calls him a 'learned clergyman.' Horace Walpole has an amusing anecdote of the value he put upon his metrical compositions. He was travelling tutor to Lord Charles Fitzroy,* who was taken dangerously ill at Genoa. Through the remedies applied by the physician, the crisis appeared to have passed; and Mr. Seward went to his room, and began a complimentary ode to the Esculapius; but before it was

* Third son of Charles, second Duke of Grafton. Lord Charles was born in 1718, and died July 1739.

finished, a relapse took place, and the patient died. The tutor, however, was so well pleased with the commencement of his poem that he finished it, despite the failure in the moral of the tale.

When Miss Seward commenced her correspondence with Mr. Whalley, her father was advanced in years, and soon began to occupy much of her thoughts and attention, and she appears to have watched over his declining years with much tenderness and affection. She was susceptible of strong attachments, two of which are frequently adverted to in the following letters: one towards Miss Honora Sneyd, a young lady of an old Shropshire family, and whom she mentions as 'her joy for seventeen years.' One of Miss Seward's most admired poems, the Monody on the Death of Major André, owed its origin to an attachment which had existed between Miss Sneyd and this officer. Miss Seward made some severe reflections on Washington for his conduct in the affair, and the value which the Father of the *late* great Republic placed on her good opinion was evinced by his sending her, when the war was over, copies of the correspondence which followed upon the Major's arrest, to prove that he had endeavoured to save André's life, instead of being, as still commonly asserted (see History of England by the late Rev. Mr. Walter), forward in promoting his execution. Miss Sneyd married, in 1773, Mr. Edgeworth, the well-known writer on education, and often alluded to in very unfavourable terms by Miss Seward. Mrs. Edgeworth died early, leaving an heir to the property. The other attachment, which is traceable in all Miss Seward's letters, is of a more questionable character, being, as we must call it, a platonic affection (and no slur was cast on her conduct) towards Mr. Saville, the leader of the choir in Lichfield Cathedral, who lived separate from his wife. Her devotion was more valuable to him than that of Queen Bess to her 'gentle Robin,' for it conferred substantial benefits during her 'Giovanni's' life; and at his death, instead of selling his effects to balance accounts, after the royal maiden's example, she settled 100*l.* a year on his daughter. If Miss Seward was strong in her attachments, she was equally so in her dislikes, as evinced by her unmeasured reflections on a certain Mr. Pratt, a publisher and bookseller at Bath, whom she suspected of writing unfriendly criticisms on her works; in her censures of Mr. Edgeworth's conduct towards his wife and children; and in the odium she endeavoured to heap on the memory of Dr. Johnson, whenever an occasion offered. Her political antipathies also were very strong, increased, doubtless, by the eventful and exciting times in which she wrote: thus, there is no abuse too strong for Pitt, or the measures of his long administration. Even the grave could not cover her ill will, and she calls him, after his death, 'the sanguinary and fallen idol.'

Her great object in life seems to have been literary fame, and no sacrifice to ease or even health was deemed too great to offer at the shrine of this goddess. In the midst of pain, unable to rise from her chair without help, suffering from vertigo, in consequence of the overtaxed powers of the brain, she still continued in her old age to indite those interminable letters of which abbreviated specimens are given. The last is dated just two months before her death, and dwells on the usual topics of politics, literature, hatred of what she calls Methodism, and her fond memory for the departed Giovanni. She died March 25, 1809, aged sixty-two, in the Episcopal residence at Lichfield, which both her father and herself had long occupied as the Bishop's tenants. She left by will twelve quarto volumes of letters to Mr. Constable for publication, which she says did not constitute a twelfth part of her correspondence, and these were given to the public in 1811. Among them are many letters addressed to Dr. Whalley, the originals of which (often varying from the printed copy) the Editor finds among his MS. These have all been omitted in the present collection, which does not contain one-half of the remainder of her letters to him. Whatever the publication of her epistles may have gained to her reputation as a prose writer—she had previously been known to the public chiefly for her poetical compositions—her memory suffered proportionably on the score of regard and delicacy of feeling. A letter written by her old enemy Pratt, to Dr. Whalley, mentions the indignation at Lichfield excited by the publicity given by her to the private interchange of thought among friends, in this posthumous publication. As more than half a century has since elapsed, it is hoped that no such feeling can now be excited by this fresh issue of her letters.

In the summer of 1783 Mr. and Mrs. Whalley broke up their establishments at Langford Court and Bath, and went to reside on the Continent for some years. A foreign tour was then a very different matter from the flying visits of the present railway days. A *désobligeant* from the remise of Dessein would not convey a gentleman, with his wife and servants, from Calais; and few were able or willing, with Goldsmith, to travel with a knapsack, and for the sake of a meal—

> To lead the sportive choir,
> With tuneless pipe, beside the murmuring Loire.

It was necessary, without travelling with the luxurious ease of the Fonthill Beckford, to incur considerable expense. Thus, the Roman adage,

> Non cuivis homini contingit adire Corinthum,

by substituting the name of an Italian for the Grecian city, still held good. Yet economy had some weight in his protracted tour in France, Italy, and Belgium, as it enabled

Mr. Whalley to diminish his expenditure, which a too large hospitality had rendered excessive. The peace of Versailles, at the conclusion of the American war, opened France again to the English, and many took advantage of it to visit Paris and Versailles. In the famous palace of the latter city, Marie Antoinette was then in the midst of her brilliant court, fascinating all admirers, as Burke describes her—'Glittering like the morning star, full of life and splendour and joy.'

On some occasion she was particularly struck by the appearance of Mr. Whalley, and afterwards alluded to him as 'Le bel Anglais.' He did not, however, remain long in the French capital or its vicinity, for we find a letter addressed to him by Miss Seward, in the middle of October, at Chamberberry, where he spent the winter, surrounded by the Alps, and from hence he made the short excursions into the neighbouring country of which he has left such a lively and amusing account in his journal. The elegant compliment Mrs. Piozzi paid him at this time, in reference to the friendships he had formed, was not flattery. Writing to him, March 1784, she says, 'Elegant and gentle manners are attractive in all nations, and you have not drawn iron to you, but gold.' He soon won golden opinions among the society of ancient Savoyard noblesse to which he was introduced, and formed a strong attachment to the Baron Chatillon, the inheritor of a remarkable feudal castle on the little lake of Bourget; but an untimely death soon ended this friendship, and Miss Seward condoles with him on his loss, saying, 'And is this all of thy Chatillon's story?'

Another friendship he formed at Chamberberry was with the Count Galateri, a young Piedmontese officer, who was destined to act a part in European politics, in the great struggle which was then not far distant. Mr. Whalley describes him, when he was his companion in his rambles amidst the Alps of

Savoy, as a fine young man, not over well educated, but good-humoured and obliging, and the gayest of the gay. Just fifty years later, the Editor arrived one morning at Alessandria, and, before sitting down to make his toilette, despatched a note to the Governor of the province, who was also commandant of that important fortress. But a few minutes had elapsed, when the aforesaid operation was interrupted by the forcible entry of a six-foot aide-de-camp, gay with decorations and plumes, who had come to take him off to the General's, with apologies that the latter could not wait on the stranger himself, as he was confined by sickness. The wish was soon complied with, and there on his bed lay the stalwart figure of His Excellency the Count D. Gabrielle Galateri di Genola, Governatore e Comandante Gen. della divisione d' Alessandria, Generale di Cavalleria, Cav. Gran Croce Insignito del Gran Cordone dell' Ordine militare de' SS. Maurizio e Lazzaro, degli Ordini Russi di S. Anna di 1ª Classe, e di S. Giorgio di 4ª Classe, Commendatore dell' Ordine Imperiale di Leopoldo d' Austria, di S. Waldimiro di Russia, Cavaliere della Spada di Svezia, Cavaliere Onorario di S. Giovanni di Gerusalemme, della Sciabola d' Oro Guernita di Brillanti coll' Iscrizione al Valore, della Medaglia del MDCCCXII. di Russia, e di quella per l' Entrata in Parigi delle Truppe Imperiali nel MDCCCXIV. Decorato dell' Ordine Supremo della SS. Annunziata, l' undecimo di Septembre, 1833. Such were the honours which fifty years had heaped upon the young Chevalier of 1783.

He received the Editor with the greatest kindness, in consideration of his relationship to his departed friend, of whose memory he spoke with the warmest affection.

The intermediate fifty years had been fraught with great changes to the young officer. When, during the French revolutionary war, his king was driven from his throne, and the country fell under foreign dominion, refusing to serve the stranger, and adopting the motto General Ludlow placed over his door in Switzerland, 'Omne solum forti patria,' he migrated to Russia, and offered his sword to the Czar. In his service he fought in various climes against the Turks and Persians, and at length had the satisfaction of opposing his old enemies, when they sought him out in his newly-adopted country. He followed them to Leipzig, in which memorable battle of giants he took part, and finally entered Paris with Alexander in 1817. During the whole of this long period he continued a close correspondence with Dr. Whalley, commenting freely upon politics, and acquainting him with many important passing events. Shortly after the Bourbons were restored to France, Dr. Whalley crossed the Channel to meet his friend, now grown old in war, covered with many honourable scars, and among which was a notable one on the top of his head, where a portion of his skull, which had been sliced off by a sabre cut, was replaced by a silver plate. When the peace of Europe was finally established, after the fresh troubles of the 'cent jours,' the King of Sardinia, sensible of the General's loyal attachment as a subject, and distinguished merit as a soldier, appointed him Governor of Nice. During the political disturbances of the Carbonari, Count Galateri made a decided stand against the liberal party. He regarded all desire of reform as tending to revolution, and he had witnessed so much misery proceeding from these political changes, that he naturally dreaded them. He continued in equal favour with Charles Felix after the abdication of Victor Emmanuel, and was finally appointed by Charles Albert (who succeeded to the throne in 1824) to the most responsible military post in the kingdom, that of Commandant of Alessandria. Whilst holding this command, he was principally concerned in repressing a new movement of the liberal party, and was considered to have acted with severity in condemning to death some of those who were compromised, and to have shown much want of feeling in witnessing their execution. It was said, as they were led out to be shot, that he sat over a cannon, dangling his legs on either side with an air of indifference. However this might be, he spoke, on the visit just alluded to, of his share in the event with an air of triumph, saying, 'J'avais le nœud dans ma main,' and added that the King had written him a flattering letter of approval with his own hand. Charles Albert, as is well known, after coming to the throne, deserted the liberal cause, which, under his cousin's reign, he had fostered; and he was so much satisfied with the old General Galateri's ability and decision in suppressing this liberal movement, that he conferred on him the highest order of the state, that of the SS. Annunziata, and styled him his 'cousin.'

The letters written to Mr. Whalley by the Count Galateri, the Baron Chatillon, who succeeded his elder brother, and other foreign correspondents, making a large packet, were inconsiderately destroyed some years since. A few were found elsewhere, and are given.

The winter of 1784-5 Mr. and Mrs. Whalley spent at Avignon, to their no great content, as the tone of society in that city did not please them; and in the spring they took a house near Vaucluse, where they passed the summer. Mrs. Whalley mentions their entertaining the Duke and Duchess of Cumberland and other distinguished guests at this country house; and Miss Seward compliments Mr. Whalley on his graphic description of the scenery. The next winter they spent at Pisa, and in the spring went on to Florence, where Mr. Whalley became acquainted with Mr. Greathead, one of the contributors to the 'Florence Miscellany,' edited the year before by Mrs. Piozzi, and with other friends of that lady, to whom she alludes in her subsequent correspondence with him. Charles Edward, the Chevalier, was also residing in that capital, as Sir N. Wraxall says, in his

Memoirs, 'exhibiting to the world a very humiliating spectacle.' At times he roused himself from his debauchery, and appeared still to have aspirations for the future, as he said on one occasion to Mr. Greathead, in good English, that 'he should soon speak to him in Westminster Hall,' and called him 'his subject.' From Florence Mr. and Mrs. Whalley turned their steps homewards, travelling by the Tyrol and Switzerland, as appears from his journal. They rested at Zurich, where Mr. Whalley was greatly interested in making the acquaintance of Lavater. They proceeded, ascending the Rhine, to Cologne, and reached Brussels, where they spent the winter of 1786-7, and the following spring. At this capital Mr. Whalley was joined by his favourite niece, Miss Sage, who was greatly admired for her general talents, especially for her music, as well as for her personal attractions. They formed the acquaintance of the Duke d'Aremberg and his family; and some letters, written by his heroic daughter, afterwards the wife of Prince Schwartzenburg, are given. This lady was burnt to death on the occasion of a fête given by the Austrian Ambassador at Paris, on the marriage of Maria Louisa with Napoleon, in 1810, when the ball-room caught fire. She had escaped, but, missing her child, she re-entered the saloon and perished. The Duke d'Aremberg invited the Whalleys and Miss Sage to visit him at their country seat, where he was fond of having a gallop on a led horse across his park with Miss Sage, though he was quite blind, both his eyes having been destroyed by the gun of the English Minister at a shooting party. After dinner, it was the custom to hand round a single glass of Tokay to each guest—wine from the Imperial cellar at Vienna, and not to be purchased. At Brussels they again met with Mrs. Piozzi, who, in some clever verses, has enumerated many other members of their agreeable society. One evening, at the theatre in that city, soon after Lavater's work on Physiognomy was published, Mr. Whalley was amusing himself with forming conjectures on the characters of persons around him, from their features, by Lavater's rules. A gentleman sat down by his side, and Mr. Whalley thought if there was any truth in Lavater's science, this gentleman must be very clever. Quite unknown to each other, they entered into conversation in French, and soon talked of the stage, and of the English Mrs. Siddons. Mr. Whalley observed that she shone both in tragedy and comedy, and that she was not only eminent on the stage, but irreproachable in her private character, elegant in her address, and in her conversation showed a fine and cultivated understanding. They both agreed that it was not common for persons so to shine in different stations and accomplishments, although there was, indeed, said Mr. Whalley, an instance of the same person shining in *different* professions (navy, army, and law)—the English Erskine. 'Erskine?' said the gentleman; '*I* am Erskine!'

Early in the summer the party returned to England, when Mr. Whalley went immediately to visit his venerable mother, at Winscombe Court. His own country house was let, and he commenced building a cottage on the lofty hill of the Mendip range, which belonged to the property. This little 'maison de plaisance' was added to from time to time till it grew into a mansion, and in the meanwhile the mountainous site on which it was erected, became clothed with firs and deciduous trees. It was the first experiment which had been made of planting upon Mendip, and ill were the general auguries of success, but the thousands of acres which now adorn the slopes of these hills, owe their origin to this beginning. In this delightful summer residence Dr. Whalley spent several months for many years, collecting around him those friends, whose regard for him is so warmly expressed in the following correspondence, and whose worth, refinement, and intellectual powers formed that society which constitutes the highest social enjoyment.

During the winter, he resided at his house in the Crescent, at Bath, where he mixed with the general company of that city to an extent that excited Miss Seward's surprise, and even called forth her remonstrance. He had always a great affection for animals, as shown in his letters to his young relative at school, and many years continued a breed of large Danish dogs, spotted white and liver colour, of great sagacity. They were fond of hunting on Doleberry Warren (a part of the Mendip Lodge estate, which abounded with rabbits), and during Dr. Whalley's winter residence in Bath, two of those dogs, named the Duke and Duchess, would absent themselves at intervals for one clear day, and it was ascertained that they spent the time in a visit to the Lodge, to enjoy their favourite pastime.

In 1799, a tragedy in blank verse, written by Mr. Whalley, called 'The Castle of Montval,' was brought out at Drury Lane Theatre, in which Mrs. Siddons, Mrs. Powell, and the two Kembles, took parts. He imagined the character of the Lady of the Castle (the heroine of the piece) was especially suited to the powers of his admired friend, and she exerted all her talent to make it acceptable to the audience. A comment written to Mrs. Sullivan, ci-devant Fanny Sage, by his brother Richard, who was then rector of Horsington, dated July 22nd of this year, marks the anxiety felt by the elder brother for the success of his play, and the disapprobation of the other that he should have written it at all. 'Your uncle Sedgwick, I suppose you know, has been in the neighbourhood of London for some time, staking his reputation on the reception of a play. 'T was a sad losing game, for, whatever the fate of the play, his reputation with all good and wise people was sure to suffer; but our vanities and our vices blind us to a degree that is hardly credible or conceivable.'

However just such a stricture might be, in reference to one 'ordained to a holy function,' who occupied his time for the furtherance of sueh amusements, we must remember that Mr. Richard Whalley's opinion would then have been regarded as unjust, even among many of the more seriously disposed. Mrs. Hannah More, though she had now renounced such writings, had recently gained great applause from her dramatic pieces. Mrs. Delany, in a letter dated December 1777, says, 'My friend Miss More succeeds prodigiously, and Percy is triumphant.' The tone also of Mr. Whalley's tragedy was strictly correct—offering, in that respect, a marked contrast to much of the drama, not only in that day, but, unhappily, also in the present. However, Mr. Richard Whalley's assertion that his brother was playing a 'losing game' was fully verified. Shortly before his tragedy appeared, another, with a plot very similar, called the 'Castle Spectre,' was produced, which so damaged the effect of his, that, after a run of nine nights, it was recalled, and never reproduced. Miss Seward considered that he possessed the imagination and taste suitable for success in the drama, and urged him to cultivate them; but he never attempted to bring forward another piece on the stage, though he left some plays in MS. He had, in 1794, published a handsome 4to. edition, illustrated by engravings, of his 'Edwy and Edilda;' also, before that time, a poem on 'Mont Blanc;' and, in 1809, a tale called 'Kenneth and Fenella,' which, with the exception of what he sent to periodicals and a pamphlet hereafter to be mentioned, is all that we know of his contributions to the *belles lettres.* Mr. Whalley's mind and pen were soon to be exercised on other subjects, than those of the fancy. The Misses More, having relinquished their school at Bristol, purchased a small property, called Cowslip Green, in the neighbourhood of Mendip Lodge. Their active and benevolent minds soon discovered the deplorable ignorance, which prevailed among the labouring population in that district, and they determined to lessen it. Their friend Mr. Wilberforce zealously seconded their wishes, and said he would find money, if they would find labour. This compact was soon concluded, and under such auspices, they commenced the establishment of their well-known Mendip Schools. But they found their benevolent exertions were met with distrust, which soon increased into open hostility. As a more complete body of evidence will be produced on the subject of the once famous Blagdon controversy, than has hitherto been seen by the public, it will not be out of place to give a view of the whole question, as Dr. Whalley was so much concerned, throughout the discussion, as the friend and adviser of, and at last, advocate for, the lady. At the same time, the Editor trusts, after the lapse of so many years, when all the actors have passed to their account before another tribunal, no ill feeling can again be engendered by the production of these letters. The deeper religious feelings of his brother Richard were more in unison with those of Mrs. H. More; but Dr. Whalley's keen sense of justice, strong attachment to his friends, and general desire to uphold what was beneficial and virtuous, caused him to throw himself into the contest with an ardour and public spirit, to which his brother Richard was a stranger. Not that the latter shrank from throwing the weight of his opinion into the controversial scale in favour of the ladies, as will be seen by an extract from a letter, written June 1802, to Mrs. Sullivan, then residing at Sydcot:—

'It is not impossible that I may call upon you ere long, as I think I shall come into the neighbourhood, provided the Misses More hold the anniversary at Shipton as usual. I am not afraid of being known as one of those clergymen who profess an attachment to her and her principles. They who endeavour to discredit them know not what they are doing, and are truly to be pitied.'

The eldest brother of Winscombe Court took, on the contrary, a decided part in favour of the curate of Blagdon. Writing to him, in reference to the meeting at that village, hereafter to be mentioned, he says:—

'As chairman, I did not give my opinion formally, it not being usual, unless a casting vote is wanted; but I sufficiently expressed myself to several gentlemen present as being of the same opinion; had I formally given in my vote, I should have added, that I thought Mr. Bere very injuriously treated.

'I am, dear Sir,

'With Mrs. Whalley's best respects to Mrs. Bere,

'Your very obedient friend and servant,

'FRS. EDWARDS WHALLEY.'

This declaration doubtless arose, in the first place, from an honest conviction of the truth of the affidavits against the conduct of the schoolmaster, submitted to him as a magistrate; but the condemnation of the former was also agreeable to his feelings, as it dealt a blow to the increase of evangelical religion, which he, with the great majority of the laity, and it may be added of the clergy also, called Methodism (another term for what they considered enthusiasm or hypocrisy). His brother Richard, whose judgements were perhaps somewhat severe, thus describes Colonel Whalley, in a letter to Mrs. Sullivan, dated June 11, 1800:

'In your uncle Whalley (who, as a natural man, is the best-tempered creature that lives, and one whom I dearly love as a brother) you will meet with a decided enemy to all serious religion—so entirely ignorant of himself, and perfectly wrapt up in his own sufficiency for *understanding*, *willing*, and doing, that he treats the Gospel as trash, when it crosses his own conceits and opinions. His character helps to confirm me, more than that of any other person I have met with, in my opinion of the deceitfulness of the human heart, and how easy it is for a man to think himself a Christian, without the least foundation of faith in the word of Christ.'

At the present day, when we are disputing about the most efficient way of carrying on popular education with the aid of Parliamentary grants, we may smile at the apprehension of danger, which the Misses More's benevolent exertions in this direction created. The gradually enlarging experience of three parts of a century has shamed the narrow selfishness of some, and dispelled the honest fears of others, and the education of the masses is promoted, not only from the dictates of benevolence, but also from motives of policy. Popular feeling was very different when, in the year 1798, Mrs. Hannah More visited Wedmore, a large parish situated in the rich vale contiguous to the southern slopes of the Mendip Hills. She was not surprised to find, from his well-known character of religious indifference, that the chief landowner, a man of much influence in the Somersetshire moorlands, was opposed to her plans; but she was scarcely prepared to have her schemes for educating the poor opposed on the dogmatical grounds, urged by the wife of the chief farmer of the parish. This woman, whose husband rented an estate of 1,000*l.* a year, told these amiable sisters, Martha and Hannah, that the 'lower class was fated to be poor, and ignorant, and wicked; and that, as wise as these ladies were, they could not alter what was *decreed.*' The husband enforced the very grave position taken up by his wife, by adding, that 'he liked the parish well enough as it was. If the young men did come and gamble before his house of a Sunday evening, when they might as well do it farther off, it was only for him to go out and curse and swear at them a little, and they went away; and what could one desire more?' (Mendip Annals.)

There were many others, at that day, of a very different class from the squire and topping farmer of Wedmore, who were likewise opposed to popular education.

Though the good effects of Mr. Raikes' Sunday-school system were beginning to be felt, and enlightened men like Wilberforce, H. Thornton, and Porteus Bishop of London, supported the efforts made by these benevolent ladies to instruct the minds of the rough Mendip miners, and of the villagers to the north and south of that range of hills, still many of the well-disposed among thinking and generally intelligent persons disapproved of the attempt; they considered that it tended to level the different grades of society, that the lower classes would lose their respect for the higher, that insolence and insubordination would be fostered, and that ere long our political institutions would be changed, and that the social disorders which were then desolating France wonld extend to this country.

The fear of enthusiasm, under the name of Methodism, was another bugbear in the minds of some of the opponents to this movement. The Psalm and Hymn-singing, and the evening religious reading — conducted generally by the schoolmaster or mistress — savoured too much of the conventicle, in the opinion of many sober-minded churchmen; and our own much fuller experience, despite the costly training schools, of the difficulty of obtaining schoolmasters qualified for their office, by sobriety of mind as well as education, suggests the possibility of miscarriage in this particular in the Misses More's benevolent designs. The irresponsible position of the teacher, in reference to the minister of the parish, was likewise an evident objection to the plan. It was when such inflammatory matter as the above, was smouldering in many places, that the torch was ignited at Blagdon. There were circumstances connected with the village calculated to fan the flame. The incumbent was non-resident, and his place supplied by an elderly clergyman of low parentage, who had risen through the various grades of a place in the grammar school, a servitorship at Oxford, and an ushership at a school, to holy orders. His boast of ancient Welsh descent, during the controversy, elicited these particulars, otherwise not deserving notice. Finally he was made a justice, and reigned supreme at Blagdon. At first he hailed the new school as a boon, but after a time took offence at the schoolmaster, and required Mrs. Hannah More to dismiss him. This she declined to do, unless sufficient charges were proved against him. On November 12, 1800, eleven gentlemen, five of whom were neighbouring clergy, with Mr. (Colonel) Whalley as their president, met, at the curate's request, in the village of Blagdon, to hear evidence on the matters in dispute. The curate produced several affidavits taken before himself by persons of the parish, affirming generally that the schoolmaster had at different times used improper language, some of which was disloyal and even treasonable, and some savouring of a religious enthusiasm, injurious to his mission as a teacher. Counter depositions were also presented. The resolution of the meeting was favourable to the curate's character, and recommended the dismissal of the master. Thus the first semi-official inquiry into the dispute between the curate of Blagdon and Mrs. H. More was favourable to the former; and the depositions, with the opinion of the meeting, being forwarded to the Chancellor of the diocese, acting for the Bishop, he recommended that the school should be closed. Mrs. H. More had wished to take this step several months before, and was only restrained by the entreaties of the non-resident rector. Now the school was closed. Further reflection on the evidence brought forward at the meeting, caused many of its members to alter their views, and four out of the five clergymen, broke off their acquaintance with the curate, and such representations were made to the Chancellor of his unworthy conduct in this affair, and of his own heterodox teaching, that some months later the Chancellor suspended the curate from his spiritual functions at Blagdon. The interest of the dispute—first carried to a distance by private correspondence and comments in the local newspapers; then gathering consequence, as the matter took a far wider range, by being discussed in the chief literary reviews of the day—obtained, when the curate was dismissed, a degree of public attention which we can only account for by considering the real principle at issue—viz., the future education, or the continued ignorance, of the lower orders. We have a list—probably an incomplete one—of no less than twenty-eight pamphlets or articles on the controversy. The virulence with which most of these were written shows the strength of party spirit which existed, and certainly does not contrast favourably with a similar class of writings at the present day. Mrs. H. More did not publicly raise her voice to rebut the charges made against her, though she was assured on high legal authority that they were libellous. Heat in argument might palliate the *odium theologicum;* but when the enemy began *ambiguas spargere voces*, in order to destroy an unblemished maiden character of so many years, he leaves himself without excuse. Though the shaft missed its object, yet its intended victim did not remain scatheless, but, as the following letters will show, was brought almost to death's door by the rancour which aimed it. The warm support of attached friends was not indeed wanting, and among them all, none was more zealous in her defence than Dr. Whalley. He shrank, indeed, from entering the lists openly, as he dreaded exposing himself to the Billingsgate language, in which the curate and some of his friends indulged. Few, however, could equal him in the power of sarcasm, as shown in the anonymous pamphlet, which the subjoined letters proved to have proceeded from his pen, entitled 'Animadversions on the Curate of Blagdon's Three Publications.' The irony with which he exposes the curate's false boast of high parentage, is as amusing as it is cutting, and can be only palliated—we can scarcely say excused—by the language which the object of it had used towards others. The whole pamphlet of fifty-five closely-printed pages is, by the variety of points it takes up, the exposure of the secret motives of the curate in the quarrel, the numerous sallies of wit, and the lucid summary of the entire matter, not unworthy of the high encomium bestowed upon it in the following letters. It appears to have acted as a *coup de grâce* to any further appeal on the part of the curate to the compassion of the public. Sympathy from various quarters had been expressed when he was deprived of his curacy, and it was argued that the Bishop, through his Chancellor, had done too much, or too little. He refused to allege the grounds on which he dismissed the curate: if they rested on his complaints against the schoolmaster, the punishment was too severe; if on his heterodox teaching (he was accused of denying the doctrine of the Trinity), the award was too lenient, for no steps were taken to deprive him of the benefice of Butcombe, which he held. The force of this reasoning was probably felt at Wells, and a reconciliation being effected between the rector and the curate, the latter was allowed to resume his functions.

So ended the controversy, but not the animosity engendered by it, which long continued to rankle in that neighbourhood. The kiss of peace, we may fear, was too much like the embrace of the 'Jungfrau,' which occasioned death; for the Blagdon school, as we see by the letter of September 1801, was then finally closed. The light was removed from a place which, by the curate's own confession, was peculiarly dark, and how will he answer, if this removal shall have been to some 'the blackness of darkness for ever?' The eminent lady, who thus withdrew from the contest, continued her active benevolence, both by her writings and her charities, with increasing success through nearly thirty succeeding years, instructing alike the palace and the cottage. At a public breakfast, given by the Duchess of Gloucester to several of the Royal Family and other distinguished guests, she introduced Mrs. Hannah More as the Authoress of 'Hints to a Princess;' and it is interesting to know that this book, written in 1805, by high advice, expressly for the benefit of the Princess Charlotte, was the last book read by the Princess before her marriage, and the last she perused before her much-lamented death.

During the height of this controversy Mr. Whalley experienced a severe calamity, in the loss of his wife, who died December 8th, 1801. She had suffered for a long time from an accident she met with by her carriage overturning. Her spine was injured by the fall, and her body became much bent; still she retained her usual cheerfulness. Upon one occasion, a neighbour called at the Lodge, bringing a child with her. The latter, not restricted by the decorum of an elder person, and vividly struck with the appearance of the little bent elderly lady, exclaimed, 'Mother Bunch, Mother Bunch!' With great presence of mind and kindly feeling, she replied, 'But, my dear, you see I am not the Mother Bunch who lived *under* the hill, as I live on the *top* of the hill.' The winter and spring following her death Mr. Whalley spent in London, avoided his Bath society, and there he wrote his animadversions on the curate's three publications. In 1803, he formed another and suitable alliance, marrying Miss Heathcote, a lady of good property and ancient family in Wiltshire. Though not young, she became a very willing bride, and expressed to some of her friends her great happiness and good fortune in being united to a gentleman 'whom she had always admired beyond any of her acquaintances, and who brought her a fortune equal to her own.' This union, however, which promised so well, was not destined to be of long duration. The second Mrs. Whalley caught cold on leaving a crowded assembly at Bath, and died a few weeks afterwards, October 10, 1805. Miss Seward, in one of her printed letters, mentions her as 'gentle, kind and good, and sensible, though reserved.' At the same time, she gives a description of Mendip Lodge, as it appeared in the year 1804 :—'Thirteen years ago I passed six weeks in that Alpine habitation. Increasing wealth and fine taste have since transformed and enlarged an elegant cottage on the brow of Mendip to an Italian villa, superbly furnished; extended every way his steep and lawny walks; and placed before his house, and to its whole length, a Tuscan veranda. It is the loveliest architectural luxury I ever traversed, peculiarly calculated for the almost dizzy elevation on which the mansion stands, and for the extreme of light which it chastises, and which was given by large sashes, the whole height of the apartments, from everyone of which, on the second floor, we step out into the gay veranda.' . . . 'Twenty-four large china jars were filled with autumnal flowers, and one of them placed under every arch. All the sitting-rooms are on the second floor; servants' apartments on the ground floor; but no culinary operations are carried on there. To this villa urbana there is a villa rustica, which is the cook's region.' . . . 'There is a noble dining-room backwards, on the second story, adorned by fine pictures, the glory of which is a full-length portrait of Mrs. Siddons, by Hamilton. It is a speaking, a beautiful, an exquisite likeness, by which her charming face and figure, drawn in the prime of her life and beauty, should go down to posterity. She is in the character of

Hill's Zara, at the moment in which she exclaims, with extended hands, "Can it be Osmyn speaks; and speaks to Zara!"'

The death of the second Mrs. Whalley, was a great loss to her husband in every point of view; but he continued to entertain company, which appeared necessary to his existence. In 1808 he went to Scotland, to receive, at the University of Edinburgh, the degree of D.D. It was not unusual in those days, amongst elderly clergymen, to take this degree; and Mr. Whalley fancied that it would come with more grace, if voluntarily conferred by another University, than if he received it from Cambridge by his own right. Sir Walter Scott was, therefore, requested to proffer the petition to the University of the Scotch capital, which accordingly conferred this degree on Mr. Whalley on the 10th of July. The names of distinguished men were added to this document, such as Professors Playfair, Brown, Leslie, Jameson, &c., who were thus content 'to get rich by degrees.' In the winter of 1809, Dr. Whalley bought a house in Baker Street, and for some subsequent years resided a portion of his time in the metropolis. This was a period in Dr. Whalley's life of much expense, and, according to his income, of extravagance, which he looked back upon with regret. He entertained sumptuously, was a collector of paintings, and had a weakness for expensive jewellery, by which Messrs. Rundell and Bridge must have considerably profited. Still he had no lady to preside at his table, and his friends had urged him to supply this want. Miss Seward often alludes to it. In the year 1813, when approaching towards seventy years of age, he, unhappily for his own peace of mind, did marry for a third time. The lady of his choice was the widow of General Horneck, an acquaintance of many years' standing, who had long formed one of the Bath society, was clever and well connected, and supposed to be in good circumstances. Dr. Whalley soon found, to his cost, that public opinion in the latter particular was erroneous, as she was, on the contrary, greatly encumbered with debts, which he had to liquidate, to the extent of many thousands. Such a discovery at the commencement of married life, was not auspicious towards the prospect of future happiness, which incompatibility of temper rendered still less probable. Consequently, the general peace of 1814 had no sooner been proclaimed than Dr. Whalley, under the plea of ill-health, which in reality offered an excuse, left England, and, carefully avoiding any proposal to his wife that she should give him her company, went to reside in France. He fixed his abode for the winter at Nevers, where, with his usual talent, he soon collected around him a select society, of which General Count Coëtlosquet, the Military Governor of the Province, formed the principal star. He gives a pleasing picture of the General in a letter written from this little provincial capital. In the midst of this agreeable society and enjoyment of social peace, his health and spirits revived, but they were soon again disturbed by the sudden landing of Napoleon from the island of Elba, on the 1st of March. We have a note, without date, from the Count Coëtlosquet, acquainting Dr. Whalley with the state of affairs, and urging him to fly with all expedition—'Partez de suite, le plutôt possible, sans vous arrêter.' He did, however, pause at Paris, doubtful where to go to. England had no charms for him, and, finding that Wellington was preparing to defend Belgium, he determined to place himself under his protection.

He barely left Paris in time, and said he never saw such villanous countenances as those of the 'canaille' who lined the Faubourg St. Antoine, as he drove through it on his way to the Belgian frontier. They were awaiting the downfall of the Bourbon Government, and appeared disposed to prevent his flight, but he reached Louvain in safety, almost to whose gates the tide of war was soon to follow him.

It was a singular circumstance that Dr. Whalley, who for so many years had defended the policy bequeathed by Pitt, of continuing the war, under the conviction that Napoleon must succumb at last, should have been within sound of the final struggle.

The great drama of European strife, whose fluctuating incidents he had been anxiously watching for twenty years, was now played out, and the curtain was about to fall upon the battle-field, and not again to be raised for forty years. Many of those in public life (as Fox and Sheridan), and among the circle of his private friends (as Miss Seward, whose arguments against the continuance of the war he had so earnestly combated), were no longer on the stage of life, to witness the ultimate triumph of his political principles. Confident in his opinions, and relying on the genius of Wellington, he took shelter behind his ægis, and without flying from the country, there awaited the shock of the contending armies. His sagacity at once detected the importance of the blow which had been struck; and in the letter to be found in the sequel, written the day after the battle, he calls it a 'day that will be famous in the annals of history.'

It is to be regretted that the letter has not been preserved entire, as it contains an interesting picture of the lights and shades of the landscape in the rear of the contending parties. The account of the military movements, though not accurate, are yet more circumstantially correct than, from the shortness of the interval between their occurrence and their recital, might have been supposed.

He spent the winter of 1815-6, at Brussels, under the roof of Mr. Mullins, afterwards the second Lord Ventry, of whose attention and kindness he speaks with gratitude.

In the summer of 1816 he travelled south, revisiting his old quarters at Chamberry, and, joining his friend Galateri in the north of Italy, spent that and the subsequent winter at Modena. Here he was seized with a dangerous illness, during which he received the greatest kindness from the Duke and the Royal Family, who insisted upon sending him meat from their own kitchen, and wine from their cellar.

After his return to England, in the spring of 1818, he despatched a case of various articles in steel to Modena, in the manufacture of which this country, at that time, greatly excelled the continent. The present was graciously accepted, and Dr. Whalley afterwards received a flattering autograph letter of enquiry from the Duke himself. In this year he purchased the centre house in Portland Place, Bath, one of the largest in that city, which he furnished in a very handsome style, in the hopes of spending in it the remainder of his days. His wife, during the whole period of his absence, had been most assiduous in her correspondence, which was always filled with expressions of affection, but in the year after he had purchased this house, during a temporary absence of a few days, she deserted him under plea of ill treatment. The legal separation which ensued was for his happiness, but as a man of the world, who respected public opinion, he was greatly distressed at the violent manner in which it was effected. She attempted to correspond with him afterwards, but he never again addressed her. She had gained a comfortable settlement, occupied a large house in Catherine Place, in the same city, where she was known for her handsome parties, and survived him some years.

After this separation he let his house in Bath, and with the exception of the winter of 1823, which he spent with his niece, Mrs. Sullivan, at Versailles, he visited among his relatives till the year 1825, when he again became a householder. He then purchased the lease of a house in Windsor

Terrace, Clifton, commanding an extensive view in front, and behind a beautiful peep of the picturesque scenery of the river Avon running between lofty rocks. This house, which he adorned according to his usual taste, with his beautiful pictures, china, &c., after occupying for a year or two, he let, imagining that the fogs which arose from the river, rendered it unhealthy. It so happened that his old and valued friend Mrs. H. More spent her last years in this house. In the spring of 1828 she wrote him an account of the ungrateful and dishonest conduct of her long-tried domestics, and her determination to leave her sweet residence of Barley Wood for ever; and as his house was not then occupied, he offered it immediately to her, deferring all arrangements as to terms for after consideration. She accepted the kind offer, and shortly afterwards turned her back upon her unfeeling household, ordered them all to be discharged that morning, and in a couple of hours was installed in her new abode, where she continued, courted and beloved, till Sept. 1833, when she resigned her active and benevolent spirit into the hands of her Maker.

In the summer of this year Dr. Whalley quitted the shores of England for the last time. His niece, Mrs. Sullivan, once the object of ill-judged pride and ambition, and still that of his tender regard, now a widow, was suddenly placed in great pecuniary embarrassment. Disregarding his extreme age and emaciated body, he determined at once to go to her relief, and avoiding the pain of a farewell visit to his relatives at home, crossed the channel for La Flèche, where she had been residing for some years. The journey, though by short stages, and in his own easy carriage, proved too fatiguing for him, and in the full possession of his intellects, and with a heart languid in its pulsation, but still strong in its affections, he breathed his last in his arm-chair, a few weeks after his arrival. The respect in which his memory was held by the leading inhabitants of the place, in which he had passed the summer of 1820 with Mrs. Sullivan, overruled the opposition raised by the clergy, to the burial of his remains in their consecrated ground, and a portion of it was railed off, where the last rites were duly performed by an English clergyman, who came for the purpose from Nantes, in the presence of General Stafford, a relative, and Mr. Torriano, a son of one of his oldest and most intimate friends, both of whom came also from a distance, to pay this tribute of respect to his memory. A handsome sarcophagus of a dark slate formation, found in the vicinity of Laval, with an inscription to this effect, marked the spot: —

M. S.
THOMÆ SEDGWICK WHALLEY, S. T. D.
EX COMITATU SOMERSETTIÆ IN ANGLIÂ,
ECCLESIÆ CATHEDRALIS WELLENSI PRÆBENDARII:
CUJUS CIVILE STUDIUM, COMITATUS IDEM, CUI MAGISTRATUS PRÆERAT,
HUMANITATEM, VILLÆ SUÆ MENDIP VICINIA,
TESTANTUR.

VIGEBANT IN EO, SPECTATA ERGA DEUM PIETAS,
BENEVOLENTIA ERGA HOMINES VERE CHRISTIANA,
ERGA EGENOS EFFUSA LIBERALITAS.

AMORE ITAQUE, QUEM PER LONGAM VITAM
INGENII EXCELLENTIÂ, ET MORUM SUAVITATE,
CONCILIÂRAT,
MORTE TANDEM IN DESIDERIUM ACERRIMUM COMMUTATO,
OMNIBUS CHARUS, SUIS CHARISSIMUS,
OBIIT TERTIO DIE SEP. A. D. M.DCCC.XXVIII.
ÆTATIS SUÆ LXXXIII.

In reviewing the character of Dr. Whalley, we see a type of English gentleman which has now passed away. The more tranquil political times, in which we happily live, the great increase in the numbers of the educated classes, the constant running to and fro by the agency of steam, tend much to raise the calibre of men's minds to the same standard. Great talkers are not tolerated in the present day; if anyone thinks he knows more than his fellows, he must let them have it on paper, not *vivâ voce.* Not so in the last century: Dr. Johnson's society was not cultivated because he had written the dictionary, nor George Selwyn's because he was a man of fashion, nor Burke's because he was a great statesman, but because they all talked well. Such were the powers for which, in a less degree, Dr. Whalley was best known. But for Miss Seward's eulogiums, few even of his cotemporaries would have heard of his 'Edwy and Edilda,' now long since passed into oblivion; but his large acquaintance with the world, his extensive and varied information, his easy and yet powerful flow of language, and his elegant manners, obtained him the distinction of the literary friends, whose correspondence is now published, and a general reputation in society, which made him a welcome guest in so many good houses.

Mr. Wilberforce, in 1813, describes him as 'the true picture of a sensible, well-informed, and educated, polished, old, well-beneficed, nobleman's and gentleman's house-frequenting, literary, and chess-playing divine — of the best sort (not adulatory) — I hope beginning to be serious.' As a dilettante, he considered himself a judge of painting, made a collection of some of the old masters, and liberally patronised living artists, especially Barker, of Bath, whose well-known picture of the 'Woodman' was painted for Dr. Whalley. He was passionately fond of music, played on the piano, and was so powerfully affected by a good military band that, when listening to it, he wept like a child. In politics, we have already mentioned, he was a strong Tory; and as he was a diligent reader of the daily news in the old 'Standard' paper, and kept up a pretty extensive correspondence with well-informed persons, he considered himself an authority, and did not easily brook contradiction, as may be seen by his letter to Miss Seward, which she returned to him. Though possessed of a handsome income, he could not confine his expenditure within its limits; and the money wasted in extravagance and vanity, caused him much regret at the close of life. It was then his great desire to arrange his affairs by selling Mendip Lodge, and securing some large sums of money advanced by him on doubtful security, in order that his relatives, after his death, might benefit by him. In writing from Brussels, December 1815, to Mr. Anstey Calvert, his friend and legal adviser, he says, 'Next summer a favourable offer may be made for Mendip Lodge, or, if not next year, the following one. However straitened in my income, I will contrive to live under it. I have been guilty of too much waste, and too many follies in money matters; but those who come after me, shall not have to reproach my memory for sacrificing their interest to the selfishness of selling, at a very inferior value, such a property as will one day not only sell for, but be well worth, the sum I now demand for it, viz. 30,000*l.*'

Though all extravagance proceeds from a selfish principle, yet Dr. Whalley was uniformly kind and generous towards his relatives and friends, and liberal to all. His largesses were excessive: Miss Seward complains of the amount of those to her servants; and at Bath the post-boys fought for the honour of driving him. He paid his tradesmen's bills with so much grace, that it appeared as if they were conferring, rather than receiving, a favour. When his executor, on his way to settle Dr. Whalley's affairs, mentioned his death at the well-known Botham's Hotel, near Hungerford, where he was in the habit of sleeping, on his journeys to the metropolis, the landlady burst into tears, and appeared really affected. It was not difficult to impose upon him once, for he readily believed a person's character to be what he wished it, and thus he was often deceived. Such disappointments, however, did not sour his temper nor tinge it with misanthropy. Writing to a young relative, in 1825, he says, 'In you the silver cord is bright and strong, and the golden bowl is sound and unblemished. In me the former is attenuated to a trembling thread, and the latter is so irreparably damaged as to be threatened with destruction. Sad and long experience of this vain world and its ways — of the hollowness of profession and promises, disappointed in some, deluded by others — deprived by death of various true and valuable friends, and far distant from a few whom I esteem, and by whom I am valued and loved — the still warm affections of my heart are concentrated within a small circle, and burn the more ardently, because, like the sunbeams on a burning-glass, converging to one focus.'

Dr. Whalley's religious creed was founded on the Tomline school, which was considered the respectable divinity of the day — free alike, from the scepticism and indifference of the past age, from the unorthodox tenets which Miss Seward held, denying the IXth Article of our Church, and from what was considered the enthusiasm, or the austerity gaining ground in his own day, of which feelings the Methodists, in reference to the former, and his brother Richard to the latter, were regarded as types. During the last years of his life, his religious views altered. The Tomline doctrine of a union of faith and good works, as the price of salvation, fell beneath such texts as, 'Ye are *bought* with a *price*.' Writing, two years before his own end, in reference to the death of a relative, he says, 'O that my last hour may be as calm, and as full of a *blessed hope* (through the stupendous sacrifice and infinite *mercy* of our Divine Redeemer, on which the best of human beings *can only* rely) of eternal salvation! With this new and solemn warning close at hand, I must work at the one thing always most needful, while a little day is still graciously left me, since that last night must ere long come on me when I shall no longer be able to work.'

HORSINGTON RECTORY:
October 1862.

Such journals as the following, written with all the unreserved freedom of an attached husband addressing his wife, possess an interest distinct from the description of scenery, &c., as they show us incidentally that the changes in the law and social habits of France, between the times of mediæval and modern history, were not more marked than the revolution in both these particulars, created by the overthrow of the ancient Bourbon dynasty. The unfortunate and forgotten victim of state intrigue, still confined in his Alpine mountain prison, long after the power of his oppressors had passed away, the jolly monks who replenished the purses emptied of their Louis d'ors, at the game of Pharo! by a fall of their mountain firs, the ruinous extent of taxation, which well-nigh consumed all the produce of the soil, exhibit a state of society totally different from the present. The modern traveller at the Convent of Mount St. Bernard may indeed contrast the frugal entertainment, for which he knows a payment in full is expected, unfavourably with the real hospitality of the well-furnished board at St. Sulpice, but he must acknowledge that the revolution which wrought this change to his disadvantage, with whatever other evil consequences it may have been attended, certainly swept away many and glaring abuses.

THREE EXCURSIONS IN SAVOY AND FRANCE,

1783, 1784.

IT is always a pleasure to retrace scenes that presented varied beauties, and hours that were gilded by the sunshine of friendly and social converse. Rarely do they glide before us unmixed with care, and, when they have done so, are too precious to be buried in oblivion. If duly prized, they multiply their charms; their first enjoyment is lively, and, if it is rendered less poignant, it becomes more touching by remembrance, which throws a soft and attractive shading over every object and every event, and consecrates trifles at the shrine of sensibility, when combined with the sentiments it delights in and the fellowship it loves. And if, added to the pleasure that arises from the concatenation of our own ideas in the recurrence to past delights, their storied recollection becomes interesting and dear to those we best love, their triumph is complete, self-love and sentiment then go hand in hand, the sweetest duty smiles on inclination, and that which would otherwise have worn the face of a frivolous amusement, takes the form of a rational and solid satisfaction.

A little excursion which I made with my beloved and amiable friend, the Baron de Chatillon, into the province of Bugey, gave rise to the above scattered reflections. It was but of three weeks and five days' continuance; but on a just and nice comparison of things, perhaps that will be found a long period for pleasure and innocence to remain in harmony, for the senses and sensibilities to act in concert together, for reason to hallow the gaiety of mirth, for health to give a new and lasting charm to variety, and for sanguine expectation to be fully gratified.

We set out about the middle of November, from my friend's country house in the neighbourhood of Chamberry, and in about two hours arrived at Aix, which is, in itself, a small and ill-built town, but celebrated for its medicinal waters. These, in their temperature, nearly resemble those of Bath, and, in their qualities and effects, both them and the waters of Harrogate, the latter of which, I was at the moment by no means pleased to perceive, they also greatly resembled in their nauseous smell. A new and handsome building has just been erected for the convenience of the numerous invalids, who flock thither in the summer from various parts, in which there are very handsome and commodious baths reserved for the Royal family. From Aix we passed on through a marshy country to the lake of Bourget, on whose curling bosom a neat boat awaited us, with four sturdy rowers, who looked as if they had stood bluff against many a hard blow from wind and weather, and whose shaggy hair floated disordered on the brisk breeze, that invited us to embark on our little voyage, and promised us a quick passage to our haven, the Castle of Chatillon. The sun had hitherto sullenly shrouded himself in clouds, and we had not rowed above five minutes before he burst through his dark veil, shot rays of gold along the dark green furrows of the crystal lake, and graced with an enchanting mixture of light and shadow, every object around. A bold shore presented itself to our eyes on either hand, formed by a chain of intermingled rocks and mountains, which nature had thrown into a thousand different relative positions, and which in some parts, rose precipitate and threatening from the water, and at others, swelled into gradual and magnificent slopes, that reached above the clouds, adorned with a variety of culture, and broken into various dells, through which the silver brooks hurried to pour their tribute to the fond lake.

As the autumn had been remarkably fine, the woods were not yet wholly stripped of their honours, but were precisely in that state when every leaf becomes interesting, when their mottled shade presents that rich variety, which speaks their near destruction; when the eye roves admiring, while the heart yearns over their drooping graces; and when one fears every blast that ruffles their remaining beauties, and snatches them hour after hour away.

Every moment, as our little bark cut its watery way, presented either new objects, or a new combination of those offered to us before. Sometimes the view was frowning and barren, but for the box, holly, and ivy that grew between the chinks of the rocks, and adorned their white crags with dark shade; sometimes it was smiling and fertile, and sometimes a mixture of both, offered a striking and pleasing contrast to the eye. Nothing could be more picturesque than to see villages hanging on lofty steeps, where, one should have thought, the laborious foot of industry could never have traced its path, basking, as it were, with an air of tranquillity in the beams of the sun, and surrounded by various patches of vineyards, woodlands, ploughed land, and pastures.

In some parts, the hamlets were scattered between the opening of the precipices, down to the very edge of the lake, in which their white faces appeared reflected, intermingled with arbours, formed by the curling tendrils of the vine, in each of which a mossy crag, broken from the neighbouring rocks by the hand of time, served for rest and refreshment, amidst the heats of summer and the labours of the vintage. Here and there, the mouldering walls of some ancient château gave new graces, in the midst of ruin, to the scene, and ranged along the edge of the green lake. At the foot of a rock, crowned with a waving wood that bore the honours of a hundred years, and which, stretching beyond the precipice to the left, swelled down with ample shade to fringe the very border of the water, a spacious convent of Bernardines presented itself constantly to the eye, as if musing over the little waves that gently broke against its walls, and in a situation that seemed at once sequestered from the world, and open to the various beauties of nature. At the end of the perspective, and towering to a point, as it were, from the bosom of the lake, the Castle of Chatillon rose to the eye with an air of solitary grandeur, and offered a proud remembrance of its past honours and renown, situated on a craggy mount of a conical form, intersected with vineyards, and adorned with various shade, on each side of which the lake formed a deep basin. As we approached its ivied walls and irregular battlements, it assumed a more picturesque and imperious air, and still seemed to frown defiance to the destroyer Time, whose hand had lain its glories in the dust, and to awe the hamlets round. It is one of the most ancient, and was once the strongest castle in Savoy. In the time of Bertoldus, the first Duke of this country, it was considerable enough to lodge him and his whole train; and, under the Counts de Seyssel, was not only the terror and scourge of all the neighbourhood, but waged a proud and long war with its sovereign, and was the last that surrendered its independence. Though by far the greatest part of its buildings is utterly destroyed, there yet remains enough to give it a lordly appearance, and to speak its ancient strength and greatness. A lofty octagon tower is still perfect, in which there are two straight dungeons,* to which you mount by

* Donjon (corrupted dungeon), the highest and strongest tower of the castle, in which prisoners were kept.

> The grete toure, that was so thick and strong,
> Which of the castle was the chief dongeon.
>
> *Chaucer quoted in Johnson's Dict.*

stone stairs cut out of the thickness of the wall, and where the groans of the wretched victims of tyrannical power still seemed to resound in my ears. One can hardly imagine a more forlorn or hopeless prison; but its moss-grown stones shall no more re-echo with sad laments, or be watered with bitter tears. Who entered it formerly, entered it with shuddering horrors, and all the misgivings of misery; who enters it now, is guided by a curiosity that loves to trace past events, and, instead of an engine of cruelty and a dwelling for despair, it at present serves as a passage to a more extensive and smiling view of the surrounding country, over which the eye roves fearless and enchanted. Who, then, can regret its lost honours, when they went linked with tyranny and oppression? Who, but must prefer it in its present desolate state, that knows its present gentle, generous, and benevolent master? Ah, it is far better to be esteemed and loved in the midst of such mouldering walls and broken battlements, than to be hated and feared in a palace brighter than the sun! We were welcomed to the castle by the farmer and his wife, who are now its humble inhabitants. I never saw a countenance fuller of plain good sense and open honesty than his, or one more expressive of innocence and gentleness than hers. Our little voyage had got us good appetites, and all hands went to work to prepare the pot and the spit. An immense wood fire in a large chimney of vast hewn stones, the relic of ancient times, both comforted and enlivened us while our dinner was preparing; and we did ample justice to the neat * and excellent cookery of the plain and wholesome viands, that soon smoked on a thick carved oaken table, turned almost black with use and

* Neat, cleanly.

> Herbs and other country messes,
> Which the *neat*-handed Phyllis dresses.
>
> *Milton quoted in Johnson's Dict.*

age, and the former servant, perhaps, of brutal carousals, and hospitality equally rude and fastidious. I slept, or rather went to bed at night, in a vast formless and forlorn-looking chamber, and lay listening with a shuddering kind of satisfaction to the tempest that wailed in the crazy windows, and shook the massy portals. All the spirits of the lake seemed to be contending in the winds, and I fancied that I distinctly heard the shock of their battle, from time to time, in the rushing blasts; while at others they seemed to skirmish afar off, and only the distant murmur of their uproar reached my ear. The next morning saluted me brightly through the narrow windows; the nightly war was hushed, or at least calmed to surly whispers, that but bickered on the bosom of the yet agitated lake. As soon as breakfast was finished, the honest Farmer Pierre, who was equally alert on land and water, and equally knew how to profit by the bounties of both, prepared his fishing-boat, and with his wife's father, a sturdy and venerable figure, whose hoary locks waved white to the green waves, the rough hind that served him, and my valet, rowed us across the frothing waters of the angry lake to the Convent of Hautecomb. There we met with a cordial and hospitable reception from the Prieur and his holy brethren, who treated us, amongst other fare, with an ombre chevalier and a dish of lavareti, the latter a fish in size and flavour between a herring and a whiting, and peculiar to this lake: the former resembling a middling-sized cod, but still more delicious, and found only in the lakes of Bourget and Geneva. The convent is well-built, large and commodious, and its revenues considerable enough to support the community (which is not a large one), in plenty, if not in elegance, and enables the brotherhood to fulfil the duties of hospitality, though perhaps unequal to the demands of luxury. After dinner the good and gentle Prieur, whose manners were alike simple and courteous, proposed a walk to a famous intermitting fountain in the wood belonging to the convent. We agreed to it with pleasure, and after mounting the hill about ten minutes by a craggy path that skirted the rocks, arrived at a little platform of beautiful verdure, adorned with the irregular shade of some scattered chestnuts, and bounded by a picturesque rock crowned with trees, whose pendent branches waved wildly over its brow, embroidered all over with ivy and moss of various hues. At its foot we saw the pebbly channel of the capricious fountain, and the aperture from whence the uncertain water was wont to flow. When we first came it was quite dry, and the pebbles looked white in the sun, but we had not stood in anxious expectation above five minutes before we heard the sound of rushing waters within the rocky cavities, and a moment after saw them gush out with petty violence from the mossy outlet into their narrow channel, which they even overflowed in their momentary pride, and then hastened winding and silvering through the dark wood to the lake below. But their triumph was short; the crystal gush soon diminished to a trickling thread, and a few minutes after entirely ceased. The circumstance that puzzles the naturalist is, that these intermissions are wholly irregular and apparently independent of seasons; the fantastic fountain sometimes refusing to flow for a whole day together, and sometimes ebbing and flowing twice or thrice in an hour, and this with equal inconstancy in dry and wet weather, in summer and winter. As it was growing late, we pursued our way from the fountain by a natural and beautiful terrace through the wood; from which the inquisitive eye, penetrating the interwoven branches that shaded the deep slopes, saw the lake below and the opposite landscapes. After a delightful walk of near an hour we arrived at the water's edge, where the boat had been ordered to await us, and from whence the passage was much shorter to the castle. Amongst the monks with whom we had dined, there was one Frenchman, who, as he chose to distinguish himself, ought to be set apart from the rest. He was bold and familiar with all the loquaciousness and vanity of his nation, and none of its grace; his countenance was dark and sallow; his eye haggard, and his brow full of bad promise. The expression of his face marked enough of what the French call *esprit,* but it was an esprit tricking, libertine, and malign. He talked at everything, and where his knowledge failed him, his address helped him through, and in a manner that showed he had long been used to shifting. He had been in England, affected to know every place and every person there of consequence, and remembered every impious and indecent expression in the language of that country, though he had forgotten every other part of it: a powerful *argumentum ad hominem,* which proved the picture in his face no liar. After his brethren had left, he would still attend us, and when we arrived at the border of the lake, on a slight invitation from my friend to accompany us to Chatillon, leapt into the boat, tucked his robes round his girdle, seized one of the oars, and rowed away for the castle. At supper he ate like a glutton, drank like a sot, and talked like the most abandoned debauchee. My friend happened to mention the old chapel at the castle; this reverend Father insisted on performing mass in it the next morning, in the holy zeal of his heart, as it was Sunday, and as a preparative begged Vincent my servant to shave his beard, which was at least of ten days' growth. As the operation was dexterously performed, he desired to see the razor, which was really an excellent one and the best I possessed, admired the temper of the English steel, and wished he was master of a similar one. In the morning Vincent shaved me, afterwards he placed the envied razor on my dressing-box, and left the latter in the room, through which the monk was to pass in order to go down stairs. A minute after he descended and hurried away to say mass, which when he had gabbled over we all sat down to breakfast together, and I desired Vincent in the mean time to pack up my clothes, &c., as we meant to leave the castle as soon as our appetites were satisfied. He returned in a moment to inform me that the razor in question was missing. All our searches were fruitless, it was nowhere to be found. My suspicions immediately fell on our reverend companion; but though I detested his principles, and was provoked at his impudent theft, I would not expose him and his holy order, before the honest Pierre and his household; but when he pretended to lament my loss, contented myself with saying that it was a trifle, which was not worth my regret, or any person losing a good name, or confirming a bad one, by thieving it from me. I fixed my eye fully and sneeringly upon him, as I said this, and in spite of his habitual effrontery and natural art, traced a hurrying emotion of guilt in his face, which he presently checked; though all his impudence could not serve him enough to enlarge further on the subject, or to insult me with his further condolences. We soon after parted, as he took one boat to join his worthier brethren of Hautecomb, and we entered into another to pursue our little voyage by the lake, and a canal cut from it to the Rhone, whose rapid current we reached in about two hours, and after sailing swiftly down it about one more, landed at the little village of Rochefort in the province of Bugey. As we were not provided with a carriage to convey us to Bellay, the little capital of this little province, and could procure none in the village, we put on a good face and sent our compliments to Madame Montillet, whose spacious château appeared with a domineering air, on a hill that towered over the lowly roofs below, praying her in the name of two English travellers, to lend us some one of her carriages to help us on in our way. The petition was graciously received, female curiosity sent three scouts in the form of two livery servants, and a rosy chaplain, to reconnoitre us, and after some chat and civilities between us and the latter, a neat curricle drove down from the château with two horses, in which we and our servants mounted, and proceeded to Bellay, through rough and dirty lanes flanked on either hand with a country, that *then* demanded no particular notice, and *now* merits no particular remembrance. The *town*, or (for, like other *little* things, it is doubtless jealous of those titles, which are not supported by personal merit), as I should have written, *city* of Bellay, is old and sufficiently ill-built, but full of poor provincial *noblesse* in the winter, who cannot afford to live in more brilliant and expensive capitals, of Chanoines who belong to the cathedral, and of *Religieux* and *Religieuses* who belong to its unnecessary convents. The Bishop's palace has a nearer resemblance to that name than one would expect, is well furnished, and possesses two treasures, in two beautiful paintings by Verney, both sea pieces, the style in which he is famous. We slept comfortably after a good supper, in a neat *auberge* at Bellay that night, and set out early the next morning for Lunes, the château of Count d'Angeville, and the termination of our tour.

The country immediately about Bellay, though not highly picturesque, is fertile and pleasing, especially some little hills, intersected with verdant pastures and soft woods, crowned with châteaux and sloping vineyards, formed at regular distances into festoons, by training the vines from tree to tree, planted on purpose for their support, and between which, either the ridges of wheat in the autumn emulate with their floating gold the purple clusters that dangle and blush above, or a verdant carpet seems to invite them to drop their riches on its soft lap. As we advanced, the objects became bolder, but less various and pleasing. Stupendous mountains, dark with forests of the formal fir, frowning rocks, and immense unshaded meads, presented themselves continually to our eyes, till we reached a steep summit above the little village of S——. From thence a varied and magnificent scene was opened before us, which extended one way, in charming perspective, across the Rhone, to the Lake of Bourget, closed in by a noble chain of interlaced rocks and mountains, and which smiled and wantoned amidst fertile meadows, scattered villages, and picturesque hills. The ruins of an old castle just below us, and the nest of tranquil and neat-looking cottages, with their little gardens and clear river, deep beneath, formed no unlovely features in the striking and diversified prospect. Yet, upon the whole, it was rather that vast and dizzy kind that, from repetition, would fatigue the eye — which is always to be admired, but which might not always delight.

Lofty as this part of the road was, we mounted continually on foot, to ease the labouring and almost jaded horses, for nearly three hours, between sombre mountains and woods of the frowning fir, till the monastery of St. Sulpice suddenly presented itself to our eyes, with an air of sequestered state, in a highly-cultivated little basin, far amidst the fir-crowned heights. A keen frosty morning had so sharpened our appetites, that the curling smoke from the chimneys of the convent had more charms, in our eyes, at that moment, than the noble sweep of the mountain and the late verdure of the meadows. As we descended to its hospitable gate, the dinner-bell sounded like sweetest music in our ears. The jolly monks assembled at the gate to meet us. Our reception was open and hearty, as we might have expected it to be, from a set of *religieux*, in whose eyes danced mirth and content, on whose cheeks sat full plenty and dimpled ease, and who had *bons vivants* written on their foreheads. A good fire was a welcome preparative to an excellent dinner, in which the holy brethren showed their connoisseurship in cookery. Their wine was not inferior, and the growth of their own vineyards. We joined them in doing ample justice to both, and all seemed to bear in mind at least that part of the Scripture which saith, 'Let us eat and drink, for to-morrow we die.' After dinner, they showed us their kitchen and cellar; the perfect convenience and nice order of both, proved of how much importance they thought them to their happiness. Indeed they were worthy of a prince, even though he were an epicure. I know not what St. Bernard *was*; but well know, that if all his disciples are like the monks of St. Sulpice, he has a set of as jolly fellows for his followers as live under the sun. I do not believe, indeed, that they will wear out their knees with praying, or the gloss off their skins with sackcloth and ashes; but I can aver that they wear good humour, and the convivial and hospitable graces, and that they become them perfectly. It is no mean merit also (and in my eyes worth a thousand vigils and fastings), to gladden the hearts of all the peasantry about them, and, by open-handed, yet well-regulated benevolence, to have made the desert smile. The beggar is never turned away empty from their doors, the industrious peasant is sure to meet from them both encouragement and reward; and while his merits are justly appreciated, his misfortunes are relieved, and his sorrows consoled. The soil all round their convent was originally ungrateful and sterile, the valley a swamp, and the mountains bare. But by their wise and benevolent system, the latter now are shaded by stately forests of pines, and the former laugh and sing with fruitfulness. Their revenue is considerable, but one of the jolliest amongst them told me, their expenses often went beyond it. But they have their remedy at hand. When they want a sum of money, the axe goes to work, and a thousand or two of their towering firs bring all matters even again. 'Voilà,' said he, pointing to them, 'de quoi payer nos dettes.'

But amongst the sleek and pampered Bernardins, on whose plump cheeks glowed the rich hues of a warm autumn, I should have distinguished one, who had scarcely passed the spring-tide of his days, but in whose cheeks the blossoms seemed untimely to have withered, and in whose eyes sat pensive melancholy. He interested me, and observed it. The conversation turning on pictures, M. Chatillon desired me to produce my darling little resemblance of Mrs. Siddons,* as a proof of the skill of our miniature-painters. It passed from hand to hand. The suffrages of the others in its favour were loud and prolix; but the young monk regarded it with fixed and silent attention, and with a rising tear, that showed it made a deeper impression upon him, and recalled touching ideas to his heart. After we had risen from table, he took occasion to invite me to his neat apartment, where, opening a little cabinet, he drew from a secret drawer a miniature picture, which he pressed, with a quick motion and a passing flush, to his bosom; and then, with a sigh that spoke more touchingly than all language, put it into my hand. It represented a beautiful young woman, with the complexion, and somewhat of the features, of Mrs. Siddons. I read in it the cause of his graceful emotions. He saw it, and said, 'But for that lovely creature, I had never renounced the world, to shut myself up within the walls of a monastery.' I supposed that she had jilted him. 'Oh no,' he cried, with emphasis, 'she was as amiable as she was beautiful; and thence my deep sorrow, which seven years' penitence and prayer have not been able to efface! I am the son of a merchant at Lyons. I passionately loved this charming girl, and won her heart. She was of equal birth; our families approved our vows, and the day was fixed for our nuptials. In the mean time one of my relations gave a ball, at which we danced together

* This was probably the miniature, the engraving of which is given.

with all the joy of young and heedless minds, that give themselves up to the pleasures of the moment, and to the delights of a fond passion, which meets no opposition and dreads no reverse. After a long and fatiguing dance, oppressed with heat, she passed into the room where they dealt out refreshments, and desired me to procure her some warm wine and water. I pressed through the crowd to demand it. In the hurry and confusion they put a basin of cold lemonade into my hand, which, through a carelessness I never shall pardon myself for, I did not observe. The object of all my wishes drank it eagerly, clapped her hand to her forehead, uttered one groan, and dropped dead upon the spot.' Tears choked his words; mine flowed with them. All I could say was, 'that it was not for man, but Heaven, to give him comfort.' He clasped his hands in agony together, and with a mixture of energy and submission in his countenance that I shall never forget, replied, 'It has taught me resignation, but when will it teach me forgetfulness?' He afterwards moved his lips a moment in silent ejaculation, then composed his countenance, and conducted me back to his merrier and happier, but less amiable and interesting companions.

As the road was both steep and rough from St. Sulpice to Lunes, we did not reach the latter till it was quite dark, though we had set out in good time, and the distance between one and the other is not above five miles.

The château of Lunes is the loftiest habitable situation I know. It was once a very strong fortress, and sometimes braved even the arms of the king; but having served as a stronghold in the civil wars against Henry the Fourth, that monarch ordered its fortifications to be dismantled, and it now proudly stands on its high and rocky hill, a memento of past times. It is no longer a terror to the present, braving only the winds of heaven, and looking harmless scorn upon the village of Hauteville, whose thatched cottages seem crowding round its base to admire its grandeur. The Count D'Angeville and the Countess, his mother, received us with the usual French politeness, and more than the usual French cordiality. We found a numerous and cheerful society assembled round their hearth, and as I spent eighteen of the happiest days of my life amongst them, it is natural that I should love to retrace their several characters, and dwell on them with pleasure.

The Countess D'Angeville is about fifty, has the remains of a handsome person, and more than the remains of a good understanding, ripened by experience and quickened by a thorough knowledge of the world. Her heart is, I believe, on the whole, good, though I would not answer for its sincerity in her common French-like professions. Her temper is even, and her cheerfulness of that composed kind that is not subject to sudden reverses. Yet she tolerates, even promotes, noisy mirth about her, and with her children has all the playfulness of a sister, and all the ease of a friend, joined to the tenderness and respectable manners of a mother. Her knowledge is rather of the prudent and necessary, than of the enlarged and elegant kind, and consistent with it, she attends more to her household affairs, and to a *procès* which she has long and successfully pursued for her son, than to the belles lettres. In consequence of this, she has sometimes the subtlety of the lawyer in her arguments, and now and then his documenting air. In her religious duties she is so exact as to be suspected for a devotee; but I could never perceive that she carried her zeal in a good cause, far enough to be offensively rigid or uncharitably austere.

Her eldest son the Count is perfectly well made, and is so firmly set together, and has so decisive an air, that I do not know a more manly figure, though he is not above five feet high. Joined to all his national good breeding, he has all the English frankness, and though he is, after all, a Frenchman, wears his *façons* and gold ear-rings with so open and honest an air, that you cannot help thinking the poison and varnish of a French education, have in vain striven to mask his countenance, or corrupt his heart. His understanding, without being highly cultivated or profoundly deep, has taken that kind of light polish which shines agreeably in society, and has a certain acuteness in it, which seems peculiar to his country, which always gives self-possession, keeps the eyes and the ears open, and supplies want of depth, with attention and address. His temper is gay and accommodating, his manners easy and friendly, his sentiments just, if not refined, and for his principles, his behaviour as a son and a brother may speak in general, and the following little scene, which I was charmed to witness, in particular. As he was lately arrived at Lunes, his old nurse, a paysanne in one of the neighbouring villages, came one morning to see him, and entering the room where we were all assembled, could not restrain herself, in the honest excess of her joy, from throwing her arms round his neck, kissing him with all her heart, and weeping on his bosom. Instead of being put to the blush (as many a fine gentleman I know would have been) by her free and coarse caresses, he wiped her eyes, patted her cheeks, kissed her heartily again and again, called her by a thousand endearing names, enquired kindly after his foster-sister, her husband, her son; told her to be sure and come to see him often; and turning to me, added, 'Is not my good old nurse a *brave femme*? — I assure you I love her dearly, and, however eager I may be in the chase, never pass her door without bidding her *bon jour*.' 'And if thou didst,' cried the honest creature, in her *patois*, with equal warmth and simplicity, 'I would shake thee soundly.'

So we will leave the dear little manly Count to chase the

wild boars and chevreuils in his fir forests, and pass on to his brother, the gentle Chevalier, whom, to look at, one should never suspect of having been aboard one of the floating batteries, that was burnt in the dreadful day before Gibraltar. He has none of his brother's vivacity, though much of his merit, and his lady-like manners do not sit well upon a lieutenant-colonel; their effeminate softness does injustice both to his understanding and courage, the latter of which has been proved intrepid, and the former, though not brilliant, being on a level with those of the people in general, and equal to all the common purposes of life and society. Nominally a Chevalier of Malta, he seems already to have much of the preciseness of an old bachelor, though scarcely six-and-twenty, and though he has not yet taken the vows of celibacy. In the service of Spain, he seems to have engrafted some of the formal gravity of that nation on French politeness, though without a grain of its repulsive pride. His constant disposition and perpetual attention to oblige, would alone make him an amiable member of society.

The Countess de Champdor, his only sister, is a fair widow of twenty-eight, and her beauty is attractive and interesting, because joined with the softness of her sex, lighted up by sense, and glowing all over with sensibility. That her manners should be graceful is no wonder, because she is a Frenchwoman; but for that very reason it is a wonder that they are *naïve.* I never saw the consciousness of a sensible and tender heart so visible in any one; it is for ever diffused through every motion and over every feature; trembles in her eyes, and adorns her cheeks with the most charming blushes, which she is wise enough never to hide with *rouge.* In her conversation she is extremely agreeable and always nicely and naturally delicate, an extraordinary merit in a Frenchwoman of quality, who is handsome, *pleine d'esprit,* and mixes much with the great world. Her temper has that warmth in it, which usually belongs to quick sensibilities, her sentiments are liberal and generous, and her soul highly susceptible of friendship and offering affection. As a wife she was remarkable for her constancy and tenderness, and as a sister, daughter, and mother, she is irreproachable. In short, in all points of view she is estimable, and in all charming.

The Marquis de Chatelet, her father-in-law, is what the French call a *beau vieillard,* though blind, but his blindness renders him at once more venerable and interesting, and the defect of his natural, seems only to have added to the perfection of his intellectual light. His *esprit* is truly *fin,* both in the French and English application of the word; the pains he has taken to cultivate his talents have been well bestowed, as they have rendered him at once highly informed and entertaining. His manners are extremely polite, and he is so full of refined and insinuating caresses, that you can scarcely forbear giving yourself up to them, though you cannot help suspecting, that they come more from the lip than the heart, and that there is more in them of French *finesse,* than English sincerity. Of penetrating judgment, and a long and acute observer of mankind, he presently reads, blind as he is, the character of the person he converses with, and accommodates his own manners and sentiments accordingly, and has the art of pleasing while he apparently flatters you, because he has always the art of putting you in a good humour for the moment with yourself. Of his principles and real disposition, I leave those to speak who know him better. A man like him is not to be understood in a few days; though in a few days one can discern enough to see, that one must not take all his fine sentiments and rare professions upon trust.

Madame Quinsieux, his daughter, was another and no inconsiderable member of the various group. She was interesting from beauty and youth, but still more so from impaired health, which always adds new softness and delicacy to female attractions, and from being destined, and perhaps against her will, to waste her cheerless days within the dreary walls of a convent: a monotonous and torpid existence, little suited to her piercing and searching spirit, and still less, peradventure, to her temperament. Bred up for the world, she would have been a refined and elegant coquette; immured early in a convent, she is an ingenious and engaging nun, who, without professing, well knows all the arts of pleasing, and gains more on the side of nature, than she has lost on that of education and a knowledge of the world. Nothing can be more insinuating than her manners, or soothing than her voice. Her smile is full of intelligence and seducing sweetness, and when it ripens to a laugh, which, with her, is never coarse and clamorous, discovers teeth as white as ivory, and gums that have all the freshness of the new-blown rose. Her eyes are of a clear dark grey, with long and bright brown lashes and brows, and express at once, acute refined sense and melting softness. She was only permitted to visit her sister-in-law, Madame Champdor, on account of her declining health. The prey of ennui and fruitless desires, and a hectic blush in her cheek, to which a sensibility, not wholly made up of refined sensations, sometimes gave a deeper and warmer dye, accorded wonderfully with her light and delicate form, beautifully white skin, and the full shading of her dark hair; of whose superior beauty she was well aware, and to whose abundant tresses, she adjusted her neat muslin cap and black gauze veil, with a care and grace that betrayed how vainly the cloister had endeavoured to mortify her female pride, and render her indifferent to beauty and its attendant admiration. Unhappily, she was not only destined to a convent, but to a convent where there was nothing either young, handsome, or ingenious but herself; and perhaps the tiresome cant and austere and superstitious devotion of her antiquated fellows, rendered her cloister not only tenfold more disgusting, but taught her curious and discerning spirit to soar above their uninformed zeal, and disdain their narrow prejudices. Her humour is equally cheerful and conforming, and her conversation intelligent, spirited, and full of female refinement.

With more than her *finesse*, the Chevalier Montillet, her brother, does not possess half her amiable qualities. He is about the height of Count d'Angeville, and what the ladies would call 'a sweet little man.' He is, in truth, perfectly well made, but instead of the open and manly air of the Count, has all the lounge and mien of a Parisian *petit maître*, a character which he seems to make the object of his ambition, and, therefore, he would take my comparison for praise. When he walks, it is upon tip-toes; when he reposes (for it cannot be called sitting), it is at his length as far as the back of his chair will admit of, and with an air of the most perfect nonchalance. His face is regularly pretty, and his eye black and bright, but full of those sly sidelong glances, that mark design and a desire to find out something at which to sneer. A finished French education, has given him what are termed all the accomplishments of a gentleman, and with them the vanity and principles and *manières factices* of a young Frenchman of *ton*, who loves nothing but himself, follows nothing but his own gratifications, and, if possible, suffers nothing to interfere with his ease, when situation and circumstance separate him awhile from his pleasures. Yet (when he would so far vouchsafe) he could be extremely agreeable; would let you see that he had a cultivated understanding, was master of many pleasing talents, and that he could even be prepossessingly amiable, but for a refined expression of art, which always accompanied everything he said, lay in ambush about his mouth, and sat retired in the corner of his eye.

The unpolished Chanoine Ruban was a character diametrically opposite. With little genius and much erudition, good humour and bad taste, coarse manners but an honest heart, he sought less to win your prepossession, than good opinion; and if he did not gain your affections, was certain, in the long run, to gain your esteem. As he had read much poesy, he thought he must be able to write it; and, as a proof of his harmonious talents in every sense, sang us two or three songs, which he had composed in compliment of Madame Champdor's beauty, made up of old ends and strange imitations of Ovid and Tibullus; and, in truth, never were voice and verse better suited to each other. They might truly be said to form a concord of discords, and it would be a thousand pities that they should ever be divided. However, he has a praise far beyond the praise of a good poet, that of being a good man; and his being a good sportsman was also of some moment to us at the time, as he and the Père Crochon, almost daily supplied the table with hares, red partridges, woodcocks, pheasants, and other game.

The Père Crochon is a monk of St. Sulpice, and I need say no more to prove that he can enjoy good company and good cheer; and as this seems not only to be his highest praise, but the utmost scope of his talents and wishes, I shall add no more of him, but make my bow to Madame Chovin, the Countess d'Angeville's sister, who is a mere old swarthy Frenchwoman, with an intriguing face, and a black eye, that rolls about and tells many tales of past days. But, alas! those days are over. She sees her earthly paradise now in a pack of cards, and makes it her greatest glory to vaunt of her former feats of *Basset*, before the cruel Court prohibited high play. Her husband is about fifty, has long served his King for poor wages, and bears in his rough and weather-beaten face the marks of arduous travail, and bold seeking for honour in the cannon's mouth. His natural understanding is remarkably keen and nervous, and he makes better songs than the Chanoine, though without erudition or a pretence to genius.

He talks little, except occasion draws him out, but what he says is full of force, and always to the point. He has a dry and powerful badinage about him, when he pleases, that there is scarcely any parrying, but he never employs it ill-naturedly. The rage of cards is also upon him, and there only he appears to disadvantage, as all his passion is awakened and interested in the cause; and their influence over his judgment (which on all other occasions seems so cool and sound), it is said, has cost him a considerable part of his fortune, and gone near to destroy his life or ruin his peace.

Of Monsieur Mongonnan and Mademoiselle La Tour, the former, Madame Chovin's son by a former husband, and the latter, a demoiselle of eighty-three, and a relation of Madame d'Angeville's, I shall say nothing, because they appeared too nothingless for anything to be said of them. On my dear Chatillon's character I need not enlarge, nor descant on his merits; those friends who are likely to read this, have been made fully acquainted with both. I shall only add, or perhaps repeat, that he was born to form the ornament of public, and charm of private society, and that all the worldly and domestic *agrémens,* joined to every domestic virtue, shine eminently in his manners and conversation, and build their seat loveliest in his bosom.

Such was our society, and, from its heterogeneous nature, it could not fail to be agreeable and entertaining. Walking, riding, cards, reading, and that kind of childish frolicking, where every one casts aside all pretence to formality and superior wisdom, and which is wont to make the heart so much lighter than philosophising, alternately occupied the winged hours that fled onwards with our lives, and left us no place for present lassitude or future remorse.

When the Château of Lunes, which is modernising and undergoing a thorough repair, is finished, it will be very handsome and spacious, and some chimney-pieces and ornamental tables of stucco appear to me to be *chefs d'œuvre.* Some are in representation of the verd antique Egyptian, and others of the most precious marbles, and are so highly finished, that this imitation exceeds the original in polish and beauty. Nothing can surpass either the exquisite taste or natural appearance of the veining: and if they prove but as durable as they are delicate, the most costly marbles would yield the palm to them in my eyes. The man who executes them is a Frenchman, is very moderate in his price, and unites the greatest industry to the utmost ingenuity. At present he is little known, but when his talents are justly appreciated, he cannot fail to make his fortune. I am sure he would soon do so were he to go to England, where nothing comparable of the kind has yet appeared; his stucco being as superior to the pillars of the Pantheon, as those are to that of the most common kind. The prospect from the château is wide, bleak, and cheerless in winter; but when the immense meadow lands are of a lively green, and covered with sheep, cattle, and various kinds of grain and pasture chequer the sides of the mountains, whose towering summits are covered deep with firs, it must be lively as well as commanding. The fir forests, indeed, form at once the striking feature and riches of the country. They are, in general, beautifully straight, and of an amazing height and thickness, and all the under lands, produce a revenue very disproportionate to their dark hosts, a part of which fall before the tyrant axe at stated periods, and are succeeded by their little offspring, who again fall to make room for a future generation; but man, who is their lord, suffers them at least to live and flourish the age of man, before their stately honours are levelled in the dust.

Amongst other delicacies, the head of a wild boar was served up at the Count's table, after the ferocious animal had been killed by his own hand, and, frightful as it looked, its delicious flavour found favour with all the company, and made them see it again and again with pleasure. The Count had tamed two of these ugly beasts, which he kept in his courtyard, and called Annette and Lubin. He often amused us by playing with, and making them follow him. But Lubin, I then thought, did it with a grudging aud surly sort of obedience, which showed his savage nature to have been rather checked for a time, than effectually conquered, and his rebellious and dangerous violences have since cost him his life. As to poor Annette, she was perfectly gentle, though completely ugly, rolled at her master's feet like a dog, and was prodigal of her uncouth caresses. But Lubin, it seems, still reigned the absolute master of her secret affections, and she took his untimely death so much to heart that, as the epitaph says, 'Awhile she tried to live without him, liked it not, and died.' The application may be thought ludicrous, but it alters not the fact, and, meanly as poor Annette may be thought of, and much as the mind may revolt at her affections, I fear the constancy and tenderness of love, is seldom to be found so perfect in the vaunted human heart.

Our time was divided between Lunes and Champdor, the château of the fair Countess, who did its honours with the utmost liberality and grace. It is about two miles from Lunes, much lower and less pretending in its situation, but more snug, and in my opinion more pleasing. The cottages in this village have an air of peculiar comfort, and every peasant was neatly clothed, and had a healthy and contented look. It was a singular pleasure to me to remark the genuine affection and delight that animated their faces, when their lady passed by their doors, and the kindness with which she received their salutations and returned their benedictions. How easy is it for superior rank to conciliate humble affection, and while it exacts the outward reverence of awe, how sure is mistaken fastidiousness to lose the real respect of the heart! I one morning attended Madame Champdor to her neat parish church, and as we passed by the font she dipped her fair hand in the holy water, and with a quick and graceful motion formed a cross on my forehead and bosom, and told me that she had now made a good Catholic of me; I thanked her for her kind care of my soul, said I must salute my belle Marraine with an holy kiss, and assured her that if it spoke truth, she would find it as warm on the side of affection, as she could possibly be on that of zeal. Thus, we passed our time in innocent mirth and harmless jesting, and I confess that I parted from my fair god-mother, and my interesting nun with much regret, real esteem, and a firm belief of having obtained a place in their memory, if I could not flatter myself with having obtained one in their friendship.

But I must not trace my steps back again to my friends in Savoy, before I have made mention of a ride I took one day with the friendly little Count, and which terminated in one of the most singular and picturesque scenes I ever saw, and which perhaps Europe produces, though so entirely out of the track of English travellers in general, that I do not recollect it to have been noticed by any one of them, frequently as the press has laboured with tours to the Continent. After tracking for about half an hour the course of a small but rapid river, which, having been swollen with late rains, went proudly eddying and foaming amidst fragments of rocks, and formed itself into numerous falls, we crossed it by a stone bridge, and entered into a field of beautiful verdure, which conducted us by a steep slope to a semicircular platform fringed all round with elms and oaks, whose interlaced branches trembled in the sharp blast, that every moment reft them of their last scanty shade. Nothing appeared beyond, and I rode carelessly chatting on till the Count halted suddenly, and seized the bridle of my horse. Awakened by this unexpected pause I looked forwards, and instead of the supposed continuance of the smooth and even lawn, found myself on the edge of a precipice, down which my eye plunged trembling to a dark gulf of fearful depth, while my ear was deafened by the thunders of rushing waters. The surprise was perfect, and gave tenfold effect to a scene, which was in itself equally romantic, beautiful, and sublime, and which the mind was never weary of contemplating with that shuddering kind of transport, which is always a tribute to the terrible graces. When the first dizzy astonishment was a little subsided, and my wondering eye began to distinguish and select the striking objects presented to it, the profound gulf appeared a vast basin formed at the bases of the surrounding rocks and mountains, which were thrown together in the noblest disorder, formed the boldest angles, and frowned darkly with the thick shade of a thousand evergreens and various brushwood, mixed with venerable oaks, chestnuts, and ashes. Their wild branches were thrown in the most fantastic and picturesque manner across the mossy crags, and seemed the haunt of every bird of prey — whose mingled screams were heard amidst the dashings of the water, and added to the terror of the scene. On the right the river, which I thought we had left far behind, boiled along to the brink of a stupendous precipice, from whence it rushed tempestuously to a rock beneath, whose craggy points broke its crystal sheet into a hundred parts, and sent it raging and foaming from crag to crag, till it threw itself at once with redoubled fury and loud bellowings into the deep and dark gulf beneath. There the eye still pursued its tortuous and rapid course, till it lost itself in the rocky cavities of the mountains; yet sublimely fine as the scene appeared to me, the Count assured me that it was much superior when all the trees were in full leaf, and a bright sun gilded partially its sombre beauties, and set the cascade on fire. The contrast between the sparkling water and the black intense is then, he assured me, the most striking picture imaginable; and as I have promised to visit him at his château again in the month of May, we are to return to this singular spot, and he affirms that my most sanguine expectations will not be disappointed. Till I had seen this gulf, I thought that of Chailles, which Rousseau celebrates in his Confessions, must be the most picturesque scene of the kind in Europe. But it is neither so greatly featured, so dark, nor so capacious as that of Charabot; shows a glimpse of the world in cheerful perspective beyond it one way, and above all, wants the noble cascade of its awful rival, to render its contrasting features and savage scenery complete. The French often talk and talk of *belles horreurs*, but here the forcible term may be justly applied.

From Champdor, in our way back, we reached the convent of St. Sulpice by 12 o'clock, accompanied by the honest Chanoine Ruban and the rough soldier Chovin. It was impossible to see the smoke of the jovial monks' kitchen with indifference, after having had a taste of their good fare, so our horses were led to their stables, and we attended them willingly to their plenteous board. As the Père Crochon had privately advertised them of the day we purposed quitting Champdor, and the probability of our calling on them by the way, the vain and luxurious old rogues, had piqued themselves on providing every delicacy that the season, and at least three of the elements, would afford, and the fourth, with the skill of a most complete cook, sent them to table in a much more tempting shape, than they need have appeared before hungry travellers on a frosty morning to stimulate their appetites. When we had eaten, and drunk, and laughed our fills, we rose up with grateful hearts and thought to have gone away; but a good fire and cards were prepared in the abbé's drawing-room, and the jolly friars seemed to have so set their minds on a bank at Pharo, that we could not find it in ours, to refuse staying at their convent that night. I am almost ashamed to add that, after having eaten their victuals and drunk their drink, we also nearly emptied their purses; but the firs, and 'voila de quoi nous dédommager,' came into my thoughts, so I pocketed their Louis, and slept on their down bed in peace. We left them early enough the next day to reach Bellay by dinner, which was prepared for us in the house of the Marquis de Chatelet, who had insisted on our eating and sleeping there, instead of returning to the auberge. In the evening we went to see a play performed by a strolling company in a wretched cockloft, ludicrously fitted up and scenefied; and harmonised in the interludes by one wretched scraper with an old scarlet coat, blue breeches patched with white, long ruffles that seemed to have served in the former capacity of dusting-rags, one eye, and half a nose—the latter of which he fed continually with snuff, whenever he ceased to torment the stale graces of Lady Coventry's minuet, the sum total of his *ars musica*, at least for that night. If I have seen comedies better, I have never seen any more divertingly, represented. The Englishman at Paris, particularly, was a chef-d'œuvre, as it was played by a tall meagre sallow figure, (supposed to be just come off his journey from London,) in a yellow threadbare coat bedizened all over with tinsel frogs, and who laboured at English with a broad patois French accent. However, the belles dames of Bellay admired him prodigiously, and cast exulting looks at me from time to time, on the excellence of the representation, which I assured them could not be sufficiently extolled for its spirit and truth. An honest fib, and much better, in my opinion, than shocking their pride by rude ridicule and illiberal sneers. It has always seemed to me a debt to society, never unnecessarily to put any of its members out of humour with themselves, or destroy the good fellowship and benevolence of the moment, by useless contradiction and ungenerous fastidiousness. The doctrine of self-love, a doctrine so dear to us all, should teach us a different conduct, if our better principles are not powerful enough to influence our behaviour on this head. The person in any company who sets himself up as a severe censor of all around him — as the critic of their judgements and the corrector of their tastes, though he may be thought clever, will never be thought amiable; may sometimes be looked up to, but never with affection, and loses more on the side of esteem, than he ever gains on that of respect.

We made a little excursion the next morning with the Chanoine Ruban to Père Chatel, a famous convent of the Chartreux, about six miles from Bellay. It is built on the point of a ragged and lofty rock, of which its dark front seems a continuance — the building being carried in a perpendicular line from the very edge of the precipice, and seeming of a piece with it. The road to the convent is so steep, that we were obliged to alight from our carriages before we had got half way up the ascent, and labour the remainder of our way on foot. But this we should have preferred doing otherwise, as the bold objects on either side, demanded frequent pauses and particular attention. The road winds through stupendous rocks on either hand, broken and varied, which in some parts overhang it with a menacing air, and which are the whole way adorned with the dark shade of the box, holly, fir, and yew, and embroidered with moss and ivy in the most picturesque style, except in one part on the left, where a craggy slope of cheerless and scanty verdure, is scattered over with oaks, whose wild branches meet at the top and form an irregular canopy over the white cliffs below. A gateway was built across the sombre chasm a little way before we reached the summit, the uncourteous porter of which denies entrance to every female foot — an omen of those austerities which are practised in the habitation above, and which refuse, either from fear or wisdom, from a dread of present, or a penitence for past frailty, to hear the voice of the charmer, or feast the eyes with the fairest work of God. When we arrived at the convent, how different our reception from that at St. Sulpice. Here all was sombre, all silent, except the wind that murmured round the walls, and the Rhone that roared sullenly beneath. We entered, and paced the long cloisters, which seemed to echo with a melancholy sound to the tread of our feet; and at last met the holy Prieur as he came from chapel, where, if strong appearance lies not, he had surely been offering up his devotions with a pure heart. He accosted us with the air of a man weaned from the world, yet who well knew its usages, and had not yet lost its polish. The simplicity of his welcome spoke humbled affections rather than unformed manners, whilst its fulness satisfied the heart. As it was cold he conducted us to his brown parlour, hung round with saints of the order, where there was a little fire, which he hasted to replenish more for our gratification than his own. Three of his brethren soon joined us. What a difference between their meek and mortified looks, and the prompt and convivial air of the Bernardines! What a difference between the sunken eyes and sallow cheeks of the one, and the laughing and well-fed countenances of the others! What a difference between the subdued appetites here, and the pampered ones there!—between the exhilarating joyousness of these, and the pensive severity so touching, so respectable, of those—between their deportment and sentiments, the turn and movements of their bodies, and the expression of their minds. It seemed to me that I relished the conversation of the one and respected that of the other; that the one awakened in me every emotion of pleasure, whilst the others inspired me with a tender interest and a sacred kind of pity; that I would have chosen these for my amusement, and those for my edification; these for my companions, and those for my instructors; that my joys should have revelled with the one, and my sorrows have been poured out with the others; in short, that my senses were with the Bernardines, and my sensibilities with the Chartreux, and that though I would have lived with the former, I would have died with the latter.

One of the monks, observing that I fixed my eye on a painting of our Saviour, which hung opposite to me, told me, with all the flames of enthusiasm in his eye, that I might well admire it, as it was the only faithful picture of that Divine personage upon earth. I humbly asked how that might be; and he took up his parable, and said, that Abrogarus, the king of Edessa, a small city in Palestine, being sick, and hearing of the fame and persecution of Jesus, despatched a messenger to pray his assistance, and to offer him an asylum in his city. Pleased with his benevolence and his faith, our Saviour sent one of his disciples to heal him, and, as a further mark of his Divine favour, a handkerchief, with which he had wiped his face, and on which he had left the exact impression of his features. From this very handkerchief the portrait I saw was painted; but how it came into the possession of the Chartreux of Père Chatel, the good monk did not explain, nor did I venture to ask. I bowed assent to all he said, and would not, for the world, have expressed a doubt, in discredit of the superstitious zeal on which his happiness so much depended. Excess of faith, in a religion of which it is the essence, never appears to me despicable, though it may often be superfluous; and surely candour would not only be inclined to excuse, but benevolence almost to rejoice, in the enthusiasm that stands in the place of every earthly good, and which is the only means of shedding the balm of peace on the heart, in the midst of so many austerities and so many privations. Wretched, indeed, must be the poor Chartreux, who have not their thoughts continually rapt to heaven, and who cast back a longing look on the world, which they have renounced for ever. A simple dinner of eggs and herbs summoned us from the dark parlour to the refectory, where sober abstinence is the constant handmaid to chastened appetite, and pampered Luxury never shows his bloated face. One of the monks waited on us with a readiness and humility that spoiled my stomach, and abased me to the dust. I never felt so little in my own sight, being served by a person whom I thought so much better, so much more respectable, than myself.

After dinner we visited their several narrow cells, in which there seemed not for nature, more than nature needs, even when her demands are most moderate. A single chair, a small table, a little hard and curtainless bed, a shelf with a few religious books — this was all the furniture of each. I forget — in one we found an elderly monk, of a majestic height and air, dusting the keys of an organ with his handkerchief. I had not seen him before. He received us with equal benevolence and courtesy. His features were finely marked—his mouth large but gracious, his smile ingenuous and benign, his nose Roman, and his eye full of clear intelligence and ardent imagination. Without the least knowledge of music, he had himself made the organ I saw in his chamber, to which he had, with infinite labour, arranged several barrels, that played, with a pedal, various airs with the utmost exactness, There was also a clavier, with a double row of keys, though useless to himself; but on which he was delighted to hear me play a few marches and minuets, whilst he blew the bellows with all the enthusiasm of a man, who has had his whole soul in an enterprise, and of which he witnesses the success. The organ was extremely well executed, both as to the ornamental and mechanical part, well toned, and in perfect tune. And all this he had achieved in the short intervals, between the necessary exercise and sustenance, and his religious duties. His whole conversation showed a mounting spirit; and he proved how impossible it is to smother the active and subtle fire of genius, which, ardent and restless, will always find some means to show its light; and in the midst of watchings and fastings, of penitence and prayer, disdains not to illumine the gloomy solitude and narrow cell of a poor Chartreusien, with its bright beams. He afterwards led me below to a little outhouse, where he had piled up his scanty winter's portion of wood; and, the instant he entered, a number of canary birds flew towards him as their friend and benefactor, perched on his head, his shoulders, and his hands, and demonstrated every token of delight and blandishment. The picture of benevolence in his countenance, while he both returned and exulted in their caresses, was wonderfully fine. 'Ah,' said he, 'comme l'homme est fait le maître, il doit être l'ami de tous les animaux, et c'est sa propre faute, s'ils n'ont pas la confiance la plus parfaite en son humanité!' His heart shone through his words, and it was surely made to be loved. We afterwards visited the chapel, which is plain and awfully sombre—consistent, as it struck me, with their order, and then stopped a few minutes to contemplate once more, before we took our leave, the site of the convent, which, on three sides encompassed with *belles horreurs*, presents an emblem of their present state; and on the fourth, open to an extensive, various, and smiling landscape, watered by the rapid Rhone, one of the world which they have left, and which, while they thus contemplate in beautiful prospect, must teach their thoughts new forbearance, whilst it lures them enchantingly on through soft scenes, bestowed by the bounty of heaven on man.

On my expressing the satisfaction I had tasted from the Prieur's informed conversation, liberal and easy manners, the Chanoine told me that he had formerly served many years in the army — had particularly distinguished himself in the last war between France and England in Germany, and acquired great military rank, as well as fame. But immediately on his return to his native country — from what motive has never been discovered — he threw himself into this convent, from whence all the tears and prayers of his family, which is a noble and rich one of Bordeaux, and of which he was the heir, proved unavailing to draw him, though enforced by the offers of new honours from his king. Finding all their endeavours ineffectual, his friends got him made superior of Père Chatel, where he is much beloved by all the monks; and he has never appeared to repent leaving the world, and giving himself up to heaven.

We slept again at Bellay that night, and the next morning set out for Chatillon. The wind being right against us and very sharp, we were a great while labouring up the Rhone, though assisted by a stout horse, which used all his efforts by land, and by two of the sturdiest and handsomest young fellows I ever saw, who used all theirs by water. I thought I should have expired with cold before we reached the canal, though buried deep in straw and wrapped up in a blanket. But when we thought all our little difficulties at an end, and began to anticipate with pleasure the good fire and dinner that awaited us at Chatillon, we were assailed by a real danger, and had nearly lost our lives in the puddle, that they call canal, between the impetuous Rhone and the proud lake. About mid-day we met a barge laden with tiles, to which were fastened two lesser ones; and in the first, a singular and most striking figure stood upon deck, and directed the rudder. He appeared about sixty, was majestically tall, and amply squared. His hair was bushy and abundant, of mixed black and grey; his face deeply indented and intersected by a thousand wrinkles. All his features were strongly marked, his air was stern and imposing, his mouth grim, his brow surly, and his eye made to threaten and command. The description of Marius occurred powerfully to me as I regarded him; and if such were the person and mien of the Roman general, I wonder not that the soldiers employed to assassinate him in his prison, dropped their swords through awe and trembling, and implored mercy. As we approached him, he deigned not to cast one regard on our little boat, but kept solemnly moving the rudder with one arm, while he rested the elbow of the other, with an air of grave dignity, on a chest. As we began to pass his bark, there was but just space enough for our boat to clear that, and the bank; but before we had passed those in his train, he steered so near that we were in the most imminent danger of being overset and crushed against it. We were — and had cause to be — alarmed. Our boatmen hallooed to inform him of our danger, and we lifted up our voices with theirs, to make him steer his barges towards the opposite side. But all in vain. He was as inexorable as Charon to the cries of the poor ghosts on the Styx, and kept on his state without once vouchsafing to turn his head. From entreaties our watermen proceeded to curses, which they vociferated in a volley, that one should have thought would have roused the most insensible and warmed the most phlegmatic. But they made no more impression upon this imperious brute, than if we had been so many frogs; and wo were at last in such a strait, that but for the utmost activity and address, on the side of our boatmen and my domestic, who found means, with the oars and a stout pole, to turn the last barge a little on one side, as it was on the point of oversetting us,— we should have run the utmost risk of losing our lives, and, at best, have had a thorough ducking in one of the severest mornings I ever felt. I wished heartily for a Sir Joshua Reynolds to have sketched out the most striking subject for a painting in its kind, that ever was seen. But all the *désagremens* in our way, only served as themes for chat afterwards, and gave a double zest to the comforts of the castle, where we soon satisfied our hungry appetites, and stretched our stiff and weary limbs, in that kind of lazy and luxurious repose that makes inactivity happiness, after cold and fatigue. But I cannot moor our little bark on the other side the lake, before I have mentioned one other personage who dined with us at Chatillon on our return, and who contributed greatly to our amusement. He had an old house, or rather the shell of one, at the foot of the castle, and as he was an assessor of the lands, as well as one of his vassals, my friend thought it politic, as well as neighbourly, to pay him some attention. He came, then, bowing and scraping to M. le Baron and my lord Anglois, in a full-trimmed suit of crimson plush, worn into a hundred different shades, black worsted stockings, white stiff-topped gloves, and a hat that might once have been black, and which, through abundant reverences, had the fore part pinched into an acute angle that shone again, with either the natural or adventitious grease of his clumsy fingers. Never was man so full of snuff and importance! He was a great haranguer, too, and when he wanted a trope applied to his horn snuff-box for timely pause, and to give a new spring to his brain. But the chief subject of his rhetoric was the view from Chatillon, which was *mignonne,* his darling expression, and which he applied on every possible occasion and to every possible thing. In our way down to the lake the next morning, he was officiously solicitous that none of the surrounding objects should escape my notice. At every moment he stopped with a 'My Lor Anglois, avez-vous fait attention à cette église? n'est-ce pas que c'est mignonne? Regardez ce petit bois, n'est-ce pas que c'est mignon? Voyez vous cette belle plaine, my lor, n'est-ce pas que c'est mignonne?' Thus he went on, till, some new object striking his eye, he paused where the path was steepest, and hurrying to finish a pinch of snuff, in order to begin his oration with one hand, whilst the other was stretched out with an important air to point out his fresh mignonne, the farmer's dog rushed by him, and throwing him off his balance he fell headlong down the rough road, and the envious wind wafting his full-trimmed coat over his head, discovered a large patch of bright orange-coloured cloth, plastered full behind on his crimson breeches. Attentive to his post of honour in the midst of his bruises, and conscious that it was somewhat out of repair, he clapped his hand backwards instinctively on the envious blot, but not in time to prevent its being exposed in the most ridiculous light. I could not help crying to myself in the midst of my laughter, 'Voilà quelque chose, en vérité, qui est mignonne dans son genre.' But if his posteriors were mignonne on the side of humour, God knows his wife was not so on the side of beauty; yet with her rough and flat visage, black teeth, pale lips, and green eyes, she had all the affectation of a pretty coquette, and all the *minauderies* of a *petite maîtresse.*

After a pleasant little voyage, we arrived safe and well at the opposite end of the lake, and rejoined our various friends at Meri, a country house of my dear Chatillon's, and from whence we had parted. Thus ends my three weeks' tour, which I should never have written, but at the instance of Amelia,* and which I doubt not will afford her, and the other friends who may read it, amusement, because they interest themselves in everything that befalls me, and read everything that comes from my pen with a favourable and partial eye. As Amelia keeps a regular journal of our tour when we are together, I am exempted from a task, which would seem a

* Mrs. Whalley.

slavery to my ideas, and which would ill suit with my habitual indolence; but she has exacted a promise from me to write one of all my little separate excursions, which I shall rouse myself to perform; and if I do it to her content, my end will be answered, and I shall find my full recompense in her approbation.

JOURNAL THE SECOND; IN THE TARANTESE.

JUNE, 1784.

As I have again been vagabonding,. I must again journalise. It is a tax that Amelia exacts for my absence from her arms, and I pay it with as much pleasure as my English sentiments of perfect liberty, and my natural aversion to everything that resembles a set task will allow. Courage, however! Avaunt, ye demons of indolence and procrastination, that have haunted me from my cradle! Let the execution of a *devoir* sacred to friendship and love, be as pleasant in the performance, as it will be agreeable in the retrospect; and what I will with all my heart, let me execute with all my understanding, lest a languid style should unjustly seem to speak languid affections, and a fault in the *physique* be mistaken for a defect in the *morale*. An earnest desire, it is said, often makes the body active, and gives warmth and energy to the efforts of the mind. I seem to feel this truth. My nerves begin to assume an elastic spring, a crowd of ideas seem suddenly to be put in motion, and flash over my mind; imagination stands trembling with ardour, dips her pencil in the life-blood of my heart, just where its choicest affection is concentred, and colours them as they pass. Now, now is the moment of my enthusiasm's quick flash, my sensibilities thrill through my frame; open the course once freely before them, and they will be sure to serve me to its end. Amelia is the god that inspires me. Far more sacred are her inspirations than those that Pythian priestess ever felt. My bosom throbs, my soul expands under their beloved influence, and thus I offer up a grateful incense at her shrine. I hate the slavery of dull dates. They would act like the celebrated talismans of romance, and steel me against thought. How I wish to charm Amelia with the magic of my ideas, but to do so I must first be charmed myself with the day-dreams, my imagination sets before me of scenes foregone. Let the revision but equal their reality. Let my pen but paint as I felt them, as my heart felt them, and we shall both be satisfied.

It was towards the middle of May that I made an excursion into the province of Tarantese. My companions were two young Italian officers, the Count Vivaldi and the Chevalier Galaté.* A glowing cheek that spoke warm desires, a lurid and wandering eye, that marked quick and changing sensibilities, a delicate face and fine-drawn person, that announced their frequently being carried to excess, genteel manners, and an insinuating address, distinguished the exterior of the former. With a fashionable education, and rather a specious than sterling understanding, his conversation was more pleasing than informed, and his language more elegant than forcible. For the time you are with him he throws an interest into his deportment, and a warmth into his sentiment, that expands the heart towards him. But he is one of the many, whose sensibilities require *presence* to awaken them; it serves as a burning-glass to concentre the wandering rays of his affection to a point, which otherwise are diffused too widely to excite any ardour in his bosom. His affections, like butterflies, flutter in the sun, and show their bright wings dropped with gold. Their sun, is the countenance of whom he calls his friend; but, rob them of its genial influence, and they shrink back, like the chrysalis to its shell,

* Galaté in French; Galateri in Italian. The General Galateri mentioned in the memoir.

and lie torpid there, till enlivened again by the cheering beams, on which almost their being and their activity depends.

Brim full of blood and vivacity, with all the frankness of an open nature uncurbed by experience, with all the thoughtlessness of youth, the extravagance of gaiety, and the impetuosity of a quick temper and ardent passions, Galaté is called by the world a *bòn diable*. As far as he appears to the world in general, which brushes the surface without penetrating further, it is precisely his character; but the nicer eye of a friend, finds in him qualities to be respected and affections to be loved. With all his slap-dash and *étourderie*, he has high sentiments of honour, strict ones of principles, and the most warm and genuine affections. His ingenuousness is so perfect, that he tells to the letter whatever is to his disadvantage, as well as what tends to his credit; and though it is a temper that always does him honour in the eyes of the candid, it often operates to his prejudice with the worthless and designing. Prompt of thought and eager to execute, his designs burn in his breast till they are put into action. What is done with him must be done quickly. The idea is like a flash of lightning, and the conduct it suggest follows as rapidly as the thunderclap. With such inflammable matter about him, one should think his sentiments would be more violent than durable. And it is the case when anger gives them birth; but on the side of friendship, his attachment is as steady as it is eager and vehement, and it must be the person's own fault to whom he vows his affection, and the defect and coldness of their own hearts, if his regard abates and his ardours languish. The reverse of Vivaldi, absence seems to add a stimulus to his affection, and fervour to his sentiments; and one of his most sensible pleasures is to pour out the effusions of his heart in frequent letters to those friends, who are far distant, and to receive frequent assurance of their regard. His natural understanding is quick, but his education has been sadly neglected; yet the frank manner in which he owns his want of erudition, wins him a new interest in the heart, and turns that to his account on the side of sensibility, which would be to his disadvantage on the side of judgment. In every respect he is void of pretensions and false colourings, and, while many others are said to do so, is the one that really carries his heart in his hand; so that, though the 'Spectator's' plan of a window in every one's bosom, was to take place, *his* might still remain unenlightened, without having more concealments than his neighbour's. His manners are too volatile, and his body too active, to attend to the rules of etiquette and the insinuating smoothnesses of polished breeding; but an original kind of spirit, and a flying haste to oblige, makes one easily dispense with his inattention to address, and sometimes, even, to the common rules of genteel decorum—making that appear always amusing, and often pleasing in him which, in a heavy body actuated by a different mind, would be tiresome and disgusting. His conversation is not wholly void of that *grossièreté* with which the Piemontois are generally reproached, but the freedom and gaiety of his character, makes it less striking in him, and one is the more ready to excuse it, as it is never united with one mean idea. Indeed, no man was ever more an enemy to baseness of soul; and the greatest indignity one could offer him, would be to suppose him capable of a low action or sordid thought. Generosity and intrepidity are two marking lines in his character, and as the one often endangers his purse, so the other has more than once endangered his life; but his spirit and address have always extricated him from the perils, that his *emportements* have brought upon him, or into which his ardent courage has made him run headlong, even when acting on the side of duty. His person is handsome, his limbs well proportioned, full of muscle, and made equally for force and agility, his countenance inspirited and open. He has a flushing cheek, and a sparkling eager eye, that speaks the activity and ardour of his mind. His eagle's nose curves forward to salute his answering chin, and a smile plays about the scarlet thread of his thin lips, that marks at once gaiety and *fierté*. He scarcely ever walks soberly, like other men, but bounds along with an active and undaunted air, like a proud stag in the season of his amours. Yet, high as he is of spirit, and impatient of control, the voice of affection may do anything with him; and he listens not only to the counsels, but reproofs of his friends with docility, and even satisfaction, as marks of their affection and the true interest that they take in his honour and welfare. He calls me his mentor. I wish I had as much the wisdom, as the wish to serve him, and that I could save him by my influence from the tempests of too irritable a disposition, and the imprudences of too ingenuous a heart. On the side of vice he needs no mentor, for he is in no respect a vicious or debauched character, and will never split on that rock. The excess of his virtues, if one may be allowed the expression, is the point of peril for him, and his great enemies are his easy faith, his tiptoed honour, and his kindling scorns. I have wrote much of him, because I love him much, and because I verily believe there are few people in the world who love me more, different as are our tempers, ages, pursuits, and callings. But a certain predilection sometimes overleaps all these obstacles to intimacy, smoothes down all differences of character, and nearly assimilates those (in all the essential points of sentiment and principle) who seem most opposite from temper, manners, and the general tenour of their conduct.

A balloon had been projected from Chamberry a few days before we left it, and the triumph and feasting that the success of this their hobby-horse occasioned, was the more enthusiastic and boundless, as all its boasted honours, too prematurely and rashly predicted by the prospectus, had been levelled with the dust in the first essay, to the disappointment of an immense crowd assembled on the occasion, the infinite mortification of the chief agents and their partisans, and the secret joy and triumph of the French, who spoke and published a thousand malicious sneers and cutting criticisms, to humble still farther the philosophers of Chamberry.

The ardent Galaté had all along taken an active part in favour of this project, and as he never does a thing by halves, had distinguished himself by his zeal for the honour of Savoy. On the day of their humiliation, he had soundly cudgelled a tall raw-boned strutting Frenchman with a long sword by his side, for saying that the poor Savoyards were not formed by nature to be philosophers, and on the day of their triumph he was the life of the cause. Mounted on the box of the Countess de Morand's coach, his hat shaded with boughs, and his lip armed, rather than adorned, with a tremendous pair of moustaches, it was he that headed the parade back to the town; it was he that marshalled the ranks and regulated the order of the cavalcade, which attended the triumphant balloon through the streets; it was he that bounded about with a naked sword, and kept the unruly mob in order; it was he that amused, enlivened, and inspired all the world. Gravity grew gay with his vivacity, and insensibility caught warmth from his enthusiasm. His humorous frolics delighted the people, and his generous ardours in behalf of the Savoyards, ardours so unusual in a Piemontois, endeared him to the noblesse, and piqued them to extraordinary exertions of spirit and demonstrations of joy. It happened that the day we set out for the Tarentese, was the one appointed for the departure of the Cadet Maistre, one of the renowned aërial voyagers, for Piemont. His brother-flyer to the clouds, his family, and a long train of his friends in coaches and whiskies, in carrioles and carts, on horseback and on muleback, were prepared to accompany him, with two broken-winded horns by way of a band of music, as far as the little town of Montmelian, and we could have done no less than join ourselves to the cortége of this great adventurer, had we not been headed by the gallant Galaté. As for his part, he no sooner kenned the heterogeneous cavalcade, than he shot from the voiture like an arrow, and the next moment I saw him driving the front coach like another Jehu, with equal spirit indeed, but with a better heart. Quickly as we arrived at Montmelian, the rumour of our triumph had got thither before us, and the principal persons of the place had prepared a handsome cold collation for our reception. I need not, if I could, repeat the congratulating, and rejoicing, and complimenting, and sympathising, that inevitably took place between the grandees of Montmelian and Chamberry. But whatever hypocrisy there might have been in their cajoleries, the gay and honest Galaté was de bonne for all jubilee and triumph. The suffocating heat of the day and a wound in his leg, occasioned by cutting his ankle with his buckle, could not keep him quiet, and he danced the valse and the Montferine as if his blood needed thawing, and his limbs had been perfectly sound; capering along the streets afterwards with all kinds of antics, and falling aboard every girl he met with as lawful prize, and with a gaiety and good-will all his own.

We pursued our route in time to get to St. Pierre that night; the road was a very fine one, and led through a picturesque country, with a grand chain of Alps on the left, and a beautifully varied and cultivated vale on the right, watered by the fantastic windings of the mischievous Lizère, and bounded by woody hills in the foreground, and in the background by the northern Alps, with all their fine breaks, their bold angles, their majestic swells, dark woods, and white rocks; their aspiring points that pierced the clouds, and their snow-crowned summits of dazzling splendour. The vale of St. Pierre does not deceive with false appearances, and the graces that weave their dance amongst its golden harvest and flowery meads, are as rich as they are lovely. The land here is esteemed the most fertile in Savoy, but the furious Lizère leaves on every side marks of devastation, and like a capricious tyrant, sometimes ruins in a few hours with its overwhelming waters, the fruitful fields and verdant pastures, that had for many years been nourished by its bounties, and had thriven under its curling smiles. It would by no means be difficult to confine this destructive river within proper bounds, and add the advantages of an external, as well as internal commerce, to the fertilising course of its waters, but poverty and oppression damps all public spirit in this charming but exhausted country; and nature offers her full-handed blessings in vain, whilst the exactions of a tyrannical Government, perverts their order and corrupts their source, and an erroneous and cruel system of politics, withers their blossoms and turns their honey into gall. The noblesse, with ruined fortunes and all the pride of illustrious blood, struggling perpetually between the forced endeavours to support a decent appearance, and the necessity that sits meagre in their secret chambers, and stalks about the gloomy walls of the mouldering chateaux, are not in a condition to undertake expensive schemes of public utility; the Bourgeoisie are content, if they can live comfortably on their gains, in a country where trade is languid and payments tardy, and the Sovereign is poisoned by the hungry Piemontois courtiers, against this his most ancient possession, and spends that, in ostentatious parade and vain attempts to equal richer and more powerful monarchs, which might be expended for the benefit of Savoy, and in the end to his own.

Many years have not elapsed, since a company of English

offered to be at the whole expense of embankments against the Lizère, and to reduce its uncertain and ravaging course within a uniform and navigable channel, on condition of being put into possession for twenty years of all the land that had been ruined by, and that should be saved from, its furious inundations. Could one have thought that there was a possibility of objecting to the offer? Especially as all the noblesse to whom the rescued property might belong, were fully convinced of its advantages and eager to accept it. But the jealous Piemontois feared that Savoy might become too flourishing, and contrived to prejudice the spirit of the King against so useful and rational an undertaking; to accomplish this, it is said they got the Queen on their side. She is a Spaniard, and has all the inflexible pride and blind bigotry of her nation. The company were reported to be Jews. A hue and cry was raised against the profanation of such a treaty on one hand, and against the disgrace of the King of Sardinia's being under pecuniary obligations to these outcasts of the earth, on the other. A thousand murmurs were heard, a thousand difficulties raised, the Queen worried incessantly a peaceable spirit, that knows not how to stand firm against her querulous pertinacity, and the proposal was rejected to the shame of reason, and the scandal of justice. Since that time the Lizère wastes at its will, and in some parts has broken itself into so many branches, that it is almost impossible to distinguish the main stream, winding its many-headed course round the ruined lands (which present the sad remains of their fruitful verdure, choked with sand and gravel), like a hydra, that poisons amidst its graceful curlings, and destroys amidst its shining evolutions.

St. Pierre is a paltry little town, in a delightful situation, as it stands on a healthy elevation with the southern Alps overhanging it, with all their woods and rocks and vineyards on one hand, and commands an extensive and diversified view of the vale on the other, behind which the northern mountains tower in magnificent piles, and present themselves in noble confusion. We supped with the commandant, a young Italian officer of illustrious family, called La Moura, and whose cooing voice and affectionate and gentle manners, seemed to answer to the dulcet accents of his name. The next morning we rose early, in order to visit the château of Miolan, before we pursued our journey to Moutiers, where my friend Galaté was ordered to command a detachment of horse, and which was to be our head-quarters. The rough path to Miolan, winds up the base of an Alpine mountain, which lowers over it, rough with rocks and various woods, through which several clear brooks silver to the valley, and seem to soften with their playful smiles, the dark frowns of the haughty mountain from whence they spring.

The castle was formerly one of those strong fortresses, the ruins of which are so frequent in the more mountainous parts of Savoy, and belonged to the counts of that title. It was one of the last which surrendered its independence to the dukes of this country, but has now lost its ancient honours and lustre, and is converted into a dread prison of state. Under this new denomination it still awes the country round, though as a vassal to a more powerful lord, and with delegated, instead of independent sway. But its gloomy walls need not regret their past splendour. They are now the terror of crimes, and the ministers of offended justice; whereas they formerly served as the oppressors of innocence, and the scourge of peace, according to the rapacious desires and private passions of the petty tyrants, who were its possessors, and whose capricious violences often desolated the blooming vale. Strangers are rarely admitted within its massy portal, but as Vivaldi was well acquainted with the antiquated governor, I obtained that favour. The crazy corps of old invalids, that bear the pompous name of guards to the castle, seemed of a piece with its time-worn walls, and tottered, under the consuming influence of age and infirmity, more than the most mouldering of its battlements. These, indeed, have been repaired; but alas! there is no repair for those, and a far straiter prison, than that of which they have the custody shall soon hold their frail bodies. The prospect from the governor's little garden is extensive and of varied grandeur and beauty.

My eye was roving over its succeeding images with wonder and delight, when it happened to glance on the grated window of a round tower, at which appeared the pensive face of a pale prisoner, whose eyes were fixed with melancholy attention on the possessors of that freedom, which he had lost. All the enchantment of the fine scene before me vanished in a moment. 'Ah!' cried I, to my troubled soul, 'to me those woods and meads, and groves and plains, those rural villages and those murmuring waters, those swelling hills and those cloud-capt mountains, present an earthly paradise, but that poor prisoner must view them afar off with haggard eyes, as Satan did the garden of Eden, and with all the throes of anguish and despair. They serve but to recall to his too faithful memory, the social comforts that he is cut off from, and the scenes that he must enjoy no more.' It was natural for me to be interested for the unfortunate captive who caused these sad reflections, and as natural to enquire who he was, and what had been his offence. The governor told me that his name was Lavin, that he was of a good family in Piemont, and that his crime had been a forgery, committed at the early age of twenty, and at the instances of the Count de Stortilian, to whom he was secretary. His natural understanding was of the first order, and his erudition astonishing for his years. To the greatest genius, also, he joined the utmost ingenuity; and excelled equally in all the powers of a strong intellect, and in all that dexterity and grace in the minutiæ, that mark ductile talents and delicate taste. In short, to all the electric spring and warmth of imagination, he joined the most perfect address and patience of execution, and united all the elegance of finish, to all the energy of thought. But all his powers and all his graces had been doomed to languish within the gloomy walls of a strait prison, till the frail body which they illumined and adorned, should be removed to its dark and narrow house, and the animating spirit shook off the fetters, with which man could bind down its mounting faculties, and curb its ardours. Yet, though the fire of genius may be damped, it cannot be wholly extinguished, by sorrow and slavery; born to dazzle, it will sometimes break through the dark clouds that intercept its beams, pervade the walls that confine its fervours, and enlighten the dungeon that chills it with horror. The enchained eagle, is an eagle still; though he cannot soar to the sun, he still gazes on it through the bars of his iron cage, shoots fire from his eye to welcome the golden beams of heaven; shakes his strong pinions, elevates his daring crest, and in the moments of his proud delirium seems rapidly mounting to the fount of light. But awakened from his trance, he bows his beak mournfully on his breast, hangs his bold wing, shuts up the lightning of his eye, and feels all the horrors of his captivity in silent anguish.

It is thus with poor Lavin; at times his imagination takes fire, his spirits mount in his breast, and he conceives and executes various works of genius, ingenuity, and taste, to amuse captivity and cheat despair; but the bright day-dream soon vanishes, and he awakes to all the sober certainty of hopeless misery. During the first years of his imprisonment, from an excess of severity equally useless and cruel, he was denied the use of pen, paper, and books, yet with straws drawn from his hard bed, did he contrive to write the most elegant things in the most beautiful characters, and to adorn the walls of his narrow cell with charming drawings, the fruits of his exhaustless fancy, or the representation of scenes recalled by fond remembrance, and traced with a yearning heart. For some years past, pen, paper and books have been granted to solace his lonely hours, at the intercessions of the Baronne de Pozer, an accomplished and lovely woman of quality in the neighbourhood, who admired his talents, and commiserated his sufferings, and he has shown his gratitude for the boon by a thousand ingenious toys and delicate compliments, which his fertile spirit and expert hands have formed for her service and amusement. But alas, these resources begin to fail him. Disease for some time past has fixed its vulture talons on his body, and through that rends his mind. Amidst the sickening languors of his nerves, his sensibilities acquire new point, and the excruciating pain he suffers, tears off the veil that fancy sometimes threw over his misfortunes, and forces his mind back to all the horrors of his fate.

The governor showed me a letter, which he had lately written to the Governor of Chamberry, praying his intercession with the King that he might be removed to the prison of State at Turin, as he should there be in the way of good medical assistance, and as he hoped for some alleviation of his sufferings from the effect of his native air. I never saw such beautiful characters, nor read a more elegant or masterly style. It was short, but how much had he expressed in a few words, and with what energy, simplicity and pathos! It might vie with the choice morsels of Rousseau, and pierced me to the heart. Yet it is said this poor boon has been denied him; if it has, hard indeed must be the hearts of kings and governors, and sadly forgetful, that neither the kingly sceptre, nor the judge's robe, become them with one-half so good a grace, as mercy does.* Oh, when poisoned by power, and hardened by ease and prosperity, how apt is that vain, feeble, and strutting being, man, to hear with indifference the miseries of his brethren, and how does the tempest of his sorrows, brush lightly over his heart.

Three-and-twenty long years, has the cell of poor Lavin echoed with his groans, and been drenched by his tears! A punishment, surely, amply severe for the backsliding of his youth, and sufficient to wash out his offence. His crime had also every extenuation to allege in its favour, committed as it was at the subtle persuasions of an experienced and artful courtier, and at the earnest instances of his master and benefactor, to whom he had been habituated to look up with respect and gratitude, and to whose commands he was accustomed to pay implicit obedience. What a hard trial for a young and sensible heart, and how impossible almost was it that it should resist such temptation? Yet, with all these alleviations, and though he reaped no profit himself from the forged drafts, that were uttered to supply the profusion and vices of his unprincipled lord, the Count Stortilian was condemned to a lighter punishment than himself. Perverse and partial justice, which discerned not motives, and confounded degrees of guilt!

I cannot quit Miolan without making mention of a remarkable fact which relates to it, and which was related to me by a lady of fashion of Chamberry, who was a witness to its truth. At a public ball in that town, not many years since, an old gentleman appeared most singularly dressed, and with his grey locks waving upon his

* Perhaps without knowing it, Dr. Whalley in this beautiful passage was quoting Shakespeare —

> "Not the king's crown, nor the deputed sword,
> The mareschall's truncheon, nor the judge's robe,
> Become them with one half so good a grace
> As mercy does." *Measure for Measure.*

shoulders. His countenance was interesting, and his air noble. An habitual melancholy seemed to have taken possession of his features, and he gazed round him with a look of wonder and estrangement, as if he had been the native of another world, and utterly unacquainted with the manners and customs of that into which he was just introduced. Every one considered him with a mixture of surprise and respect. A whisper of 'Who is he?' circulated round the room, but it was a universal demand to which no one could give a satisfactory reply. On entering into conversation, however, with some gentleman near, he observed himself that they must be astonished to see a stranger of his appearance amongst them, and thence took occasion to gratify their curiosity by the following short tale:—Born of a noble family in France, he had connected himself with the party in opposition to the Prime Minister, and was deep in all its intrigues. They proved abortive. All the anti-ministerial plots were discovered, and he was known to be a chief agent in them; he fled into Piemont, to save himself from the vengeance of the arbitrary engine of despotic power. But his asylum was ill-chosen. An absolute monarchy was an unsafe refuge, for the bold opposer of tyrannic measures. His vindictive enemy discovered his retreat, and, aided by the abused authority of his master, prevailed with the Court of Turin to become the base agents of his private revenge, and to seize and shut up secretly the unfortunate stranger in a state prison at Miolan. In the changeable course of things his enemy was disgraced, and the whole system of politics changed; but as his family and friends supposed him dead, and the Ministers at Turin, were too attentive to private interests and pleasures to throw away a remembrance on an unfortunate stranger, he still continued to languish in a severe captivity, the rigours of which were uniformly enforced, as they had never been countermanded. Shut out from society, never leaving his gloomy cell but to go between a double rank of guards to mass, forbidden the use of pen and paper, and every inlet blocked up, from whence he might have been informed how things went on in the world, he patiently resigned himself to his fate; and giving up all his hopes and joys in this life, calmly attended the moment, when he should be removed from the proud man's wrongs and the oppressor's injuries, and awaited that *arrêt* which awaits us all, and which is the instrument of impartial and unerring justice. His slavery had begun in the proudest prime of his life, but year had passed on after year, till age had joined care, to deepen the wrinkles in his face and shed snows upon his head.

After forty years' imprisonment, which had rendered him almost forgetful of the world by which he was forgotten, the old governor paid his last debt to nature. The one appointed in his stead, by an etiquette of office, was obliged to give in the state of his prison, and names of its prisoners, to the Government; and behold the unfortunate Frenchman on the list! His name excited curiosity, and it happily led to enquire the nature of his offence. But here every one was in the dark; the Ministers of the moment were either dead or disgraced at Turin, as at Versailles, and no one could discover why this stranger had been doomed to captivity. On a strict enquiry, however, as well as from an application to himself, the truth came out, and it was known that he had been sacrificed to gratify the personal resentment of a French Minister, who had long been dust and ashes, and whose power was no more remembered. An immediate order was given to release the noble captive; and in his way to his native country, he heard of the ball of Chamberry, and his curiosity led him to make one in a gay scene, to which he had so long been a stranger, and to observe the change of fashions and manners that had taken place, during the dull uniformity of his long imprisonment. He added that he knew not yet whether he ought to consider his freedom as a blessing, or a curse; that he was hurried back to a world, which he had long ceased to make an object of his wishes, and found himself dazzled and bewildered in it by a thousand new objects, and the immense difference in his own ideas at the time he was rent from, and the hour in which he was restored to it; that most of his friends must be dead, that the rest had forgotten him, and that his family would probably be chagrined to see a person rise, as it were, from the tomb, to claim honours they had long been decked with, and possessions they had long enjoyed; that his was not a time of life to form new connections of any kind, unknowing as he was of the world as it then went, and with blunted sensibilities and broken spirits; that he should walk amongst men single, as it were, and uninterested in their actions, exciting only on their part emotions of curiosity and a tale for the day; and, in short, that if he did not find mankind more generous than he expected, and less selfish than he had left, he should often sigh to return to his prison, to the torpor of affections from whence he had been roused, and the still tranquillity that he should taste no more. Everyone who had the least sense or feeling, took a lively part in the interests and extraordinary fate of so informed and amiable a man; and he parted from Chamberry with universal admiration, and a general wish for his future peace.

From Miolan we wound our path down the wooded base of the mountain to the great road, where our coach awaited, and where the gay Galaté was seated in doleful dumps, reposing his lame leg on the opposite cushion; a misfortune which caused him to fret and fume like a fiery and restive horse, who seeks in vain to free himself from the restraint of his curb. The route between Miolan and l'Hôpital, the village where we purposed dining, was very pleasant; and the eye failed not, as usual in this country, to mount from the soft graces of the vale, to the lordly Alps, and from their bold rocks and towering pinnacles, to skim again the level lines and mingling beauties of the even vale. Just above l'Hôpital, and hanging on the sunny side of a verdant hill, the little town of Conflans presented itself in front of the road, in one of the most picturesque points of view imaginable. The sunbeams glancing brightly on its buildings, it seemed to welcome us with the most attractive smiles, and to rejoice amidst the various verdure of its velvet pastures and tufted vineyards, its pendent gardens, and its walnut groves, while the Lizère and the Ader rolled their proud waves at its foot, and the sheltering mountains rose with a benign, though lofty air, behind and on each side, as if to protect its blooming beauties from the bitter blasts. I know not a more tempting object for a painter, or one that more pleasingly unites the rural with the bold beauties of nature.

Just as we alighted at our inn, hungry and thirsty, and half choked with dust, my charming countrywoman the Marquise de la Pierre,* who has not yet forgot in this land of noble *paresseuses*, that a lovely Englishwoman can walk to see how nature paints her colour,† fearless of complexion and fatigue, passed by from her usual morning strolls, which preserve the blooming health in her cheeks, and help to give new spring to that amiable spirit that always zests her conversation, but which is never carried beyond the just bounds of politeness, delicacy, and judgment. She insisted on our

* Several of her letters are given in the sequel.

† "But who can paint
Like Nature? Can imagination boast,
Amid its gay creation, hues like hers?
Or can it mix them with that matchless skill,
And lose them in each other, as appears
In every bud that blows?" *Thomson's Seasons.*

all partaking of a friendly dinner at her *campagne.* Galaté excused himself on account of his lame leg, which, in truth, stood sorely in the way of his reverence to a *belle dame,* as well as his *bienêtre.* Vivaldi could not think of taking the liberty to present himself at Madame la Marquise's table in so slovenly a plight; but, for my part, I treated her with the honest frankness of an Englishman, and told her that, as she was ready to excuse my deranged coiffure and dirty clothes, I should be a booby to make objections that would deprive me of the pleasure of her society. '*Allons donc!*' cried the amiable Marquise, taking my offered arm, and away we walked to her château, laughing at the extreme etiquette of foreigners in the minutiæ, and their indecent and unbounded freedoms in matters of consequence. I found her table served with all the elegant neatness of an English board, at which she presided with all the English sincerity, joined with more than the English ease. I never spent three hours more agreeably. But the best dish she presented to me amongst all her delicacies, was a dish of English chat at the dessert, which was garnished on her part with the utmost taste, and was in itself of the most delicious flavour. The well-bred Vivaldi, after having brushed his coat and new-powdered his hair, joined us at our coffee, and it was not without regret that I received a summons to rejoin our invalid *étourdi,* who attended us in the coach at the bottom of the court. If the objects between St. Pierre and l'Hôpital were finely varied, they were enchanting between the latter and Moutiers, though the views were less extensive and diversified. We followed upwards the winding course of the rolling Lizère, and there was but just space enough for the river and the road, between the haughty mountains on either hand. But those mountains offered a continual succession of romantic pictures, where a few striking objects were distinctly marked and happily grouped, and where the soft and the savage graces, where rural and imposing images, were finely contrasted, and contended for the palm of taste. Here smiling cottages and fertile little pastures were scattered between frowning rocks and barren precipices, there huddled together. They seemed to dread the threatening crag that jutted over them. Here groups of gloomy firs added a sombre grace to the scenery, and there cornfields and vineyards hanging about amongst the heights, gave it an air of plenty and peace. The rocks themselves were broken into a thousand grand and fantastic forms, everywhere of the richest colouring; and frequent cascades, hurried frothing down the steeps, flashed between the wood, or dashed from rock to rock; on one hand, formed repeated falls—and, on the other, threw themselves with furious precipitation from the imperious heights, to add their tribute to the river in the strait valley, giving life and energy to the various pictures and completing the striking imagery. As it was the season for the great melting of the Alpine snows, as well as that, when the parti-coloured spring, putting on her robe of mottled green, begins to encroach on the empire of summer, and to mingle his luxuriant shades with her freshness and fragrance—every part of nature was presented to me in the happiest point of view, and I devoured her charms with all the enthusiasm of one, who is always her idolater, and who sees them renewed with a peculiar rapture, after being long bound in the icy chains of a most rigorous winter.

About a mile from Moutiers the mountains retired, as it were, on either hand, and formed themselves into an august amphitheatre. On the right, they presented a sublime boundary to one of the most picturesque basins I ever saw, where nature was adorned with all her soft and smiling charms, and where hill, dale, shady wood and sunny plain, and liquid lapse of murmuring streams, offered a beautiful contrast to the abrupt precipices and snow-capt Alps, that formed an irregular chain round them. Several sweet villages and finely-situated châteaux, gave new life and variety to the picture, and left the eye nothing to wish for.

For the last half-mile the disjointed crags hung frightfully menacing over our heads, and threatened us with instant destruction. Nor are their menaces always vain. They often send thundering ruins to the road beneath, and it is only last year, that a poor paysanne and six sheep were crushed to atoms in a moment, under an enormous fragment that was suddenly rent by a gust of wind, from the nodding masses of superincumbent rock. In its destructive violence it bore down a part of the wall, built as a defence for nightly passengers against the deep gulf, where the Lizère rages below. The wide ruins occasioned by these rocky fragments of the mountain strewed the road, and almost blocked up our way.

Immediately on quitting this little Eden, defended by a more sublime wall, than even Milton's pen could have given a just idea of, we mounted again between dark-browed rocks, which became more forbidding, and the mountains more bleak and barren, every step we took.

Moutiers, the small capital of the Tarentese, is very old, very ill-built, and very beggarly; but its situation offers a singular and picturesque *coup d'œil* in a little plain, so entirely surrounded by dark and stupendous mountains, that when there, it is difficult to trace an outlet to the world. It is built in the form of a triangle, on each side of which rolls a rapid river, whose confluence is at the narrow end. Each of these rivers, rushes out of a dark and narrow chasm on either hand between the mountains; each rages and foams along its rocky bed; and each, in its swelling pride, after heavy rains or a great melt of snow, threatens the affrighted city with destruction. More than once have the trembling inhabitants near their banks, been obliged to fly to their upper stories for shelter; and more than once have these torrents swept away whole houses in their wrath. One is called the Dorean and the other the Lizère. Their confluence offers a remarkable spectacle. As the Dorean runs over a bed of clay, its waters are of a muddy yellow, whilst the bed of the Lizère being of slate, its inky waves frown like a tyrant, that hastens to mark his steps with desolation. At their confluence their proud waters seem to be in furious contention for the mastery. Here the flashing surges wear the tawny hue of the Dorean, and there the dark-browed Lizère swells triumphant. Now divided by the interposing crags, they roll with a furious and menacing air, side by side, and now the fierce conflict rages again, and the whirling eddies are yet tinted with their respective colors, till by degrees these discriminating shades grow less perceptible, and at last their waters, are so entirely mixed that all distinction is lost, and the victorious Lizère, swallowing up, as it were, its vanquished rival, rushes with new fury through the vales of Savoy to Grenoble. Here, after receiving the tribute of another river, it pays its own, with humbled pride, to the majestic Rhone, in which it loses both its waters and its name.

Thus it is that little tyrants, after ravaging the unprotected villages and the defenceless plains, fall a prey in themselves to more powerful conquerors, who, in the midst of their own crimes and devastations, become the avengers of the innocent and the scourge of the oppressor. Thus it was that the former tyrants of the numberless castles in Savoy, whose ruins moulder on every rock and mountain, and offer a useful memento of ages foregone, fell, one after another, under the yoke of a single despot — and amidst all their poverty and oppression, the Savoyards may yet cast an eye of satisfaction on their fruitful pastures and unmolested herds, and cry, 'It is better to pay a third of what these yield us, to a single lord, and to enjoy the rest in security and peace, than to be at the mercy of a thousand rapacious little tyrants, and never to lie down with a fearless heart.

Insignificant as Moutiers is, its archbishopric is the richest preferment in Savoy, and one of the most ancient sees in Europe. It was founded at the beginning of the fourth century; and the walls of a large saloon in the archiepiscopal palace are adorned with half-length portraits of all its prelates, down to this day, in the different dresses of their times. There are numerous great names amongst them; and the noblesse of Moutiers point out the scarlet cardinals with no small pride, and even reckon a pope — one of the Johns — amongst the former prelates of their capital. A poor subject for boasting! But vanity, like the polypus, shoots out its feelers on every side, catches flies when it is unable to draw to itself a better sustenance, and will even gorge itself with the shell, when it cannot seize the nutritive substance, that filled it. But nothing diverted me so much at Moutiers as a strutting old gentleman in a long gold brocade waistcoat and a tarnished sword by his side, from his uprising to his downlying, who piqued himself on his love for the English and his knowledge of their history, and who, amongst a thousand other ideas equally absurd and ludicrous, supposed that we had no potatoes, ate no bread, and never made butter or cheese. But if his galimathias amused, the informed and elegant conversation of the Père Reinari charmed me. He was a monk of the Society of the Cordeliers, but neither his mind nor manners savoured of the cloister. Polite, cheerful, enlightened, with profound erudition and delicate taste, his noble air, open countenance, and sparkling eye, prejudiced in his favour before his entertaining and instructive converse, liberal sentiments, and benevolent principles, inspired one with affection and respect. Yet formed as he is to adorn the first stations, his brilliant talents and captivating graces, are buried in this obscure corner of the world, where he is doomed to hear the superstitious cant of a convent of nuns, as their confessor to lend a patient ear to the dull and endless catalogue of their petty sins, to quiet their weak consciences, and to calm their bigot fears. Between these narrow-souled religieuses, and a dozen boobies of Moutiers, to whom, as being professor of natural philosophy, he is obliged to teach what they can never profit by, his precious hours are wasted, his powers thrown away, and his virtues lost. What a life for the friend of the illustrious and immortal Ganganelli, who, different as were their ages, distinguished his merits and honoured him with his esteem. He told me that he once lived ten months in strict intimacy at Rome with that best of all possible popes, in his own apartments, when he was cardinal. His cheek flushed and his eloquence warmed, as he celebrated the talents and virtues of that great man, and the tears of grateful love and indignant sorrow flowed from his eyes, when he assured me that his illustrious benefactor and friend surely fell a sacrifice to black Jesuitical vengeance, which had the atrocity to pursue him to the very altar, and to poison him in the emblem of that common Saviour, whose doctrines are the very essence of mercy and forgiveness.

I passed my time very agreeably at Moutiers in every respect. My lively friend (who was the commandant, and in whose quarters I was commodiously lodged) used his utmost efforts to amuse me, and we received a thousand polite attentions from the few people of fashion there, and in the neighbourhood. Amongst others we visited the Baron and Baronne de Vergey, whose campagne is most advantageously situated in the little paradise before named. The house is an ancient one in Savoy, but surely noble blood never animated a more ignoble figure, than that of the old tapestry baron—if the automaton kind of movements of a body like a stuffed pudding, and marked with eyes, nose, and mouth, deserve the name of animation. But what he lacked in wit he made up in bows, and I thought his poor old back would never have ceased forming a villainous curve, whilst his forehead almost touched the ground, and his arms dangled right downward on each side, as if hanging by swivels. Messieurs, j'ai l'honneur de vous saluer; and, Messieurs, vous me faites bien de l'honneur — forming all the while the alternate sauce to his endless reverences. As to Madame the Baronne, she did the honours of her chateau to a *merveil* in a black stuff sack trimmed with crimson, and had been the wit as well as the *belle* of the province forty years before, when her bright eyes and quick *repartie* discomposed the dignity of many a grave Spaniard quartered at Moutiers, and conquered the conquerors. At present her sparkling glances are quenched in envious rheum, and she is so deaf that she can no longer hear the applauses offered to her *bon mots*, which in truth are powerful enough, armed as they are by her breath, to keep one at an awful distance, or make one pay dearly for being too near. Next to her wit she seemed to admire her chateau, every window of which she and the puffing old baron bustled to unbar, that not a morsel of the old tapestry or antiquated furniture might be lost upon us. The incredible volubility with which she enumerated the charms and conveniences of her campagne, is not to be conceived. I thought that *belle pièce* and *beau salon* would never have ceased ringing from her tongue, which might with reason have applied the terms of *belle vue* and *beau coup d'œil* to the enchanting landscape without. But in this she only resembled the generality of her countrywomen, who, amidst all the most bold and luxuriant beauties of nature, seem only to have eyes to discern, and taste to relish, the productions of art, and to throw away their admiration even on her offals, whilst the sublimest objects and most graceful pictures of her great mistress, pass before them unnoticed. Unluckily, the old baron was fully as deaf as his wife, so that our poor lungs had no quarter; and the wicked Galaté, taking advantage of this circumstance, continually assured him, amidst the most profound and reverential bows, that he was a superlative ass — a blockhead of the first magnitude. 'Monsieur, vous êtes une grande bête; Monsieur, vous êtes un âne comme il n'y en a point,' repeated he, casting such sly leers upon me at the same time, that it was with the utmost difficulty I could forbear laughing out. But the poor old baron took all in good part, and answered at all times with 'Wy, monsieur; wy?' his cant expression, which he uttered every moment, and pronounced broad as I have spelt it, lifting up his peruke at the same time above his left ear, as if to regale his blunted sense with the harmonious emphasis of his darling word.

We had made our last bows at the bottom of the hall steps, and were about to mount our horses, when the baron bustled down to us in great haste, and taking me by the sleeve, cried, 'Mais, monsieur, monsieur — wy, wy; monsieur, il y a une chose — wy, wy — il y a une chose que j'ai oublié — wy, wy — que j'ai oublié de vous montrer — wy, wy.' Accordingly he dragged me back again to his *salle-à-manger*, and, pointing with exultation to the portrait of a puffy, tallow-faced young officer, stuck out in full regimentals, and bridling as stiff as buckram behind his expanded chest. 'Voici, monsieur — wy, wy — voici,' cried the enraptured baron, 'mon portrait!—wy, wy — mon portrait, quand j'étais jeune— wy, wy — quand j'étais dans le service — wy, wy — dans le service. C'est moi, monsieur — wy, wy. C'est moi, moi,' repeated he, pointing his forefinger with a quick and reiterated motion to his breast, and with redoubled self-satisfaction, as if enraptured with his former youth and proud of his former charms, which in truth were as like to his aged ones, as is a ripe to a withered pumpkin. After paying due homage to this precious portrait, where art and nature may have been said to rival each other, I took a second *congé* with as grave a face as I could of the noble *moi, moi*, and, rejoining my arch friend, we went laughing and galloping back to Moutiers, entertained with the visit of the day.

From Moutiers, also, I visited the silver mines at Pezay, which are distant about half-a-day's journey, and the road to which lay through a country abounding with all the magnificence of rocks and mountains, while the terrible graces were frowning amongst the precipices, or rushed with dishevelled hair through the gulf below, where the dark Lizère raged amidst the rocky cavities, and bellowed through the over-arching cliffs. These were shaded by the fantastic bushes that took their root in their humid crevices, or with the thick gloom of the embattled fir, which stood in deep squadrons on every mountain, and sometimes lifted up their dark honours above the dazzling snows, that sat upon the extremest heights. I had left Moutiers before sunrise, or at least before his golden chariot had rode up the eastern Alps, which lay heaped one upon another in sublime disorder right before me, or dispersed the sombre mists incumbent on their haughty brows. The perfect stillness of the air, and the solemn twilight that reflected a doubtful *day* on the projecting features of the great objects round, infused a deep calmness into the mind, and disposed it to a musing meditation, that was only interrupted by the sullen surges of the river beneath, and by the plaintive notes of the nightingales, that seemed to wail the setting of their beloved moon, and the approach of garish day. In this disposition of soul, and lost in a luxurious pensiveness of thought, my horse gently mounting, with the bridle loose on his neck, the light of many tapers suddenly shot to my eye at the distant point of the steep ascent, and a long procession of white figures issued by pairs, from between dark and stupendous rocks, and slowly descended to the sound of a solemn air, sung by a mixture of shrill and deep voices, the blended tones of which echoed among the cliffs, and resounded from mountain to mountain. It was a magic moment; a sudden awe crept through my blood. It seemed to me that the spirits of the mountain had left their dark recesses and their secret caverns on some high errand, and were coming to tell tales of fear and wonder to the world: the surprise of sense was perfect, and the enchantment of the imagination complete. Every object round added to the delusions of fancy, and every concomitant circumstance was in keeping with the main action, and deepened the enthusiasm of the instant. In short, it was one of those happy moments which so seldom arrive, and worthy of the pen of Ossian to have worked up into the wonderful and the terrible. I felt, though I cannot describe it, like him. But as I cannot charm with the fiction, let me at least satisfy with the fact; and what is wanting in the phrenzy of enthusiastic imagination let me supply by the soberness of truth.

This extraordinary appearance, then, proved nothing more nor less than a procession of the peasants of Eme, a little town in my road, who were trudging barefoot in white sheets, and with contrite hearts, to the cathedral of Moutiers, in order to call down rain from heaven on their thirsty land, by the power of their penitence and prayers. But should your petitions not be granted? demanded I of an old peasant who brought up the rear. Monsieur, in that case, replied he, the peasants of a neighbouring parish will take their turn, and try the effect of their faith. But, my good friend, should the fattening showers still tarry to descend? Another and another procession, answered he, will go to the great church to supplicate the Bon Dieu till our prayers are granted. A sure way of being enabled to cry miracle sooner or later, and of maintaining the credit of their oily priests. This may literally be called wearying heaven with importunity. But happy is the procession on these occasions that proffers its petitions in the nick of time, and honoured is the priest that heads it. The righteousness of that parish is held in high reverence, and becomes a tale for their children's children. Between Eme and Moutiers, in a soft vale, between the right-hand Alps and the river, and picturesquely scattered amongst abundant and beautiful shade, lies the village of Ceintron, which was ages ago the capital of the Tarentese, and of which Cæsar makes mention in his commentaries. As its situation is so much more charming and favourable than that of Moutiers, in a rich plain that has all the air of a fine park, and is watered and fertilised by the Lizère, which has not yet begun to change his beneficent smiles into a destructive rage; it is difficult to divine what chance or caprice, exalted the latter at the expense of the former. At Eme I visited the mouldering remains of an altar in honour of Diana, erected by the Romans in gratitude to the divine huntress for her supposed protection of their hosts amongst the difficult and dangerous passes of the mountains. Their goddess was certainly well chosen, as an ardent passion for the chase, could only have induced one of the tenants of heaven to have explored their gloomy wilds, and sought pleasure amongst their rocky fastnesses and inaccessible heights.

From Eme I still followed the Lizère as far as the village of Belle Autre, which lies a little on the other side of that river, and from which the road took a direction almost straight to the northern Alps. Belle Autre merits a particular mention, situated as its straggling cottages are in the midst of savage nature, and with an air of the most solitary wildness. A precipitate river that rushes down from the near mountains over a wide course, all scattered over with fragments of rock, and which the melting of the snows had swelled to an impetuous torrent, difficult to pass, formed as it were the street of the village, the little wooden houses of which were irregularly grouped along its banks, with narrow wooden bridges here and there, over a main branch of the many-armed water, for the convenience of the inhabitants, and to pass over their mules loaded with charcoal, in order to gain the road that led to the mines. On each hand the rocks and mountains shot up frightfully sombre, and a dark chasm yawned in front, through which the torrent raged, bounded by steep Alps, whose sharp points shone covered with eternal snows, above the volume of clouds that slept heavily beneath. Yet, amidst this desolate prospect, the village *clocher* shot up its taper spire on the brow of a little soft hillock of lovely verdure and delicious shade, as if accidentally dropped there by the hand of a fugitive grace in her passage to adorn the flowery bosom of some fruitful vale.

As there was no other road but the irregular course of the torrent, we were obliged to pick our way as we could along the beds of gravel between its branches and in its shallows, towards the dark chasm, at the entrance of which, a little rough path presented itself on the left hand that led to the mountains. By it we climbed, sometimes with tolerable ease on our horses, and sometimes with much labour on foot, for three hours, through a most forlorn country, and often on the edge of a deep precipice, at the bottom of which always appeared the torrent. Yet now and then fine savage scenes beguiled our steps, and a sublime sweep of imperial mountains awed and charmed the eye. Amongst the former I must not pass by a lofty Alp, that offered itself on our right hand as we crept along the edge of a profound gulf, alive and roaring with foaming waters. Its haughty brow and steep sides were gloomy with a massy forest of firs; a nest of quiet little cottages, with a peep of their tiny pastures, hung as it were in the clouds on the left, at the extreme point of a glade, and from the right a torrent of water shone on the dizzy summit, and precipitating itself down the rocky opening and between the dark firs, which seemed to have retired their deep ranks on either hand to open a passage for its fury, thundered to the profound. The still solemnity of all the objects round, formed an enchanting contrast with the impetuous motion of the noble cascade, and its foaming waters still seemed to retain the whiteness of their parent snows, that sat majestic on the extreme heights, and which amidst all their apparent calmness incessantly fed the rage of a whirling torrent.

The mines of Pezay are in the bowels of the Alps, and shut out from the cheerful haunts of men, by a surrounding chain of the most blank and barren of the mountains. Stupendous and frightful rocks, precipitate steeps russet with heath, wild and melancholy heights rough with short brushwood, or bleakly bare to the piercing blasts, intermixed with precipices glazed with perpetual ice, and towering summits white with eternal snows, formed the striking features of the widely desolate scene. On each side torrents of water rushed down the chasms of the mountains, and in one part four cascades fell from the edge of an enormous rock a hundred and fifty feet high, whose dashing waters found an endless supply in the mass of snows that glistened far above; and those mingled streams formed the origin of the rapid torrent, whose raging course we had traced upwards from Belle Autre. These four cascades were so small a space asunder, that they were concentred as it were in the same point of view; and one more abundant and turbulent than the rest, disdaining to pour leisurely down the rock, proudly shot its lucid sheet of water in a curve from its brow, which being caught by the strong breath of a contrary wind, was formed into the most beautiful feathers and picturesque waves of humid dust, before it reached half way to the ground. These, pierced by the sunbeams, shone with a thousand radiant colours, and played, and sparkled, floating lightly in the air, till, condensed near the ground into a body, they fell thundering upon the crags that time, tempests, and the constant wear of waters, had disjointed from the frowning cliffs above. I was particularly lucky to see it in this favourable moment, and was enchanted with the beauty and novelty of the effect.

I descended into every part of the mines by damp galleries, where the low vault obliged me almost everywhere to stoop, and often to bend myself nearly double, and passed from one to the other by villainous ladders to a great depth, and with much fatigue. I have often found my extraordinary height very troublesome, but never so much so as on this occasion. After having been exalting my eyes to stupendous objects all day, that made me appear an atom in my own sight, it was difficult to remember that it was necessary to stoop. But half-a-hundred stunning blows against the points of the rocky roof, proved a severe memorandum, though I only saved myself from a broken head at the expense of a broken back; and it appears a miracle to me that my half-and-half could ever set themselves seemly together again. When arrived at the caverns in the profound, where a few dim lamps only served to render darkness more visible, and the lost lamp of day more dear, the pale and squalid spectres that laboured riches from the living rock, struck me with horror and compassion. What a fate! To be deprived of the various charms of nature, the cheering light of the sun, the vivifying air; to be cut off from every comfort of life, and breathe a thousand noxious vapours, to poison and shorten its course; and for what? For four-and-twenty sols a day. For sufficient to eat a little bread in bitterness of spirit and drink a little sour wine, mixed with faint sweats and salt tears! But, no! the picture, thank God! is heightened, and expression forced beyond the truth. Born to rags and the most abject poverty, with few ideas, and those bounded to the mere necessaries of life, with sensibilities as gross and rigid as the lines of their countenances, with the rough-drawn sentiments of nature and the coarse habits of education, they find little difficulty in tempering their feelings to their situation, and even consider these twenty-four sols per day as an object of ambition, and a comfortable means of existence. The locality signifies little to them, the wherewithal is the grand point, and, born and bred as they are, they form a right judgment. The poor miner can seat himself on the crag of a rock in the dark and humid caverns of earth, and eat his well-earned bread by the sombre light of his little lamp, from day to day, with a kind of pride and independence of spirit, as being obliged only to his own travail for his subsistence; while the squalid beggar crawls upon its surface, insensible to the various beauties of nature around him, uncheered by the glorious sun, because petitioning from day to day for a precarious subsistence, humbled every moment by brutal refusals, and crushed by earthly scorns.

These mines were first opened by a company of English, but from heavy expenses in the first place, disputes amongst themselves after, and the wiliness and rapaciousness of some Savoyards, who pretended to have discovered a material breach of their covenants, and who wished to turn the rising profits to their own advantage, the English enterprisers were wearied and worried out of their rights, and quitted them just as it began to make them some return for the risks and toils of many years. However, the mines have by no means realised the sanguine expectations of their greedy encroachers, and they still continue to dream of treasures which they are never likely to produce. The thread of silver is pure, but inconsiderable. The director told me that, after a most expensive and laborious process, two ounces only could be obtained from sixty-four pounds of ore, as it comes from the mine. The neighbouring mountains are utterly despoiled of their former abundant shade, and they are forced annually to search at a greater distance for the immense quantities of wood, reduced to charcoal, necessary to supply the devouring flames, without which all their hopes must expire, and which yet burn up almost all their profits. Were it not for the lead, in which their ore is abundant, they must give up their works; and, as it is, it not unfrequently happens that they are obliged to draw on their funds, for a part of their annual interest money. However, they still feed themselves with brilliant hopes, talk big, dazzle those who have not taken pains to examine into the real state of things with pompous relations, and, possibly, will in the end cheat themselves as much in substance, as they have striven to do others in words. In a country, however, so poor as Savoy, where works of taste and elegance afford little to the craving many, and where there are abundantly more hands than are sufficient for the cultivation of the soil, the mines at Pezay are of material service, by supplying above five hundred poor creatures with a comfortable existence, as far as wholesome sustenance goes; and in this light I hope, they will always produce their owners sufficient profit to continue their undertaking.

I forgot to mention the Salines at Moutiers, which are well worth notice. The buildings are on the most improved plan, and the whole process of extracting the salt by evaporation very curious, and most ably superintended by the Chevalier de Butet, who is esteemed an excellent mathematician, and bears the better reputation, as well as appearance, of a man of great probity and worth. The Salines are entirely worked for the King of Sardinia's emolument, and are productive of a considerable revenue. But nothing either in Moutiers or its neighbourhood charmed me half as much as some little excursions I made amongst, or rather up, the Tarantese mountains. From below they appear very majestic, and form a sublime bulwark to the little valley; but, crowned as they are with rocks, or a deep phalanx of firs, one has not an idea of any new cultivation, of any smiling and habitable scenes, beyond their airy summits. What an error! what a surprise! After mounting four hours by the most steep and rugged paths, which a mule only could climb, and sometimes not without peril, a new world was opened to my eye. And what a world! How full of enchantment! How different at once, and how much more picturesque and attractive than that below. Could anything be more striking than to see, amidst these stupendous heights, the most fertile and varied scenes of pastoral landscape stretching on every side between Alps and Alps, here hiding themselves, as it were, amidst their precipices; there climbing sportively up their rugged sides, and here again nestling beneath their overarching cliffs? The most verdant pastures and the most luxuriant corn-fields appeared everywhere intermixed, and lending new graces to each other; and wherever the lordly Alps seemed rent asunder, and yawned horribly to the gulf below, it offered a most picturesque view to see little fertile patches clinging on the very brink of the precipice, and looking down, as it were, with terror to the deep profound. And what nests of cottages, huddled together amongst their stately walnut groves! And what pure rills gurgling along the meads or hurrying down the rocks! What shady hillocks and what romantic dells! Here and there a taper steeple seemed to have mounted a little eminence, on purpose to invite the pious, with a modest and smiling air to pay the tribute of thanksgiving and prayer to that Deity, who delights in humility, and to whom the devotions of the simple and lonely are the most acceptable sacrifice.

It is not possible to give an adequate idea of the picturesque effect of these cottages, here scattered more thinly, and there grouped in large masses together; here reposing tranquilly in the valleys, there hanging amongst the crags, or running up the mountain's ridge to the very edge of the snow, and seeming to dare every bitter blast. Nor was there the least perceivable difference either in their form, size, or materials; no brow-beating château to awe them, nor even the ampler volume of a richer *fermier's* habitation, swelling amongst them with an air of fastidious superiority. In short, the most perfect equality seemed to reign throughout the populous scene, and presented a homefelt idea of that sufficiency, good, simplicity, and peace, which must have been the distinguishing features of the golden age, and which, in the polished nations of Europe, are so rarely found in this. I have erred. The curé's mansion always appeared smiling, with its white face and a more polished air, by the side of the parish church, but with a distinction that denoted no arrogance, no luxury, no vanity. It seemed to invite with its benevolent aspect, and to say, 'the good pastor within, whom your pious duty feeds, and by whose doctrines and example ye are taught to seek the bread of life, and to drink of the fountains of living water, courts you to my walls, and wishes to afford all its comforts to your necessities and your sorrows.' The transport with which I explored and roved amidst scenes so new and romantic, from day to day, is not to be described. It was wonder, it was delight, it was enthusiasm unknown before. I seemed to glory in scenes which appeared uncorrupted by vice, and where pride and luxury were visibly unknown, and to grow at once more satisfied with myself and mankind. With what ecstacy did I climb up the extremest heights, and plunge myself deep into the forests of pines that darkened their brows! How charming to hear them vocal at once with birds and the bells of the numerous herds, that grazed the mossy herb! But how much more picturesque and delightful still, to see a number of children sporting amidst the shade, whilst following their flocks, lying about upon the grass, surrounded by their sheep and mottled goats, or frolicking with the innocent animals, which gambolled with fearless familiarity, and made playfellows of their jocund little keepers! In many parts, too, the fields and mountains were enamelled with the most beautiful flowers; and wild laburnums and pomegranates made the valley glow with their scarlet blossoms, or enriched it with their floating gold. And as the inhabitants of this new Arcadia appear equal in all other respects, so are they also in their dress. *La pragmatique* has existed there time out of mind, which forbids the least distinction or innovation in this article; and, of course, it is extremely singular, and wholly different from anything I ever saw before.

I happened to be roaming amongst these delicious mountains on a *jour de fête*, and saw above five hundred peasants assembled in a churchyard, waiting the hour of mass. The men's habiliments were not very particular, though all alike, consisting of a suit of coarse drab cloth (if it deserves the name), manufactured amongst them; but the women's was very odd and striking. Each was arrayed in a kind of puce-coloured serge petticoat, that reached only to the ankles, bound round with four lists of worsted lace — the two outward ones of red, and the inner ones of green. A loose jacket of the same, with large sleeves as far as the elbows, was thrown over a straight vest of green serge, set close to the shape, like a bodice, and which was laced with red before. A deep collar, of coarse thread lace, fell over their shoulders and breast, and left their necks bare, which were ornamented with gold crosses; and their wide shift sleeves, which appeared beneath the short ones of the jacket, were edged with the same lace as at the bosom. Each wore a little red cap, like a child's skull-cap, bordered with a green and yellow lace, and their hair was strained up under it before; whilst behind, it was twisted into tight tresses, one within another, stuck up flat against the pole, in the exact form of a plate of sausages, as they are served up, ring within ring, in Savoy.

If they were a spectacle to us, Vincent and myself were no less so to them; and three pretty arch-looking girls, that were cuddled together under a walnut tree, looked, and tittered, and blushed, and looked again, till their surprise and amusement at our strange and, what doubtless appeared to them, ludicrous dresses almost totally got the better of their diffidence and good manners. Our round white hats, and English leather breeches, seemed to be the great objects of their attention and mirth. However, they became more composed on our accosting them, and a further familiarity with our outlandish raiment abated their astonishment. I reconciled them still better to it by a *douze-sols pièce à chacune,* and was endeavouring to make out their *patois* and make them comprehend my French, when the good curé approached, with his grey locks and an air of primitive simplicity and hospitality, and invited us to repose ourselves in his mansion. 'Ce n'est qu'un pays de montagne, Monsieur,' said he, 'mais j'ai de bon beurre, d'assez bon vin, des œufs frais, quelque fromage, et tout ce que j'ai, je vous offre de bon cœur.' Who could resist such a patriarchal invitation from so patriarchal a figure, and amidst such patriarchal scenes? The inside of his house was just what its outside promised — neat, plain, and unpretending; but with an inconceivable air of peace and comfort, of philosophic solitude and pious sequestration. And his little garden and his little field! with what an appetite did I eat of his victuals and drink of his drink, and how insatiate was my ear of his plain and sensible converse, as I sat beside him in the seat of honour — his walnut arm-chair — leaning my elbow upon his deal table, and steadfastly eyeing him with equal philanthropy and delight! He told me that he had resided in this parish forty-two years, that his situation at first seemed rather desolate; but that he had not only, long been reconciled to, but so enamoured of it, that he would not change it for all the splendours and dignities of the world. 'Mes paroissiens, dit-il, sont de bons gens, ils m'aiment et me respectent, et je leur fais tout le bien que je puisse.' He informed me, that the peasants of these mountains were at once the most industrious and opulent in Savoy. Not one, he said, who did not maintain his family honestly, and live at his ease. Not a spot of ground, even if hanging amidst the most frightful precipices, but their hands had cultivated with incredible labour, and not a production of the mountains that they did not turn to account. The firs, he told me, served equally for their firing and for the construction of their houses, which are built entirely of wood, huddled together for mutual protection, covered with wooden tiles, secured against the weight of sudden and violent gusts of wind by large stones, laid here and there upon their roofs. The great source of their commerce, he said, was their oats, cattle, sheep, and mules, vast abundance of which they sold at the large fairs; while their pigs, goats, and poultry, supported their households. He assured me that no less an annual sum than four-and-twenty thousand louis, was returned in cash for the commodities of the Tarantese Alps. But they carry their industry still further, for the ease and comfort of their families. At the dead season of the year, the poorest of the men descend from their mountains; and dispersing themselves through the nearest provinces of France, follow various employments, leaving their wives and children to take care of the live stock at home, and return, as the genial season approaches, to crop their fields and reap their own harvests, with four or five louis clear gains in their pockets; happy, if with the fruits of their honest labours, they bring not back to their Alpine abodes some taint of the dishonest vices of the country they return from, and the men with whom they must necessarily have mixed!

Adieu, dear smiling and romantic scenes, which nature seems to have fostered with such partial fondness, placed amongst her rocky fastnesses and Alpine heights, and guarded with all her mountain sublimities, that, if possible, they may be out of the vanities that disgrace, the vices that pollute, and the violences that desolate, all her graces below! Never never, shall I see your like again!

As in a strange country, especially, I never wish to return from any excursion by the same road, and as I had heard there were three convents worth attention placed high amidst the Alps, and which I could visit, with some toil, in my way back, I determined to satisfy my curiosity, and return by the mountains to Chamberry. My gay friend Galaté accompanied me to the first, which is called Tamier, and which we reached on a hot morning, after much climbing and much fatigue. The ascent thither was diversified, as usual amongst the Alps — now with smiling, and now with frowning, objects; and barrenness and fertility went hand in hand, and mutually gave relief to each other.

The first *coup-d'œil* of Tamier was striking and beautiful. It is situated in the centre of a lovely and luxuriant valley, hemmed in between the mountains; and those mountains, above, waving with various graceful and abundant shades, where stern Winter does not chill and repulse fruitfulness with his snows, and, below, cultivated with grain and pastures by the cares of the monks, who never fail to carry plenty with them wherever they settle, and, in the midst of their austerities, to make the desert smile. This convent is of the rigid order of the celebrated La Trappe, and its inhabitants are famous for their hospitality and piety. They maintain a perpetual silence, except when they have any advice to ask, or commissions to execute, from the Superior, or he has any orders to give them. Their regimen is still stricter than that of the Chartreux, their fastings more frequent, and their watchings and religious duties longer and more severe. Every day they sally out in a body, headed by their Prieur, to labour, in silence, a portion of their lands; each digs his own grave, and each prepares the various requisites for his interment, which he daily contemplates before his awful call to his long home, and at the dread hour of death, each is laid in his hair shirt on a bed of ashes, where he is attended with the last solemn rites of his religion by all his brethren, to whom he offers a striking, and, after so much penitence and so many privations and sufferings, I trust, salutary example at once of earthly weakness and misery, and of the sustaining power of faith, at the fearful moment when all the possessions and splendours of the world become nothing, and when the chamber of state and the bed of down only add new throes to conscious and expiring nature, and give new regrets to fond and failing thought.

We were received with great benevolence and humility by the Prieur and coadjuteur, who spread our board with a profusion, which they themselves partook of but sparingly. They afterwards showed us their demesne, which was extensive, picturesque, and highly improved, and at about the distance of three hundred yards from the convent, the good Prieur pointed smilingly to a neat building, where he told me the wives of those gentlemen, who did them the honour to visit them might be admitted: 'quoique nous n'osions pas,' said he, 'les admettre dans l'enceinte même du couvent.' To this he added a polite and even cordial invitation to me to bring my wife, and to pass a month amongst them. 'L'air de notre montagne, Monsieur, est bon et bien épuré dans la belle saison, faites nous donc le plaisir d'amener Madame, et quoique nous ne puissions pas aller la rendre nos respects dans sa retraite, nous prendrons garde qu'elle soit bien servie de tout ce qu'est à notre portée, et selon nos règles. Mais il y a une chose à vous dire, Monsieur, il ne faut pas que vous restiez ensemble la nuit; vous coucherez toujours dans le couvent: il serait de blesser la bienséance de notre ordre d'agir différemment, cependant un petit divorce ne vous ferait point de mal.' I thanked him for his hospitable and, I will answer for it, sincere invitation, which, would circumstances and other engagements have allowed it, I should readily have accepted.

At night I was conducted to sleep in a neat apartment, and in the bed where Victor Amadeus, grandfather to the present King of Sardinia, had lain several nights. If in the shrine of my body, so bold and comprehensive a spirit, and such strong and improved talent, did not rest, I trust at least, that with it reposed a less ambitious, crafty, and ungrateful heart. If my slumbers were not then, they ought to have been, sweeter than his, and my waking surely was sweeter, as I waked full of philanthropy, without one dark or vengeful thought, and hailed the balmy breezes from heaven with a cheerful and thankful mind. Yet, amidst all their meekness and mortification, the monks of Tamier seemed weakly vain of the honour formerly done to their convent by this royal guest: a strong proof how difficult it is in any state, to close the eyes utterly to the dazzling splendours of the world, and expel all remains of its prepossessing vanities from the heart. But if the good Prieur of Tamier was indulgent to the dark, violent, and artificial character of Victor, he thundered out his anathemas with an unsparing tongue against those of our Harry VIII., and his able, unfeeling, and politic daughter Elizabeth — rightly enough, it is true, had he not from zealous prejudice unjustly slipped over the detested memory of her elder sister, the bloody and bigoted Mary. But I gave him no useless and ungrateful mementos on the subject, and took all his fervent prayers for my conversion, as they were meant, in good part. How vain, indeed, how absurd, how almost impious, all contests about modes of faith, where the meaning is *right*, and the *right* God worshipped. Oh! I have never doubted, I never can doubt, that He looks down from His high and holy place with a smile, on all our little bickerings in matters of religious controversy, and that *that* smile is mercy. But when a difference in religious opinions rouses the bloody fury Persecution, that fierce hell-bound that cries havock on mankind, then it is that his wrath is justly awakened, and his red right arm laid bare, to avenge his outraged prerogative on those, who have dared usurp his vengeance. To worship our God and our Saviour in spirit and in truth, as far as our weakness and frailties will admit, to relieve and comfort the wretched and destitute, to be benevolent, tolerant, and just, and to judge no man, that we ourselves be not judged; such has always seemed to me the sum and substance of a religion, which we are assured he that runs may read, and which yet so many, by priestly pride and a vain wish to distinguish themselves, have blasted by their dissensions, and marred and perplexed by their needless interpretations and intemperate spirit, to the shame of candour and the scandal of Christianity. May God preserve me from so great a sin!

As I have touched on heavenly subjects without meaning to do so, I cannot help mentioning a large picture of heaven, and as we are assured, very exactly delineated, which decorated the room where we dined. In it was precisely marked out the rank of angels, archangels, saints, and hierarchies, even up to the throne of God, with all the different roads leading thither from this nether world. Here wives were scaling the steep way, and there maidens climbing by a gentler ascent: on one side, the bachelors squinted on the latter, and on the other, husbands seemed to turn their backs on the former.

Here lawyers seemed to slip into heaven by craft, and there soldiers took it by storm; here little folks toiled and sweated up a rugged, and strait, and winding path, and there great ones jogged sociably along an evener way; but the main road of all, and where there appeared no let nor hindrance, was occupied by a long train of bishops, cardinals, and popes, marching in all their paraphernalia and with becoming state, and followed by a numerous cortége of fat chested monks, elbowing each other to make room for them, while the saints and apostles seemed in the higher places of the divine regions. But woe to him that stumbled in his way up, for below a thousand devils of different forms, and differently armed with pitch-forks, hooks, and red hot pincers, and other such delicate hellish weapons, grinned horribly, and haled* about in fiend-like triumph the poor culprits, who had fallen within their clutches. But, however one may laugh at their easy belief, one cannot but respect their unaffected piety and noble benevolence.

An unequivocal instance of this happened a few months before I visited them, and amidst their little prejudices and follies will speak trumpet-tongued in their favour. By some accident a large mountain village had been burned a few miles from their convent. As it was in the night and in winter, its industrious habitants lost all their live and dead stock in the conflagration, as well as their furniture, and scarcely escaped naked and alive. Horrid was the desolation of these honest peasants! The Alps echoed with their cries, and as their only refuge they begged a temporary shelter within the walls of Tamier. It was granted them with all the eagerness and sympathy which distress loves. But this was not all; the compassionate and generous monks furnished them abun-

* We find hale still used instead of haul, as in the Bible translation. Saul 'made havock of the Church, entering into every house, and *haling* men and women.'

dantly with every necessary that could render their abode in the convent comfortable, and having privately informed themselves of the full extent of their losses, supplied a sum of money to the amount of 1,600*l.* to purchase new furniture, clothes, and implements of husbandry to stock their little fields again with flocks, and their barns with fodder; and, after entertaining them all at Tamier till their village was completely rebuilt, sent each home with money in his purse, happier and richer than before the disaster, that seemed to have overwhelmed them with helpless ruin. Let them, then, in God's name, abuse King Harry and Queen Bess, till their tongues are weary, and cover the walls of their brown parlours with plans of heaven, contrasted with their divine charity, religious candour will but smile at the one, and patriotic zeal be mute at the other, however rejoiced that England is free from the intolerant zeal of similar bigotry, and the blind credulity of similar superstition.

I parted with my lively friend at Tamier, and whilst he trod back his steps to Moutiers, pursued my wild way over the mountain grandeurs and solitudes to Belleveaux, a convent of Benedictines. After alternately mounting and descending four hours, attended by the Prieur of Tamier's ancient servant, by almost untrodden ways, and surrounded by a glorious sweep of Alps, that rose up sublimely as far as the eye could reach, with new features and in new directions, the fertile and populous vale, that leads to the sombre solitudes of Belleveaux, suddenly presented itself to our eyes, stretching beyond the reach of the sight between a chain of mountains, on either hand up whose steep and rugged sides, the valley-graces seemed sportively climbing, scattering their blooms and their verdure as they mounted, and wreathing their fruitful dance round the barren rocks. How unexpected to see a wide and good road leading through the centre of the valley, and extending among these stupendous heights from hamlet to hamlet for many miles. It is reckoned the most populous vale amongst the Savoy Alps, and counts thirteen parishes. Yet pleasing and singular as the view was, it both surprised and charmed me the less after the superior beauties, sublimities, and free and fantastic graces of the mountains above Moutiers.

At the entrance of this vale our guide left us, as he said we could easily enquire, and scarcely miss, our way to Belleveaux. After ambling along this Alpine turnpike for about an hour and a half, we turned from it to the right, and followed up a narrow path by the side of a torrent, that rushed down a dark chasm between dreary rocks. The lonely convent soon appeared at a distance, looking down with a melancholy air, from its lofty eyry in the bosom of a dark wood, that feathered far below it to the torrent, and reached above its head in a conical form to a height, that almost rivalled that of the stupendous rocks and snow-capt mountains crowded in tumultuous hosts all round. As we wound up our gloomy way, the convent sank in a mass of shade from our eyes, the rocks grew more awful and overhung us with a more threatening air, the torrent roared louder, every trace of smiling and cultivated nature disappeared, and an iron forge, worked by the surging water, whose appalling thunders were heard from afar, and which perpetually vomited volumes of smoke mixed with ruddy black flames, completed the terrors of the scenery. After passing the forge we expected to mount immediately to the convent; but vain the hope! Like the airy palace of some enchanter, it seemed only to have been lifted up to our sight in order to tempt our feet to trackless wilds, and betray us, amidst all the magic horrors of the tremendous scenes around, with malicious delusions. We actually wandered at first by the edge, and at last up the torrent, amidst fragments of rocks and the most black and terrific objects, near an hour in hopeless pursuit of a path, that might lead us to the convent, which, hungry, thirsty, and weary as we were, seemed like the land of promise to the children of Israel, and which seemed to flee us, like them, to try our patience and faith in the dreary desert. At last we had advanced so far, that looking back we saw the lowering rocks lift themselves in gloomy bulwarks across the winding path by which we had advanced, as if to bar our return to the cheerful haunts of men. From this change in their direction to the eye, we knew that the secret path, so long and anxiously sought, must lie somewhere behind us, and that interested as we were to find, we yet had missed it. With cautious steps and searching glances, then, we now went *with* the stream, and found that, as in most other worldly cases, it answered better to us, than to have striven *against* it. In short, the long-desired path appeared, lurking in the shade, at the water's brink, and we spurred our mules up it with delight. Half an hour's difficult climbing by one of the most impracticable of all the mountain roads, landed us safe at the convent's gate, and just as its bell sounded sweetly to dinner,—to dinner! The ring of bells that warned Whittington to turn back and saluted him as Lord Mayor of London town, was less grateful than the voice of the clapper on the house-top at Belleveaux.

A warm and hearty welcome is always pleasing; but who can speak its transport under our circumstances? Oh! thou dear little Prieur, when I forget thy round belly, thy sleek front, thy ruddy cheeks, thy twinkling eyes, thy cordial smile, may my right hand forget its cunning, if indeed it has any to forget. I had brought him a letter of recommendation from Tamier, but needed none to a soul so brimful of hospitality, conviviality, and the very custard of human kindness. How he bowed, and bowed and smiled, as he led me to the refectoire; and how did he stand tiptoe, as a duck might do to a crane, to look up in my face! I really longed to finish my dinner, that I might have a full relish of his benevolence and sociable spirit; and after the cravings of my appetite, which stood so much in the way of sentiment, were satisfied, found not only a fund of good sense and good humour in my little Prieur, but natural good breeding, liberal sentiments, and a disdain of narrow prejudices. And he fiddled, as if his face had been full of touching sensibility, and the pale and pensive graces, had embellished his person and formed every limb. Luckily, too, he had a young curé with him from Annecy, who played deliciously on the hautboy; and as they had been wont to accord their notes to each other, they played in the sweetest and most perfect unison.

The situation of the convent is extremely singular, and sequestered beyond description. The little recess that is formed at the bases of the rocks and mountains, which tower immediately around it, is only of capacity just to admit of the convent which is not a large one, a moderate-sized court and a good garden. From these the ascent directly begins, though the monks with their wonted attention to improvements, have hung verdant pastures on their swelling sides, as far as they would admit of cultivation. There is really a something terrific in the solitude, from the stern features of the haughty and rugged rocks, and the roar of two impetuous torrents that rush down the clefts of the mountains on each side, and the depth of gloom all round. From the loftiness and near approach of the mountains, the Prieur assured me that during six months in the year, the sun was only two hours above their horizon. But such a social, cheerful, courteous, benevolent spirit as thine, my little round man, secures sunshine wherever thou art, and will enliven the deepest solitude and illumine the darkest shade! The day had been of chequered sunshine and storm, and I cannot describe the magical effect of partial gleams of the former lighting up the advanced angles of the rocks, and setting a portion of the dark woods on fire; and still less the enchantments of the latter, which varied their features every moment — now sitting with fleecy pride on the extreme heights; now sailing with solemn majesty from cliff to cliff, first reflecting a thousand luminous and radiant tints, then growing dark with vengeance, and, gathering their gloomy squadrons together in their wrath, showing horrid glimpses of the red thunderbolt that muttered in their lurid bosoms. As the kind Prieur saw my real feelings of the imposing scenery, he proposed an excursion the next morning to the summit of a neighbouring Alp, which he told me was esteemed one of the highest in Savoy. Accordingly he loaded a mule with wine and provisions, and attended by two stout mountaineers we set out. About mid-way up, and after two hours' clambering, we arrived at some large fertile meadows, which were part of his demesnes, and where he showed me his *vacheries*, occupied by fifty as fine cows as I ever saw, and whose delicious milk afforded us a most grateful refreshment. In about two hours more we reached the desired spot, but not till after having plunged through a mass of snow almost up to our mules' bellies, where surly winter still maintains a post *in terrorem*, and in defiance of summer. As it was the latter end of June, and an ardent sun had darted its beams on our head all the way up, we arrived scorched and exhausted at the desired summit. How delicious, then, to throw ourselves down by the side of the snow, and court the fresh breezes that brush eternally the Alpine heights. And on how beautiful, how fragrant a couch did we stretch our languid limbs!

Ye luxurious monarchs of the East, who ransack all nature to contribute to your voluptuousness and ease, can ye show one like it? Nature had here painted all her choicest colours, and blended them with the most bewitching harmony. The lustrous blue of the lovely gentianella vied with the vivid blush of the pink; the rich purple of the powdered auricula with the deep scarlet of the trumpet flower; the anemone pure and silver-white with the gaudy ranunculus's flaming gold, and they, with a thousand other unknown sweets, were not scattered by nature with a parsimonious hand. It was a bright bed of unsparing lustre, impossible to express, unless my pen possessed its rich colouring and endless variety. And what perfume when the passing breezes whispered amongst their sweets, and brushed their glowing heads with their light wings!

What transport to breathe at once such refreshing and fragrant airs, and to quaff the ruddy tribute of the grape, cooled in the congealed snow that edged our flowery couch, and which showed, in immediate contact, the seemingly wide contrast, between the chilling and barren rigours of winter and the warm and fruitful graces of the luxuriant spring! How did I gaze with wonder and ecstacy from object to object, now wantoning with the crisp snow on one side, and now plucking the various blossoms on the other, and forming a garland with them about my hat, and hanging them round my neck. Never did Flora present Zephyr with more fragrant or more glowing wreaths. The scenery of rocks and mountains round, too, was sublime, and from the extreme edge of the mountain, the sight plunged down at once without the break of one interposing object, shuddering to the vale. What a depth, and how giddy did my head grow, as my eye hurried trembling over the dazzling lines of the chequered world beneath; I felt almost frightened at the aspiring heights to which I had dared to mount. St. Pierre really appeared, like a town of cards, on a level with the Castle of Miolan, while from below, it towers so proudly above. At night my courteous host had prepared a surprise and pleasure of another kind, and formed to excite softer emotions, and touch every tender chord in the heart. It was just two days before the full moon, and it may easily be supposed how charming her mild light must appear amidst such magnificent scenery, and what new charm and solemnity it must give to every sublime object round. After supper, then, the Prieur led me to a little grotto at the skirt of the wood, above the convent, in which rose a limpid fountain that bubbled to a narrow channel, and from thence murmured to pay a pure tribute to the imperious torrent beneath. While one of the religieux was pointing out to me the limpid source, and I was hanging over it with pensive pleasure, the most dulcet sounds struck my ear, and every rock and mountain seemed to reply to the pathetic strains of an air, which the Prieur had heard me particularly admire, and which of all others undulated the most melodiously, between the soft breathing notes of his friend's hautboy, and the silver and expressive tones of his own violin.

Our pleasure of all kinds is relative, and depends in a great measure on circumstance and situation, and particularly those of sentiment united with sense, which owe their fine point to the state of our nerves, our bent of thought, foregone feelings, and the objects present. On every side what I felt within, and saw without, served to render mine exquisite. The awful serenity of the general scene, the more garish delights of the foregone day, the pensiveness of mind occasioned by the glooms and stillness of night, mixed with the pale beams of the moon, that gleamed partial light on the sublime objects round, and the softer affections, more awake than usual, from the warm benevolence and kind attentions of my host, all united to harmonise every nerve, and make them apt to thrill with rapture at the sounds, that awakened so deliciously the drowsy night; and though I often have heard, and probably often shall hear, much finer music, I most likely never shall hear any, that falls with such full effect upon my heart. I leaned my back against a rock, and folding my arms upon my breast, listened with rapt attention to the various airs that now swelled and now sank on the ear, which echo multiplied round, and to which the rustling leaves, the moaning wind, and the gurgling water formed irregular, and wild, yet soft cadences. I started from my posture as out of a profound sleep, when the Prieur hung up his sweet lyre, and approaching told me it was midnight, and followed him in deep silence to the convent, as if afraid of interrupting the melody that still sounded in my ears, and jarring the chord of melancholy, that still vibrated so sweetly plaintive in my bosom. Now, God go with thee, gentle Friar, for all thy courtesy shown to me!

But I must not quit his holy house without observing that its whole society, which consists but of six Religieux, treated me with the utmost hospitality, and that they seem to live together with that spirit of meekness, love, piety, and peace, which are sufficient to enlighten the darkest solitude, and of power alone to open Paradise in the wild. An old monk, who had resided there near threescore years, told me I was the first Englishman he had ever seen. I was here dubbed with the title of Monsieur le Chevalier, as I had been at Tamier with that of Marquis, and as I am going to be at Allezon, another Alpine convent, and one of the order of Chartreux, with that of 'my Lor'—yet all the while nothing but a simple parson, though one that has been bedecked with as many titles, on the continent, as a German prince or an Eastern mogul — so easily are they acquired. But are they as easily worn, and worn as meekly, were they really mine? Should I not swell, and feel screwed up with them in every limb?

Leaving these points to be resolved by those, who are more learned in worldly honours than myself, I resume the thread of my journal, which is, and had need be, spun almost out, and invite Amelia to sit down with me to an excellent maigre dinner at Allezon, after a long and fatiguing ride over the mountains. This convent is spacious and rich; but its demesne, though equally lofty, and somewhat similar in feature, is by no means so picturesque, so fertile, and so abundant in fine shade, as that of Tamier.

As I had journeyed thither on my good little Prieur's own mule, and attended by his own servant, both of which were gone back to Belleveaux, the Prieur of Allezon had his favourite beast caparisoned for me to return to Chamberry, and set me thereon. Now, at first I thought it was a sturdy, wicked-looking mule; but on eyeing him again and again, my belief was staggered, and I asked the Prieur's man, who followed me, what manner of brute it might be. 'C'est un jumarre,* mi Lor.' 'Et qu'est ce que c'est qu'un jumarre, mon ami?' 'O my Lor, c'est une bête qui est faite, entre un taureau de montagne et une jument.' On I went, then, on my jumarre, examining him from head to foot, and, above all things, having an eye to his vile dispositions to break my neck down the rocks, as we descended the rugged and sometimes almost perpendicular paths, that led to Chamberry. Did Vincent's mule dare approach it, a bite and a kick were his sure welcome. Did even the Prieur's man presume to come too near, his malicious posteriors were presently turned in a convenient attitude to have a fling at him. Thus I crept down the mountains, sometimes with bodily fear, and

* This very remarkable hybrid animal, is particularly described in the scarce history of the Vaudois Church settled from time immemorial in three Alpine valleys of Piedmont, published in folio by Jean Leger, the Moderator, in the year 1669. He gives a drawing of the beast, and mentions his travelling eighteen leagues through the mountains on one, with greater ease than on horseback. The jumarre is a cross between the bull and the horse, or the bull and the ass; the head and tail resembling the former, though without horns. As the upper and lower jaws do not meet together, they can only feed where the grass is long enough to be broken off with the tongue. The editor, when he was formerly in the Vaudois valleys, found the animal was still known.

sometimes worked up to spite myself, by the spite of my beast, till landed, at length, safely in the vale, I jogged on with less apprehension, and with relaxed reins. All was well till we were crossing a little river, at the end of the town, when my strangely-begotten animal, resolving to avenge himself, with the true spirit of a Catholic beast, on his heretic rider, stopped short, gave himself one rude shake, and in an instant, and without time for prevention or even thought, I found myself in the middle of the river, and the gentle jumarre making repeated efforts to finish all my worldly cares by kicking out my brains. And his kind purpose would doubtless have been fulfilled, had not Vincent leaped into the water, and saved me from his charitable hoofs. Yet I mounted him again, drenched as I was, and ornamented as he was with a large silk net, fringed above and below, together with bells and with tassels — clapped my spurs in his sides, swore, and rated, and went, dripping and clattering and ringing, through Chamberry, in all possible state. Methought I only wanted rings to my fingers, and bells to my toes, to complete my triumph, and outfigure the old woman of famous memory. However, past peril often becomes a theme for present mirth, and mine only served to heighten my sense of home-felt comforts, and the joy of finding myself safe again in my dear and tender Amelia's arms.

TOUR THE THIRD.

JUNE, 1784.

AGAIN I take up my pen, but with all the misgivings of a heavy heart, bleeding with remembrance of the past and trembling at a view of the future. That I set myself down to fulfil my promised task at all, may be considered by Amelia as one of the strongest proofs of my affection, and of my readiness to sacrifice my ease to her pleasure. Dull as they might appear to an indifferent eye, in hers the foregone tours are precious, and she presses their completion; but I am perfectly conscious myself that they are, at best, but of paste-like value, and that the eye of discernment and taste must, like hers, see them with the foil of affection to see them sparkle with genuine lustre.

But let me hasten to the dreaded task, which it must cost me a thousand pangs to finish, and which my heart pants to hurry through, that it may return from impatient murmurs to its former patient resignation, and sink from the storms of sensibility to those calmer regrets, over which it was wont to brood, and which it holds alike sacred and dear. Ah! Hope, as enchanting as it appears, and balmy as are the breezes that it wafts o'er my soul, I dare not trust thy lovely, but shadowy perspective, lest it should suddenly be shut in eternal darkness from my yearning eyes. Yet shall it be closed eternally? Let but a point of time, to which mortality so fondly clings and gives such ideal extent, pass, and death through momentary and gloomy terrors, shall open those bright and eternal abodes, where joy and friendship shall reign purified, exalted, and immortal, and where my dear Chatillon shall read distinctly, with how warm gratitude and what true and tender affection my soul expanded towards him on earth.

Soon after my return from Moutiers, I set out with my beloved friend on our long-concerted tour to Bugey. Ill omens accompanied us from the first moment. Unforeseen yet necessary delays prevented our leaving Chamberry till towards the evening, and long ere we reached the Lake of Bourget* the gathering clouds threatened elemental war. However, we persevered; and, accompanied by the sensible and upright Du Molard; his third brother, the gentle, wise, and benevolent Senator Santier, whose countenance says, 'Place unlimited confidence in me,' and whose heart will justify its promises; the composed, and queer but well-informed, keen, and caustic Chevalier de Châteauneuf; we embarked for the castle of Chatillon. At pushing off from the shore, an old fisherman warned us against trusting the angry lake at so late an hour, with so crazy a boat and such unskillful boatmen, as he assured us we had engaged. But as Chatillon's affairs pressed his arrival at the castle, and interest and jealousy might have prompted the old mentor of the lake, we prayed God speed us, and rowed away. In less than half an hour we had cause to repent our temerity; the sky grew horribly black, a violent wind lashed the indignant wave into boiling foam, thunders began to mutter, and every surge that beat against our open boat, to menace us with quick destruction. We durst not venture far out on the lake, and yet it was perilous to keep too near the rocky shore, dark as it was and ignorant as we found our conductors. What was to be done? Du Molard and Châteauneuf were for returning, or landing at the first possible place, and passing a comfortless night under the rocks. My dear Chatillon and Monsieur Santier, thought we might as well proceed; and the former, knowing the lake and being

* Usually called the Lac de Bourget, or Borgetto.

a good steersman, believed that with Vincent's help, who is an excellent rower, there would be little real danger of drowning, though a moral certainty of being drenched with the rain, that already began to pour on our unsheltered heads. 'Courage; donc!' we cried, unanimously, and kept on our watery and weary way. But for the dread of regaling the monstrous trouts and pikes of the lake with my carcase, I should have enjoyed the terrible beauties of the angry lake, all white with foam; the deep gloom of the heavens, rendered more distinct from time to time by the lightning that flashed through the dark rolling clouds, the rush of the howling wind, and the dreadful majesty of the rocks on either hand, which frowned awfully to the nightly terrors, and, while they menaced the clouds, caught and seemed vengefully to launch back to them their thunders. In short, about midnight we arrived at our desired haven wet, hungry, and tired, and hailed the mouldering honours of the tempest-beaten castle with joyful and thankful hearts. Was ever fire so cordial, supper so welcome, beds so soft, or sleep so refreshing?

After passing three convivial days at Chatillon, and amusing ourselves amongst other things with the snuffy pomposity of the renowned knight of the patched breeches, Messieurs Châteauneuf, Santier, and Du Molard returned to Chamberry, and myself and Chatillon pursued our way to Bellay, where the first object we saw was Madame Chovin's meretricious face thrust like Jezebel's out of a window, and painted full as gaudily, though the adroit Frenchwoman would scarcely ever be found accompanied by eunuchs in her chamber, like the Israelitish queen. 'Eh! bonjour Madame Chovin!' 'Eh! bonjour Messieurs; soyez les bienvenus.' So we alighted and mounted, and were presented in form to her daughter-in-law, a bride of ten days and a Dijon fortune, to the no small joy of the family, and the no small emolument of the family estate, which needed much piecing and many repairs. What though the teeth of *la nouvelle mariée* were notched and black, her face as rough as a cross-road, her nose like that of a squab pigeon, her eyes placed here and there like the famous Johnny Wilkes's, her neck the colour of mahogany, her throat with a goître-like protuberance, robbing her scraggy bosom of its swell—she was quite alive to her own consequence, showed off the tonish airs of a high-bred coquette, set up for a wit with the help of old proverbs, and for a *bel esprit* with the fag end of old songs, and made the family into which she was just engrafted, thoroughly sensible of the honour she had done them, by leaving the *beau monde* of Dijon and transplanting her person and her money-bags, to the distant and unmodish little capital of Bugey. And her brother! Her very counterpart! strutting about from day-break to midnight in his flaming French silk *habit de noces*, long dirty-laced ruffles, a sword by his side, a *chapeau de bras* befeathered under one arm, and twirling for ever his snuff-box in his hand, that one might admire the portrait of one of his *belles maîtresses* on the lid (if such an one he had, how he must have paid her), whilst a false bottom offered to your eyes, the most offensively obscene picture that imagination can suppose, or a Frenchman ever cherished. How dear has Madame Chovin paid for her rich daughter-in-law! how much dearer still, I should think, the husband of the belle, who is really a genteel and pleasing young man.

But what has liking to do with French marriages! In their own words: 'Ils ne sont que des liens de convenance, et c'est une sottise que de chercher son amante dans sa femme.' And their wives are fully even with them, for I believe it is very rare indeed that a Frenchwoman of quality thinks of seeking her lover in her husband.

The next day was the fête of the tutelary saint, a former Bishop of Bellay, and of course a grand gala. All the neighbourhood round, high, low, rich, and poor, one with another, gathered together on this occasion in their holiday clothes, and paraded the streets to the cathedral, which was dressed up in all its finery, and where the Bishop performed the high mass in his robes of state, attended by the Chanoines and other dignitaries of the Church in their paraphernalia, and sweating like over-driven hogs in a hot July day under their load of gold brocade. I never saw a more noble figure than that of the Bishop, nor heard sacred service performed to the Almighty with so much dignity and such captivating devotion. But at pauses, hymns and spiritual songs were performed by a concert of vocal and instrumental music, that was anything but spiritual; for as the noblesse of Bellay made a point of twanging their artificial lyres in honour of their saint, and some added thereunto the natural twang of their pipes, it was a Babel of sounds impossible to describe, and, as I felt to the cost of my nerves, almost intolerable to hear.

How I pitied the poor Bishop, in the finer modulations of whose voice there was true harmony, and who was assaulted on every side by this worse than caterwauling band, placed just behind on each side the altar. And the spirit of St. Anselm, if saint he be above, and really habituated to the melody of the spheres, how must such gross discords have shocked and shaken his incorporeal essence, as, in duty bound, he leaned from heaven to hear the notes vocal with his praise. At least, saint as he is, he must suffer one day in the year like any sinner, except spirits above be as sensible to flattery and panegyric as spirits below; and then, indeed, the most savage sounds would seem harmonious, and the grossest incense please.

But, talking of St. Anselm's spirit, I had well nigh forgotten his body, which remains still uncorrupted on earth, and was found fresh and fair, as all Bellay will witness, some two hundred years after its interment, such respect had the worms for such holy flesh. In a little chapel particularly dedicated to him, and where he was buried, one of the Chanoines watches his former earthly tabernacle, on this his commemoration day, with all due solemnity, and shows it to the gaping multitude. A wicked heretic curiosity, tempted me to wedge myself in amongst the pious and credulous crowd, that pressed to see the miraculous remains. With much elbowing and fervent heat, I at length arrived at the crystal shrine, in which he lay extended in rich robes. The chapel was very dark, and the shrine only illuminated with one little wax taper; however, I pried into it as keenly as I could, and discovered something in the shape of a human corpse, but so enveloped in finery, and so muffled up about the head, that nothing could be distinguished resembling a human face, where a face should have been; nor could I for my life see anything but a dark blotch at the end of the body trappings, to which neither shape nor name could be given, and which, from its colour one should have supposed the work of some envious fiend, if fiends indeed be black.

However, I dropped a piece of money into the proffered dish, like all the rest; and after having paid for peeping, like my namesake of Coventry, bit my tongue, and lifted up my eyes, as if with reverential astonishment, for I would not, by unseasonable ridicule, even in a smile, shock the innocent credulity of the crowd and wound the rights of decency. The good or politic canon (which shall I call him?) seemed to triumph in my devotion, and the people appeared edified by my faith. A long-winded narration of St. Anselm's virtues on earth, and power in heaven, followed, under the title of a sermon, to hear which novelty kept me awake, even though Monseigneur the Bishop, more accustomed to and less allured by such droning panegyrics, snored manfully in chorus to the twang of the Predicateur's nose; a sad affront, methought, to the saintship of his predecessor, and which made one more apt to call his faith in question, than his judgment. We partook, afterwards, of a grand festal dinner, which the old Marquis de Chatelard, who, blind as he is, has always his mental eyes about him, sagaciously arranged in mutual honour of the saint and the bride. Whether the former gave me a good digestion I know not; but I well remember that the latter, added the piquante sauce of her *bons mots* to that of the numerous *bons plats*, though I am afraid I was vulgar and tasteless enough to relish the latter, more than the former. But what would you have an hungry Englishman do, who is more *au faite de la cuisine, que de l'esprit Français?* Besides, as the honey-moon was not half expired, it seemed to me injustice, rank as her breath, to rob her husband of any of her *bonnes bouches*. My poor Chatillon, how did he affect to envy me, and how did he rally me with his dear badinage! Alas! those days are fled—will such ever return? But I must drive from me such ideas, or the pen that trembles in my hand will never perform its task.

The day after we set out for the Château de Lunes, where Count d'Angeville expected us; but *gourmandise* and gratitude equally forbade our passing the hospitable gate of St. Sulpice. Oh, how many *embrassements* and *bien venus* did we receive from the jovial fraternity. The interesting young monk pressed my hand with much affection, to which mine returned sympathetic greeting; and he told me it would make him as happy as anything in this world could do, if I could find occasion to pass a week with him in the convent. 'À vous, monsieur,' dit-il, 'je pourrais bien ouvrir mon cœur, et verser mes larmes dans votre sein. Vous les recevriez avec pitié et bonté, parceque vous vous êtes montré sensible à ma douleur; mais ces moines mes frères ils n'en comprennent rien, et d'eux je cache soigneusement tous les chagrins qui me déchirent.' I told him how happy it would make me to afford him so trifling a consolation, should my necessary engagements admit of it; and assured him that, at all events, I should always remember and deplore his misfortunes, and interest myself in his welfare. The bell summoned us to dinner, and we both joined his convivial brethren at their plenteous board, where the bottle was pushed about briskly enough to make me forget my own cares, as well as those of others, and to send me half tipsy on my way. On our entering the Count's village, we spied our little hero at a distance, mounted on a cart, and encouraging, with his voice and gesture, a multitude of peasants, who were repairing the highway in the mud below, and just covering a watercourse, to which they had given a new direction, with a tiny bridge of flag-stones. 'Bravo, mes amis,' cried the little Count; 'travaillez bien;' and at the same instant seeing us, he leaped from his post of honour, and ran through the dirt to embrace us with his wonted frankness and gaiety. Away we went to the chief *rentier's* smart house, which stood smiling with its white face on a little hill above, under the shelter of the lofty castle, and where we found the amiable Madame Champdor. 'Eh bien, restez-là, mes messieurs, un petit moment sous la protection de cette belle dame, pendant que je vais finir mon pont, et après je reviendrai vous rejoindre.' 'Non, non,' we cried out with one voice, 'nous irons finir ce fameux pont ensemble.' 'Allons donc,' replied the sturdy little man, and we descended to the labourers in his road, together, to the disgrace of Madame Champdor's white stockings, and the praise of her handsome legs.

Mounted, with one consent, in the cart, we looked down as from a triumphal car, but not with contempt, on lesser folks below; and, by our encomiums and familiarity, made their labours at once more vigorous and light. At length the bridge was finished. 'Allons,' cried the Count, 'il faut lui donner le baptême, mais avec du vin au lieu d'eau.' Accordingly, his servant was despatched for wine to the château, and in the mean time, we gossips consulted about a name for the young bridge. 'Supposons que nous l'appellions le Pont d'Amitié,' said the Count. 'Non pas,' replied Madame Champdor, 'cela est fade.' 'Ou le Pont de l'Hospitalité,' cried Chatillon. 'Non,' answered our lady fair, again, 'cela ne me plaît pas, non plus. C'est usée.' 'Il faut donc,' said I, 'que vous le nommiez, ma belle marraine.' 'Volontiers,' replied she; 'laissons-nous donc l'appeler le Pont d'Alliance.' 'Bravo, bravo!' echoed round the outhouse where our cart stood. So down we leaped, handed the marraine to the bridge, and, giving three cheers as we stood perched upon it, poured out a goblet of wine upon the largest stone, and cried, 'Buvons à la stabilité du Pont d'Alliance entre l'Angleterre et la France.' 'Et à la santé,' added Madame Champdor, 'du brave Anglais, qui est venu ici comme plénipotentiaire, entre les deux plus puissantes nations du monde.' The peasants grinned and stared, but seconded the health with true French gaiety and a true French air; and a strutting, sly-looking, consequential old man, after wiping his lips in a red night-cap, which he had taken off in honour of the ceremony, and which discovered his grey locks papered stiffly up for the next fête day, cried out, 'Mais ne faudrait-il pas que Monsieur l'Anglais bût aussi à la santé du Roi de France?' 'De tout mon cœur,' I replied, 'mon ami;' so, taking a goblet and filling it to the brim, I shouted out, 'À la santé et au bonheur du Roi et de la Reine de France, et de toute la famille royale, autant qu'ils restent les bons amis de l'Angleterre.' A loud and long acclamation followed my toast, and we then bade *le bon soir* to the honest peasants, whom we left as gay, as if they had not a want or care upon earth. It is true that the Pont d'Alliance may not be so famous in history as many others; but has any other ever exhibited a scene of greater or more innocent festivity? Let not the Pont d'Alliance, then, be jealous of its greater rivals, or mourn the want of celebrity, which would perhaps be purchased with crimes and blood.

After staying a night at Lunes, we accompanied my fair marraine to Champdor, where we spent two social and pleasant days, and then set out all together in our cariole, Madame Champdor's chaise following, for Meriaz, a convent of Chartreux in Bugey, where we were to part; the Countess and her gay brother, on affairs of consequence for another part of the province, and my dear Chatillon and myself, for a convent of Chartreusines called La Sallette, on the borders of Dauphiné, and in the immediate neighbourhood of the Grande Grotte de la Balme, which was our principal object. Ah, what forgetfulness! what ingratitude! I had well nigh been seduced to cabriole away with the fair Champdor, without casting one thought behind in remembrance of the dear *belles horreurs* de Charabot, though they afforded me so much new delight and deserve all honour. As I had in my former excursion thither viewed them from above, so did I in the present one from below, and though always charming and always sublime, yet they derived new gloomy magnificence, new terrors, and new graces from the situation in which they were now presented to me.

My dear Chatillon, d'Angeville, and myself rode thither one morning from Champdor. They were contented with the noble *coup d'œil* above; but insatiable to explore every part of a scene so full of great enchantment, and where Nature holds out, to the enthusiasm of pensive and romantic fancy, those images that she holds most dear, I took a sturdy peasant for my guide, and partly aided by his robust hand, and partly by the interwoven boughs that canopied over my steep and uncertain descent, after near an hour's excessive toil, arrived safely at the bottom of the admired gulf. How was I repaid! What objects! What scenery! What a plentitude of the sublime and beautiful, of fine contrast and magic combination. The river, or rather torrent from the distant mountains, that supplies the cascade, is often in summer diminished to a mere shred, but luckily violent thunder-storms for several succeeding days, and an almost continued deluge the whole preceding night, had swollen it to a raging flood. How impossible to give a just idea of its effect, as it rushed from the brink of its channel high o'er my head, and dashed and sparkled and boiled from rock to rock and from fall to fall! And those falls, how much finer than they appeared from above; and those rocks, how rugged, how shaggy, and how grandly featured! And at each point, undistinguished from my former position, appeared the ruins of an ancient castle, looking down from its mouldering walls upon the roaring torrent, and seeming mournfully to say—Still ye remain with undiminished force and undecaying honours! We were once! but are no more. Our honours are past, like your waters in a dry summer, and our glory, like the thunders that roll over your rocks. But the heavens shall be covered with clouds, and your waters shall return. With black clouds shall they be covered, and the thunders shall roll over your rocks. But our glory is past like that of the lords that possessed us, and our honours, like theirs, shall return no more.

Ah, how perishing are thy works, O Art! and how durable are thine, O Nature! But, contrasted with these proud mementoes of time past, more humble but more pastoral and smiling images of present days were offered to the eye, on the green slope at the summit of the mountain, at the other end of the gulf, as well as in its very depth below. Here a mill with the miller's cottage and a few outhouses, were grouped in a most picturesque style, under the thick woody edge of the river, that eddied through the rocky bottom, and there a village lay scattered, cottage climbing above cottage, amidst its little pastures and its peculiar groves, and looking down, as it were, to the roofs below with terror and astonishment, as if they had fallen from the heights and were shut out for ever, in the dark, deep and lonely gulf, from all intercourse with men. And what a theatre of various shade, and what a sweep of inclosing rocks and mountains, and what sources of crystal water, forming so many lesser cascades, gushing out of the rocky caverns, and murmuring and shining amongst the intermingled branches, that bowered over the precipitate steeps. How did the ardent sun set the great cascade on fire, and seem to wanton amidst its flashing waters; here shedding warm day upon the thick foliage, and there, from contrast, giving deeper hue and new grace to the night of shade. From the season, too, every tree was full of verdant honours, and by looking upwards, every object became more grand and distinct, and every angle acquired new force, and every feature finer projection and dignity. Adieu ye *belles horreurs!* Adieu! &c.

Adieu, admired Charabot; when Nature puts on her majesty, thou art surely, if not her crown itself, one of the jewels that she loves best to place there; and who meets her in her solemn walks, shall look up to thee with wonder and delight.

But I must now whisk back again to our cabriole, seat myself by the fair Countess's side, and hold cheerful and friendly chat with her, and Chatillon, and d'Angeville, along our short way to the Convent of Meriaz. What! a lady, and a fair lady, too, set her foot within the austere rounds of walls dedicated to St. Bruno. What a tale! What pollution! How must the holy anchorites' blood have frozen with horror, as they peeped at her through the narrow windows of their cells, and when her delicate feet touched the hallowed threshold, within which carnal thoughts never entered, and whence are banished every lust of the flesh. Dreadful profanation! Be at peace, ye disturbed spirits of severe sanctity. Let not your chaste souls glow and flutter in your breast; the voice of the charmer was not heard within your gates, neither did her steps pollute your threshold.

The good Prieur and his coadjuteur, awaited her at the entrance of a pretty pavilion, built at the issue of a picturesque wood, through which we had descended, and at a sufficient distance from the holy ground, to leave your consciences in perfect repose. Here we dined; and as it may be supposed that the superiors of the Chartreux, have a superior portion of chastened appetites to their brethren, and surpass in continence of thought those sons of God, who were formerly tempted by the daughters of men, the Prieur and coadjuteur ate *maigre* with us, to all appearance with *tres bon appetit,* quaffing their excellent wine between whiles, with an air that seemed rather to belong to the jolly Bernardines of St. Sulpice, than the mortified monks of a Chartreusian convent. And the Prieur talked much of war and politics, themes methought that did not become his mouth, and the profession of austerities, and that total disregard for the world, which belonged to his order. He showed me their cells, too, with an air of exultation, even boasting of their superior convenience to those of Père Chatel. I grudged him none of his comforts, and had eyed with a sacred kind of pity, the severities and privations at his brother convent; yet an emotion of, I know not what kind, struggled in my soul as he talked. It was not vexation, it was not indignation, it was not contempt, and yet there seemed to be a something of each striving in it. Certain it is that I had both looked at, and listened to the Prieur of Père Chatel with far greater satisfaction. Why was this? I wished them both cheerful and happy, and was pleased to see them both so in their different ways, but one seemed to fulfil his particular vows with more simplicity, piety, and dignity than the other.

Meriaz is a solitude, not destitute of beauty on the side of nature, situated as it is in a verdant and fertile little valley, and quite surrounded by mountains adorned with a deep border of firs, which forms a bold and undulating line at their summits, of fine and singular effect. The way from Meriaz to the great road between Geneva and Lyons lay through a chasm between the mountains, and was extremely picturesque. Its length was near a mile and a half. The mountains, though similar in general feature the whole way, were finely varied in point of sink and swell, light and shade, and the rocks that thrust their rough heads between, or towered above the mass of firs, were fantastically grand and of beautiful effect. The road ran gently winding, and on the left hand a large brook followed its course, gurgling under the luxuriant boughs, that in return for its refreshing waters screened it from the thirsty sun, and hailed its murmurs with the song of a thousand birds. On our entrance upon the great road, our fair fellow-traveller, after due *embrassemens*, a la Françaiso, mounted into her chariot with her gay brother, and turned the horses' heads towards Geneva, while we turned ours towards Lyons.

From thence to Cerdon the objects were not remarkable; but the view of that village from the brow of a steep hill that leads to it, was very beautiful. On each hand were rocky mountains, and on the lofty brows of each towered the ruins of castles, which still seemed to regard each other with a watchful and menacing eye, as in times of yore, when the jealousies and heart-burnings of their several petty sovereigns, spread scenes of barbarity and destruction round. The left-hand rocks were more particularly bold, curved into the form of a bow, and crested with two of these castles at the opposite ends, the remains of which were still ample. A narrow and steep road, had been laboured with great toil up to the rock, on which one was perched, and even through that rock to the castle itself; and at a little distance a pure and abundant source of water, threw itself in a beautiful cascade from amongst the towering cliffs, to the valley below, where its liquid duct, that had seemed to be almost dissipated in air, collected itself into refreshing streams to feed the lovely verdure, and slake at once the thirst of the shepherd and his flock.

At the end of this semicircular valley, and seemingly deep in the bosom of a stately walnut grove, appeared the village, charmingly nestled in shade, and forming various clusters of cottages inexpressibly picturesque. The near approaching mountains rose up like stern guardians on each side; and beyond it another castle appeared, with an air of sovereignty, on the point of a high and rocky mount, that towered in the form of a sugar-loaf abruptly from the plain, and which, being quite isolated, seemed to disdain all league and companionship with the neighbouring heights. Indeed, every eminence, more naturally commanding, and of more difficult access than the rest, through the mountainous provinces of Bugey, Dauphiné, and Vivarois, is crowned with the ruins of these ancient scourges of the peaceable inhabitants of the vales; perched like so many birds of rapine upon rocks, these little tyrants formerly used to watch the convenient moment for seizing their prey, and then pounce at once upon it from their aerial heights. Happy he, who could escape their cruel talons, which the divine justice often turned against each other in punishment of their general wrongs; and thus one tyrant tore another piecemeal to avenge innocent blood, crying against them on all sides, like so many ravenous wolves fighting for the slaughtered lambs.

All tyranny is bad; but the multiplied horrors of little tyrants the worst of all. Amidst all the oppressions caused her, by the violence and ambition of Cardinal Richelieu, and amidst all the noble blood that he sacrificed to his stern revenge, France may yet bless his memory, for destroying utterly every remnant of this bane to her prosperity and her peace. With it, were destroyed the fermenting seeds of those civil wars, and of those intestine broils, that had for ages vexed her quiet, impoverished her coffers, and pressed down her glory.

From Cerdon, we went gently near half a day's journey on the great road, and then turning off to the left, soon reached the banks of the Rhone, crossing which into Dauphiné, a little hour brought us to the gate of the Convent de la Salette.* Few men are admitted within its walls; but as Madame d'Angeville's daughter-in-law had been its superieure, and much beloved and respected by the community, a letter of warm recommendation from her hand, was sure to be received with favour.

Four Chartreusian monks are appointed to manage the worldly affairs of these holy sisters (who are rich), as well as to perform mass, receive their confessions, and fulfil other such services, as may be deemed necessary and fitting.

* Since famous for the miraculous appearance, in the year 1846, of the so-called Lady of La Salette to two shepherd children on the mountains surrounding that village. This mysterious apparition of a lady, clad in white and silver, and resplendent with light, caused an enormous sensation all over that bigoted district, and thousands flocked to the spot where the Holy Virgin was said to have uttered her warnings to the surrounding population, and drank of the fountain which was declared to have sprung up on her disappearance. A church was erected on the venerated site, and bishops and prelates vied with each other in celebrating the miracles wrought there. At length, in 1852, some enemies rose up to doubt the authenticity of this apparition; an action was commenced, and finally they succeeded in tracing the appearance to a certain Madame Lainarlière, of a noble house, once a nun, and now enthusiastic for the honours of the 'Lady de la Salette.' She was tried in 1857, and, although defended by the celebrated Jules Favre, she was convicted by the whole court.

They have their proper apartments and domestics, see and converse, indeed, with the Chartreusines through their grated parlour; but are never permitted (as we were assured), except in the case of urgent religious duties, such as to administer extreme unction, &c., to penetrate beyond the veil of the Tabernacle, and enter into the Sanctum Sanctorum. We found all these monks courteous and hospitable, and the Père Procureur vivacious, intelligent, and full of kind attentions. Nothing ever surpassed his volubility; and it was scarcely excelled by his readiness to oblige; for as to his readiness to communicate, it was an indulgence to himself, as it indulged his rage for talking. He was a convincing proof that all the Chartreux are not pensive and of few words; and that abstinence, prayer, and fasting do not, in all, subdue the animal spirits, and render the blood cooler and the thoughts more sedate. But it must be considered, that his lot had fallen in a fair ground, and that he lived in a constant course of near communication with fifty religious virgins: and how they could talk we had a sufficient specimen of, by chatting an hour with, or rather listening to, three of them through the grated curtain that divided their oratory from the great chapel.

Such a peal I never heard, since tongues were called clappers. And such a striving for the ball of speech, and such insatiable curiosity! And such a tide of questions, that knew no reflux, and which, swallowing up greedily the small streams of our lips, would not wait for full answers, but bore us down with their vehemence! I might say, with Falconbridge, that I was never so bethumped with words; and not being then so ready at French as I now am, their tongues at last fairly ran away with all my ideas, and with them the possibility of expressing myself; so that, the very opposite of the Saviour, whose example they strove to follow, and whose doctrines they adored, instead of restoring the deaf to hearing and the dumb to speech, they made me both deaf and dumb, and seemed to have robbed me of my understanding into the bargain.

Pretty damsels ye are, to make vows of silence, are ye not? And doubtless ye keep them as devoutly as did Falstaff his, to quit sack and sugar. I observed that they boasted of nothing so much as the fine carp and tench in their ponds, which, perhaps, they loved the better for being mute. In truth, we found them excellent, and the *maigre* table covered, the two days we tarried, with wherewithal to make a man fat. It naturally occurred to me, that when the Procureur confessed these loquacious virgins, he must be outrageously impatient, while, descanting voluminously on twopenny-halfpenny sins, they indulged their talking dispositions; but then I reflected that he would have his revenge, while he worried them, in turn, with endless lectures and exhortations.

The chapel is handsome, in a common style; but the oratory of the Chartreusines pleased me extremely. The wainscot is all composed of inlaid woods, unpainted and nicely varnished, and the ornaments are so modest that they can scarcely be termed such. The whole is of singular elegance and simplicity, and reminded me of a line of Thomson's, in his description of Lavinia, 'When unadorned, adorned the most:' which always seems to me the case, and ought to be the characteristic of the temples of that great and only God, who tells us Himself that he delights not in pomps and shows, but loves the sacrifices of the poor and lowly, offered up with a pure and contrite heart.

But I must not forget our main object, the Grotte de Balme, which is not above three-quarters of a mile from the convent. Dom Procureur, who was always for a little gadding, and whose body, like his tongue, was in perpetual motion, desired he might attend us thither, and accordingly we set out in due order, with candles and lanterns, &c., and soon arrived at the cavern's mouth. Nothing ever struck me more than the entrance, and, indeed, it far surpassed, in my eyes, every object of curiosity in the humid courts far within. It appeared like an august temple, not made, indeed, with hands, but whose builder and maker was God. The vaulted roof of rock was of a prodigious height, and the dimensions below proportionable and ample. The irregularities of its rocky bottom and craggy walls, only served to render it more noble, as if disdainful of the petty rules of art, and triumphing over their nice proportions; and the beds of rock that formed a natural staircase at the farther end, by which to enter its inner recesses, had a more grand and striking effect than the most superb staircase of the most superb palace on earth. The solemn kind of day, also, that reflected partial light throughout the cavern, made it more awful and august; and as we entered, some strangers, drawn thither by a curiosity like our own, just showed themselves with their lighted candles at the extremity of the staircase, and then disappeared.

What a magical effect! What enchantment did it give to the distant gloom! Kindly imagination caught at them as they seemed to glide along, and cried—Behold the enchanter and his imps or the spirits of the secret caves, where night and silence reign, and which the echoing step of worldly intruders, have roused from their dark doings in the abysses deep below! I have never loved groping about in the damp, chilly, and cheerless caves of earth, yet these pleased me more than any I had ever explored.

We first went almost straight onwards from the top of the grand staircase, and as we advanced found streams of living water, gushing from the rocks, which had worn them below with the lapse of ages, into curious basons incrusted with a kind of scallop shell of the most beautiful fretwork. By the perpetual drippings also from the roof, and the trickling all round, fine clusters of crystallisations of various and fantastic forms, appeared pendant from above, or encrusted every part of the rocky walls beneath. After walking, and without difficulty, a considerable distance, we arrived at a little lake, which is said to be unfathomable, and which lost itself to the eye amidst the winding of the lowering rocks.

An Englishman some years since, whose name I could not learn, tempted by a daring curiosity, resolved to explore this lake and attempt to discover its issue at the other end. Accordingly he got a little boat made after his directions, and just large enough to contain one person, and, like another Theseus, pushed off from the dark shore of this new Styx, to visit the regions of Erebus on the other side. But if his temerity was not punished, his curiosity was not gratified. After paddling with difficulty and danger between the near approaching and winding rocks, beyond sight of the shore, he had left, the closing crags pressed the lake into so narrow a space, and hung so low over it, that it was impossible to proceed, and the daring voyager in these realms of night, was forced to return vexed and disappointed after a petty, yet most comfortless and nauseous voyage, some risk, and much fatigue. We saw the wrecks of his boat, which still remain on the edge of the lake. On our way back we turned to our left, and mounted by a more difficult way into caverns less worth regard, except for a fountain of curious petrifaction at their extremity, and always supplied with the most limpid waters.

The wonderful power of Time and exhaustless fancies of Nature, in the ornamental work of a kind of pyramid, from whence gushes the pure source, as well as in that of the basin which it fills, is well worth present attention and future reflection. It is the absolute and visible transformation of one element to another, for what was water once, is now a kind of crustaceous earth, resembling indeed, but more beautiful, than stone. And as is the supply of water, so must the transformation be, endless. Yet the beauties of the fountain and the fine drapery of petrifaction, on the walls round, can scarcely reward one for the horrible nastiness and stench, that one must encounter to arrive at them. A part of the cavern that leads thither is peopled by innumerable bats, whose droppings were equally incommodious to the smell and the feet, and whose incessant flittings flurried the nerves, and threatened to extinguish our lights. Their shrill cries seemed, at once, the tokens of their regret at being awakened out of their beloved sleep, and their anger at our invasion of their dark domain, where they had sought the blessing, succour, and protection of Morpheus, silence, and night, far from the garish haunts and disturbing clamours of men.

At our return from this range of caverns, we entered into another on the opposite side, where there were also curious groups of petrifactions, but the passage to them was low, and horribly tiresome to a man like me, six feet two inches high, which my head and my loins alternately found, as I now stretched myself up to ease the latter, and now ducked like a cock at shrovetide,* to save the former. But nothing I saw within, was half so striking and beautiful as the first awful view that I caught of the noble entrance. Nothing either above or under ground could awe the tongue of our loquacious Chartreux, and it was very diverting to see him with his bald pate, and his long cloth habit trussed round his loins, scuttle along the sombre galleries, and clamber like a goat up the rocks, talking all the while, and running backwards and forwards, on this side and on that, to point out the

* It would appear that the barbarous sport of throwing at cocks was still practised. It was regularly introduced into our public schools in the reign of Elizabeth.

beauties of the humid walls. Would we have patiently awaited the end of all his harangue in our underground expedition, I really believe we should have left our bones with old Mother Nox, or at best have slept a sweet slumber amidst the perfumes of Bat Hall. But God bless thee, thou soul of Mercury; for thy heart is in thy hand, and it seems to be as innocent as it is light.

We did not return to the convent from the grotto, but went on our way towards the cascade of Glandieu, which we were told was of celebrated grandeur and beauty, and by which also, making an elbow, we could return to Bellay. Crossing the Rhone again into Bugey, we followed the great road till towards evening, and then turned off on the right, by a picturesque village called Ambrieu; passing which, and continuing our journey through a mountainous, and romantic country, we arrived at nightfall at a little town, the name of which I have forgotten, because it merited no particular remembrance. From thence we reached a well-situated village, called Roussillon, to dinner; dominated over, like most of the others we had passed, by a castle which had been very famous in its day, and the ruins of which were singularly grand and beautiful.

The old Marquis de Chatelet told me an anecdote relating to this castle, which he assured me was authentic, and which deserves mention. One of the ancient Counts of Roussillon, who was powerful, brave, and amorous, had seen the Princess of Genoa at her father's court, and fallen desperately in love with her. She was then affianced to the King of Burgundy, and was speedily to be sent, with her train, to her royal husband. Her way necessarily lay through a part of the Count's territories, and knowing the day of her departure from Genoa, he lay in ambush for her, with a resolute band of his followers, and putting her escort to flight, carried her off in triumph to his castle. Enraged at the affront offered to his dignity, and afflicted at the loss of the most beautiful princess of her time, the King of Burgundy levied a powerful army, to revenge his outraged honour and his love; and after laying waste the Count's demesnes, besieged him in his stronghold. But, valiant as bold, the dauntless ravisher, knew how to maintain by force, what he had obtained by fraud; and the King, cooled, perhaps, in his appetite for a fruit, which had been so often tasted, and wearied with his losses and fruitless efforts to reduce the castle, patched up an ignominious peace with his invincible adversary, and left him in quiet possession of his mistress and estates. The site of the castle is equally strong and noble; and the above anecdote, made me regard it with double interest and pleasure.

As we dined very early, we had time to reach Glandieu, at five in the afternoon, by one of the most dreary roads, amongst cheerless and barren mountains, that I ever travelled. The cascade is formed by a branch of the Rhone, the main body of which it hastens to rejoin from the fall, in the rich and beautiful vale, in view on the other side of the road. As the sudden swell of waters, from the storm a few days before, had ceased, and the water was very low, we by no means saw the cascade in its beauty. However, from what we saw, it was very easy to judge that it must be very noble and picturesque when in all its glory. The rock it throws itself from is ninety feet high, and bending round in a semicircular form with a broken and uneven edge; the water, dividing itself, rushes through three or four different channels, as it approaches the brink, and forms as many falls, though the main sheet darts over the centre of the rock, and when the river is full, must be very striking. The rock, too, is beautifully fringed all round and ornamented with bushes of varied green, and the scattered village lies at its foot.

The charming view opposite, bounded by the Dauphiné Alps, forms a fine contrast to the near objects, and by offering so different a picture to the eye, relieves and makes it return with new pleasure to the home scene, whose rough, grand, and distinct features lend new graces in turn to the smiling beauties, endless variety, and airy perspective of the vast and fertile vale. From Glandieu we returned to Bellay, which we did not reach till near eleven o'clock, and where we were very glad to satisfy our craving hunger, and rest our weary limbs. At Bellay we again met the amiable Madame Champdor and the little Count, and I reproach myself for having, till now, delayed making honourable mention of the lovely and interesting Madame Guinsieux, my fair nun of Bellay, in whose society I had passed so many agreeable hours, at Lunes and Champdor, the foregoing winter. She seemed by no means to have forgotten her promise to think of an English heretic with friendship, and, if the falsehood of the world has not crept within the cloister, the warmth of her greeting at seeing me, again proved that I had won a place in her esteem. As her health was much mended, she was not permitted to go without the gloomy convent walls, to join our social party and partake of our innocent festivities, but we visited her several times in the parlour, where she one afternoon gave us a *goûté* of choice Burgundy, and various fruits, the flavour of which was much heightened by her refined and spirited converse.

What a pity that such charms, such graces, and such talents, should be buried alive in a cloister, and, what is still worse, enslaved to the society of five or six ignorant and bigoted old nuns, who, with every advantage and improvement that the most liberal education could have given them, would never, in the world, have been chosen as meet companions for a soul like hers. From Bellay, Madame Champdor, a demoiselle of the town, the fair and witty bride, her *à la mode de province* brother, and ourselves, made a little excursion to La petite Grotte de la Balme, which hangs, as it were, under the guardian brow of Père Chattel, on the side of the rock that lowers immediately over the Rhone. The cavern in itself is capacious, but little worth regard after its greater namesake. But if its internal beauties are inferior, its external ones far surpass those of its rival. Nothing can be more romantic or picturesque than its situation and the view which it commands; the rock that hangs over the entrance is awfully grand, and forms a vault of singular magnificence. A count of illustrious family, whose title I have forgotten, but whose wonderful simplicity and noble courtesy, I remember with respect and gratitude, has built a little pavilion just by the cavern, which seems formed out of the rock, as the stairs that lead to it from thence really are. His neat and modern chateau lies directly on the other brink of the Rhone, in a beautiful vale, rejoicing as it were amidst the vineyards and pastures, that surround and belong to it. Its hospitable and polite lord ferried over to us immediately on our arrival, attended by two servants loaded with choice wines, liqueurs, fruits, and conserves.

The evening was very fine, and nothing could be more delicious than such a *goûté*. Cheerfulness and good-fellowship reigned within, and from the windows and balcony of the pavilion a captivating scene was offered to the eye. The woody rocks, crowned with the convent, lay above our head, and formed a wall and a curtain behind us; at our feet flowed the Rhone through the ruins of a bridge built by the Romans, and by which they first entered into this part of France; beyond the river, the bold and dark-browed rocks of Savoy stood marshalled in lone array; and to the right, cultivated and shady hills, and a fruitful and varied vale, stretched away as far as the eye could reach, fertilised and adorned by the tortuous course of the majestic flood. How well, then, were we repaid for the pains we had taken in toiling up the steep path to the Grotte and the pavilion, under the influence of a burning sun! My pleasure would have been complete, could I have stolen an hour to have greeted once more with cordiality and reverence, the holy anchorites above, and to have bidden a last farewell to the gentle, amiable, and interesting Prieur, whose winning courtesy and unaffected humility, had made so deep an impression on my heart.

Two days after, we set out on our way home, accompanied by Madame d'Angeville in our carriole, and followed by an old family coach, belonging to a Bugey Count whose name I have forgotten, which was crammed up to its roof with various female luggage, added to that of Madame la Comtesse, her two daughters, their waiting-woman, and the young Count d'Ambrieu. The first had been very handsome, and was very sensible, agreeable, and well-bred, without the remains of coquetry, or the least affectation of those oscillations (if I may so call them) of wit, which French ladies are so fond of exhibiting. In short, she appeared like a tender and discreet mother of a large family, to whose interests and welfare all her thoughts and desires were devoted. One of the demoiselles was going to Aix to bathe for rheumatic pains, which seemed to have still more soured a naturally fretful temper. Her pert peevishness was sometimes very improperly exerted towards her mother, who bore it with the indulgence of a kind parent, who allows much for ill-health, and the prudence of a woman who was always unwilling to humiliate her daughter by reprimands, or expose both, by querulous altercations before strangers. The younger demoiselle was very handsome, very graceful, and very engaging, modest without *mauvaise honte*, and lively without *étourderie*; her open and noble countenance did justice to her mind, which seemed the heiress to her mother's merits, as much as the former was of her beauty.

The Count d'Ambrieu was a young man of about twenty, with good parts, improved in some degree by education, but, with the true French *amour propre*, estimating himself far above his real value. He had all the positiveness of half instruction, and all the decisiveness of inexperience, with fortune and youth. Music was one of his passions, but the fashionable mania of mesmerism raged with uncurbed violence in his soul. Mesmer was with him a sage, a prophet, an earthly God, an angel of light, sent in mercy to heal alike our bodies, and irradiate our minds. The issues of life and death were in his hand, and he held immortality, as it were, betwixt his finger and thumb. 'Oh, monsieur, je vous assure, que jamais un tel homme ne se fit paraître sur la terre. Quel savoir, quelle dignité, quelle modestie, quelle bienveillance! Non, monsieur, il n'a point, il n'a jamais, eu de semblable.' Thus he ran on, whilst I in broken French endeavoured, now and then, to oppose the tide of his words, and to contest the certainty of his deity's miraculous powers. 'Et vous ne croyez donc pas, monsieur, au magnétisme animal?' 'Pas tout-à-fait.'—'Et vous n'en avez jamais vu des expériences?' 'Non, monsieur, et peut-être je n'en verrai jamais.'—'Mais si vous étiez d'en voir de très fortes.' 'Peut-être je n'y croirais pas d'avantage.'—'Mais, mon Dieu, monsieur, monsieur, quelle infidelité donc, quelle opiniâtreté!' 'Peut-être, monsieur, je suis un peu infidèle quand il s'agit des miracles.'—'Mais, monsieur, tout le monde à Paris vous est contraire.' 'Pas tout, monsieur; pour instance, vos meilleurs médecins.'—'Quel argument! Ils sont des intéressés, des envieux.' 'Peut-être; mais moi qui ne suis pas envieux, je suis de leur avis. C'est vrai que mon opinion vaut très peu de chose.'—'Mais vous ne jugez, monsieur, qu'après des idées abstraites.' 'Ils me suffisent, monsieur; je n'en demande point d'autres.'—'Mais si vous étiez de voir avec vos propres yeux?' 'Tous les sens sont quelquefois bien trompeurs, et particulièrement quand on a envie d'être trompé.'—'Mais si vous étiez de sentir vous-même, oui, monsieur, dans votre propre corps, les effets les plus marqués de cette divine science?' 'O! monsieur, cela seroit tout-à-fait une autre chose. Cependant il ne vaudrait pas la peine, que je courusse à Paris après de telles preuves.'—'Pardonnez moi, monsieur, il vous vaudrait bien la peine de courir au bout du monde pour voir de telles merveilles, et pour être convaincu de verités si utiles et si sublimes.' 'Ah! monsieur, les miracles ne sont rien sans foi, et comme je la manque, je ne mérite pas de les voir.'—'Que diriez-vous, monsieur, si moi, moi-même, fusse à la porté de vaincre votre infidelité, et ce jour même?' 'Je dirais assurement, monsieur, que vous eussiez plus de raison et de savoir que je ne pensasse.'—'Mais voudriez-vous être convaincu de bonne foi?' 'Certainement, monsieur; j'ai grande envie de voir un miracle une fois dans ma vie. Montrez m'en avec des preuves convaincantes, et je crierez tout aussi haut que vous: Mesmer n'est pas un rusé, Mesmer n'est pas un fourbe; c'est un vrai sage, c'est un vrai prophète, c'est un ange, c'est une divinité, admirons, adorons le.'—'Vous badinez à présent, monsieur; mais vous parlerez tout autrement, je crois, avant la fin du jour.' 'Mais de grace, monsieur le Comte, dépêchons-nous. Convertissez moi à la face de ces belles personnes et de notre ami Chatillon? Si j'ai péché, j'ai péché trop longtemps; et mon repentir ne pourra pas être trop prompt.'—'Monsieur, ce bateau n'est pas un lieu propre, pour exercer mon pouvoir, il faudrait que nous fussions à terre. La terre a plus d'électricité, plus d'attraction, et la matière subtile et fluide qui se communique de corps à autres, aura plus d'effet.' 'A la bonne heure, monsieur; mais de grâce instruissez moi comment avez-vous pu obtenir cette science divine?'—'Monsieur, je l'ai achetée.' 'Oh! monsieur, je le crois, et sans doute un si beau savoir se vend, très chèrement.'—'Pas trop; il ne m'a couté que deux cent louis.' 'Que deux cent louis, monsieur! Ce n'est rien; c'est absolument rien. Deux cent louis seulement, pour savoir faire des miracles; pour guérir vous-même, vos amis;

pour exercer votre bienveillance; et pour ne pas monter en ciel que quand il vous plaira. Jamais rien n'a été vendu à si bon marché.'—'Moquez-vous de moi à présent, monsieur, mon triomphe est à venir; mais il sera le triomphe de vérité et d'humanité.' 'Tant mieux, il sera beau, et vous m'attacherez en esclave fidèle à votre char.'

Here the contest ended for the present. It had begun as we entered the canal between the lake and the Rhone, and lasted till we approached the shore of the latter, between Hautcombe and the Castle of Chatillon, where a sloping turf, canopied over by tall chestnuts, with a cottage. peeping here and there between them, invited us to land and enjoy our breakfast at ease, and sheltered from the beams of the sun, which began, though it was not eight o'clock, to pierce through our awning, and incommode us with ardent heat. We had brought with us a provision of rolls, wine, sausages, and cold ham; and a fisherman's cottage at hand supplied us with trouts, just taken out of the lake, and with the best omelette I ever tasted. A clear rivulet bubbled at our side, amongst the half-exposed and fantastic roots of the trees, to mix with our wine, and cool our hands and face. The raw cold of the dawning day had whetted our appetites, and never did people do more justice to a plentiful and heterogeneous breakfast. From the blue bosom of the watery expanse, which a whispering breeze gently curled into the most inviting smiles, we must have appeared a most attractive group to any accidental voyagers—while the lake, the various fishermen's boats, the Castle of Chatillon, and the bold opposite shore, formed to us a picture of the finest colouring and most picturesque features.

Never had I felt myself so loth to leave any spot. The scene was so calm, so delicious, the shade so refreshing, and the rays of a hot sun sparkled so brightly, and formidably from the water. Ah! it was surely a sad presentiment! But let me turn away a moment from such melancholy ideas. They will press upon me but too soon with redoubled force. After suffering extremely from an intense sun, which the awning over our boat only served to render more suffocating, we landed about a mile from Aix; and while the ladies went on their way thither (escorted by my dear Chatillon), the young mesmerian sage led me with a confident and mysterious air, into a retired little field, where, spying a large chestnut tree, he cried, exultingly, 'Voilà ce que je souhaitais. Cet arbre sera très-favorable à mes procédés, et aidera bien la fluide électrique, et l'attraction insensible entre nos deux corps, qui forment l'essence, et pour ainsi dire l'âme, de mon art.' Accordingly, he placed me with my back against the tree, with great ceremony and gravity, and setting himself in order, cried: 'Mais, monsieur, avant que je commence, il me sera très-important de savoir une chose. Vos nerfs, monsieur, sont ils faibles?' 'Au dernier point. J'ai failli deux fois d'en mourir. Ils sont toujours sensibles, souvent tremblants, et ont toujours été les vrais et cruels ennemis de ma santé et de ma paix.'—'Je suis bien aise, monsieur, que vous m'en avez averti à temps, parce qu'il, me faudra adoucir mes preuves, et ne vous donner que des secousses très modérées et beaucoup au dessous de mon pouvoir.' 'Vous êtes bien généreux, monsieur le Comte, et par reconnaissance il faut que je vous avertisse aussi d'une chose. Ne contez rien sur mon imagination, parce qu'elle ne fera rien pour vous servir.'—'Monsieur, monsieur, épargnez moi de grâce! Croyez-vous que ceci est un jeu d'enfant?' 'Je sais bien, monsieur, qu'il y a bien des enfants, de tous les âges et de toutes les conditions.'—'Allons, monsieur, je ne cherche pas de gagner votre imagination, c'est à votre raison seulement que je m'addresse; mais agissons de bonne foi.' 'Soyez sure, monsieur, que je guetterai bien mes sensations, et que le moment que je sens quelque impression, quelque mouvement extraordinaire, je vous le dirai franchement.'

Now, then, he set himself in earnest about his conjurations, and with as muchparade and solemnity as the witch of Endor when she forced the yawning grave to give up, of yore, the spirit of Samuel—or as when Glendower summoned the imps, his ministers, from their dark abodes, to do his fearful bidding—who shall tell the various gesticulations, writhings, and contortions of this my little magician? Now his hands formed various motions and figures above my head, and now widely separated, and, with the fingers spread abroad, they descended in parallel lines on each side of my body, flourished over my forehead, or were pointed to my breast; all the god of mystery, as it were, swelling and panting the while, in his own bosom, and his eyes fixed upon mine with the frantic stare of a Pythian priestess, crying out, from time to time, 'Mais monsieur, ne sentez-vous rien?' 'Rien, monsieur.'—'Mais présentement?' 'Rien, monsieur.'—'Mais, le diable! maintenant, monsieur? 'Toujours rien.'—'Pas une petite chaleur coulante à la tete, ou dans la poitrine?' 'Non, monsieur.'—'Mais à présent assurément vous sentez un je ne sais quoi, une petite agitation, un serrement du cœur?' 'J'ai toujours chaud, monsieur, parceque j'ai été bien cuite au soleil tantôt; et mon cœur palpite aussi.'—'Mais, monsieur, ne badinez pas, je vous en prie; ce n'est pas le temps. Prenez votre sérieux, et guettez bien vos émotions.'

Again, then, he set himself to work, perspiring with contortions and vexation; but all in vain: my head remained clear, my breast composed, and my heart beat with perfect tranquillity. 'Mais, monsieur, qu'est ce que ça donc? Certainement vous m'avez trompé, vos nerfs ne peuvent pas être faibles.' 'Plut au Dieu, monsieur, qu'ils ne le fussent pas!'—'Assurément donc ce changement d'air, l'exercise, et l'amusement de notre petit voyage, leur ont bien fortifiés aujourd'hui.'

'Tant mieux, monsieur.'—'Pas pour l'honneur de ma science.' 'Réellement, monsieur, je vous plains; ce contretemps me fache; mais comment faire avec mes diables de nerfs, qui sont si résolus de n'être pas ébranlés.'—'Pour cela, monsieur, je vous assure que je leur ébranlerais rien, si vous voudriez bien me le permettre.' 'Comment?'—'Croyez-vous, monsieur, que je me suis servi de toutes mes forces?' 'Je n'en sais rien.'—'Voudriez-vous éprouver des sensations très-decidées et douleureuses même?' 'Volontiers; je suis dans vos mains. Faites votre possible, monsieur, excepté de me donner la mort; parceque cela m'empêcheroit bien de célébrer votre belle science, et de crier miracle.'—'Mais savez vous monsieur, que vous risquez même d'avoir quelques convulsions? J'en ai bien données.' 'J'ai bien vu, monsieur, que vous vous en êtes données à vous-même; faites m'en sentir donc, aussitôt que vous pourrez, si ce ne seroit que par sympathie. Mais dépêchez-vous, je vous en prie, monsieur le Comte, parceque, pour dire la vérité, je suis un peu las, et j'ai grande faim.'

Behold my little wizard now exerting all the power of his art. What twistings and turnings — what goggling and muttering — what sweating and sweating! Sometimes all his might was levelled at my head, sometimes at my side, and at others at my breast. All kinds of geometrical, necromantical, and bacchantical figures and gestures were formed by his body and his limbs. Now my head was assaulted with right lines, triangles, and circles; now my side was attacked by zigzags, crescents, and squares. And now the main battery of paraboles and parallelograms, hexagons, and pentagons, and rhomboids, with a thousand other figures unknown, were played off against my breast. But all in vain; my hard heart was equally proof against persuasion and menaces, fraud and force, and my risible nerves were alone shaken by his efforts. 'Mais, mon Dieu!

mon Dieu! monsieur; vos nerfs sont d'une force, mais d'une force comme il n'y en a point. Quel tempérament de fer, que le votre! Jamais je n'ai rien trouvé de semblable. Il faut absolument que toutes les humeurs, et tous les éléments dans votre corps, soient dans un parfait équilibre. Oui, monsieur, je le répète, dans un parfait équilibre. Non jamais,' repeated he, panting, wiping his reeking brows, and fanning himself with his snuffy handkerchief;—'jamais je n'ai rencontré une santé si parfaite.' 'J'en suis charmé, monsieur! Quelle heureuse nouvelle pour moi! Elle vaut presque le miracle que j'esperais prouver de vos mains'——

We regret that the remainder of this journal has been obliterated through damp.

His friend Chatillon, so often spoken of in this tour and in his letters, appears to have died suddenly before they reached home, as the editor thinks, from the effects of a *coup de soleil.*

NOTES ON A JOURNEY FROM ITALY

THROUGH THE

TYROL, SWITZERLAND, AND BY THE RHINE TO MALINES,

IN THE SUMMER OF 1786.

VICENZA.

THE most admired specimens of Palladio's architecture are to be seen at Vicenza, of which place he was a native. A theatre, built after the plan of Vitruvius, and in the manner of those of ancient Greece, is particularly to be admired; the scene unchanging, and representing two streets of a town, of which, from the seats of the audience, the perspective is admirable, and one of the very best *lusum visûs* I have ever seen. The form of the theatre is semicircular, and of most beautiful architecture.*

The country about Vicenza is pretty, but about Verona it is beautiful. The situation of the latter is also very fine, being placed among lovely hills, with the Alps to the north,

* Beckford, who visited Vicenza, 1780, thus speaks of this wonderful triumph of art:—'The morning being overcast, I went to Palladio's Theatre. It is impossible to conceive a structure more truly classical, or to point out a single ornament which has not the best antique authority. I am not in the least surprised that the citizens of Vicenza enthusiastically gave in to this great architect's plan, and sacrificed large sums to erect so beautiful a model. When finished, they procured, at a vast expense, the representation of a Grecian tragedy, with its chorus an dmajestic decorations.' This remarkable building still remains in perfect preservation.—ED.

and a rich plain to the south. The Adige runs through the town, adorned with very handsome bridges. The town itself is old, but very large, populous, and ornamented with some fine architecture, particularly by Michel Micheli. The amphitheatre is well preserved, but neither so large nor of such fine architecture as that of Nismes. The country from Verona to the entrance of the Tyrol, is cultivated with vines and corn, but not marked with any fine features.

TYROL.

May 1786.—The Tyrol is picturesque for the first twenty miles, the Alps forming a noble and varied, though barren bulwark, on each hand. The little valley between is fertile and populous, and watered by the Adige rolling rapidly in the midst of it. The view for the next five or six miles is the most wretched and displeasing imaginable. Not only every tree, but every shrub and blade of grass seem to have been turned by some Medusa's head, into so many stones, which lie about in heaps of the most ugly confusion. The view then changes to a fertile, populous, and picturesque valley, that leads to the town of Roveredo, where we dined; and from thence to Trent, and especially about the latter, the scenery is very beautiful and picturesque.

Trent has 25,000 inhabitants, and is in itself old and indifferently built. From Trent, the next day's journey was very pleasant, the valley between the mountains sometimes enlarging itself to the width of several miles, and varying its culture between vines, corn, and pastures. The sides of the mountains also appeared more picturesque, being clothed with wood on the right; with houses and villages and ruins here and there, scattered about on the heights, and having their lofty sides beautifully cultivated, and very populous on the left. The Adige sometimes wound at the side of the road, and at others lost itself to our sight, on the farther side of the valley. We slept at Bolzano, which is a pretty large and very flourishing town, carrying on a considerable commerce, especially in raw silk; its situation most beautiful. From Bolzano to a village where we dined, the mountains on each side were more picturesque than can be described: their wild, natural, and majestic breaks and beauties being intermingled with hanging vineyards, cornfields, and cottages, steeples, country seats, and ruins; the river boiling rapidly over the rocks at the bottom, and its banks, where there was space enough, adorned with mills, villages, and various culture. Our little inn was exquisitely neat, and the view from the room where we dined confined, but charmingly romantic. Mem.: We have set our hearts, if it should please God to spare our lives, on staying to dine and sleep at this inn, hereafter, with our dear Mrs. Jackson.*

Prospect to the south from the windows—the river, rolling rapidly and foaming over its rocky channel, with the road winding by it, and on each side the mountains, drawn near together, rising up grandly, of various forms, and very finely broken, here with bold swells, and there in easy slopes, adorned beautifully with firs and other wood, and cultivated with corn pastures and vineyards in a style singularly picturesque; the vines being trained so as to form so many pent-houses or light arcades, as it were, of graceful shade, and curling in and out round the little fields, like a snake, to a great height, so as at once to form their exact limits and most

* This lady's name often occurs in the subsequent letters. Mr. and Mrs. Whalley visited her in Bath shortly before they left England. Miss Seward in one place mentions her as 'the accomplished Mrs. Jackson of Bath;' and on another occasion says, in 1791, 'We were guests of Mr. Whalley's charming friend, Mrs. Jackson, a woman of first-rate abilities and virtues.' Mrs. Siddons mentions the death of her husband, who probably held an appointment in India, which must have been a great pecuniary loss to her. She published, in 1806, 'Dialogues on the Doctrines and Duties of Christianity,' in two vols., in the sale of which we find Dr. Whalley interesting himself.

pleasing ornament. On the right a whited church and steeple, happily perched on the very summit of a sugar-loaf mountain; some picturesque cottages, here singly, and there in clusters, hanging about declivities and on the slopes, or seated snugly on the river's banks; the mountains drawing their august curtain round the end of the perspective to the south, except where they opened their dark drapery to discover a last, loftier, and more distant one, rising to a point, and covered with snow. A side view of the village and church, climbing the mountain, formed the home scene on the right, together with some handsome trees scattered singly, and the neat little garden of the inn with its bowers of vines. From the west window the eye looked over the village to a woody mountain that towered above it, and from the awful heights of which an abundant cascade threw itself, in successive sheets of foam and three distinct gushes, down a rock in lengthened floats. The name of the village is Colman.

A very little way from Colman, on the right, a most picturesque convent, like a castle, and two or three houses, situated on the edge of a high and woody rock, with the ruins of a round tower on another directly above them.

Road from Colman to the pretty town of Brixen through the most beautiful country, the banks of the river adorned with the richest meadow ground, often resembling a park and most graceful groves; the mountains cultivated to their summits, with a picturesque intermixture of woods, cottages, country seats, and churches. Brixen a more open and less romantic, but not inferior situation to Colman. The river runs through Brixen.

Neat inn again, and most honest, simple, and obliging people belonging to it. From Brixen to the little town of Sterzingen, where we dined, the valley straightened very much, and the mountains were steeper and less favourable for cultivation, though always grand, with their dark and abundant shade of firs. From time to time, however, the road was ornamented on either side with groves of walnuts, sweet chestnuts, and beeches, and the valley widened and presented beautiful meadows and picturesque villages, with cultivation and cottage scenery on the declivities of the mountains, but no vines were to be seen, and the snowy summits drew nearer and nearer to the eye. Sterzingen: situated at the end of a plain, with picturesque views on the steeps on each side, and lofty mountains clothed with firs and crowned with snow to the north behind it; but the large pastures leading immediately to it swampy and unwholesome. The river on the left skirts the foot of the mountains. A neat inn again, with the same civility and simplicity of manners.

From Sterzingen to the village of Brenner, the road mounts almost continually between the Alps, which are drawn so near together in many parts as almost to overhang it, and which present very fine scenery in the savage and romantic style, with here and there a cultivated spot and a few quiet cottages. Many beautiful cascades fall from the rocks, or foam from between the dark firs, and add their tribute to the river, which, diminishing fast as we ascended, dwindled at last to a mere transparent rivulet gurgling over its pebbly channel; and just before our arrival at Brenner, we discovered its source in a beautiful cascade that gushed out of, and fell a long way down a black rock, fringed on one side with firs and larches, and with a picturesque cottage at its foot.

Another neat inn, with a most obliging hostess.

The scenery from Brenner to Inspruck is gloriously romantic and sublime. The valley very straight, and the eye chiefly plunging down from the elevated road to the shady beauties of the deep dell, with the river foaming between the dark firs at its bottom. Inspruck is finely situated in a verdant plain that opens between the receding mountains, one very lofty, one towering immediately behind it to the north, and another to the south, towering above nearer to me, highly cultivated, and finely shaded with firs and larches. The river Inn runs through the suburbs from west to east, the vale stretching along it each way between walls of mountains, most beautifully enlivened with numerous villages and country seats.

In the church of the Franciscan Friars, brass statues, larger than the life, on each side the nave, of the sovereigns of the Tyrol down from the fifteenth century, with several of their queens, in the dress or armour of the times. The tomb of the Emperor Maximilian in the midst of the nave, surrounded with ornamented iron palisades, and with his effigy kneeling upon it. The entrance to Inspruck is remarkably fine; the street nobly wide, the buildings handsome, and most of them gaily and differently painted on the outside.

The golden roof and its history are remarkable. The ancient edifice it covers, is of yellow veined marble, erected in the year 500, and adorned with three broad bands, one to each story, of curious carving in the same marble, and antique paintings. The carving of the lower part, arms and devices, and of the second, groups of little figures, but what they represent unknown. The third story, a balcony, from the balustrades of which rise handsome gothic pillars, not heavy or inelegant, to support the costly roof, every round tile of which is plated with solid gold, near as thick as half-a-crown. Built by a Prince Frederic, who had been sneered at by the nobles of his town and time, as a prodigal whose foolish splendour and munificence had ruined his fortune, as a proof of his remaining treasures and their blind envy and malice. Kept up with the greatest care, in the highest preservation, and the pilfering any part of its precious covering, made a capital crime. This little building, which now projects to the street from a large modern one, formerly a part of the prince's palace, which has long been destroyed.

From Inspruck to Barwis: the vale wider, and runs straight almost between the mountains, watered by the river Inn, and wholly cultivated to pasture. The mountains, on the left a good deal fertilised with corn and pasture, but with here and there a bleak and barren one covered with snow; on the right rising up close by the road, and finely clothed with deep woods of firs, which in one part gave a new feature to the scenery, standing in thick groves at the bottom of bare and most stupendous rocks. This part of the view, on both sides and in all respects, very noble and picturesque, with fine woods by the river-side for a continuance of six or seven miles from Inspruck. The valley then flatter and wider, and the mountains, though always bold and various, less romantic and beautiful.

Winter come again from Inspruck to Barwis, and much snow fallen on the surrounding Alps the preceding night, May 19th.

From Barwis to Nazareth, we plunged deep amongst the Alps, the road first mounting for a long time and to a great height, and then descending as much. The scenery very savage, sublime, and at times beautiful; the Alps rising to a stupendous height on all sides, and of the boldest forms; some covered with snow, and others with firs; most beautiful and noble groves of the latter, mixed with the lighter shade and featherings of the larch, skirted the road for many miles, sometimes in grand avenues, and at others grouped variously and in the most graceful style, as in a fine park, on the verdant and unequal turf, that led the eye to a great distance; and most agreeably between them, the mountains appeared through the deep and feathered veil of their intermingled branches, with that kind of indistinct and shadowy state which had a something more awful and sublime in it, and more attractive to the imagination, than an open and decisive view of their imperial features. We lost the river before we reached Barwis. Nazareth, where we passed the night, is a desolate situation, sunk deep in a little basin, and overwhelmed, as it were, by rocky and sterile mountains of a prodigious volume and height, without any graceful shading to soften their terrific frowns.

N.B.—The host of the inn where we dined, of a character strikingly frank and simple. He jabbered out a little broken Italian with such overflowing civility and goodness of heart, that Amelia wept with the touch of virtuous joy—a sure sign of the excellence of her own spirit.

From Nazareth to Hetterwang, the mountains stood in heaps all round us, so that the eye was often at a loss to discover the pass between them. Many of them were covered with snow, as well as the groves of firs hanging on the neighbouring ones, much snow having fallen on the preceding night. Little cultivation to be seen, yet here and there a pretty verdant spot in the hollows, of fine pasture, and enlivened by cottages and hamlets. One point of view, about three miles from Nazareth, charmingly clothed, and the summits of some are covered with snow, rising round in an august theatre; with a beautiful fall of water foaming down them on each hand, the one forming immediately a clear brook, and the other discharging itself into a lovely little blue lake, which held up its mirror to three soft and beautiful hills, highly adorned with wood, and rising to a point—the lake lying between them, and a fine ruin of an ancient castle placed on the summit of the middle one. The vale, where we dined also, very pastoral, with wide-extended meadows of the finest herbs, and verdure spotted over with the huts where the numerous cows are housed and milked in summer, and animated with three or four considerable villages; the mountains rising boldly to the south, and running eastwards and westwards, snowy or shaded as usual, but with humbler heights, as if spent with towering above the clouds, and as the earnest of a more level and habitable, though less sublime country.

The host of our inn, a frank, handsome, honest German; but, wearing a scarlet waistcoat laced with silver, touching simplicity was out of the question.

From Hetterwang to a village where we slept, twelve miles distant, the mountains were less awful and sublime, but for a part of the way were very finely clothed on the right, the lofty firs forming a light, unbroken, and undulating fringe on their summits, and reaching down in full ranks quite to the level vale at the bottom. As we went on the mountains gradually diminished, and a little before we reached our quarters, they stopped entirely their bold phalanx, and a wide extended vale just opened by twilight to us a far different face of nature for to-morrow's journey. The little wood-built inn resounded with rustic jollity, and the thump of the peasants' feet were audible, as we entered, in cadence to the fiddles that inspired them. I never saw greater mirth and conviviality than among a dozen clowns and their lasses, joined to greater cordiality and simplicity. They seemed delighted with our pleased attention to their merriment, as we were with their innocent, natural, and unclouded joys. Can there, indeed, be a more interesting spectacle, than to see honest industry solacing itself in its recess from labour, and giving itself up to a mirth and good fellowship untainted with envy, vanity, or vice? If bitter is sometimes the sweat of their brow, grateful is that which follows from it in the vacant and frolicsome moments of the heart; and, when given wholly up to the hilarity of the moment, to-morrow and its cares are left to shift for themselves, till the morning.

For seven or eight miles towards the city of Kempten, the pasture ground fell and rose prettily enough, but little worthy of remark after the magnificent and beautiful scenery we had been accustomed to for the preceding days. A most noble road afterwards led us winding, and alternately mounting and descending, through a most charming country, which appeared on all hands as far as the eye could reach like a beautiful park, adorned with the finest verdure, and numberless groves of firs and larches, disposed, as it were, by the hand of taste to make it picturesque. Large herds of cows were seen feeding here and there along the rich vale or between the trees, and many farm houses happily spotted about at the foot of the groves.

Kempten is an old but pretty large and most cheerful town, situated partly on the banks of the Iller and partly on a pleasant and healthy hill. The city, properly so called, belongs to the Empire, but is free, and is wholly Lutheran; the suburbs, which are large and well-built, Catholic, and the property of the Prince of Campidomo, who is at once bishop and sovereign, and resides in a large convent, of which he is superior, and where he has a handsome palace; it is an order religious and military, consisting of twenty-eight cavaliers, all noble.

The most attractive civility and simplicity seem to be the real characteristics of the Campidonians. Our inn, a good one, was neat, charmingly situated on a rising ground in the suburbs, and the host and waiter ready and obliging beyond expression.

From Kempten to Leutkirch (where we slept) the road and country were similar to those in the morning. I forgot to observe that the houses, especially those we saw during our earlier stages in the Tyrol, have a singular and not bad effect, being either painted in fresco, with various figures and ornaments round the windows and scripture subjects between, or, being chiefly built of fir wood, are chequered in a kind of whimsical mosaic work of an endless variety.

The rafters and cross-pieces employed in their construction, before the plaster fills up the intervening spaces, have the appearance of a large cage of various and fantastic open work. When the building is completed, they paint this wood-work either black or red, which, with the white of the plaster between, forms the whimsical *coup d'œil* before mentioned. Leutkirch, a moderate sized, but dirty ill-built town, situated on the banks of the Iller, and belonging to the Emperor.

From Leutkirch to Bergartrent the country, for the first five or six miles, is flat, and not worth remark as to prospect, though very rich in soil. The ground then became finely broken, but chiefly cultivated with grain, and ornamented as before with groves of firs, between a most noble vista of which, the eye caught a beautiful and rich perspective of the country for many miles. Bergartrent is a wretched village, and the inn dirty and poverty-stricken; but it was not possible to complain of anything, or not seem to be pleased, while the poor creatures to whom it belonged, behaved with such touching humility, and such alacrity to serve and do to the best of their ability.

From Bergartrent to Weingarten is an open vale, rich and finely wooded, with soft and well cultivated hills on each side, the road in one part winding through a wood of firs and limes, broken and grouped in a charming manner, their various green relieving the eye, and giving new effect to each other. A most noble wood of both rose on a gentle elevation on the left near Weingarten, and at the end of it a picturesque and magnificent convent, with a fine church adjoining, and a large village climbing up the hill, on whose summit they stood with a royal air, as if preparing to receive the homage of their vassals below. Weingarten is an old and rather large town, surrounded with ancient walls; the houses chiefly built of wood, and painted and flourished off with the nicky-nacky rafters at all rates. The situation fine, on a rising ground, and with a vale and hills on each side, that would have appeared most captivating in our eyes, had we not so lately quitted the various and enchanting beauties and sublimities of the Tyrol. Our little inn, six miles from Weingarten, is a single house, with a pleasant view of the country, and interesting from its own neatness and the simple and obliging manners of its possessors. The German children, in the part of the country we have seen, are generally handsome, stout, ruddy, and to appearance as hardy as the firs they grow up with all around.

From our little inn to Mörsburg the country was fertile, but without any striking features, till we came in view of the noble lake of Constance, and of the smiling hills, villages, towns, seats, and other buildings that adorn its banks, with a long ridge of very lofty Alps, covered with snow on the east and north-east. Our passage over the lake to a hamlet about two miles from Constance was very agreeable, as the weather was brilliant, and the lake like a beautiful looking mirror, tinged with bright blue, and reflecting the clouds that lay rolled back in grand fleeces all around. The country, from the place of our disembarkment, was adorned with soft hills of charming shade and verdure, and cultivated on every hand with vines, which would have a much more pleasing effect, did not the stakes to which they are fastened, rise three feet above the topmost tendrils, so that at a distance the country appears all over bristled with bare sticks.

Constance is finely placed at the western extremity of the lake, just where the Rhine issues from it, winding, below the town, through a rich and beautiful country. The town, not large, is very ancient and ill-built, but famous for the great council once held in it, governed by the Prince Bishop of Constance, under the Emperor, who about six months since suppressed the Dominican Friars, and gave their large and finely situated convent to a number of Genevans, whom the disputes and discontents of that place had caused to be disgusted with their native home, and who have at this moment every thing prepared for the establishment of a manufacture of fine painted linens, the same as those at Geneva. One of them showed me the *locale*, which is finely calculated for such a fabric, as it forms a little island on the lake, a long bridge leading to it from Constance. The winter refectory of the monks is converted into a Calvinist chapel, and the former large chapel into the chief apartment for the manufactory. Such wonderful and sudden changes are caused by absolute power, and it is happy when it is thus exerted for the encouragement of honest industry, and the support of hundreds. I also saw, in the now abandoned cloister in the courtyard of the quondam convent, the dance of the dead, which, in point of idea, has moral and merit, but being painted in fresco, poor Death, though habituated to his bare bones, with nothing to defend them from wind and weather, has here suffered so much from the latter, as in some of the departments to be scarcely visible. But it may be said that he is commonly sooner felt than seen.

The Bishop of Constance is an independent sovereign, under the title of Prince of Mörsburg, where he has a handsome palace, and almost constantly resides. A pretty considerable territory round belongs to him.

From Constance to the neat and pleasant little town of Frauenfeld, belonging to the eight oldest Cantons, the country is very fertile, well cultivated, and beautifully divided between hill and vale, and finely wooded. The most picturesque part of the country was in the Canton of Lucerne, and our little neat inn, half way between Constance and Zurich, commanded a sweet pastoral view. About six miles back we passed the river, which is narrow, very rapid, and must be extremely disagreeable, and sometimes even dangerous, to pass in stormy weather, as the boat, or rather raft, is clumsy and unmanageable, and the men who guide it have only their poles to stem the force of the current.

From our dining place to Zurich, the country is similar to that before. The situation of Zurich is singularly fine on the border of its own lake, the banks of which rise round it on the south east, in a beautiful amphitheatre, and present the most smiling, graceful, animated and picturesque scenery to the eye imaginable; the first order of snowy Alps towering above the cultivated hills in sublime state, and with their ridges broken in the finest manner. As the lake is not more than four miles wide, the objects on each side are presented to the view distinctly, forming a succession of pictures equally various and charming. And I would write again in raptures of clouds, were I not apprehensive that you would think me enamoured of them, like another Ixion, though, as my passion is more pure than his, I trust it would neither meet, nor deserve, a similar punishment.

Our situation at Zurich is charming. The clear and noble Limmat rushes from the lake just under our eastern windows, which look over it to a square, crowded in a morning with peasants offering to sell their various commodities, as well as to a part of the town running over its banks and cultivated hills rising above it. The beautiful lake spreads lengthways to the south, broken to the eye just where it gives current to the infant river, by a long, light, wooden bridge, with a steeple in the centre, a pretty house grown as it were out of its bottom, and a mill always in motion by its side. Beyond, the lake forms a majestic basin animated with little vessels. Its circular borders to the right are adorned with soft and populous hills in the foreground, backed by woody mountains, and to the left, by a succession of rising grounds, richly enlivened by numberless houses, picturesquely placed amongst the luxuriant foliage.

The gracefully curving southern extremity of the lake forms a noble amphitheatre of three distinct stages, the first composed of beautiful and populous hills, the second of more lofty ones, with wilder features and darker shade, the third elevating itself with the first order of Alps, above the clouds, awfully grand, picturesquely piled and broken, and laced all over with eternal snows.

When three miles on the lake, its form appears a beautiful oval, with various and delicious scenery all round it—Zurich, with cultivated hills behind it, forming the perspective at one end, and the sublimest of the Alps, resplendent with snow, towering above the soft hills and humbler mountains at the other, and giving the grandest and most picturesque finish imaginable. On each side a succession of swelling, finely-shaded and cultivated hills, ravish the eye with a continued change of sweet pictures, in which the cottage and village scenery is singularly attractive, with here and there a house of larger volume, and more elegant form, though neither frequent nor proud enough to browbeat their neat, smiling, and more humble neighbours.

As the lake also is not more than half as wide, or long, as those of Geneva and Constance, when upon it, the eye distinctly views and enjoys the charming and various scenery of its surrounding banks, with all which you seem at home without any of that oppressive vastness, or obscure perspective, which at once excite and cheat curiosity, confuse the ideas, and bewilder the eye.

Unfortunately for me, Mr. Lavater was so wholly occupied on my arrival at Zurich, between a conflict in his mind whether to remain in his native town amongst his old connections, or to accept a most pressing invitation to the living of Bremen, 200 leagues distant in Germany, his decision on which was necessarily to be declared in a few days, that I could only procure half an hour of his conversation,* but he rendered that short period very precious by his courtesy, benevolence, and genius. I shall never forget the manner with which he presented me a print of himself, and dear as the latter will always be to me, and striking as is the resemblance, the former has made a still deeper impression of him on my heart. His face, like Sterne's monk, is pale and penetrating, but not mild; a keen and eager intelligence and mounting fire lurk about his mouth, and in his fine eyes, which search you to the soul, and yet are tempered with so much benevolence that you are not afraid of their regards. Every motion, every look, every gesture, and almost every word, marks enthusiasm, but an enthusiasm engendered by glowing fancy, active knowledge, and exquisite sensibility. The turn of his countenance is at once beautiful, and noble, and engages alike affection and reverence. Intense thought has forestalled time in furrowing his cheeks, and the fervours of an ardent imagination continually kept alive by new and deep researches, seem to have consumed his flesh, and burned the colour on his cheeks to ashes. But, amidst all his flushing ardours, a shade of melancholy, of tender and pensive thought, now and then passes over his face, that touches you to the soul, like a cloud before the sun. His manners are at once vivacious and simple, with the information of a first-rate understanding, and the captivating courtesy of a warm and good heart, disdainful of little forms, and, from right feeling, never neglecting the more essential attentions, which win, satisfy, and put you at your ease.

He told me, that he was to set out with his son for Germany in a few days, where the amiable and clever youth is to study physic, but that he hoped to find me here at his return, and to see me often. I could wish it might be, but

* Owing to his great goodness, I did see him many times.

his absence will probably be extended beyond the limits of my stay here. You will not laugh at me, for being eager to hear him preach, though wholly ignorant of the German language. Do the eyes, the voice, the air, the gestures of such a man say nothing? Yes, they speak always in the most forcible, and often in the most intelligible, language. This extraordinary genius was born a great orator. He seems to move the passions at his pleasure. His tones are finely varied according to his matter, and when turned to the pathetic are irresistible. I found the tears often starting from my eyes, and saw the numerous audience melting all round. His action is equally animated and graceful, and is so far from being affected or studied, to set off his own eloquence, and work upon the feelings of others, that it apparently proceeds from the impulse of the moment, and his natural fire and sensibility. As he preached extempore, his elegant hands were at full liberty, and they always said just enough and no more, without one false flourish of pathos, or one wild movement of weak and flaming enthusiasm. How much did I regret that I could not comprehend his language! But I have been well informed that his style is what I supposed it—fine, flowing, energetic, and full of fire. His application is uncommon, and the readings of his spirit wonderful. He has published above sixty volumes, most of them in 4to, on various subjects, but his principal favourite, most extraordinary, and most celebrated work, is that on physiognomy, which he has reduced almost to a system. You have doubtless heard that it is not confined to man, but extended through the whole living creation. Of the former, as more strongly marked and fit for observation, he judges, not only from the real presence, but by the portrait, handwriting, and even shadowy profile, seeming even to prefer the last, as more true to nature, however wanting in colouring and animation, to anything but the *viva persona*; and for this reason, that though the portrait is more striking, the profile is more exact. The gestures, air, and back of the head, are also in many subjects sufficient to lead him, as he avers, to a knowledge of their understanding, temper, and dispositions. In general, he appears to judge of the understanding under all its modifications from the form of the head, in particular the proportion of the front, with the back part of it, the greater or less projection of the forehead, and the angles formed jointly between it, and the other features. The dispositions, qualities, and passions of the heart, he rather reads from the play of the muscles and expression of the countenance, seeming to lay more stress on the mouth and brows, than on the eyes. In some points one is inclined to think that his natural warmth of temper has made him push a favourite system too far, yet how be master of a criterion to aver this, without his science; and how venture to declare anything he has advanced visionary, without having studied his particular subject profoundly as himself and with equal capacity and penetration? One thing is certain, that his virtuous, upright, and every way respectable principles and character, exclude in the eye of candour the slightest suspicion of imposture, or wish to build a fabric to tinsel vanity and disgraceful fame, on the sandy foundations of novelty and credulity. Nor is it less sure that his divinations have been wonderfully just, and in a thousand instances where he had never seen the person whose capacity and disposition he made known.

Surely Mr. Coxe * let fall a strange absurdity from his able pen, when he supposed that, though somewhat may be judged of the dispositions of a horse, or any other large animal, from its face, yet that it was ridiculous to imagine the countenance of an insect the index to its mind. What

* Archdeacon Coxe's *Tour in Switzerland*, published shortly before.

are the terms of great and little, thus applied, but comparative, and in the contemplation of immensity how does their difference shrink into nothing. Surely it is much less surprising, that a mite's countenance should mark its temper, qualities, and intelligence, than that it should live, and move, and have a being, by the means of arteries, nerves, muscles, the circulation of the blood, and all the various springs and ducts, that are necessary to the coexistence of matter and spirit. If a mite's or a horse's countenance indicate his turn of mind, by fair analogy (for nature is uniform and simple in her plans) one may suppose the same of the smallest reptile; though our natural powers, with the help of art, incapacitate us from forming a judgment of them from distinct and discriminate vision. I have only yet read scraps of Mr. Lavater's ingenious and extraordinary publication on this subject, but long to consider the whole, and mean to purchase it before I quit Zurich, as a good French copy is just completed here.

Nothing can be more delightful to a contemplative mind and a lover of nature, than the walks round Zurich—by those little private paths, that look as if they had never been trodden by the proud or great, but seem formed by the foot of happy and innocent industry, trudging to or from the labours of the day. How dear are they always amongst the woodlands by the tattling rivulet's side, to tender sentiment and pensive thought!

The cottages also satisfy taste without, and benevolence within. Their form and situation, their little neat gardens and fruitful shade, their peculiar and relative features, their various dispositions and similar cheerfulness, enchant the eye, whilst their internal neatness, and a certain air of ease and comfort, gratify the mind. On such habitations, I can never look without a secret, however erroneous, conviction of their owners being at once amongst the happiest and least corrupt of human beings, and could scarcely help despising the man that could view them without a tender delight. For my part, now that I know what they are, and how their inhabitants live, they appear with tenfold charms on every side of me, as I ramble about the hills or sail along the lake.

I never shall forget the sad revolution I felt on this subject in Savoy. Amongst my strolls, and a little after my arrival in that lovely and sublime country, I descried a whitened cottage, smiling sweetly through its walnut shade on the side of a verdant hill, with a view equally picturesque and noble of the world without, whilst a clear brook hurried down the steep at its side. The golden corn waved richly in its own enclosure, round which the luxuriant vine wantoned with interlaced tendrils, laden with fair promise of an abundant vintage. Before the door an arbour was formed, the whole roof of which was embroidered with the already swelling clusters. The evening sun sparkled amongst, without piercing through, its thick foliage, and in it sat an elderly man, just returned from labour, and wiping the sweat from his brows. I accosted him with all the dilatation of heart, which one felt at the presentiment of humble comfort and content, and asked him if the field and the vineyard, and the walnut trees and cottage were not his own. He answered in the affirmative. 'How happy are you,' said I, 'to possess corn and wine and oil, thus at your own pleasant door, and sufficient for your wants.' He shook his head, and smiled as one does at a person who errs in judgment, though with respect for his motive. 'Ah! sir, I possess, it is true, but others enjoy the fruits of all these.' 'How,' cried I, with surprise and chagrin. 'Do you not eat your own grapes and your own bread, drink your own wine, and trim your winter's lamp with your own oil?' 'Credit, sir, the word of a poor, but honest old man. Our taxes are so grievous, that I am obliged to sell the produce of all I possess,'— and here he went into his humble dwelling, but returning in a moment, continued,—'and the money it yields me, after our king is paid, hardly suffices to buy me this bread and this oil, and it is rarely that I drink of anything but that brook. But God grant me strength to labour still, and I shall be content, for many poor creatures round me have often not this bread to eat.' And what was it? black and disgusting to the eye and nauseous to the taste, for I tasted it, that I might retain a deeper feeling of my error, of hardships which it is salutary to remember, though cruel that one cannot remove. I cannot describe to you the sensations I felt, and to you need not add, that not only the charms of the present lovely scene vanished, but that in all my future rambles, wherever I saw a nest of picturesque cottages, the image of the old man started up, to damp my enthusiasm and deaden my pleasure.

I do not agree with Mr. Coxe. The situation of Lucerne appears less beautiful to me, than that of Zurich. It is true that the mountains are piled in grand confusion, round the part of the lake one sees from the town, but that part is very narrow and insignificant, and frequently hides itself behind the advancing rocks between which it winds. As one sails up it, indeed, the scenery becomes sublimely savage, and the rocks and mountains are varied with all the bold angles, points, swells, woods, different colouring, barrenness and fertility, that form the enchantment of the Alps, and fill the mind at once with awe and admiration; and the lively and recent impression of these successive pictures naturally made Lucerne appear to Mr. Coxe, as he approached it from the lake, in a point of view unusually favourable. The enthusiasm excited in his mind had not begun to subside, and what he saw was united to what he had seen in too near a relation to be divided from each other. As I entered Lucerne by land, and with calm ideas, its position towards the lake, though picturesque, fell far short of my expectations.

In my way back to Zurich, I walked up to the summit of Mount Albis, from the inn where I had dined, with my wife and a young Dutch merchant of Amsterdam, who was our *compagnon de voyage.* The prospect was extensive, various, and grand. To the east, the lake of Zurich stretched its mirror between the cultivated and populous hills, rising gradually from its edge, and showing the town, situated at its extreme end, northwards. To the south, a noble ridge of snowy Alps, that divide the pastures of Zurich and Glarus, broke through the clouds, scattered in soft fleeces about them, with their irregular and pointed summits. To the west and south-west appeared the lake and town of Zug, and beyond them, deep amongst its awful rocks, a part of the Lake of Lucerne, the mountains closing it in presently from the searching eye, and rising in confused and imperious heaps, dark with impending storms, that at times looked angrily and awfully red with the beams of the declining sun. Its rays strove in vain to gild the clouds with splendid and cheerful light, and could only force from their lowering brows that kind of fiery and malignant lustre, that seemed like a tyrant's dark smile—the forerunner of vengeance. In the near ground the view was finely broken by steeps rough with wood, and a mountain of lesser size, that rose to a point, covered with firs.

As I contemplated this glorious scene in deep admiration, the Hollander shook himself from his lethargic wonder, and cried, 'What a terrible silence; I cannot bear it! Mein Gott! how different to Amsterdam!' Used only to speculation, and unowned by contemplation, it was no marvel that the awe he felt influenced and compressed, instead of pleasing and expanding, his soul. But to mine, how captivating this solemn silence of nature amidst her greater works! How commanding in her stillness! how sublime in her repose! How divinely does she sit amongst her rocks and her mountains, her dark forests and her deep glens, and from her unseen and sacred throne, issues out laws to govern the nether world, sends down torrents to form and swell rivers, ripens in her mountains the precious metals of the various mines, dispenses her treasures of rain, arrests the winds in their furious and destructive course, and wakes the busy hum of men in cities and countries, who, knowing not what they owe, make use of her bounties without once tracing them to their source.

Notre Dame des Hermites is a magnificent convent of Benedictines, a short day's journey from Zurich, the road from one to the other running continually in view of the lake till within a few miles of the convent, and abounding in fine scenery, all of the picturesque and pastoral kind. Its first foundation was a chapel, built in the midst of the desert of Einsiedlen, in the cantons of Switzerland, by a hermit called Meinrad, who was murdered by robbers. These robbers were miraculously pursued to Zurich by two black constables of the air, called crows (birds, you know, even with the heathen, of ill omen), discovered, and executed. Miracle upon miracle, performed by the dead hermit's perishing bones, spread his renown far and near. His saintship began to assume importance, and pilgrims offered up adoration at his shrine. A succeeding saint retired to the same spot, doubly hallowed it, and erected another chapel, and laid the foundations of the abbey, which priestly craft and religious zeal soon increased and augmented to the majestic volume now extant. Who placed the figure of the holy Virgin, with our Saviour in her arms, in the beautiful chapel of black and white marble, erected just within the great door of the church, is not known; but it is well known that the chapel was consecrated by the Almighty, for a certain Bishop Conrad affirmed it, and can bishops lie? No! you will answer. Far be it from me to suppose such sin in the holy pillars of the Church, but they may dream, and verily in a dream (but whether sleeping or waking is not determined) the Bishop of Constance received these tidings from an angelic messenger.

We know the blessed Virgin was a native of a hot country, but did you ever hear that she was a black? And not only she, but our Saviour also. It is true the sombre complexion of both, may be attributed to the hidden light that is always diffusing splendour on the silver and golden glory with which, being in need of earthly riches, she is surrounded — and all earthly light at least, you know, is accompanied with some smoke. But, though her skin has suffered, her clothes appear little the worse for wear; and what wonder, when she has a complete suit for every week, all rich, and often renewed. Not being a gala-day, when she puts on her court dress, she was only arrayed in a vesture of brocade and gold when I saw her, with fine drop garnet earrings. But her wardrobe is supplied, for great occasions, with rich embroidery composed of pearls and other precious stones. A profusion of jewels then strive to illuminate her dark countenance, which I think they might paint *à la mode de Paris* in honour of the most Catholic king whose court first brought *de se farder* into fashion. But, if I smiled at the absurd inconsistencies and low mummery about these vile representations of such divine personages, I looked with a sacred kind of pity on the crowds of poor pilgrims happily arrived at their desired post, and kissing the earth before their shrine in all the fervour of true, however mistaken, devotion. They are never a just object of ridicule, whatever may be the priests who cherish their blind superstition, and favour, I had almost said, their idolatry.

The church is a noble and spacious building, but loaded and daubed all over with trumpery pictures and barbarous ornaments. The convent forms a long wing to it, in front of each side, and both are commandingly situated on a platform, to which you mount from the village by a long majestic sweep of steps. The village itself is wholly composed of inns (there being no less than 70), and little shops for the 'vente' of rosaries, medals, crosses, and other trifling objects of Catholic zeal and priestly commerce, &c. But numerous as are, the inns they are often found insufficient to contain the pilgrims, who flock to visit the wonderful Madonna from all quarters. Their annual number is said to amount to 100,000. Such sway have bigotry and superstition over the minds of the vulgar, where indeed they are quickest to enter and slowest to depart. But the days of princely pilgrimages and offerings are over, and silver saints and precious crowns are rarely sent to Einsiedlen now-a-days to bribe the virgin's aid. The treasures preserved in the convent are of immense value, and strangely heterogeneous.

Would you not start back with a mingled emotion of disgust, mirth, and scorn, from all kinds of pretended holy bones, dressed up in satin and velvet, and enriched with gold and silver? Yet what are these to half a dozen skeletons of pretended saints, decked out with sumptuous robes, their poor skulls plastered all over with pearls and coloured stones, discovering through their open breast (for they are all hollow like those of many other saints) their ribs and backbone, embroidered with the same precious materials in the most clumsy fantastic style. Two or three had green silk gloves on, velvet slippers, and the empty sockets of their eyes goggled at you, with protuberant roses of large pearls! What a shocking prodigality of wealth, and how absurd and loathsome to see the wretched carcase of the dead, adorned with the costly show and vanities that even disgrace the living!

It gives me so much pain to behold such masses of treasure sleeping in the presses of monks, and under the idea, or at least pretence, of doing honour to God and his elect, that I think those at Notre Dame des Hermites shall be the last I will ever visit. I forgot to mention five large holes in a chased silver plate, over the outward door of the chapel, which the poor pilgrims firmly believe to have been formed by the fingers of the Almighty, when He consecrated the chapel. One smiles at their credulity, as one sees them eagerly cramming their fingers into these supposed vestiges of divine power, and praying with redoubled fervour, but one shudders at the impiety that can dare nourish such a supposition.

The village and convent are surrounded by fir-clad hills, which with us would be called mountains, and pastures covered with cattle occupy the valley. The scenery is picturesque enough, but appeared nothing in my eyes after the sublime awful solitude of the Grande Chartreuse and Belleveux, the latter of which deserves to be more known and celebrated, as it far surpasses in grand scenery many of the most vaunted situations amongst the Alps, and indeed vies with that of Chartreuse itself.

I cannot resist my wish to make you a partaker, as far as my imperfect description will allow me, of the famous fall of the Rhine about a mile and a half from Schaffhausen, where the river is no longer navigable. From thence, continually more straitened in its bed, it rolls rapidly to the place of its fall, between Newhausen a village belonging to Schaffhausen, and the Château Bellival de Lauffen belonging to Zurich. Two rocks lift themselves proudly up in the middle of the cataract, ornamented with tufts of wood, and divide it into three fine and noble falls, besides a gash through the larger of them, absolutely dividing it into two distinct parts, which seem to have been formed by the continual and powerful action of the water. The château itself, and a pretty village crowded behind it, as if waiting to satisfy its curiosity afterwards by a peep at the thundering cascade below (rendered at once curious, and encouraged by the example of its lord), with a steeple standing quietly at a small distance, shaded and embosomed by trees, are disposed very picturesquely on the summit of a dark rock.

Beneath, a light wooden bridge constructed on purpose, with a small covered porch which has the air of a little pavilion, allows one to advance to the very edge of the fall. On the Schaffhausen side, a cluster of picturesque cottages, beautifully grouped, partly edges the rock, and partly retires under the shade, on the declivity of the soft hill that swells above, cultivated with vines. One of these houses has a mill; a silver thread of the river is conducted by a shallow wooden shoot to work the latter, and from thence frothing down a rock forms another pretty little fall, under a second wooden bridge. In the front, hill appears gradually above hill, and the last rising with a round head, and almost wholly covered with wood, closes the perspective very beautifully.

I first approached the fall from the Schaffhausen side, and looked down on it with less wonder than I expected. I then descended to the lower bed of the river, and seating myself opposite to the centre of the fall, viewed the scene with still and raptured attention.

The vast volume and thick sheets of foam of the purest and most dazzling whiteness, the fast mounting clouds of liquid smoke that diffuse their dews all round, the deep thunders and impetuous motion of the water, are here finely contrasted with the black rocks in their centre, the dark shade and tranquil scenery on each side, and the various tints of bright blue and green, that so eminently distinguish the beautiful Rhine. The river appears agitated from the violence of the fall to a considerable distance, rolling its azure waves rapidly along, fringed, so to speak, with the light and silver foam yet undissolved.

We then crossed the Rhine to view the principal cataract on the Lauffen branch of the cataract, which we first saw from a pavilion of the chateau, and on the very brink of the rock above. It was very noble, in this position, to trace the river raging along its rocky channel for a considerable distance from its fall, and increasing in anger and foam as it went along. Near the cataract its contention with the impeding crags was more violent, and one could see it hurry and dash and whirl about in every possible direction, till, worked up as it were to a paroxysm of fury, it rushed in one volume with incredible swiftness and impetuosity over every obstacle, shaking the rocks and the pavilion above in the power of its wrath. An awe mixed with admiration and terror seized me, when by means of a light scaffolding I approached almost close to the utmost verge of the cataract. The very sublime of waters was here! Above, it mounted with indignant waves of foam, as if it would assail the clouds in its rage: the indistinct abyss below, seemed the boiling cauldron of all the furies. What a whirlpool and whirlwind of water!

As you look at it, your confused soul seems forced along with the thundering cataract, whose impetuous swiftness, far outstripping the ideas, whirls them round in giddy and tremendous transport. Let age come here and be calm! Let pride look on and feel itself annihilated! Let bold presumption hide its head, and shrink blushing and trembling back, with confusion and dismay!

The road from Zurich to Berne is remarkably fine, and the whole country, especially within the last thirty miles of Berne, extremely fertile, abundantly wooded with oaks and firs, and divided into rich vales of mixed pasture and cornland, watered by the Aar. The horizon is closed in towards Berne by a ridge of rocky and woody mountains on the right, which rise up in earnest of more lofty ones to come. No vineyards are seen in this part of Switzerland, and the cottages are far less pretty, comfortable, and picturesque than those about Zurich; but in point of fine cultivation, soft hills, graceful shade, and verdure, equal to any thing I have seen. The inns are good and neat, and the charges not unreasonable. We saw many storks' nests in the roofs of two or three villages about thirty miles from Berne, and these birds are unmolested by the inhabitants from a superstitious idea, of their being lucky and acting the parts of good geniuses, to their hosts and protectors. On the roof of a good-looking inn I remarked a wooden frame, commodiously fixed, and spread over with the first materials used in binding their nests, in hopes of tempting them to choose and favour the house. But, on enquiry, I found the anxious wishes of its owner had hitherto remained ungratified, though the long-legged bird of good omen had chosen, to appearance, less advantageous establishments on the cottages round. I know not whether a family of storks might bring guests to this inn, but assuredly, if it did, they would not eat more trouts from the neighbouring river, on account of the fishermen over their heads.

Berne is beautifully built on a hill, which forms a peninsula, the Aar running from the west and winding round it to the east and south. The banks of the river being high and steep, form two deep and narrow valleys to the north and south, between the town and the graceful hills that rise above it in charming succession of lovely verdure and shade. To the south the river falls over a long weir, and the neat and gay little hanging gardens of the town, rising in terraces one above another, supported by walls to keep up their earth from falling into the river, that rolls rapidly beneath, answer with pleasing variety to the sloping pastures and groves, enlivened on the opposite side with a variety of houses. The horizon to the east is finely bounded by majestic mountains, shining with snow, and crested with glorious helmets of clouds.

Berne is long, but narrow. It is in general well built,

with a greyish stone, and the principal street is above a mile long, wide enough for eight or nine coaches abreast, with a running water through the middle, various fountains and statues, and, in general, good houses. I cannot, with Mr. Coxe, admire the arcades, as they are supported by very heavy masonry (for columns they are not), deformed with buttresses, mean flights of steps in different directions, queer blind doors that jut outwards in the form of garret windows to shoot wood, &c., into the cellars beneath. The arcades themselves are irregular, and so low that, being of a stature above par, I had always the idea of breaking my head against their arches, and felt oppressed by their weight and gloom. The roofs of the houses are also of unequal heights, and project several feet over the windows, in a manner that put me in mind of the old-fashioned pokes to the caps worn by our grandmothers. Yet, on the whole, the street has a noble appearance, though the town is far inferior in beauty and architecture to Bath, with which Mr. Coxe brings it in competition, and not half as large.

Three strange statues excited my curiosity and attention in the streets. One is a Swiss warrior, perhaps William Tell, holding a flag in his right hand, and with a young bear between his legs, standing on its hind paws, and in the act of firing off a gun with its fore ones. Another statue must certainly be meant for the giant Fe Fa Fum, as he is crunching the head of a poor naked infant between his horrid fangs, whilst half a dozen more are hanging about him, to be cracked in turn, and finish his dinner. The third statue is that of a huge bear, clad in armour, and standing up with a champion-like air. In one paw he holds a shield, in the other a flag of triumph; a long sword is girt to his left, and a cutlass to his right side, and he grins dismay through the open and gilded bars of a towering helmet crowned with a gilt ball. Though the Bernites have chosen a bear for their arms, I should not suppose that they would really choose one for their general, and therefore think they may as well leave him in *puris naturalibus* and on his all fours, instead of humanising his savage figure and rendering him ludicrous, instead of formidable, by arming him cap-a-pie— a parody on human nature.

The views from Berne, setting aside the snow mountains that on one side close the perspective, consist of that distinct kind of scenery where the eye is always pleased and never distracted, over which it can wander and on which it can repose with cool attention and calm delight, but where the mind is never warmed into high admiration, nor wound up to rapture.

The walks on the ramparts are charming, well shaded, and command a view of all the hills round. The prospect from the platform of the cathedral is also picturesque, though very far from being one of the finest in Switzerland; and I wonder Mr. Coxe's eyes should be so deceived, after having seen so much of its matchless and magnificent scenery.

The route from Berne to Soleure, for near two leagues, is the same in character as that from Zurich to Berne. The next two present little worth remarking, especially in a country so abounding in all kinds of fine scenery as Switzerland. The two last leagues are very richly featured, and charmingly wooded, and broken into hill and valley, the Aar flowing through the latter with a wide channel. Soleure is situated in the centre of a most fertile vale, with the river running through its faubourg on the south side. The town is small, indifferently built, far inferior in neatness, and with a much less flourishing air than Zurich, Schaffhausen, and Berne. The cathedral, which is built of a beautiful white stone, and has only been finished fourteen years, is a noble edifice, the freshness and sumptuousness of which makes poor Soleure look more insignificant, dirty, and shabby, than it would otherwise appear. The flight of thirty-six steps divided into three ascents, leading to the platform of the cathedral, adds much to the grandeur of its air, as well as two handsome fountains, exactly similar, that stand in the returns of the stone balustrades, with which the flight is adorned and surrounded. The front is very beautiful, but rather overcharged with ornament. The inside of the building would be altogether nobly simple, were it not for the daubs of painting placed over and disgracing all the elegant marble altars, and the vile frescoes, that are meant partially to ornament the ceiling and cupola. The organ is finely placed in a graceful curve at one end, and has a magnificent appearance; the pulpit is the most elegant, though not the most curious and valuable, that I have seen. The ramparts, in my opinion, command at once nobler and more varied views than those at Berne.

To the west, and north-west, the horizon is bounded by Mount Jura, which proudly lifts up its white rocks, shaggy with dark firs, and cries 'Respect me, for I am a child of the Alps.' As he descends towards the vale, a deep curtain of foliage is thrown over his lofty sides, and the aspiring hills lift up their graceful woods of blended oak and firs, to meet his forests and mingle shade with shade. A rank lower, meadows, intermixed with country seats, cottages, sloping gardens and separate groves, offer a new picture to the eye, and to the south-west the rich vale stretches far away, and loftier mounds in grand heaps finish the blue perspective. To the east and south, the river appears winding through the vale, a rich but narrow plain, which is presently closed in by bold hills. These are alternately covered with the noblest woods of firs and oaks that can be imagined, their green foliage of various hues and verdant meadows, stretching between, relieving the eye with their various colours. Behind rise up, in sublime ranks, the first order of Alps, piercing the clouds with a hundred points, and mossy with eternal snow. To the south the river forms a majestic sweep, and the same noble and rich scenery of hills, and woods, and pastures, reach to its very banks.

The inn at Soleure is one of the best I was ever at in any country, and its hostess was particularly obliging. The ladies at Soleure, I observed (for it was Sunday), were dressed in all the elegance and frippery of French *ton*, and with the toss of *ton*, and airs in proportion. But what wonder that Swiss simplicity is less apparent at Soleure, than at Zurich and Berne, when a French ambassador resides there. Even the genteel son of our hostess was dressed in *boue de Paris* silk breeches and stockings, with a tamboured waistcoat, worked ruffles, and an enamelled watch. Ah! Swiss simplicity, thou hast had thy day, and been deservedly vaunted; but one must no longer expect to find thee with all thy integrity and charms in that beautiful and sublime country, except amongst the recesses of the Alps, far from the thronged streets and the frequented vales.

Near Soleure, and in the shady bosom of Mount Jura, we went to see a hermitage, happily placed under the projections of a bold and bare rock, with a tufted top-knot of firs,— another rock of similar height and feature, answering to it, and bending forward as it were to meet a murmuring brook of limpid water, edging the narrow path between them with its winding course. A chapel of different form springs out of each rock, one of which is entered by a bridge thrown lightly over the rivulet, mounting many stone stairs, the other chapel and a few stairs has been laboured out of the hollow bosom of the very rock, by the first hermit who fixed on this pretty solitude, with great patience, and after the toil of twenty-five years. It is of considerable depth, the entrance roomy and lofty, but narrowing and lowering as one approaches what may be denominated the choir. I fear all the fervours of my devotion would not be sufficient to defend me from the humidity of the spongy walls and roof, which are for ever dripping. A little platform before the entrance, which is covered by a portico supported by four light columns, has a very pleasing effect, as well as the bell, which appears at the summit of the rock in a little turret that pierces through the shade. In a cavity in the same rock close by, is an *oratoire*, enclosed by rails, within which are seen three wretched figures of saints reposing on a bank of moss, with a miniature of the new Jerusalem in tawdry toy work, over their heads. A lamp suspended from the roof within, has a pleasing and solemn effect, especially in the evening. A rustic little wooden bridge, with a doorway and a fountain at its entrance, leads across the brook to the hermit's simple dwelling and little paled garden, which are shaded by a few walnut trees. A dog and two hens composed his family, and the companions of his solitary hours. The winding path leading to this sweet retirement, with the deep and solemn shade all round, as well as an *echappée de vue* between the rocks, of a few little verdant and quiet pastures, soon terminated by the rocky and woody heights of Mount Jura, rendered the whole scene very delightful, and perfectly analogous to one's cherished ideas of the romantic tranquillity of a hermit's solitude.

From Soleure to Basle the road lies, for the greater part of the way, through the centre of Mount Jura, which lifts up its grand, white, and finely-shaded rocks as a lofty wall on each side. The entrance to the little valley, where stands the pretty village of Balstal, is very romantic, and the rocks nobly featured. As one goes on, several châteaux are seen most picturesquely situated on the points of rocks, with a deep shade all round. Half a mile from the village, and quite across the pastures of the valley, I walked to see a cascade, which falls in three gushes over a rock to the depth of about sixty feet. The volume of water is not very considerable, but the solitude of the spot, hidden quite from the vale in the very bosom of the mountain, the scenery of shady heights bending over it, and the grand and fantastic form and features of the near-approaching rocks, between which the cascade is seen at some distance, falling from the dark recesses within, while they are so interlaced as quite to hide its falls from the heights above, make the whole a finely-marked and striking picture. I was almost sorry to leave the romantic pass between Mount Jura, rich and beautiful as were the hills and vale that led from it to Basle.

Surely no country in the world is so finely, abundantly, and variously wooded as Switzerland. Basle is much the largest town in Switzerland, not ill-built, but thinly peopled. The Rhine flows most majestically through it with fine sweeps, the noblest of which descends with a vast and profound volume of water. One has only to lament that its natural beautiful colour has been mudded by the turbulent Aar. The houses on each side, forming long curves, have a picturesque appearance, especially those on the south side, which are elevated on a green and shady bank, but in other parts Basle is inferior in situation to Berne, Soleure, or Zurich, as the borders of the river are flatter, and the hills and mountains that appear at a considerable distance, are less finely picturesque and beautiful, than those about the above-mentioned towns.

From Basle, about forty miles north of Soleure, we went to what is called the English garden, nearly five miles distant. There is a chapter of rich German Catholics just by, two of whom have employed the time that lay heavy on their hands, in contriving pleasant walks through a wood that grows on the side of a rocky hill, and ornamenting, without overcharging them, with rustic seats and buildings. Nature has formed three fine caverns in the beautifully shaded rocks, and all possible advantage has been taken of the circumstance. The first is converted into a banqueting-hall, with a platform edged with trees in the front, between the trunks of which, a delightful prospect opens of the opposite hills and neighbouring village and vale. The second is much more fantastic and picturesque, and is pierced by the able and all-various hand of nature, through and through, in several parts, so as to form romantic vistas, and to admit of rough stone stairs leading from the cavern on one side, to that on the other.

The view here, from several well-disposed rustic seats, is more retired, the eye looking down to a little clear lake in the verdant bottom, strictly enclosed by bold hills, which are finely featured and rough with a variety of trees. This cavern is called the Temple of Proserpine, and an image, intended to represent that goddess, is distinguished at the farthest end of the perspective, and through the natural aperture of the rock, by means of a few little lamps, that just admit light enough for one to discern dimly the vaulted roof, and the various angles and objects round, without destroying that pleasing gloom, which takes possession of the imagination, and is so favourable to the place and its title. One approaches the mock goddess by means of a long and steep staircase, that leads up and between the juttings and arches of the rock; but adieu to the delusion one loves, the instant one has a distinct idea of the wretched pasteboard image, that personates the queen of night. Even from below, she appears much less majestic, and less darkly charming than she might do, were the good canons as well acquainted with the queen of hell, as they think they are with their Madonna, the queen of heaven.

On another rock, beautifully tufted and rough with bushes and trees, is an inscription under the arched hollow of one equally picturesque: the figure of a hermit is seen asleep, and a clear stream falls in shining threads over the rock, and murmurs from thence to the valley. A pretty little neat garden, divided into parterres and glowing with flowers, in the front of the grotto, added much to the scenery. From hence you mount by winding stairs between the rocks to the hermitage, which is perfectly well imagined for the dwelling of an anchorite, as it is buried deep in three sides in shade, and open on the other to a partial view of the wood beneath and opposite hills, so that the solitude appears much more perfect than it really is. The outside of the hermitage is entirely covered with the bark of trees, neatly joined together, crowned with rough logs of wood, which themselves form a cross, and which are terminated with another, a bell also hanging from a cross-bar between them. The inside of the cell is extremely neat, furnished amply for a hermit's needs, and ornamented with painted glass windows, the noble arms blazoned on which, the canon could not help pointing out to me with an air, somewhat foreign to the character of the spot, as belonging to his own family. And indeed, to enjoy the ease and luxury of 1,200*l.* per annum in the convent below, each canon must prove his noble descent by sixteen quarterings at least, without the mixture and contamination of plebeian blood. Another little pavilion represents with perfect and pleasing deception a pile of wood, and from its windows a confined but most wild and romantic view is discovered of the little lake, a field or two, and a cottage hemmed in by the lofty and woody hills of different forms, but running in a connected chain quite round.

Descending from hence to the opposite hill, one descries from a winding walk along its shady base, a nobly featured and picturesque château, on the summit above the hermitage, as well as partial peeps at the objects in succession that one had just left, and a beautiful *echappée de vue* to the distant country at the end of the valley. The whole is really laid out with sentiment and taste, and the good canons have the more merit in this, as all the gardens in Switzerland, as well as Germany, France, and Italy, are in the old and unnatural style, with forced terrace after terrace, mince-pie parterres, cropped hedges, Chinese arbours, yews cut into all figures on earth, and under earth, and crowded, according to the state and fortune of the proprietor, with jets d'eau, and temples, and grottoes, and images without number.

But I should not forget in justice, to mention that various spots are dedicated in this pleasing retreat, to the sports of the neighbouring peasants. In one part there is a swing, and near it an alley to play at nine-pins, and a platform for dancing, with benches for the spectators; in others, there is a beam nicely balanced to indulge them in their dashing amusement of see-saw, with four seats at the end of horizontal posts, elevated three feet above ground, and contrived so as, with a little exertion, to whirl swiftly round an upright post which forms their axle. There is also a natural bower formed by the trees, in which are placed tables and benches for the honest rustics to regale on Sundays and fête days with cake, fruit, and wine. Five hundred are sometimes assembled there at a time, and a most picturesque effect it must have, to see them engaged in their various pastimes, or scattered in little groups about the hanging paths. Free access is given them to this sweet retirement on holidays, and they have never been known in the slightest instance to abuse the benevolent indulgence of the Chanoines, who have a manifest and excusable pride in the little Eden they have created within the last eighteen months, and who have been encouraged, by the influx and approbation of numerous travellers, to continue with ardour their improvements, and to extend greatly their original plan. As nature offers herself most temptingly for the exercise of their talents and taste, and the whole glen and shady steeps around belong to them, there is no doubt of their rendering their English garden still more famous, and more worthy the attention of the curious and nice observer.

ROUTE FROM STRASBOURG TO MAYENCE.

FROM Strasbourg to Brenheim the road is very fine, but through a flat country, offering little variety to the eye, though fertile and cultivated with all kinds of common grain, besides quantities of Indian corn, hemp, and potatoes. Lauterbourg, the next post, is a small fortified town belonging to the Bishop of Spire, but with a French garrison of 450 hussars, always kept there by right of treaty. Soon after quitting Lauterbourg we entered a most beautiful wood of mixed oaks and beeches, nineteen miles long and nine broad, belonging to the Bishop of Spire.

The country between Rheinzabern and Germersheim is well cultivated, but flat and mountainous. The latter is a pretty little town, but after leaving it, the country is again similarly featured to Spire. Spire is a free German town, governed by its own magistrates, though the bishop is its nominal head, as he is also of the chapter, consisting of fifty canons, half noble and half of lower birth—the revenues of the former, much exceeding those of the latter: the former also independent in great measure of the bishop. One handsome street of Spire terminated with the cathedral, a noble and spacious building, and attractively simple within, excepting the choir, which is laden with gilding.

Spire has been a large and flourishing town, but has never held up its head since the greatest part of it was burnt by the French, in the reign of Louis XIV., at the end of the last century. They pursued the troops of the Palatine thither, who entrenched themselves in the principal houses, bishop's palace, and churches, where their enemies attacked and utterly defeated them. The ruins of the churches and bishop's palace still offer sad mementoes of the disastrous day. I have rarely seen a town with so melancholy and deserted an air.

From Spire to Manheim the country is little varied, though a few vineyards formed into low espaliers and intermixed alternately with stripes of white poppies, (which are much cultivated in this country,) somewhat varied the cultivation. Here and there also in both days' route, we saw some thriving plantations of tobacco. The country, immediately before we crossed the Rhine to Manheim on a long bridge of boats, was very swampy and ungracious. The city stands on the very borders of the river, which flows majestically with a prodigious volume, the Neckar throwing itself into it just above the town. The Elector's palace, which is a vast and noble edifice, appears above the river and ramparts with a royal air, as one approaches the latter. The town is large, regularly and well built, populous, and strongly fortified, setting aside the mighty barrier which the Rhine forms to protect it from insult on the French side, while the Neckar defends it on the other to the north, so that the town stands on a peninsula, the neck of which is extremely well fortified, and in itself of difficult approach, the ground being very marshy all round. The Elector keeps up a constant garrison of 5,500 men, but has deserted Manheim for Munich since his accession ten years ago to the Electorate of Bavaria.

Manheim consists of twelve streets, cut at right angles by eight, all of an equal breadth, except the principal one, which is wider than the others, though all are nobly wide; and were the houses a stage higher, it would be the most regularly beautiful town perhaps, for its size, in Europe. As it is, few can be compared to it, but since the desertion of its sovereign, it has languished greatly, and is less populous. The collection of paintings in the palace, which fill nine large rooms, is a fine one, especially with respect to those of the best Flemish masters, which are in the highest preservation. But of all the pictures in this gallery, none are so rare, precious, or natural, as two heads of an old man and woman, by Denners,* which when examined through a magnifying glass, seem to live and speak in every feature and every line. For the detail, the minutiæ, the very cunning labour of nature, I did not think it possible that art could have mimicked her with such exact fidelity. Two pictures by Weinix, of a hare and peacock, and other birds, were superior to anything of the kind, both as to nature and exquisite finish, that I ever saw. In their way they are as perfect as those by Denners.

I was much pleased also with a masterly idea of Quintus Bohl's, in a large painting in which Abraham is represented offering up Isaac. The picture has great merit in all respects, particularly the head of Abraham; but I was charmed with the sensibility of the painter, as well as the justness of his conception, in making the father cover the face of his son, in the act of lifting up his hand to spill his blood. In every other painting on the subject—and I have seen many, and by great masters—the face of Isaac is bare, and they have exerted their skill in giving it natural grace, and touching expression and resignation; but how much more powerfully does one feel Bohl's idea. It penetrates immediately to the heart, and shows at once, as plain as words, or, rather, as the living scene could speak, the agonies of the fond father who dreaded lest his rebellious affections should interfere with his perfect obedience to the commands of his God. The idea of Agamemnon's turning away his face from the sacrifice of his daughter is fine; but this of Abraham, the sacrifice of his only darling to the will of heaven, and whose action in covering Isaac's face, expresses at once the extent of his resignation and his tenderness, is sublime.

The Flemish pictures on subjects of common life, and low

* Denners painted in Germany in the earlier part of the 18th century.

and humorous scenes, as well as their perspectives of various buildings and some landscapes, are beautiful; but those, even of the best masters, which attempt to express high and inspired themes in miniature, appeared in my eye, as usual, miserably inferior to their subject; the very polish of their finish has a *faiblesse* in it when applied to such scenes, and injures the expression of their figures. The passionate and sublime have nothing to do with such minutiæ, such exactitude. What is laboriously correct will generally be cold on the side of pathos, and can give one no idea of those rapid emotions, that ardent enthusiasm, which war in the artist's bosom, when he would touch and put in delicious tumult the feelings of others. What has needed infinite precision in the execution, must require too near an inspection, and too close an attention in the observer, to leave room in his soul for the strong emotions and the quick and lively interest which such subjects demand, and should excite. Would a mouse ever excite the strong sensations of the noble, and rouse the passions of admiration and terror, like the lion? Or, rather, would a lion no bigger than a mouse have the same effect as one of its natural size, especially if placed near several of its more majestic kind? The mind supplies bulk, and metamorphoses the pigmy to the giant, it is true, with wonderful facility; yet, rapid as her powers are in this way, while she is employing them the still more rapid flash of first strong impression vanishes, and is supplied by the cold applause of the judgment, which precedes feeling in this case, as it is preceded by it in the other. In scenes of still or every-day life strong feeling has nothing to do, and a sense of the truth to nature is the impression required, and the best tribute of praise. In scenes of low humour there is always a strong trait of the grotesque that helps the effect of miniature figures, and atones for the deficiency of natural bulk. Besides, in one and the other case the finer sensibilities, more delicate feelings, and energetic passions, are out of the question; but in subjects of pathos, where the tender, the noble, the sublime, are required, and where they ought to strike with an electrical shock at the first *coup d'œil*, the utmost force of the miniature falls far short of our conceptions, and will be regarded at best with still admiration.

For these reasons the best Flemish painters always appear, in my eye, to have thrown away their labour and sacrificed their genius in their miniatures of high and noble subjects; and admire their fine conceptions, natural colouring, and exquisite finish as one will, the heart always murmurs in secret that it is a *coup manqué*—that the pretty is substituted for the beautiful, the correct for the daring, delicacy for spirit, precision for grandeur, and nothing for the sublime. In short, my mind feels precisely the difference that it has always felt between the best Liliputian actors in buskins and grown men and women in the same heroics. And let this serve to explain my idea, if others find it contrary to theirs, on the subject. I love to examine some things in detail; but when required to do so by others, cry, a sun should not be like the stars, fly out into impatience, see nothing properly, and feel not at all.

The library is worth seeing for the beautiful arrangement of the books, and elegant lightness of the noble room which contains them, otherwise I should not have visited it; for what signifies my being told on such occasions that there are forty or fifty or a hundred thousand volumes, in I know not how many languages, on I know not how many subjects, and in a thousand various styles. One can only look at the outside of them, and of the binding of books, however rich or gay, I have never been enamoured; and what is it to see half a dozen leaves of half a dozen musty (though perhaps precious) manuscripts, turned hastily whilst the librarian tells you that this is Persian, that

Arabic, and the other 1,000 years old? Much one is the wiser or better for such knowledge. Perhaps, too, on such occasions my *amour propre* is mortified at knowing itself surrounded with so much entertaining, curious, and useful literature, which it would not comprehend, even had it time to examine the volumes that contain it; and when the *amour propre* is dissatisfied, all the world knows that everything goes wrong. For these manifest causes, I never go to see libraries, except there be somewhat else in them worth visiting besides books.

Let me not forget to mention the Cabinet of treasures, and those of Natural History. The first is extremely precious, consisting of all kinds of ancient cups, vases, dishes, vessels, and many other articles in gold and silver, curiously embossed agate, lapis lazuli, alabaster; cabinets of amber, tortoise-shell, and ivory, many of them set with precious stones; curious old delf and porcelain, and, above all, one large glass case entirely filled with a great number of vases, cups, dishes, &c., of rock crystal of various colours, amongst which are some of black crystal (the rarest of all kinds), the finest known. This crystal apparatus, is always sent to Frankfort, to serve at the Emperor's table, the day of his coronation. The cabinets of natural history contain specimens of every kind of marble, granite, agate, porphyry, and a great variety of petrifactions of wood, ammonites, shell-fish, serpents, &c.; a collection of beautiful shells, specimens of all kinds of minerals, and the *lusus naturæ* found in different mines; birds and beasts preserved with their natural hair, attitude, and plumage, and fish, serpents, &c. But as to the latter articles, they appeared trifling after those of Sir Ashton Cevers' admirable museum, and some others we had seen in France and Italy. These cabinets are all most judiciously arranged, and with taste as well as order. They are all on the ground floor of the palace, which, after that of

Versailles, is the largest and has the noblest air of any I have seen.

Besides the public Mall through the centre of the principal street in Manheim, there are four handsome 'Places,' well shaded with plane trees. The walk round the ramparts is also pleasantly shaded, well kept up, and commands various views of the river and adjacent country. But I should have mentioned a group of celebrated statues which ornament a fountain in the middle of the great 'Place,' and which represent a flying Mercury, who places the figure of a city, under the form of a beautiful woman crowned with battlements, between the river gods of the Rhine and Neckar. It is well imagined, and there is some spirit in the execution; but what in the name of wonder has Mercury to do with the sun (a greater god than himself in heathen mythology) fastened to a string round his wrist, and glittering with a blubber face and pert gingerbread air, in the beams of the real lamp of day? Did he force him down from his flaming chariot, *nolens volens*, merely to give him a nearer peep at his new hobby-horse? But unluckily the fountains are without water.

In mentioning the destruction — the wanton and malicious destruction — of Manheim and Spire by the French troops, in 1688, I should have observed that those two cities, as well as Heidelberg, Frankenstahl, Worms, and Oppenheim were burnt the same day — a cold-blooded plan of vengeance, unworthy of a nation that piques itself on its urbanity, humanity, and generosity of spirit. It is easy to see that the barbarous deed still rankles in the breast of the Germans, and that it will be long ere it is forgiven. 'Vous avez une jolie ville,' said I to the aubergiste at Spire, as I descended from the carriage. 'Ah, monsieur, elle l'était, mais les François l'ont ruinée.' 'Votre ville de Manheim est superbe,' said I to my host there. 'Oui, monsieur, les François n'auraient pas si beau jeu, fortifiée, comme elle est actuellement, en cas qu'ils tentassent de la brûler comme ils le firent autrefois. Mais, monsieur,' added he with a sigh, 'il faut voir les ruines qu'ils ont laissés derrière leurs pas à Spire, Oppenheim, Worms, et Frankestahl. Oh! le beau château qu'ils détruirent à Heidelbourg. Il faut bien voir ça pour détester leur malice, et apprécier le tort qu'ils ont fait à notre souverain.' So much for Manheim.

From Manheim to Worms the road is unentertaining. Between them we passed through a pretty little town, where the Electress Palatine has an elegant summer palace, with extensive and pleasant gardens, laid out in a formal style, though with abundant shade. Worms is an old and ill-built town, a considerable part of which still mourns in ruins the fury of the French. Near Oppenheim the view is more varied, the eye looking across the Rhine to fine woods on the opposite bank, with a background of distant mountains. Oppenheim is commandingly situated on the slope of a hill, covered with vineyards, that reaches to the river. Its conspicuous ruins, recall more powerfully to the mind than ever, the cold-blooded vengeance of France. The country is richly cultivated, especially with vineyards, which produce the most delicious Rhenish, between Oppenheim and Mayence, and less flat than what we had seen on the preceding days.

Mayence is very old and ill-built, and the streets, remarkably narrow and gloomy, run partly on a hill and partly on a flat, close to the Rhine. Though well fortified, being only defended by dry ditches, under and between the ramparts on the higher ground, and in some degree commanded by a height to the south-east, it is not so strong as Manheim. It is, however, a large, populous, and very flourishing town, carrying on a considerable commerce by the Rhine with the Low Countries. One can easily distinguish that the Roman Catholic is its predominant eligion, by the multitude of its churches, two of the largest of which stand so close together, that it seems almost possible to reach from one to the other.

The cathedral is a large and lofty edifice, with a tribune at each end of the great nave, of a semicircular form, which has a singular and good effect. The ornaments are in general heavy, tawdry, and in bad taste; but there are some tolerable pieces of sculpture over several of the altars, representing, in miniature figures, stories taken from Holy Writ; and the sculpture of the panels of the pulpit has more merit than the rest, each representing a part of our Divine Teacher's benevolent command to feed the hungry, clothe the naked, free the prisoner, &c. The outside of the church is spoiled by being daubed to the very top, of its Gothic tower and steeple, with a vile colouring like dingy bricks.* The ancient part of the elector's palace, on the banks of the river, which is built in the form of a fort, is blazoned with the same glaring wash, and looks like an old woman of eighty, painted with brickdust up to her eyes. A long bridge of boats extends across the Rhine from Mayence to a large and handsome village opposite, which forms a kind of suburb to the town. There is just such another to enter Manheim from the side of France. Mayence is the first ecclesiastical electorate, and its elector is also its Archbishop and Bishop of Worms.

For about five hours the southern banks of the river, presented rather a flat, in front cultivated with corn, and backed by woody hills; but scarcely a single village appeared to animate the scene. On the German side, the northern slopes were covered with vineyards, interspersed here and there with corn; and a quick succession of towns and villages at the river's edge, rendered the scene very gay and animated. The Rhine then formed a noble bay to the eye, so surrounded

* This noble pile of building is now in the course of complete restoration. Ed.

by high and rocky banks, differently broken and with different projections, that it was difficult to discover the passage between them even when near it. And here began the grand and romantic scenery, which seemed to grow more interesting every moment. As we advanced between the rocky mounds, the windings of the majestic river between them, formed so many distinct bays, but variously shaped, and narrower or broader according to the advancing or receding of the bold shores.

The northern steeps showed terrace above terrace of vines, teeming with the precious fruit, the wine of which is so famed under the names of Rhenish and old Hock; and it was at once curious and picturesque, to see how the indefatigable hand of industry had cultivated every little spot of earth, and led the vines, winding and wantoning round the bare crags that refused to be fertilised, and the frowning sterility of which added new charms to the scene: a tuft of bushes or a light feathering of trees on the highest summits, also added their quota to the picture. The southern declivities were rich with intermixed patches of corn, and sometimes of vines, where the perpendicular ridges, offered one way a favourable aspect for the purpose. Both sides swarmed with the most picturesque and cheerful-looking towns and villages, with the ruins of ancient castles, towering on the point of some advanced rock almost above every one of them, and casting melancholy but interesting looks at each other from the opposite steeps. The ruined towers and the long sweep of a wall of one, served to shelter a little vineyard on the south bank, from the bitter blasts of the north and north-west, and attentive industry had taken advantage of the favourable circumstance, and thus planted the purple fruit of joy and gladness, in the very bosom of pensive ruin, which encircles and shelters them with her decayed and weatherbeaten arms, and offers the singular image of barrenness and destruction, serving as the nursing mother and guardian, to fertility and plenty. In another bay a bold castle, of picturesque features and majestic size, seemed to start up haughtily from the very midst of the river, and to cry from its rocky base and lofty battlements, 'I stand yet, though many are fallen; I yet am strong and dauntless, and the owl and the bat sing their sad and nightly orgies, from the ivied walls and crumbling towers of my fellows all round.' This château, which is large and in perfect repair, was formerly erected by a prince of Manheim, and still belongs to the Elector Palatine. It is built on a rock in the bosom of a river, and occupies so perfectly its whole space, the crags having been beaten away, to form a smooth and circular foundation of masonry of the body of the rock, that it appears as if springing at once from the bed of the river without a previous base. But if it appears formidable without, it is far from being so within, its inhabitants being a number of invalid soldiers, to whom the Elector has given this singular asylum, with a pension for their support, and whose age and infirmities would little enable them to defend their fortress, proud and formidable as is its air.

We stopped to pass the night at the beautiful little town of St. Goar, which runs along the water's edge, with every house charmingly neat, and almost every one painted or washed of a different colour. The neat inn is kept by three pretty hostesses, sisters, who have had their black eyes praised so much, that they think it impossible to charge travellers too high for the felicity of looking at them; but as Amelia was not of the sex, and too wise to be fascinated by their sweet looks and sugared words, she had the *malhonnêteté* to assure mademoiselle, the principal manager, that she was a Jew and an impostor. At St. Goar the Rhine again forms a noble basin, and I cannot forbear mentioning its surrounding scenery.

On the south bank stands the above town, domineered in a

most picturesque manner by the fortress of Rheinfels, built on a shaded and cultivated rock above it to the left. Beyond it, to the right, a number of little neat gardens, with pretty summer-houses and little pavilions, run along the shore; and behind the broken steeps rise boldly, finely shaded, and smiling here and there, with the tender verdure of tufted vineyards turned towards the east. Opposite, three separate mounts swell up conically, planted with terraces of vines between the jutting rocks, and a light fringe of wood running round their summits, and down their ridgy sides. Between the first two a little town was nestled in the prettiest manner imaginable, overlooked by the ruins of a château with a round tower that has almost escaped the ravages of time, and rises up high above the mouldering battlements. Farther on along the river's edge, appears here a cluster of cottages, and there four or five neat houses sprinkled along the bank, with a long walk of trees and cloth bleaching under them; and beyond these again a beautiful clump of trees seems to grow out of the water, other cultivated and woody steeps broken from each other, and showing deep and shady dells between, appearing to close round the gulf beyond, with a town peeping out from behind one of them, and another ruin appearing perched high above it, on its detached rock.

Such are the general features of the romantic view; but its particular combinations, its nice and various shadings, its thousand discriminate though similar features, escape the imperfect powers of language, and only remain delineated with sweet confusion on the heart.

St. Goar belongs to the Landgrave of Hesse Cassel, who keeps a garrison in the château of Rheinfels, at the foot of whose picturesque mount, is a handsome building which serves as barracks, pretty gardens running from them quite to the town. Before our arrival at St. Goar we passed by a little town and small territory, belonging to the Elector of Treves, and soon after quitting our lodging, we again rowed chiefly between his possessions on each side, and which continued two leagues beyond Coblentz, about six leagues in the whole from St. Goar. A beautiful village on the German side, I was informed, belonged jointly to the Electors of Treves, Palatine, and Cologne.

About two leagues and a half from St. Goar the hills on the French side, beautifully clothed with pastures and scattered shade, thin groves running along the shore, and mixing with the villages; a bolder bank on the other side cultivated as before with vines, but with a lovely village embosomed in trees on the brink of the river. Oh, the fog! the fog! out upon it; out upon it!

The fog was sufficiently dissipated to see a change of scene from the elbowing of the river, the declivities on the French side being covered with vines wherever nature will admit of it, while the German presents villages embosomed in groves, the eye just distinguishing enough of the steeps behind, through the fleeting mist, to regret that it cannot discover them more perfectly. The view then changes on the German side to woody hills, which come down close to the water, with vineyards on their slopes, that are turned towards the south-east; the French side, presenting a succession of beautiful hills that fall back behind villages, varied with trees in the foreground, and the fronts of which are cultivated with vineyards, intermixed with underwood, a nobler and more graceful shade running down low upon their brows and covering their sides, broken here and there with cornfields where their exposition is not favourable to the grape. Soon after, a proud rock lifts itself up, precipitate and rugged, set with patches of vines hanging between its crags, crowned with a strong château in good repair, and with a picturesque village belonging to Hesse Cassel at its foot. The view here on each side is varied and striking; hill succeeding hill, in charming order, clothed with wood or with vineyards, tufted groves, and orchards, cultivated with various roots and grain in the foreground, and extending their riches to the river's brink.

Nearer Coblentz we met with similar scenery, but charmingly varied, the vines being more abundant on either side, richly intermixed with wood and corn, the hills on the left coming down quite to the water, and on the right falling back behind a fertile and lovely plain, of various culture and graceful shade. The territories of Cassel, Mayence, Treves, and Cologne are here intermixed, as if contending for the possession of so beautiful and fruitful a country. We touched at the last village belonging, in this direction, to Mayence. The French shore is very beautiful, rich, and charmingly varied and broken, a chain of hills swelling down to the river, with a most picturesque village, and the ruins of a château, under and on the rocky side of one of them, the ruins of another answering to it on the point of a hill opposite. A little church, with a steeple worth particular remark, stands on the French side, on a detached bank above the village, with a tuft of trees behind, and a little semicircular vineyard before it, by way of a churchyard. The banks of the river present in great measure similar features, and is equally beautiful, almost as far as Coblentz, though with fewer vines, and more corn on the hills to the right, and er woods on either hand. Just before our arrival at Coblentz, six leagues from Goar, the plain vanished from the left, and seemed to have crossed over to the right, reaching from thence to the town without any background of hills, those on the German side, being also diminished to a sloping bank covered with vines.

Coblentz is a considerable town and the residence of the Elector of Treves, who has almost finished an elegant new palace on the bank of the river. The view of the town on the Cologne side is very beautiful, with a handsome stone bridge thrown over the Moselle, which enters the Rhine just at Coblentz. But a suburb opposite, across the river, is almost wholly built of handsome houses — the Elector's old palace, where he yet resides, appearing preeminent amongst them. A bold and rugged rock rises immediately behind, crowned with a large and ancient castle where a garrison is kept* — its various works, detached buildings, and road running round and winding about the rock.

The shore on each side, as one goes on, is populous, but quite flat and monotonous; on the left rises a chain of hills tufted with trees, and cultivated with vines rising up on the right. Many patches of corn appear as we advance, intermingled with the wood and vines on the right hand, the chain of hills falling farther back, and taking a larger sweep round the fertile plain between them and the river. The left bank was still, flat, and uninteresting. Two picturesque villages spread along the opposite banks, with rival but various charms; that on the right boasting two houses of stately and elegant appearance, which it holds out in front with a proud air, while that on the left modestly shows a long line of simple cottages with chequered faces, and their neat and unassuming little church in the centre, as if the guardian of their humility and the preserver of their peace. Alas! the enchanting scenes are fled, and monotonous flatness reigns on either hand.

[Dr. Whalley's journal continues from this point to Bonn, minutely noting down the intermediate scenery of the Rhine, evidently as memoranda for his own use, and without any mention of names, which renders its perusal uninteresting to the general reader, acquainted as many are, with all the features of this now so much visited and well-known river. We must, therefore, omit further mention of it till he arrives at Cologne.]

* Now the famous fortress of Ehrenbreitstein.

Cologne is a very large, but gloomy and ancient-looking city, founded by Agrippina. It carries on a great commerce with the Low Countries in the commodities of lace, tobacco, and wine; and a great quantity of the latter is also exported to Russia, and other countries. The cathedral is a superb Gothic edifice, but unfinished, owing, as it is said, to a quarrel which a certain Archbishop of Cologne, named Arimbert, had with the citizens on account of a tax which he attempted to charge them with, and which they refused to pay. In the course of the contest, arms were taken up by both parties, and the Archbishop was finally driven from the city, about the beginning of the fifteenth century, since which period no archbishop has ever made Cologne his residence; the Electors having always lived at Bonn, where they have a noble palace, or at an elegant country palace about three leagues from Cologne. After the expulsion of Arimbert, the building of the cathedral was discontinued, to the disgrace of the city.

Behind the tribune of the cathedral, is seen the famous tomb of the Three Kings, enclosed in an elegant little chapel of black and white marble. It is a most exquisite, as well as precious piece of workmanship; its height in front is nine feet, the upper part is gold and the lower silver, forming two stages, each of which is adorned quite round the tomb, with embossed human figures, miniature full length, in silver. The front is most richly and elegantly adorned with enameled columns, various precious stones of a considerable size, and beautiful cameos and intaglios of great value. Within are seen the three skulls of the supposed kings, arranged in a line, with each a gold crown upon its polished scalp set with jewels, and each with an elegant aigrette of diamonds in front. Their history, it is said, is this: that they were brought by some Italian pilgrim of high quality from the Holy Land, and deposited in a convent at Milan, not, in fact, as the relics of three kings, but three famous martyrs to religion in the early ages of Christianity. The odour of their saintly reputation, drew immense crowds of adorers, and consequently numberless offerings to the convent. Some time after, Milan was besieged by the Emperor Ferdinand the Second, whose army was chiefly commanded by the Bishop of Cologne. Sorely pressed, the abbess of the above convent, who was sister to the Governor of Milan, treated secretly with the Emperor and Bishop, and, on condition of safety for her brother and the inhabitants, promised to deliver the city and three sacred and, through superstition, most valuable skulls, which she had concealed in a place known only to herself, into their hands. The offer in those days was too tempting to be refused; the conditions were accepted and fulfilled, and the inestimable relics given to the bishop as a reward for his services. Returning to Cologne about the end of the twelfth century, he set about erecting the present cathedral, on purpose to give them a shrine worthy of their sanctity, but the noble edifice was never completed, as I have before observed, owing to the quarrels of his successor with the citizens. About forty years afterwards the greatest part of the inside, however, was perfected; and about 400 years since, the celebrated and most precious shrine, where the holy skulls now repose in state, was made from the rich offerings that had been presented to them by bigot zeal, amongst which those of a king of Portugal stood foremost in value. Such is the tale of the *Tombeau des Trois Rois*, though, remember, I do not entirely vouch for its truth.

The road from Cologne to Dusseldorf is very bad, consisting of a deep sand the whole way, that must, after heavy rains, be in some parts almost impassable; the country is also, in general, flat and ill cultivated, though of pleasanter appearance and more fertile. Near Dusseldorf there are great patches of the black corn, which, when in flower, has a beautiful effect, being intermingled with the other corn, potatoes, &c. Dusseldorf is rather a large and very handsome town, situated on a bank over the Rhine, and very well fortified. Just without the gates of the town, to the north, there is a small palace belonging to the Elector, with a spacious garden prettily laid out in walls, and a variety of winding walks, well shaded with different trees and shrubs, which is kept open for the amusement of the inhabitants, Dusseldorf being wholly abandoned by the Elector since his accession to Bavaria, to the great regret and loss of his more ancient subjects. As strongly fortified, however, as the town appears to be, and in fact is, in the last war in Germany, about twenty-four years since, it was surrendered to Prince Ferdinand, after a siege of three days, by a cowardly governor, who was seized with a panic at two or three bombs falling into the town and burning some of the houses.

All the world has heard of the famous gallery of paintings in the palace of Dusseldorf; they were sent away to Manheim on the attack by the Hanoverians and English, but restored to the town after the peace—the Elector John William, *avant predecesseur* of the present sovereign, who collected them about eighty years since, having forbidden their removal from Dusseldorf by his testament, so that when the present Elector wished to take them to his palace of Manheim, a few years since, the Regency of Dusseldorf remonstrated warmly against it, and the scheme proved abortive. Indeed, it is but just to leave them in their ancient quarters, as they draw a concourse of strangers from all parts of Europe to the town, and in some measure make amends for the desertion of its sovereign. The collection of paintings is certainly very fine, though altogether less interesting than those in the gallery at Florence. The collection of Rubens' works is perhaps the finest single one in

Europe. The last room in the gallery is adorned with no less than forty-six capital paintings by that great master, amongst which a group of naked boys with a burden of various fruits, a Dying Seneca, a Virgin and Child in a large and exquisite garland of flowers, sustained by eleven naked boys as large as life, (the flowers by the famous Brughel,) the Nativity of Christ, the Fall of the Rebellious Angels into Hell, with Michael launching thunderbolts at them from above, the Martyrdom of St. Lawrence, a Battle of the Amazons, Samson seized by Philistines after having lost his hair in the lap of the treacherous Delilah, Rape of the Two Sisters by Castor and Pollux, a Drunken Silenus with Bacchanals, and a Hero crowned by Glory, whom he embraces, appeared the finest in my eyes, or at least the most striking. In the other rooms the five wise and five foolish Virgins, by Schalken; a Christ scourged, (by the same painter,) as large as life, in which our Saviour's countenance is highly expressive of divine meekness, resignation, and patience; Susanna and the Elders, a St. Sebastian, and a half-length portrait of himself, about twenty-two or three years old, with the head of inexpressible beauty and grace, by Vandyke; the Appearance of Christ after his resurrection to Mary Magdalene, by Barrocci; the Descent from the Cross, and portraits of himself and father, by Lucca Giordano; a Holy Family, by Andrea del Sarto; ditto, very fine, by Cesaro Stroccacino; Sarah giving Hagar to Abraham; Christ arguing when a Child with the Doctors in the Temple, above a dozen other Scripture stories equally fine by Vanderwerf; two admirable portraits by Rembrandt; Death of Dido by Guercino; Antiope and Jupiter, and a Holy Family, by Vandyke; two glorious landscapes by Millet; several highly natural and finished pieces by Dowe; some exquisite fruit and flower-pieces by the best Dutch painters in that style; most masterly ones of dead game by

Snyders, Füt, and Weinix; and St. John in the Wilderness by Raphael, struck me the most; and I always speak and judge, as to what immediately regards my senses, after my own feelings, though perhaps many pictures more highly valued by connoisseurs, than some of those I have noted, have been unmentioned by me.

The famous St. John in the Wilderness, by Raphael, is, in age as well as attitude and action, different from the similar and celebrated ones in the Palais Royal at Paris, and gallery at Florence, and it is difficult to determine which is the most interesting and expressive of genius; the former with his eyes closed, and sitting on the edge of a fountain, expresses in his countenance the inspired reveries of a soul touched and rapt to heaven: the man is formed here with nervous and manly beauty. The other represents a youth of fourteen or fifteen, with all the fire and sublime wildness of inspiration in his eyes, flowing hair, and the elastic spring of every limb and feature, joined to exquisite sweetness, innocence, and simplicity, but I feel that this description decides for my taste in favour of the latter, though I scarcely perceived it before. My admiration, however, of the divine painter's high and just conceptions and wonderful execution, must always remain in equipoise between these the first of his works. I could not help regretting, however, a clear perspective of the busy world, which appears in that at Dusseldorf, and which seems out of character with the inspired musings of St. John in the Wilderness. Am I right? Methought all should have been darkly shaded and expressive of solitude and silence, round the almost naked figure of the divine harbinger of Christ. In the other two paintings the solitude is perfect, yet after all, perhaps, if there is more of the fire of genius in them, there is more of the energy of thought in their glorious rival. It would be difficult to decide which is the most sublime.

From Dusseldorf to Juliers the route is uninteresting, through an open country, cultivated with all kinds of grain, with here and there a village embosomed in trees, that had a pretty effect enough. The road, as before, a heavy sand. Juliers is a most wretched dismal-looking old town, with regular fortifications, and a citadel which, I suppose, would be capable of little resistance in time of need, as they are commanded by a high ground on one side.

From Juliers to Aix la Chapelle the road is better; and on approaching the latter the country becomes more rich and pleasing. The situation of Aix la Chapelle is advantageous, on an easy eminence that overlooks a most fertile vale, and with a cultivated hill rising directly behind it. The town is rather large, populous, and flourishing: its famous hot baths drawing a concourse of strangers thither, and carrying on otherwise a considerable commerce with cloth and needles, the latter of which are much esteemed. But it is an ill built and dirty place, full of ditches and dunghills, and of course stinks, of all kinds. It is a free imperial town, governed by its proper burgomaster and magistrates, in times of concord; but the gentlemen citizens of Aix have followed the example of the Genevans, and some other little states, and made such a hubbub and pother, the last two months, about their liberty and rights, that it is ten to one but they tempt some one of their powerful neighbours in the end to interfere in their petty quarrels, and deprive them of both. On the last day of annual election of a burgomaster, the bourgeois and populace broke into the Council-house, and kicked the old burgomaster, who, they pretend, had plotted to continue himself in office for life, and destroy their rights of election. They kicked his excellentissimoship, I say, downstairs, and all his privy councillors after him, bruising many terribly, and breaking the arm and leg of one, who died a few days after. The two parties had many obstinate battles, with some bloodshed and broken limbs, but without murder, for many successive nights; but the new party, as they dub themselves, at last obtained the complete mastery over their enemies, and drove all the heads of them, as well as the usual military under their command, from the town.

Since that time the citizens mount guard with all due form and solemnity, though not with the most soldier-like air and grace in the world, each street taking its turn to protect the town. The disgraced and well pommelled burgomaster and councillors, have retired to a village about half a league from the town, where they consult together on the means to reinstate themselves in their credit and authority; and for that purpose have applied to the Emperor for assistance. Woe be to the citizens if his sacred and imperial Majesty interferes! As to Messieurs the Burgomaster and Councillors, they will regret little the loss of their constitution and independency, judging according to the usual temper and rancours of us poor little mortals, so that they can usurp the chief sway under the protecting wing of the imperial eagle, and revenge themselves on the insolent and turbulent populace. Was it not the same at Geneva a few years since? And, talk as their grand and *petit* council may, is not their independence lost as a republic; and do they not behind the curtain (sometimes even before it) follow the behests of the Grand Monarque? In such frays, however, what the powerful and great call, with so much scorn and nonchalance, *la canaille*, is sure to suffer, when in the right, as if they were in the wrong; so different are right and might.

The road from Aix to Liège is in general very bad, and most infamous through a part of the territory of the Prince Bishop of Liège, who looks down with contempt, from his elegant palace on its high and pleasant hill, on distressed travellers that are sweating and floundering through his mud-holes, and thinks little about their frights and cares, whilst they pay turnpike at every corner to his myrmidons, for breaking their limbs and endangering their lives in order to arrive at his capital. Liège is a large, populous, and flourishing town, surrounded by a little river, which also divides it with two of its branches into three parts, and the houses appeared handsome, that followed the curve of one of them. In the valley, immediately under the walls of the town, there are abundance of hops, and the slopes of the hills that rise above it on the other side, are covered with vines, so that the liquors of Bacchus and Ceres contend for the pre-eminence to gladden the heart of man, and make him of a joyful countenance, in this little state. The latter, however, gained a complete victory as we passed onwards to St. Tron, the last town in the conscientious bishop's empire; and grain of every kind, as well as barley, took the place wholly of the vineyards, which had still appeared by patches basking in the south sun, or at least laying open their tufted bosoms, to invite his prolific beams as far as Liège. About that town, however, there are more pastures than corn-fields, and the small inclosures all round, as well as the face of the country, divided into gentle hills and soft and verdant vales, reminded me perfectly of the beautiful landscapes in the finest parts of Somersetshire and Devon.

From St. Tron to Tirlemont, all was an open corn country again. The latter town is the first, on this side, that belongs to the Emperor, and is pretty considerable, though not worth remark for its beauty or commerce. The same kind of country, though more richly cultivated, attended us to Louvain, which is a much more considerable and handsome place than Tirlemont, and the town hall* of which struck me as one of the most beautiful Gothic struc-

* This beautiful building has recently, with all its rich sculptures, been perfectly restored, and now presents probably the finest specimen of domestic Gothic architecture which exists.

tures I ever saw. The road from Liège to Malines is a broad and good *pavé*, but from Louvain to the latter singularly fine; and for three parts of the way so straight, running between an avenue of oaks, that the high tower of the cathedral at Malines, appears at the termination of the vista, the whole three leagues, as if inviting you to it, and guiding you on your way.

FUGITIVE PIECES.

LINES ADDRESSED TO MRS. WHALLEY, BY HER HUSBAND, JAN. 6, 1775, THE FIRST ANNIVERSARY OF THEIR WEDDING-DAY.

All hail to thee, bright ruler of the day!
May every cloud fleet from thy fervent ray,
And may thy course triumphant, on this morn,
Make glad the earth, and heaven itself adorn!
Far be remov'd each sorrowing sigh, and far
Each jealous scowl and frown, each brow of care.
Nor thou, dread Anger, show thy scarlet face,
Nor Doubt, nor Envy, dare pollute this place.
But Mirth and Joy, and Confidence and Peace,
Be *ye* all present on a day like this!
Thus Love invokes; and let it be thy care,
O honour'd Hymen! to indulge the prayer;
Since on a sister day, and sister hour,
Parent of chaste desires! thy fav'ring power
First pointed out the certain path to rest,
Beguil'd my pains, and calm'd my tortur'd breast.
For whilom, in my bosom pallid Care,
And languid Sickness,* beckon'd to Despair;
Thought, lost in pensiveness, there held her sway,
And jealous doubtings drank my life away,
Disease triumphant totter'd in the van,
With constant Anguish, squalid, spare, and wan;

* The dangerous illness to which Dr. Whalley alludes was occasioned by a fall from his horse, causing concussion of the brain.

From her swoln eye still dropp'd the scalding tear:
Weakness was at her side, and in the rear
Sat Watchfulness and Woe; from off his stand,
The horrid dart pois'd in his wither'd hand,
In act to strike, appear'd the monster Death,
And grimly smil'd upon his prey beneath;
But smil'd in vain: Eliza saw my need,
And flew to save me with an angel's speed;
Kindly she spake; Despair conceal'd his head,
And every jealous fear and doubting fled:
Before her soothings Sorrow sank away,
And with her smiles my soul rehail'd the day.
Sick as I was, she took me to her breast,
Hush'd every sigh, and lull'd my cares to rest:
No more my mind sat brooding o'er its woe,
No more my heart all comfort would forego;
Peace once again outspread her balmy wing,
And jocund Pleasure put forth buds of spring;
Soft Sleep his downy pinions light spread o'er
The bed, where Watchfulness had toss'd before;
And streaks of ruddy health began to break
Through the sad pale, that sallow'd my sunk check.
Death fled appall'd at that detested sight,
And with him fled the gloomy shades of night.
O thou! whose generous unexampled love,
Did all these evils and far more remove,
How shall my heart speak on that happy morn,
In which my blessings seem to be re-born!
From thy dear hand I date my life; from thee
My health, my peace, my independency!
O blest, most blest above the sons of men!
How shall my feelings breathe along my pen,
When my full soul its gratitude would speak,
Or tell thy virtues? Language is too weak,

To give the one or other equal fire,
Poor is my pen, but potent my desire!
Yet to be dumb, when gratitude, when love,
When every generous impulse that can move
The throbbing heart, demand the debt of praise,
Would speak that heart still colder than my lays;
And such I know is thy humility,
That still the wish to please, will pleasure thee.
Grace, then, with smiles, this tribute of my pen,
Since love, and love alone, indites the strain!
O dearer, than the dearest terms of life,
My cheerful kind companion, friend, and wife!
Thy converse sweet this spark of life endears,
And smoothes my passage through this vale of tears.
Sweet is thy temper, sweeter far thy mind;
To every softness, every grace inclin'd.
Complacent, humble, tender, meek, and good,
By thee no wiles were ever understood;
On thy dear brow enthron'd we always see,
Mild sense, chaste mirth, and sweet simplicity;
The govern'd passions, and the temper'd smile,
And all the serpent's wit — without his guile.
Still candid, gentle, generous are thy ways,
Still kind, still prudent, past the words of praise!
Still is thy heart alive to every woe;
Still has thine eye the tear humane to flow;
Transcendent still thou art, in earthly love,
Transcendent still thy faith in God above.
O may that Being, whose almighty will
Best pleased thou art at all times to fulfil,
Long, long, preserve thy precious life, and please
Thy health, thy joys, thy comforts to increase!
Oft may'st thou hail this blest returning morn,
And may thy virtues long the earth adorn!

And when shall come, as sure will come, the day
That frees thy spirit from surrounding clay,
Grant, O All Merciful! that from its bands,
Its passage may be easy to thy hands!
O my Eliza! best of womankind,
Pardon, if here my fond, my faltering mind,
Sickens, and weakly turns, distrest, aside
At that dread thought, which Faith and Hope deride.
And well may they deride; since souls so fine,
So free from every spot and stain as thine,
Look far beyond this world for happiness,
And in the realms above expect their bliss.
Ah! happiest far of all, that hour of fate
When souls like thine no more their freedom wait!
Glowing with fervent love, and hope, and faith,
How will thy spirit scorn the bed of death!
How will she pant for that immortal joy,
Which ne'er will perish, and can never cloy!
How joyful will she seek her blest abode!
For pure she is, and meet to dwell with God.

BATH-EASTON VASE.

LADY MILLER.

Her 'Vase' and its objects are thus alluded to by Horace Walpole: 'They hold a Parnassus fair every Thursday, give out rhymes and themes; and all the flux of quality in Bath contend for the prizes. A Roman vase, dressed with pink ribbons and myrtles, receives the poetry, which is drawn out every festival. Six judges of these Olympic games retire, and select the brightest compositions, which the respective successful ten candidates acknowledge, kneel to Mrs.

Calliope (Miller), kiss her fair hand, and are crowned by it with myrtle. You may think this a fiction or exaggeration. Be dumb, unbelievers! The collection is printed, published,*—yes, on my faith, there are "bouts rimés" on a buttered muffin, by her Grace the Duchess of Northumberland,' &c.

The following are taken promiscuously from among many pieces headed 'Prize Poems at Bath-Easton.'

ON A HOBBY HORSE.

'On bards' immortal provender
The Nag surviveth still.'

THUS saith a wag of former times,
And you will readily agree,
That what by such a wag is said,
May as a motto serve for me.

But he did write of Pegasus,
That proud and antiquated steed,
Which muses and their paramours
Alone can mount, and ride full speed.

Whilst I, though wanting much his wit,
Yet praise a horse of mightier graces,
That prances with all human kind,
With various mien and various paces.

A greater necromancer, too,
I well this hobby-horse may call,
Than that rare nag at Westminster,
Who lives and conjures in a stall.

* Four volumes were published: the first in 1775, which has an engraving of the vase and pedestal; the last is dated 1781, the year Lady Miller died. They are entitled 'Poetical Amusements at a Villa near Bath;' and among the contributors to the last volume, in which only the names are given, are Christopher Anstey, Miss Seward, Garrick, Hayley, besides Dr. Whalley, Pratt, and others. The poems here given are not in the printed collection.

Since at his will this wiser nag,
  Plays wondrous tricks in every nation,
All manners and all parts assumes,
  And rules alike in every station.

An hydra, poets wrote about,
  Whose poisonous pates so quickly grew,
That, soon as one was fairly lopt,
  Upon its stump, there sprang up two.

But still his multiplying pates,
  By hobby-horses are outnumber'd,
Who, for one head that wisdom lops,
  Will quickly sprout you up a hundred.

Than Proteus he more changeful is,
  His form more difficult to spy;
And by his impulses alone,
  Is known to the discerning eye.

For, scorning words as airy things,
  By *actions*, more substantial far,
The hobby speaks, and best through them
  His temper, and his shape appear.

When on his Dalilah's soft lap,
  The fond believing Jew was laid,
And to her false and cruel hand,
  Trusted the honours of his head;

When mighty Hercules his club,
  Resign'd to Omphales' fair hand,
And, crouching base beneath her frown,
  The distaff held at her command;

And when at Actium, Antony,
  With every fluttering sail unfurl'd,
Ignobly fled, in victory's eye,
  And for a *minion*, lost a *world*;

The hobby-horse, in passion's form,
  Trod under foot the nobler mind,
And, galloping with headlong speed,
  Left fame and virtue far behind.

These instances, 'midst thousands more,
  I think it fitting to relate,
And these may well suffice to prove,
  That hobby oft o'errules our fate.

Nor less his present sway, I ween,
  Than it was known in times of yore;
Still every age, condition, sex,
  He governs with a lordly power.

'Tis true that craft and prudence strive,
  To hide his image in *their* breast,
Since those become the dupes of art,
  With whom his features stand confest.

Yet still to rule this restive nag
  With bit and bridle, strive in vain;
And feel at times his headstrong force,
  In spite of all their care and pain.

Seen, or unseen, the hobby still,
  Resides in every human heart;
Of every foible wears the face,
  Of every passion acts the part.

Here heaps of gold alone can please,
 The wayward hobby's greedy eye;
There, feats of arms, or feats of love,
 A fossil, or a butterfly.

Here, all enamour'd of the dice,
 He wantonly with ruin sports;
And there, his victim plunges deep,
 In all the treachery of courts.

With mad ambition mounting *here*,
 He seeks the tempest he might shun;
Disdaining guile, his victim there,
 Is by simplicity undone.

Here, flattery only wins his heart,
 Or ostentation charms his eye;
There, riot, fashion, folly, dress,
 Intemperance, or vanity.

With these he curvets, foams, and rears,
 And makes them spectacles of mirth;
With those, drives furiously along,
 To every misery on earth.

Yet not with all, this dangerous nag
 Gallops, to sorrow, scorn, and strife;
With some, he gently ambles on,
 And sweetens every scene of life.

Thrice happy! who with virtue's voice,
 And wisdom's hand, control his will;
And make the lofty nag submit,
 By gently tempering force with skill.

Yet happier still, who find the art
  To twine the common foe, to use,
And, from his skilful guidance, know
  Mirth with instruction to produce.

And sure, who view this teeming lion,
  Will own that 'Miller's hobby' here,
By virtue ruled, by taste adorn'd,
  Doth in the loveliest form appear.

And who that views those fragrant wreaths,
  But must allow each verdant spray,
In candour's eye, may well deserve
  To be the hobby of the day.

IRREGULAR ODE ON THE POWER OF FANCY, FOR THE VASE AT BATH-EASTON.

HARK! 'tis Fancy strikes the lyre;
How wildly sweet the notes ascend!
With rapid hand, and eye of fire;
With floating robes and flowing hair;
Impassion'd cheek and raptur'd air,
O'er the responsive strings I see her graceful bend.
What magic breathes along her strain!
Lo! at her voice the groans of pain
Are hushed; the tears forbear to flow,
And pleasure tints the cheek of woe.
What notes! how strong! how clear! how high!
    Now they sink, and now they soar;
Now in rich cadences they pour,
And fill, with echoing sweetness, earth and sky.

Again the sweet enthusiast sings,
Again she sweeps the silver strings;
See at her song the jocund year,
A fresher, fairer livery wear;
See Zephyrs in the lap of Spring,
A gayer, fresher garland throw,
And loftier woods the charmer bring,
To shadow Summer's sultry brow;
See Autumn bend with richer stores,
Than boundless Nature ever gave,
And waft them to the distant shores,
Upon a more majestic wave;
See Winter, in his robe of snow,
Come shiv'ring at the magic skain,
With deeper furrows on his brow,
And louder torrents in his train.
See his stern hand, a wider rain is spread,
And bitterer blastings howling round;
While haughty fancy smiles in nature's scorn,
Now decks with brighter beams her radiant morn,
Now softer tints her setting sun,
Or gives new graces to the silver moon;
Anon adds fury to the flaming tide,
That rushes down dread Etna's lab'ring side;
With more tremendous Thunder plays,
More swiftly darts the lightning's blaze;
Tinges the tempest with a darker shade,
Or frolics with the fiercer whirlwind she has made.

Hark! what bold, what threat'ning airs!
Aloft the fury Discord rears
Her blood-stain'd tresses at the sound,
And shakes them to the nations round.

G Romney Pinxt — Scott Brown sc.

[illegible]

BORN [illegible] . D. [illegible]

How the War's deep Thunders roar!
How Havock strides from shore to shore!
How they fight, and how they fly!
How Glory, flashing from his car,
Whirls through the iron ranks of war,
While myriads basely fall, or bravely die!
'Tis Fancy animates the page
And bids the battle doubly rage.
'Tis she revives the warrior's name,
Exalts his courage and adorns his fame;
Stamps her bright fiat on the rolls of Fate,
Triumphs o'er death, with deathless rhyme,
And from the envious hand of Time,
Wrests from her fav'rite sons a fairer, longer date.

Nations within her piercing eye,
Rise and struggle, sink and die;
As she pours her strains along,
Years on years before them roll;
They echo round from pole to pole,
And distant ages wait upon her song.

But now a bolder pitch she soars,
And scorning earth's contracted bounds,
Glances thro' all creation in her rounds:
Trusted to Milton's hand, her lyre
A sudden flood of glory pours!
Aloft the raptured notes aspire;
Now set before our ravished eyes
The blooming scenes of Paradise.
Now open Heaven's own golden doors;
And now, with rapid, downward flight,
Pierce thro' the gloomy realms of night;

Burst open Chaos with their potent spell,
And harmonise the dreary depths of Hell.

Once more she sings; a wilder song
Now fascinates the list'ning throng;
'Tis her own Shakspeare strikes the lyre!
Creation's self beneath his fire
Sinks insufficient! At his strains
A new Creation trip the plains;
Hover in air, or with their monstrous birth,
Deform and fright the wand'ring earth.
All Nature's treasures open lie,
To the bright glances of his eye;
His hand alone can touch with art,
The master-key of every heart.
Whether he leads the laughing loves,
In silken bands through shady groves,
Or, mounted on his rapid car,
Directs the thunder of the war;
Or whether, at his high behest,
Stern Conscience goads the guilty breast,
High-soul'd Ambition sweeps along,
Or frolic Humour leads the throng;
Terror demands the lifted eye,
Or Grief the sympathetic sigh;
Wild Madness raves, or witchcraft's force,
Turns Nature from her wonted course;
Light fairies dance, or spirits sing,
Or Wit displays his brilliant wing;
Alike his magic strains control,
Charm, harrow, melt, or mend the soul;
Bright Fancy lends his bosom all her fire,
And to his hand alone,
Without reserve, made known
Each sweet, each pow'rful note that lives within his lyre.

O might a grace descend on me,
From Fancy's hand, my minstrelsy
So sweet should echo thro' these groves,
That all the Graces and the Loves,
From far and near should gather round,
And Envy sicken at the sound!
Envy! whose malice long hath made,
A *vain* attempt to blast this shade,
And spoil the sweet, the native flowers
That bloom around these festive bowers;
But, tho' *my* hand must ne'er aspire,
To sweep the chords of Fancy's lyre,
Some *happier* spirits yet attain,
The notes that speak her magic strain;
In Anstey's Muse they still prevail,
And lighten from the lips of Thrale;
Breathe living sweets from Beattie's polished song,
And pour, from Seward's hand, a glowing tide along.

VERSES READ AT BATH-EASTON.

SUBJECT: WISHES.

From Monday's full ball, just return'd in a pet,
Where Celia nor ogling, nor partner could get,
She flounced into bed, and in pitiful plight,
Lay tumbling and grumbling at least half the night.
'Why did Nature,' she cried, 'make poor Celia so plain?
'Twere better to die, than to live thus in vain;
For in vain must one live, whose nothingless charms,
No incense can raise, and can wake no alarms.
On every ball-night, when this belle and t' other
Sweeps in, and can put all the beaux in a pother;

While this for her shape or complexion they prize,
And that for her dancing, her wit, or her eyes;
Then ogle, and sigh, and gallant them all night,
Till my heart overflows with grief, envy, and spite.'
Poor Celia, alas! tho' she's dress'd to a hair,
Tho' befeather'd and trimm'd with exorbitant care,
Still night after night sits unthought of, unseen,
Tho' but just in the bloom of alluring nineteen!
'It is not that dancing I value one mite,
For one's hair and complexion it makes quite a fright;
But thus to be dressing and brid'ling for ever,
Yet never be mention'd as anything clever,
Is enough to distract one! Would Heav'n but grant
One moderate wish; nothing more should I want!
O! let it but give me a beautiful face,
An elegant person, fine taste, wit, or grace;
Such charms, such attractions alone let it grant me,
That every pert miss may not think to supplant me,
And Celia, contented for ever and ever,
Should grateful and thankful remain for the favour.'
Behold, at the word, a bright figure is seen,
With a heavenly grace and benevolent mien,
Who thus to the begging, disconsolate maid,
With melodious accent enchantingly said: —
'With pity I've heard your complaint and your prayer,
And therefore to comfort and please you appear;
Whatever perfections a mortal can bless,
You freely may ask, and as freely possess.
Then tell me the charms which your heart will relieve;
What with reason you ask, I have power to give.'
Amazed and delighted, the maiden replied:
'Dear angel, that point I can quickly decide.
From Wroughton and Stanley my form and my face,
I leave it to you to select as you please.

And to render the whole free from blemish, I would
Have the taste of a Miller, and wit of a Gould;
A Grenville's soft grace, both to charm and command;
Her ineffable smile and harmonious hand.
Thus armed at all points, at the rout, ball, or play,
I like lightning should pierce all that came in my
  way;
No rivals' bright beauties should tremble to trace,
While my envious heart drew the blood from my face;
My pow'r to my wish quite despotic would be;
Tout ou rien! has e'er been the motto for me.'
She ended. The Vision, thus frowning, replied:
'Your wish you have lost by your measureless pride.
'Tis true that in pity, when bathed in your tears,
You begged, as you'd been at your very last prayers;
Far beyond your desires, I offered you all
The perfections that e'er to a mortal can fall.
But how could you dream that the singular charms,
Which, divided 'mongst five, set the world in alarms,
Could ever united, on this side the grave,
In one perfect being their residence have?
Had your wishes been bounded, they'd surely been
  granted,
But an angel to be, not a woman, you wanted.
Thus ever it happens, with mortals below,
To their wants and their wishes no limits they know;
And thus still they forfeit a moderate bliss,
By catching at one they can never possess!'
The Vision departed. And Celia, tormented
With grief and disgrace, thus her misery vented:
'Ambition most fatal has poison'd my heart;
I've caus'd my own pain, and must e'en bear the smart;
Yet what if I put my adventure in verse,
And at Miller's next Thursday the vision rehearse?

Should it win the sweet wreath, yet poor Celia would smile,
And the envied reward all her woes should beguile.'
She did as she thought, and behold, the strange story,
To comfort the maid, I've recited before ye.

'During the confinement of a large party at Langford Court for several days, in consequence of a deep snow, Miss Luders made a pen for Mr. S. Whalley, and insisted on his writing her a copy of verses with it. He immediately complied, supposing the pen to speak.'— Preface by Mrs. Torriano, to the copy she wrote from memory in 1829.

VERSES ON THE COMPANY ASSEMBLED AT LANGFORD IN THE TIME OF THE HEAVY SNOW IN 1776.

LUCRETIA has made me, and now in despite,
She vows I shall pluck up my courage and write.
But what can I say? For the weather's so chill,
That it freezes my wit, and dispirits my will.
Say anything, nothing, as long as you write.
Then let it be what you shall please to indite;
And if, like yourself, I protest and declare,
The theme will be pleasing and subject full fair.
Pooh, pooh! that sha'n't serve you, so e'en set about,
The task I insist on; of what is without,
Or within you may write, it matters not what,
So the subject be merry and measure is pat.
Without or within you may write; why without,
There's nothing but snow, whisking each way about.
In such a cold cause, it is past all dispute,
My genius must languish, both barren and mute.

Or, should she bring forth, you would see in a trice,
Her offspring transformed into morsels of ice;
And surely, my mistress, pray think me not bold,
Can never approve of an offspring so cold.
Within then, perforce, I my subject must find;
I have it! 'tis suited exact to my mind.
And first my fair maker shall furnish a theme,
Bright as poets e'er fancied, and poets can dream;
But a fig for their dreams; Lucretia was made
As fair as her namesake, but not half so sad.
Far distant from pouting, and making a pother,
'Bout I scarce can tell what, and calling in brother,
And father, and husband, to hear an oration
For the loss of a bauble, not worth the relation.
Then, changing her curling-tongs into a sword,
And ripping her breast for the love of her Lord,
Our Lucy * takes care no such slip shall undo her,
So keeps at arm's distance each buxom young wooer;
Yet smiles upon all, and, in spite of their wills,
Still murders in mirth, and subdues with her smiles.
All jaunty and tasty in manner and dress,
Full of English affection and French politesse,
Coquetting and rioting, gambling and flirting,
To the next I'll proceed, and on her drop the curtain.
Behold her co-equal in spirit and mirth,
Mad Hester, † whose star jigged about at her birth,
As ne'er star jigged before; for fuller of fun,
No jolly soul ever lived under the sun.
Merry Momus stood by at the font with his darling,
And answered, as God-Dad, while Gravity, snarling,

* Mrs. G. Anstey.

† Miss La Faussille, afterwards married to Major Torriano, killed at Toulon, when retaken by Buonaparte, 1793.

Bit her nails out of madness; and starch Prudery
Found her gizzard in dole; such a dread enemy
She knew there was born to her squint; and, fy, fy!
But Comus, and Venus, and Euphrosyne
Joined Momus and giggled that christ'ning to see;
And swore, since their Godheads were honour'd on earth,
They ne'er were so pleased as at La Faussille's birth.
But why, in the legend of Humour and Laughter,
Should tight little * Wickham come hobbling after?
Since first, 'midst the foremost she ever will be,
In each scene of cheerfulness, frolic, and glee;
Her motions all spirit, her looks are all fun;
Those looks speak her mind, and her smart flippant tongue
To her mind or her eyes never does any wrong.
Such a trio never lived since old Momus had birth,
And with Comus and Venus enlivened the earth;
And Venus her Wickham has blest with good store
Of her charms and her graces, and, what is still more,
Tho' at variance in common, yet here Madame Die,
That Goddess so stupid, so cold, and so shy,
Relenting, has lent without scruple her aid,
With Venus, to Wickham, as wife and as maid:
As one, all her virtue and modesty gear
She lent her; as t'other,—attend and you'll hear,—
Tho' nine times invoked, with loud squalls and a pother,
To dub Madame Dapper with title of mother,
Still, cautious has been to preserve her from harms,
And has helped to re-touch and awaken her charms.
But enough of these flippants; a number of faces,
I yet spy around me who all demand places.
Stand by; clear the way; first approaching, I see
A lady of merit and high quality.

* His sister Mary, born 1742, ob. 1817.

Your Ladyship's humble; how does Lady Mary? *
To tell you the truth, I am in a quandary,
For my fingers with cold, you may see, are quite dead,
And the frost is got into my stomach and head.
Alas! my dear lady, the matter is sad;
But ne'er regard trifles; e'en let us be glad,
That we've got a sound roof hanging over our heads,
And can bid frost defiance with mirth and warm beds.
For while we are up, we will keep warm with laughing,
And strengthen our stomachs with eating and quaffing;
So I trust you'll do well, for a worthier dame
Never lived, I declare, in the annals of fame.
But what says fair Jenkyns to all this bad weather?
And why are her placid brows wrinkled together?
Indeed, Gaffer Care, you are somewhat too rude,
In a party so jovial as ours to intrude;
Tho' husbands are precious, yet husbands awhile
May be trusted to Heav'n; then let us beguile
The moments with mirth; and leave till to-morrow
Each murmuring sigh, and each symptom of sorrow,
Tho' gentle and civil, and kind and composed,
Yet still at the bottom full archly disposed.
I know the fair Jenkyns; and know sans all doubt
That a jest she can merrily bandy about;
Then clear let her brow be, and jocund her heart,
For merry we met, and in mirth let us part.
Ah, wags! t' espy you, a couple you are
Of as social spirits as e'er breathed the air.
There's Madam, the hostess of this company,
Will laugh and will jest till she scarcely can see;
And Sanford,† though sometimes so grave and demure,
Each frolic will mend and each joke will secure,

* Knollis. † Mrs. Rodd.

And add of her own, too, at pleasure (none better),
A cargo of wit, in a legible letter.
To honour, good humour, and friendship, and sense,
No pair now alive can make better pretence;
Allied as in blood, so in manners and mind
I would not disjoin, who so aptly are joined.
Behold, Madam Susan,* to bring up the rear,
So easy, an' please ye, so plump and sincere;
So hearty she laughs, that it does one's heart good,
And her song charms the ear, and enlivens the blood.
Pass on, my sleek Susan, and sing while ye can;
Short is life, and 'tis wise to enliven the span.
So much for the 'belles;' but pray where are the 'beaux?'
Oh! not far behind them, as you may suppose;
And first (as 't is fitting he should be) the chief,
See, bowing, the gallant Monsieur Zenovief.
What mortal can wonder we make no small fuss,
To see French politeness, engrafted on Russ;
And the Great Chamberlain of Russia's Majesty,
Appearing to grace such poor rustics as we?
But silence there! silence! not a word nor a squeak,
For Monsieur the Russian is going to speak.
'Votre humble, Madame, Ma'mselle Ludres; très votre;
Madame Week, très agréable; and you be, vous autres,
De fort jolies Anglaises.' Oh, Monsieur, Monsieur!
Your most humble servant! I cannot endure,
To be tongue-tied so vilely. Miss Luders, explain
My good wishes to Monsieur, and say with disdain,
I hold the embargo that's laid on my tongue,
Which does my esteem for the Count so much wrong.
Lucretia interprets; and like a sly elf,
Says one word for Wicky, and two for herself;

* His sister, Mrs. Crane.

While Monsieur, the Chamberlain, capers and chatters,
Salutes their soft hands, sighs, and ogles, and flatters;
Now talks broken English, now puts on the droll;
First plays like a monkey, then looks like a fool;
Acts the sot and the sick man, with each merry trick,
Making laughter re-echo, and gravity sick.
Agreeable, sensible, easy, polite;
The gentlemen's envy, and ladies' delight;
With the strength of a Samson, and humour of Foote;
A Mercury active, and loving to boot;
Can any one wonder, this gallant young Russ,
Has power our fair ones to charm and amuse?
But should they at any time put on their rude airs,
Behold at his elbow, his 'aide de camp,' Luders;
Than whom upon earth, either sober or mellow,
There lives not, I swear, a more sprack little fellow.
Gay as youth can proclaim him, and jocund as day;
Full of mirth and good humour, and laughter and play;
A better companion can never be found,
To make a dull season run merrily round.
This Hetty can witness, whose lips seldom fail,
The effects of his raptures and prowess to tell;
But surely you 'll think me a fool or a sot,
Should Wickham,* so courteous and calm, be forgot,
Whose carriage so gentle, and manners so easy,
Can't fail, if you know what *is* pleasing, to please ye.
With a soul full of goodness, and kindness, and spirit,
As loved for good humour, as honoured for merit;
Sense, tempered with candour, resides in his breast,
And mirth fills his bosom, in soberness drest;
When aces and faces skim over the green,
And the conflict grows hot, betwixt knave, king and queen,

* Mr. Wickham, of Frome, who married Dr. Whalley's sister, Mary. He died 1791.

'Midst the din of the battle, who better can wield,
Of the mighty god Whist, or the sword or the shield
Yet vanquished or victor, while tumults increase,
Unmov'd he is conquer'd, and conquers in peace.
But who, says Lucretia, pray who must appear,
In so social a party, to bring up the rear?
Can you ask, my sweet Lucy? why, maugre all doubt,
Who conducted them in, ought to wait on them out.
Behold, then, their host, as alert as a bee,
As 't is proper he should be, in such company;
Tho' skinny and lank, yet he 'll laugh with the best,
And never be guilty of marring a jest.
Full of joy, hospitality, peace, and good-will,
From the crown of his head, to the tip of his heel;
And when you reflect that he 's tall as a steeple,
You will fancy his portion is large, my good people;
But think once again, that he 's slender as tall,
And then you may fancy his portion is small.
Be that as it may, a more social party—
More jolly, more frolicsome, free, or more hearty,
Ne'er met since Don Sancho embraced his dear Dapple,
Since Israel danced hornpipes, or Eve ate the apple.
So met and so suited, each wind may blow round;
Rain rattle, frost chill, and snow whiten the ground,
On themselves and their mirth, they repose full reliance,
And to winter, and all his assaults, bid defiance.

VERSES ON LOVE.

SAY, dearest Nancy, does thy breast,
Those soft emotions feel,
Which (when the heart is most oppressed)
Deep heaving sighs reveal?

Say, dearest Nancy, does thy soul,
  Those powerful feelings know,
Which ev'ry other thought control —
  From whence such sorrows flow?

Say, do thy weary, waking eyes,
  Ne'er watch the sleepless night;
Thy breast, with frequent throbbings rise;
  Thy mind refuse delight?

On one dear object, do thy thoughts
  Perpetually dwell?
Blind to his follies and his faults,
  His merit seen *too well.*

Say, do his virtues in thy sight,
  With double splendour shine;
Do not his eyes seem wondrous bright,
  When they encounter thine?

Say, dost thou grudge those looks that dwell,
  Upon another fair;
Does not thy heart with rapture swell,
  When bent on thee they are?

Say, is thy anxious soul a prey
  To doubts, and hopes, and fears;
Do tender glances ne'er betray,
  The cause of all thy cares?

Say, when his hand takes hold of thine,
  Do conscious blushes rise?
Do soft desires and pleasure join,
  To fill with tears thy eyes?

If haply at the ball or play,
Thy favourite should appear,
And unexpected pass that way,
Where you reclining are;

Say, would your palpitating heart,
With sudden flutt'rings beat;
And heat and cold, through ev'ry part,
In quick succession fleet?

Say, if these symptoms, if this care,
Your breast did ever prove?
And if it has, believe, my dear,
You'll not miscall it, love.

Perhaps indeed thy tender breast,
Glows with this subtle fire?
Perhaps, thy bosom robb'd of rest,
May heave with fond desire.

But oh! I dare not hope thy heart,
Feels ought of this for me;
Though mine (unconscious of all art),
Feels more, far more, for thee.

And yet, since hate engenders hate,
As usually we prove;
Why is it not the will of fate,
That love should meet with love?

But if the adverse stars decree,
Thy hand must ne'er be mine;
Whatever misery falls on me,
May ev'ry bliss be thine!

VERSES ADDRESSED TO MISS WROUGHTON*

ON HER DESIRING TO HAVE THE TALE OF CORIN AND JESSY.

FAIR Wroughton ask'd the dismal tale
Of hapless Corin's woes;
And while she ask'd, upon her cheek
The deep'ning colour rose.

Upon her cheek, the colour rose,
And in her speaking eye,
A gracious smile shone through the tear
Of sensibility.

O! may the swain her heart approves,
As feeling, as sincere!
Know how to cherish — such a smile!
And value — such a tear!

MINUTES FOR AN ANSWER TO JULIA'S† LETTER ON THE SUBJECT OF SONNETS.

The sonnet, a miniature, that requires fine and delicate touches, would be glaring and coarse, if touched strongly like a large picture. Majesty not so much its characteristic as grace, and energy less adapted to it, than sweetness and fine colouring. Inharmonious cadence not a proof of, or indispensable to energy. Many of Milton's, Shakspeare's, Virgil's, and other the best poets' finest and most energetic lines, very

* A distinguished living authority on taste, speaking of the musical talent Bath has produced, says, 'And was there not *the* Wroughton, the patroness of Rauzzini, who for so long not only led the musical world, but was in the circles of fashion looked up to as "the Queen of Bath?"' Whatever this lady's foibles might have been — and who is without them? — she had many excellent qualities, and her death was much regretted.— *Monkland on the Literature of Bath*, 1855.

† The name under which he corresponded with Miss Seward.

harmonious. Their roughest breaks chiefly adapted to show and set off the sense by the sound, but such rough breaks no beauty, but a deformity in poetry, when that is the case. 'Boreal coruscations,' the break here very rough, and not the least expressive or analogous to the sense. The rumbling of the double *r*, and the hiss of the double *s*, with the sudden stop at the latter, remind me of the thumping of hammers in a forge, and the hiss of the hot iron, plunged suddenly in the water. The sonnets of Petrarch, equally and universally admired by the learned and unlearned in Italy. This far from being the case with Milton's, who is only an imitator, and surely a coarse one, of this master and inventor of the sonnet. Milton's fame has given a celebrity to his sonnets, which but for that fame, they never would have had, nor, exclusive of his other poetry, would they ever have handed down his name to posterity. Gray and Johnson, two great authorities, thought little of Milton's sonnets. A little woman affecting great majesty of deportment, rather ridiculous. She may have all the grace imaginable, and grace becomes her, as it does the beautiful lapdog, but would not the latter appear laughable, if affecting in its looks and motions, the energetic dignity and grave resolute air of the mastiff? The Miltonic sonnet, is like the pigmy affecting the strut of the giant. Swift's Liliputian's grace and delicacy and tenderness become him, and you love and take a lively interest in the dear little creature; but when he puts on the hero, and talks with grave importance of high and mighty deeds, you laugh at and despise him. The oak-leaved myrtle has always appeared to me the most insignificant of plants, because, while the form of its foliage ridiculously reminds one of the most majestic of trees, it possesses neither the fragrant odour nor lovely blossoms of the plant whose name it bears. The first impressions, you must give me leave to think, in a mind like yours, are generally right. The critical coldness of a Boothby, a Hardinge, or a Tighe, applied to damp the enthusiastic glow of your native feelings, resemble oil poured over wine, which confines without destroying its spirit. Forgive me, if I say, that the contracted dignity, the forced majesty of the Miltonic sonnet, too often reminds me of the diminutive hero Tom Thumb, who swaggers and slashes with a sword, as long and as stout as any stocking needle.

THOUGHTS ON DIVINE REVELATION.

It is the error and the vanity of human knowledge and genius, to oppose their fallible reasonings to the infallible counsels and decrees of an almighty and all-wise God, instead of implicitly depending on his revealed words, and submitting to his divine ordinances. But how should finite faculties comprehend infinite wisdom, or those imperfect beings who cannot foresee the events of to-morrow, or even of the passing hour, presume to set up their purblind intellectual powers, against that all-comprehensive intelligence, which takes in at one, to us, incomprehensible view, millions of worlds, and not only all events, but all thoughts and every pulse and spring of action, of innumerable and innumerable gifted and various beings, past, present, and to come? In perusing the word of God, as delivered to us by the prophets in the Old, and our divine Saviour in the New Testament, what we read, and not what we think, should be our polar star. Such oracles were more offered to our humble belief, than to our arrogant reason. What would you think of a naked savage in the wilds of America, who should pretend to argue against or analyse the reasonings of a Bossuet, or the problems of a Newton? Yet he would be much more competent to this, than a Newton or a Bossuet would be, to comprehend the Almighty mind, to analyse infinite power, or to reason against perfect wisdom. Let reason be satisfied, as it well may, with what divine goodness has vouchsafed to place within its narrow limits; but never let it absurdly and impiously presume to cavil at, or attempt to explain those mysteries, which are offered from heaven, as the subject and the trial of its faith.

EPITAPH, ON THE DOG'S TOMB IN THE WOOD AT MENDIP LODGE.

IF zealous service to thy soul is dear,
Or faith or gratitude demand the tear;
Check not thy pity, while thine eye is bent
On gentle Sappho's simple monument!
And when from man, proud man, the heart shall prove
As firm a friendship and as warm a love,
Then dash away with scorn the bursting tear,
And cry — Thou shalt not flow, *a dog lies here!*

EPITAPH TO THE MEMORY OF MRS. WHALLEY, WHO DIED THE FOURTEENTH OF SEPTEMBER, 1803, IN THE 97TH YEAR OF HER AGE.

SHAME on the son who, bending o'er the shrine
That holds the last remains of worth like thine,
Most honoured mother! — O! eternal shame,
If he once thought this marble could proclaim,

The various excellence that marked thy days,
Surpassing far all monumental praise.
Yet greater shame should overwhelm his soul,
Could the deep sense of duty brook control,
And the full sorrows of his swelling heart,
No proof of love or reverence impart!
Formed to delight, adorn, and to improve
A sex, where honour should unite with love,
As friend, as neighbour, mother, daughter, wife,
Thy perfect pattern was confess'd through life;
Unto a period, very rarely given
To feeble mortals by the will of heaven,
Near to the limits of thy hundredth span,
Thy life, thy senses, thy affections ran.
Sustained by faith and fortitude serene,
The Christian watch'd the slowly closing scene;
Held her firm temper, to her latest breath,
And, smiling, sank into the arms of death.
E'en to the last, upon her reverend face,
Her early charms the eye could clearly trace:
Those charms, which wisdom with grey hairs refine,
To something more impressive, more divine —
Blending an awful grace, a calm sublime,
With the strong touches of consuming time!
O! soul of honour, tenderness, and truth,
How well in thee did age become thy youth!
Accomplished, courteous, cheerful, generous, just:
Long as this marble o'er thy sacred dust
Recording lasts, thy venerated name
To every Whalley shall give pride and fame.
O! may they all — all who from thee have sprung,
And caught their best instruction from thy tongue,
Follow the bright example thou hast given,
And, lost on earth, be found with thee in Heaven!

VERSES BY DR. WHALLEY ON THE THREATENED AND THEN EXPECTED INVASION OF ENGLAND BY BUONAPARTE, IN 1807.

BRITONS, awake! Be found in arms!
When from the adverse coast of France,
Not sounding now, with vain alarms,
The foe, relentless, shall advance.

Eluding your resistless fleet,
Fierce Bony's forces crowding o'er,
Shall tread your shores with hostile feet,
But tread them to return no more!

No more! If, true to your renown —
True to yourselves, your king, your God —
With valour greater than their own,
You make them kiss the chast'ning rod.

Shall vaunting Frenchmen, abject slaves
To Bony's art and Bony's state —
Shall Frenchmen, skulking o'er the waves,
Eclipse your fame and seal your fate?

Shall they, so long your scorn and jest,
Beneath their yoke your spirits bow—
Rend every blessing from your breast,
And all the laurels from your brow?

So lately on the Egyptian coast,
Uncheck'd by sand or burning sky,
Did Britons crush the Gallic host,
Basely at home, to fear and fly?

Then let them come; let fav'ring gales
Conduct them to the British shores;
From numerous ports let crowded sails
Their thousands and ten thousands pour.

Let the fell Corsican advance
With all the furies in his train;
Let savage Hatred point his lance,
And all his vultures scent the slain.

While the whole world, in awful pause,
Appall'd, the mighty shock shall view,
Confiding in her righteous cause,
Britain her purpose shall pursue.

Both earth and heaven shall hail the hour,
When vanquished France shall stoop to shame,
And all its tyrant's boasted power
Serve to exalt Britannia's fame.

Dr. Whalley, with patriotic zeal, often contributed verses and articles to the newspapers and reviews to aid the popular enthusiasm, when the French invasion was expected, of which the above is a specimen. He also wrote satirical verses on members of the opposition; one set, in George Canning's style, on Sheridan's resigning the office of Treasurer of the Navy in 1808, deserve to be preserved, but are unfortunately not forthcoming.

N. B. In the following correspondence, the letters, especially in the case of those of Miss Seward (which are very voluminous), it has not been deemed desirable to give in their entirety, as they do not possess sufficient public interest.

CORRESPONDENCE.

Richard Whalley, from whom the following and other letters are given, possessed a talent for painting; and, with a view of becoming a historical painter, went at this time, being twenty-five years of age, to study the art at Rome. It appears he was already attached to Elizabeth Frances, daughter of the Rev. John Payne, canon of Wells, whom he afterwards married. Mr. Harford, of Blaize Castle, who has written his memoir, states that at this time he imbibed the sceptical opinions of Rousseau and Voltaire, and the tone of his letters offer a marked contrast to those written at a later period.

He resided two years at Rome, and Mr. Harford thus describes him on his return: — 'Mr. Whalley returned to his native country with opinions, tastes, and habits uncongenial with those of the friends and associates among whom he was to live. The elegance of his manners, his refined tastes, and his familiarity with foreign scenes and objects, naturally made his company sought after. His elder brother, the late Dr. Whalley, once said to me: "You are well acquainted, I believe, with my brother Richard; but unless you can compare him, as I can, with his former self, you can scarcely imagine what religion has done for him. I well remember him one of the proudest and most fastidious of human beings. He was, in fact, the proudest man I ever knew." The late Mrs. Hannah More and her sisters, who were well acquainted with him at the time now referred to, have occasionally described him to me as a man of refined elegance, but chilling fastidiousness.' In June, 1787, his brother-in-law, Mr. Wickham, offered to present him to the living of Horsington, which he held for twelve years, when he resigned it in favour of his nephew, and shortly after he was presented by his relative, Dr. Beadon, Bishop of Bath and Wells, to the small rectory of Chelwood, in the same diocese, which he held during the rest of his life.

Mr. Harford thus describes Mr. R. Whalley and his *ménage* at Chelwood:—'The house was small but neat; the appendages of his table were plain but inviting; and a due attention was paid to the little minor comforts which befit the residence of a gentleman. It always appeared to myself, when I enjoyed the privilege of spending a few days with him, that I had been admitted to converse with a sort of human angel.'

MR. RICHARD WHALLEY TO DR. WHALLEY.

Rome, June 10, 1773.

My dear Brother,—When I first heard of your departure into Wales, I was plagued by many apprehensions that my correspondence with my Fanny would not be so easily conducted in your absence. You will not wonder at this. A heart harassed with afflictions, is as a head disordered by sickness; it conceives a thousand phantoms and terrors, which neither do, nor, perhaps, will exist, and, as if its real evils were not a sufficient load, is continually aggravating them by a train of restless imaginations. Sometimes, even,

(I am ashamed to say it,) I have not been an utter stranger to such apprehensions, as I ought to be persuaded have no foundation in *possibility*.

But I think I have at length shaken off every suspicion that she can have an idea of happiness independent of me, and I have now only to combat the cursed uncertainty of my being ever in a condition to overcome the obstacles that now lie in the way of her peace. I need not tell you what my present situation is; you can figure it to yourself. You may suppose I am by this time reconciled to our separation as much as I ever shall be. It is not in the mind of man to endure for a length of time such excessive grief, as I felt on leaving Wells. But, though *not* a continuation, I have known frequent returns of it; and I know not whether the ingratitude, which I have now and then experienced since my coming hither, were not more poignant than at my departure. The hurry of a sudden removal, and a long journey, were something like a diversion to my regrets. In solitude they have returned with increase of violence. You take pains to convince me of the tolerableness and even the felicity of my lot; I myself confess that I ought to be happy. Nevertheless, I am not.

If I am persuaded that the deprivation of such a treasure, as my Fanny is, ought incessantly to be deplored, I am for that very reason capable of every effort to obtain it; and I am convinced of this by the ease with which I have passed from a life of dissipation to a life of study, and by my great contempt for such things as were once the objects of my attention. I cannot yet determine whether it be at all probable that I shall become a painter of any excellence. You know very well that I knew nothing when I left England, and can therefore imagine that I have yet the laborious part of the art to go through. I think I have neither lost nor misemployed any of my time in Rome, for I have been perpetually busied, and in the way which I believe will soonest lead me to what I want. It will most infallibly be a comfortable reflection, though all my views should be disappointed, that I have not been slack in my endeavours to *deserve* happiness. Adversity, it is said, is the best school for virtue. But I would not have you suppose me one of those unwilling scholars, who quit the study so soon as the rod ceases to lay heavy on them. I am persuaded were I at this instant to attain every wish of my heart, I should continue to think and act as blamelessly as I now do. Nay, it is impossible that the man whose affections are placed upon such a woman, as mine are, should not become a worthy character. If it does not argue absolute merit to praise and love it in others, it certainly indicates a quick approach to it; so that, unless despair should intervene to deaden its growth, you may expect one day to be proud of me as a brother.

We live very well here, but upon scraps in comparison with English provision. In nothing are people more deceived than in the notion that this is so cheap a country. Almost every article (at least to us Englishmen) is as dear as in our island. The difference principally consists in the retirement in which we live here, for want of company and public diversions.

Religious raree-shows are very frequent here; some of them I have seen. The Feast of Corpus Domini, not long since past, was celebrated by an immense procession to St. Peter's Church; it was composed of innumerable friars of the several orders, and multitudes of black men bearing torches. Afterwards, the ecclesiastics of higher denominations, such as bishops, &c., next all the cardinals in pontificalibus, and lastly the Pontifex Maximus himself, who is carried upon men's shoulders, kneeling at a kind of altar richly o'ercanopied. Any one who sees such a *magnificent* company of prelates, will not be surprised at the poverty of the flock which they have in their hands. The poor people here do not perceive their wretchedness, they are blinded by this trumpery: trumpery I must call it, for though it be striking, it carries nothing with it of real religion, which, in my thinking, is never so well attired as in simplicity. But you being a divine, I shall leave you to draw your own observations on this matter.

The clime here I find rather of the warmest, but the great heats are not yet arrived. I have a dress suited to the occasion. The Romans have a custom of sleeping in the middle of the day. I see no necessity for it, but they are fond of any excuse to be idle.

You have not so many correspondents as I have, you can therefore afford to write more frequently than myself. Yet from time to time you shall hear from me. At all times, I hope you are persuaded I am,

Yours most affectionately,

R. Whalley.

Addressed to Rev. Mr. Warrington's,
Little Acton, Wrexham.

MRS. SAGE TO DR. WHALLEY.

Queen Anne Street, July, 1773.

My dearest Rev. Brother,—You will doubtless think me a sad lazy correspondent. I know not how it is, that I never now can find time to write. A train of events has concurred to prevent my addressing you so long. At the time I received yours, Mr. and Mrs. Walters were with me. They were at our house in town three weeks, and the morning after they left us we set out for Mr. Batson's, where we had long been engaged to be, during Ascot Races, and are returned to town but a few hours since. We spent ten days in the Forest, all which time we were so fully engaged that I assure you I am glad to sit down quiet a little in my own house. I think I told you Captain Stables was married; he and his lady were of the party to Mr. Batson's; the lively Mr. Taylor also, whom you have heard me speak of, so that we were very jolly. There was exceeding good sport on the hill, a great show of company, and in the evening a ball alternately at Sunning Hill and Windsor. The Duke of Cumberland * was at two of the Sunning Hill balls, and danced all the evening; he behaved with a great deal of ease, and appeared much pleased. His Duchess was on the hill every day, where there was a booth built up, with some kind of elegance, for her and her company, which were Mrs. Hoghes and the Luttrells. She herself was dressed each day in a riding habit, and looked very charming. I cannot say the like of her sister, who is a sad pug. Count Hippesley † made his appearance at the balls, hand and glove, none more intimate than he and the Luttrells. Apropos, do you know that the society of which you are a member have elected Mr. Sage? Your friend the Count Hippesley put him up. Mr. Sage has never been among them.

My dear little girls are at Stanmore. Mrs. Sage requested their company in my absence; but I shall send for them to-morrow, as home is most uncomfortable without them, and I flatter myself I shall see them much improved by a little country air. In about a fortnight we go down to Bristol, where we propose staying some time. How shall I miss my dear brother among my friends in that neighbourhood. It

* Duke of Cumberland, brother to George the Third. He married, 1771, the Lady Anne Luttrell, eldest daughter of the first Earl of Carhampton, and widow of Christopher Horton, Esq. The Duke died 1790, the Duchess 1803, without issue.

† Afterwards long known in Somersetshire as Sir John Cox Hippesley. He was created a baronet in 1796, and married for his second wife the widow of Hippesley Cox, Esq., of Ston Easton. He was many years in Parliament, and died in 1825. The title *Count* must have been a *sobriquet.*

will greatly lessen the joy I shall feel at seeing them. But our pleasures are ever imperfect. I am at present tolerably well; I hope the Bristol waters will quite set me up. We have promised to spend a few days at General Smith's in our way down; and in the autumn are to go for a little time to Mr. Rumbold's.* We dined one day there, while we were at Mr. Batson's, and a most delightful place they have, about eight miles from him. You know she was Miss Law, a good agreeable woman, but not handsome. What a match! Rumbold can *spend* ten thousand a year, and is a very agreeable man; she has a little boy, about four months old. I am almost ashamed to ask to hear *soon* from you, and yet I must wish it, nay, I do not know whether I shall not expect it, knowing your goodness.

E. SAGE.

Mrs. Tudway I saw often in the winter. Miss is married to the Saint,† and gone down to Wells. The Stanmore family are all well — full of inquiries after you whenever I see them. Of all things in the world a square letter is the most horrid, but I never can leave more than a square vacant when I write to you. My brother Whalley spent a week in town with us lately; he was very well. Adieu!

MRS. SAGE TO DR. WHALLEY.

Clifton, August 21, 1773.

To make up for my former tardiness, I am now become a very punctual correspondent. I received yours but yesterday, and was more sorry than surprised to find it reached

* He was afterwards involved in Hastings' impeachment.

† In a letter not given, dated 24th March of this year, Mrs. Sage says: 'Miss Tudway is near marriage with the great teacher of this dangerous doctrine, Rowland Hill.'

your hands so long after date, as all the letters from this place take a circuit before they arrive at the destined port. Never was so strange a post; my letters are a week going to Winscombe, and my mother's take the same time in travelling to me. Mr. Sage has made the purchase of Thornhill,* in which I am more happy than I can well express, as it is so near my best and dearest friends, and the only place of all which I should like to spend my life at. The situation is delightful, the house a charming one, and the land very fine; and all lies immediately round the house, and interferes with no one's property, which is a pleasing circumstance. I promise myself great happiness at this place, but everything in this life is so uncertain, that I must not be too sanguine. We shall take another ride to Winscombe before we leave this place, but only for a day. We propose returning to town in about a fortnight, from thence go down to spend a little time at Mr. Rumbold's, whose place is in the Forest. After that I cannot determine how long we may continue in London, as Mr. Sage will be impatient to settle his house at Thornhill, which will take some time in furnishing, &c.

I hear of your leaving Wales with pleasure; I have been somewhat jealous of their detaining you there so long already. I shall look on the hopes you give me of spending *a few days* with us in town, as a promise, and if you should exceed that time we shall not show you the *door*. A pretty gentleman you are to talk of *days*, when you visit a sister whom you have not seen for this, I don't know how long; it appears to me *an age*, as I measure the time by my affection. If you are in the widow's good graces, you should not boast of her favours; at least, defer your information till we are *tête-à-tête*. In truth, I shall begin to harbour some sus-

* Whilst at Thornhill, he served, in 1784, the office of High Sheriff for the county of Dorset.

picions, if you stay at Acton much longer. The first wish of my heart is to see my dear favourite brother well settled; no one is more formed for domestic happiness, and I trust the good Bishop will, ere it is long, enable you to offer your hand and heart to some woman who is worthy of you, if among *women* there is such to be found.

I have the pleasure to inform you that my health mends every day, and that I hope to leave this place quite well. We spend our time very pleasantly in riding and dining parties. Such a series of fine weather I have seldom or ever known. My husband and little girl are quite well; my Fanny grows an angel.

Adieu! my amiable brother. Love me as I do you, and you will seldom cease to think of and pray for the happiness of

Your affectionate sister,

ELIZA SAGE.

My best respects to all Mr. Warrington's family, particularly to Mrs. Simpson.

I sometimes wish for your clever pen to exercise it in a few lines upon *three cats* here, who give themselves great airs, and do so particularly to me. They are stiff old maids, who value themselves on being a Baronet's daughters, though their grandfather was butler to a gentleman's family I know. They live but to speak to great people, and are never out of company. The eldest, a fury, beats her maids, and starves all her servants. If anything occurs to you in the poetical way on these things, let me have it in your next. The eldest is very *pert* and looks always in a fright. The carriage waits to carry me to the Wells. I write in a hurry. Pardon faults, numberless. Write soon. Adieu! adieu!

MRS. SAGE TO DR. WHALLEY.

Bristol Wells.
(After August, 1773.)

YOUR very kind letter, my dearest Tom, met me at Wells, and I hope you pardon my not thanking you for it before. The time I spent at Wells was so short, that I could not lose any of mother's company by taking up my pen; but, believe me, I wished much to do it, if only to express the sense I felt of your goodness. But in what instance through life has the fondest and best of brothers, omitted to show a sister, unworthy of so much attention, every proof of affection which was in his power. All the return I can offer him is a most sincere and warm regard, and such a one as can only cease with my existence.

Since ever I was capable of making distinctions, you, my brother, were the dear loadstone to my affections; and, except the claims as *wife* and *mother*, my heart can never admit a rival to the love it bears you. Your absence from Wells was such a vacancy as nothing could supply; I myself did not imagine I could have missed you so much; indeed, it is too, too long since we met. It makes me happy to hear you are well, and spend your time agreeably; but I was rather alarmed to hear that you had taken a curacy in Wales, as it seems to indicate a long stay there. Sure you cannot have thoughts of making it a home? I am more particularly *interested* in your return to Wells now, as Mr. Sage is about making a purchase in Dorsetshire; the place is but five or six and twenty miles from Wells, so that if we live there, I may hope to see you often. We have been to see the estate, which is a sweet one, between 300*l.* and 400*l.* a year, and a good house on it. Mr. Sage is very warm about this affair, as he is delighted with the spot; it is a *farm*, and we propose keeping it in hand, which will be both amusement and profit; the latter certainly, as it is all meadow land, which you know may be managed by a *gentleman* without his being imposed on. You will see by the date of this that we are at the Hot Well, where I am very sanguine in my hopes of receiving benefit. The waters have greatly relieved my complaints already. I have brought my dear Fanny with me, and left Emily with my mother, who was to carry her over to Winscombe to be there while I am here, which will be six weeks if the waters continue to agree with me. My Fanny is so good a girl, and so *very sensible* (I think I may say so impartially), that she is a very agreeable companion to me. Your god-daughter is a sweet cherub, and now runs quite alone, and begins to chatter; you would not love either of them. Would to God you could see them and their mother; but I must wait with patience, unless you will spend a little time in town with us in the winter. Why can't you, when you return from Wales, go up, if only for a little while?

There is not much company here this season. I was at a ball last night, which was a very full one, but there was a good deal of company from Bristol. We had a very agreeable journey down; we travelled in the phaeton, and, as we had our own horses, made short stages. First went to Mr. Batson's, where we stayed two days; then went to General Smith's, by Hungerford, and stayed three days; then to Frome for one night, and on to Wells. We have promised to make a visit at Winscombe and another at Frome before we leave Somersetshire, and then are engaged to go for some time to Mr. Rumbold's, which is in the Forest, to spend a fortnight or three weeks, after calling at Chilton Lodge—General Smith's. This is our route for the summer. We then return to town, whether Mr. Sage buys Thornhill or not. I have now only to add my respects to the good family you are with, and my husband, who now sits by me,

sends kind love to you. Adieu, my dearest brother; and believe me,
Yours faithfully,
E. SAGE.

I rejoice to hear poor Mrs. Potter is settled so well. Pray, if you see her again, present my compliments, and assure her of my best wishes for her happiness. Kindly, very kindly remember me to Miss Stanley.

You ask me whether I am in the way to bring another brat, or whether you dreamt it? Certainly the latter.

Direct at Mrs. Brotherton's, on the Parade. I flatter myself you will write soon.

MR. RICHARD WHALLEY TO DR. WHALLEY.

Rome, Sept. 3, 1773.

MY DEAR BROTHER. — I rely a second time upon your indolence and attachment to your friends, for I believe by the time this reaches Denbighshire the three months of happiness which you told me you still proposed to yourself will have been expired. The life you have described to me is much too endearing to be easily quitted by a man of any complexion, much less by you who are of so easy a disposition as to do anything with anybody, provided, as Sterne says, 'there be no sin in it;' and I fancy I may venture to pronounce that the yielding in this instance to the importunities of your friends will never be ranked in the catalogue of such actions as your conscience will produce in judgment against you. Go on, then, to enjoy them, and yourself, and the objects about you; and while you have a Kemar, or some such weighty preacher, to keep your flock at home, content yourself with the resolution of giving them a Christmas sermon.

I must remark to you the compliment I pay you in supposing that your welcome in Wales can continue perfect for so long a time. It is much more difficult to preserve than to gain good opinions. A slight acquaintance, a fortunate concurrence of circumstances, nay, a mere prejudice in others, will sometimes gain us a great share of their esteem; but the continuance of it, is a sign of real merit in the possessor. You have now experienced the happiness which is to be found in a cottage, and can judge whether it be superior to that which palaces afford; I, for my part, become daily more and more a villager in my desires; they are fast declining from all great resorts of mankind, and I believe not so much through a disgust, at not being able to make a shining figure in them, as from an experience of the insolidity of their pleasures. Even Rome, that offers entertainments of a much higher kind, I would gladly quit to be established in such peace and content as, in certain circumstances, I figure to myself I should find in any obscure corner of my own country. As the ideas contained in these last lines are perfectly homespun, it will be for my credit perhaps that you do not reveal them.

But how much are you deceived, if you think Nature's charms are insignificant in this country. It is probably more rich in her beauties, than in those of vertu. The misery is that they are neglected and despised. The great people here, not only never betake themselves to a country life, but they even neglect to cultivate their estates in such a manner, as would enable them to enjoy more at their ease their city residence, if it can be termed an enjoyment to loll on couches and in coaches, for in these, as far as I can learn, they spend the greatest part of their time. They have their private assemblies, but I believe there is nothing in them of that sociality, which reigns in an English circle. That they are a tasteless, if not a corrupt people, I think appears from their insensibility to Nature's charms. In a country in which she is disposed to be most luxuriant, she is reckoned of no account. It seems so, at least; for, although many of the nobility here have beautiful country seats and villas, few of them pass any time in them. Some of these sweet places I have seen actually in ruins, and those that are kept up are almost deserted. There are a good many within a very small distance from Rome that, although they are all laid out in the old-fashioned style, are absolutely enchanting. The views from them surpass in grandeur everything you can conceive. And this is what Italy is remarkable for. The scale of the country is quite different from ours; it is composed of immense plains and immense hills; on these are vast forests and in the others great lakes. In short, it is not broke into so many different parts as present themselves in all our landscapes; and of consequence it must have a grander effect. But so pleasing a one it has not, I am sure. Here is not that neatness of cultivation, that sweet variety of hill and dale, of meadows and corn-fields, of woods and streams, that we have so often trod; nor are there those flocks and herds scattered up and down the land. I do not think this a pastoral country by any means. I know not what it may have been in Virgil's time, but at present I cannot see from whence he took many of his images. But what alterations and ravages does time make! No doubt in his days whole tracts of land were beautified with corn and trees that are now shadeless and barren.

Let me now answer your questions, or otherwise my paper will fail me, and cease to harrow up this poor land which has been so long unmolested. I wish I may not have harrowed your patience too. Notwithstanding you have made use of the strongest means to work your purposes—flattery—I cannot do as you wish me. I am much more unconscious of merit in my art than I ever was; so much the better, for I am convinced that the man who can see the works I daily see without despair and wretchedness, will never attain to any of their beauties.

To-morrow I begin to paint from the figures of the Capella Sistina of Michael Angelo,—in the afternoons I mean. In the mornings I shall draw from the antique, and when I come home at night shall study the anatomy, or be always doing or thinking of something to improve myself. But after all I can do, I shall never be but as a lackey to one man here, a Swiss, who, supposing the art of painting to be again rising to what it was, I am persuaded is a full age before all his brethren of the brush, either in England or here. He intends settling in London. If he is not well received, it will demonstrate that the public has not taste for an art which they all affect a knowledge of. How lucky is West to be born at a time when there is no one, good or bad, to oppose him; he is but a child to the person I am speaking of. Let him make the most of his reputation, for I think it will all die, when the above-mentioned person makes his appearance. There is a Scotchman who studies portraits who will be great in his way, and a sculptor, an Englishman, who is a wonder. These two are the only ones of all the British subjects, that bid fair for a character in after times.

Pray remember to give my affectionate compliments to Warrington, and I know not why I may not add to all that family. I am much obliged to them for thinking of me. Write to me soon and often; you have nothing else to do; but excuse me if you hear but very seldom; writing has hitherto taken up too much of my time. The next two years and a half, I wish to dedicate entirely to one object; nor will it be, but against my will even to blot a sheet of paper for anyone else. I am entering upon a truly solitary life. I have quitted the world, in order to return to it with satisfaction. God bless you.

R. C. WHALLEY.

MRS. SAGE TO DR. WHALLEY.

Queen Anne Street, Autumn of 1773.
Thursday night.
(I have too many things to think of to remember the day of the month.)

ON my return from South Hill this evening, I found no less than three letters from my dearest brother. We went to Mr. Rumbold's on Sunday morning, and returned from thence about two hours since. Our stay was shorter than we could have wished, both from the agreeable manner in which we spent our time, and from their kind entreaties to continue longer with them; but Mr. Sage has at this time a good deal of business, to call him to, and keep him in town. I was equally surprised and delighted to find by yours, that our friend G. Warrington is in this part of the world, as there is not a creature I can be more rejoiced to see out of my own family. Mr. Sage, as well as myself, will be disposed to show him every civility that lays in our power. To-morrow morning Mr. Sage will go to wait on both the Mr. Warringtons, and ask the favour of seeing them in Queen Anne Street; till that time arrives I shall be all impatience. Pray present my kind compliments to the amiable widow of your friend: I feel for her in the absence of a beloved husband. Trying, provoking mortal, dare you talk of Christmas after the hopes you have given me? Why did you teach me to expect so soon the long wished-for pleasure of seeing you, and then draw a gloomy veil over the cheerful picture which you yourself had painted? This is not kind. Pack up your alls and begone from Little Acton, I'm sure your friends must be heartily tired of you by this. We long to be so plagued in our turn. I have the pleasure to tell you that I am vastly well, and in good spirits, but still of Pharaoh's lean kine. My dear girls are quite well, and as — but come and see them, I will not give you any account of them or any thing else.

Miss Seymour,* oh, heavens! I have not yet got the better of my astonishment. When I was at Wells she herself mentioned Mr. Hyde to me, and told me of his advantageous appointment. I observed that I thought she could not do better — a fine fortune, an amiable man, and one who had proved the steadiness of his regard for her. Her reply was, 'Oh! Mrs. Sage, talk not of him — I hate, I detest him; were the Indies in his possession I could not *marry* that man.' The very next news I heard from Wells was, that Miss Seymour and Mr. Hyde were to be married in a few days. *Can happiness ensue from such a union?*

Lord and Lady Francis are with the young couple in town; I found cards on my table which had been left in my absence. To-morrow I go to wait on her, but I shall meet her both with *pity* and *dis*esteem. If she recollects a late conversation (which I have above repeated) sure she must sink at the sight of me. What a sacrifice has she made to jewels and fine clothes! Fine feathers make fine birds, but they do not make happy ones.

If you read as fast as I write, I'm sure you will not distinguish one word from another. I have three letters to despatch by this post, so must bid you adieu; my husband is gone to the play. I have no love or compliments to send you, but those of

Your fondly affectionate sister,

E. SAGE.

* Mary, daughter of Lord Francis Seymour, Dean of Wells and vicar of Henstridge, youngest brother of Edward, eighth Duke of Somerset, married September 1773 John Hyde, Esq., Judge of the Supreme Court of Calcutta.

MRS. SAGE TO DR. WHALLEY.

Christmas, 1773.
Lovel Hill, Sunday morning.

I HAVE just taken up my pen, my dearest brother, to inquire after your health. I feel myself extremely uneasy at being separated from you at this time; and more particularly as I forgot to request the favour of a line from you while absent, to tell me how you fare. I hope in God that the quietude of your chamber has promoted sleep, and that I shall have the happiness to observe the good consequences of it when I come home again.* I hope you take care of yourself, and order what you like, and that you take what exercise the weather will admit of. I hope by this you have had a good account of dear Mrs. Sherwood.† I wish, my dear, you were of our party here, which is a very agreeable one. We sat down a large company to dinner yesterday, and spent a most joyous evening. In the morning we went to church, and in the afternoon were engaged at the card table; and after supper music took place, and we sung songs and catches till twelve o'clock. Two-and-fifty people dined in the house yesterday; and the servants were as merry as their masters. The weather is very uncomfortable; so our amusements must be confined within doors. How do my dear girls? I fear they miss me sadly. Here are a fine troop, six of them, the eldest not eight years old. Sweeter children you never saw. As you are circumstanced, I should in vain wish you a merry Christmas; but with confidence I wish you a happy New Year, and hope a number of them will return, replete with blessings.

Adieu, my dear brother, and believe me most truly and affectionately yours,

ELIZA SAGE.

* This illness was occasioned by a fall from his horse, and is alluded to in his verses on the first anniversary of his marriage, p. 215.

† He shortly after married this lady.

P.S. Give my love to dear Fanny and Emily, with a kiss; and remember me to nurse. Pray present my compliments to Lady Mary Knollis.

[The object in giving this letter, dated 1774, and another written more than a half century later, is to justify the remark which has been made of the steadiness of Dr. W.'s friendships.]

DR. WARRINGTON TO DR. WHALLEY.

Little Acton, October 26, 1774.

DEAR WHALLEY,—I cannot let Mrs. Price go to Somersetshire, without giving you my reasons why it cannot be in my power to visit you this winter. We have had more favourable accounts from Jamaica lately, than any we had before received. The estate has been taken out of the hands of the mortgagee by the Chancellor, upon a presumption that his demands were satisfied; and was placed in the care of one of Mr. Strudwicke's executors for the payment of the other creditors. This gentleman lately died; and the only surviving executor to Mr. Strudwicke is now on the point of sailing from England to Jamaica, and earnestly desires that my wife and I will come up to town, and consult with him upon the expediency of the measures intended to be pursued. It was but last year I offered our whole interest in the estate for two thousand pounds, and the proposal (according to my present sentiments) was luckily refused: so very unfavourable were our accounts, and so little expectation had we of receiving any future advantage from it. If ever we should live to be in possession of it, I shall always acknowledge the truth of that sentiment in Hamlet, that 'Our *indiscretion* sometimes serves us well, when our deep plots do fail; and that should teach us, there 's a Divinity that shapes our ends, *rough-hew* them how we will.'

We shall set out for London in a few days. Luckily, Travis and his wife are going; so we have contrived to travel together. Let me hear from you whilst I am in town. We shall be at our old quarters, Mrs. Clarke's, Duke Street, Piccadilly.

My sister Simpson desires me to ask (and you to answer) what is become of the picture she has so long expected to receive from Rome? Answer, thou son of inattention, answer!

Mrs. Price will tell you that my wife and I mean to visit you in the spring: she, I imagine, will hardly have left you by that time. If ever she returns into this neighbourhood, send the fat doctor to take care of her.

My wife joins me in good wishes to you and Mrs. Whalley.

I am, always, your affectionate friend,

George Warrington.

MRS. SAGE TO DR. WHALLEY.

October 1, 1775.

My dearest Brother,—I fear you have thought me very tardy in neglecting thus long to reply to your kind letter. My dear good brother and sister at Langford never forget me, or are they less present to my mind, with the remembrance of all their kindness, though I have omitted to tell them so. You will believe me when I say, my head and time have been fully engaged in business for some time past. When I wrote last I told you I was going to town, where I stayed two days, and went aboard the ship, where I found the captain quite at my command, owing to my good friend, Mr. Stables, who had made large promises, if he accommodated me well. Accordingly, he told me I was to choose my cabin in any part of the ship, and also my company, as he should admit no lady whatsoever, or any other passenger, without my permission; that he then had had several applications to take ladies, but would refuse them all, unless I took a lady myself, and then he would provide for her in the best manner he was able. This was everything I could wish, and much more than I had any right to expect, or could ever have obtained, but through Mr. Stables, who, as a director, had great power over an India captain. You know, at first, that Mr. Stables advised me not to take a companion. We have since had a deal of conversation on the subject, and on weighing the *con*veniences and *in*conveniences, it is determined that I must take a lady with me. I have had various applications, and have partly fixed on a Miss Brooke, who has been represented to me as a very well-brèd clever girl. Her father is a major in the King's service. Mr. Wheeler, who is one of the directors, and was the chairman when Mr. Sage was appointed, was the person who applied to me to take Miss Brooke, who is going out to an uncle in Counsel.

I cannot think that Susan's going * would answer any purpose but that of distressing my mother's pocket and mind, and adding to my anxiety. She is not young enough for such a scheme, or equal in any respect to the things she would have to encounter with. I have a support: the thought of seeing a beloved husband, for whom I would make every sacrifice, will fortify my mind (weak as it is) against every horror. Within the last week I received a letter from Mr. Sage, dated the 5th February, from the boat going up to Patna. I thank God he was tolerably well; but expresses his misery in still stronger terms, though he does not name a word of my following him. His tenderness and my own weighs down every obstacle which fear can place in the way.

My brother gives me a good account of your health, which you will believe I rejoice in. My dear sister, I also hear, is

* Susanna Whalley, born at Cambridge, 1739, married —— Crane, M.D., died at Henstridge, where she was buried 1809.

well; pray give my kindest love to her, and tell her that her Fanny talks of her perpetually, and that she now reads a chapter in the Bible.

I shall go to town very shortly, and as soon as I get there shall write to you again. I have taken a house in Pall Mall.

God preserve you, my dear brother, and continue to love your affectionate sister,

E. SAGE.

I wrote to Keate* as soon as I received yours.

Mr. Sage desires his kind remembrance to your whole selves.

Thornhill, Monday morn.

MRS. SAGE TO DR. WHALLEY.

Preparing to sail to India.
Pall Mall, November 2, 1775.

I SHALL be extremely obliged to my dear Sedgwick if he will procure me some Bristol water to take aboard ship. I would not give you this trouble, but am entirely at a loss who to apply to, either at Bristol or the Wells. I could have it here, but cannot depend on its being fresh; and it would answer little purpose to carry it stale. I shall want two chests, twelve dozen in each, and it must be in town by this day three weeks, as about that time the ship sails from Gravesend, and then I must have all my things on board; so you may imagine I am not a little hurried. My wardrobe is in hand, and furniture for my cabin making. The captain has behaved in the most polite manner, and complies with every request, nay even thinks for me. Miss Brooke has been to see me, and is quite an accomplished sweet girl. Mr. Rumbold has made application to me to

* Father or uncle to Dr. Keate, late head-master of Eton.

take a niece of his; and in so pressing a manner—in short, presses it in the light of such a favour—that I cannot refuse a person to whom I am so much obliged, and such a particular friend of Mr. Sage's. This young lady's name is Northall, and she is to be in Miss Brooke's cabin.

I give you joy of our new sister.* Poor Dick is at last united to the object of all his wishes, and I hope in God will be happy. I expect them in town next Monday. How does my dear sister? Present her my kindest love, and tell her that poor Fanny never forgets her tenderness, and longs to go to Langford.

Adieu my dear brother, and be assured I can never cease to think of you with the utmost affection,

E. SAGE.

Best respects to Lady Mary Knollis.

If my sister will let Mrs. Bishop make me a little pickled cabbage, it would be a high favour to me.

MRS. SAGE TO JAMES WICKHAM, ESQ., FROME, SOMERSET.

December, 1775.

MY DEAR GOOD SIR,—I have this moment received your kind, your affectionate letter, for which my heart returns you more ample thanks, than my pen can do. I am extremely obliged to my dear Mr. Wickham for his attention to my concerns at Thornhill, which I have long neglected, having such various other matters to think on. I would now wish to have the estate advertised and let, according to your judgment, as to the rent; but on these conditions, that the farmer must give up as many acres as you think necessary to go with the

* Richard Whalley, having returned from Rome, had now married the object of his long attachment, Eliz. Frances, daughter of Rev. John Paine, Canon of Wells.

house, provided that should be tenanted. I must farther entreat the favour of you to receive the rents, and out of them pay my little girl's expenses at Langford. I have insisted on my brothers receiving 100*l.* per annum for her board, Mrs. Mazell's and nurse's. Mrs. Mazell is to have 25 guineas per annum, and nurse ten. Mrs. Mazell will receive from me for the first year, and nurse will acquaint you that I am in her debt. You will also be kind enough to answer any little bills, which Tom may send you on Fanny's account; the overplus you will remit to Mr. Stables, who has the management of Mr. Sage's money. And now, my ever dear Sir, let me return you my most grateful acknowledgements for all your good wishes, and believe that they are repaid you tenfold. I can scarcely write for tears—tears of affection, and the warmest friendship! Be assured that I am sensible of all your kindness, and that your worth and goodness to me will ever be recent in my memory. Was not my heart warmed with the strongest affections, I should go without a pang. I feel no fear but that of leaving those I love; and my dear brother and sister, Wickham, must ever hold the first place in my heart. Ten thousand thanks to my kind sister for her proposal, but I could not see you without suffering more than I could support with any degree of fortitude.

I know not how to bid you farewell. God protect and preserve you, my beloved sister, and your sweet children. Be assured, my dear Sir, that my esteem and affection for you can only cease with my existence!

Your affectionate and obliged sister,

E. Sage.

I shall omit no opportunity of writing.

I shall send down a gown of mine to my sister, which, I trust, she will wear for my sake. I should not take this liberty with her, was it not my own work. You will present her and the dear children my kind love.

MRS. SAGE TO DR. WHALLEY.

Pall Mall, December 6, 1775.

You urge me, my dearest brother, to hasten my journey to Langford, which visit I had indulged myself in reflecting on; but as the time approaches that I am to bid you adieu, my resolution weakens. My hand is only equal to the task. Thus, then, accept my warmest and tenderest wishes for your health, happiness, and every felicity this world can give, in which my dear sisters are included. 'Tis but a few hours since, that I prevailed on myself to give up the pleasure of seeing you, but indeed I fear it would soften my mind and affect yours, more than might be right; and the short time I have to command would make it impossible for me to stay with you more than a few hours. Do not think I have had any time to spare which I might have passed in Somersetshire. So far from it, that I have not been at leisure even to go so little a way as Stanmore,* but once for a day.

My dear brother will be pleased to hear that I have every

* Mr. Sage's younger brother Joseph resided at Stanmore, and Dr. Whalley narrated a remarkable story connected with him. On returning one Sunday from Stanmore Church, the elder brother passed some sceptical comments on the story of the Witch of Endor, which had been introduced into the sermon. After bearing with this ridicule for some time, the younger brother was much moved, and said, in order to disabuse his scepticism as to the appearance of ghosts, he would reveal a circumstance in his life which he had never before mentioned. 'It has probably,' said he, 'appeared strange to you, that having so large a family of my own, I should have brought up with them a boy no way connected with me. I will now explain my motive. The boy's father, an excellent man, was my particular friend. He had been unfortunate in several commercial speculations, and at length collecting all his remaining resources, he embarked them on a last venture. I was conversant of the fact; and not long after he sailed, judge of my surprise, at seeing him one night standing by my bedside. In solemn accents he told me, that his ship with all her passengers and freight had foundered at sea, and that he had been permitted to appear to me, in order to intercede in behalf of his only son now left friendless and penniless in the wide world. The apparition of my friend disappeared, and from that moment I adopted his son as my own.'

satisfaction to expect in my passage. My friends, equally kind and powerful, have obtained every comfort for me that it is possible to have, and the captain has refused every lady that has applied to go in his ship, that I may not be incommoded. I shall have all the great cabin to myself, except a part, which I spare to the two young ladies whom I take with me. My spirits keep up; nor should I cast one look behind, but for the friends I leave, they ever must be dear! No time or distance can remove their idea, or the remembrance of the tenderness I have received, particularly from my dear Sedgwick and my sister. All the love you would continue to show me, bestow on my poor Fanny, your Fanny now; I give her up to you with this confidence, that she will never feel the loss of father or mother, while under your care. Protect her innocence, and foster her virtues.

I expect to be called on in about ten days. If to reflect on me intrudes upon your time, banish from your mind a sister who never can cease to love you most faithfully. Present my kind remembrance to my sister. Excuse me, I can add no more. Adieu!

E. SAGE.

My respects and very good wishes attend dear Lady Mary.

MRS. SAGE TO MRS. WICKHAM.

Pall-Mall, December 8, 1775.

I had indulged the pleasurable idea of seeing my dear Mr. and Mrs. Wickham again, but, alas! I must relinquish that happiness. My spirits have undergone so great fatigue, that I am not able to encounter the pain of bidding a personal adieu to the friends my heart holds so dear. Indeed, my dearest Sir, I am unequal to the task. My time is now so short, that were I to pursue my scheme of going into Somersetshire, I could only stay a few hours at any place. Accept, then, this farewell. Accept, my ever dear brother and sister, my warmest wishes for your health, happiness, and every felicity this world can give. Believe that these wishes flow from the heart, and that no time or distance can weaken my affection for you and yours, or remove from my mind a grateful remembrance of the friendship and favours I have received from my dear Mr. Wickham and yourself.

I expect to be called on in about ten days. I go with no other regret than that of leaving my child and friends. I have every comfort to expect that can be afforded in a ship; powerful friends and money have procured me every advantage and convenience, and the captain has in all respects been studious to oblige me. I told you I had promised to take a Miss Brooke, since which time Mr. Rumbold solicited me to permit a niece of his to go with me. These will be my female companions. The captain refused every other lady, that I might have just what room I liked. I fear I shall not be able to write again while on terra firma, but hope in a short time to address you from some other shore. Let me have a parting line from you. Farewell! bestow a thought sometimes on a sister, who can never cease to regard you with the warmest and tenderest affection.

ELIZA SAGE.

P.S. Present my kindest love to dear Mr. Wickham, Moll and the other sweet children. God preserve them to you!

Remember me kindly to Mr. and Mrs. Whitchurch and to my friends at Frome Field. I wished to have seen them once more.

Pray don't forget to present my best compliments and

good wishes to Mr. and Mrs. Horner. Once more, my dear sir, I bid you adieu. Remember me to poor Mary.

MRS. SAGE TO MRS. WICKHAM.

Portsmouth, January 6, 1776.

MY DEAR SISTER,—I am in a kind of disagreeable situation, I will not say a distressed one, because I am perfectly well, and have great reason to be thankful to Providence and my friends. As this is dated from Portsmouth, you will be surprised to hear that I have been at sea. Wednesday morning, the wind fair, we sailed, all in spirits. The commissioner, who had with his lady before showed me every civility, ordered his boats and yacht to convey me to the ship, and himself accompanied us. Never was a finer day, or could anything be more delightful. The commissioner, who is one of the most polite men in the world, had prepared in the state cabin a collation to regale us till we reached the ship, which was many miles from shore. Thus we sailed in state—for the king when here was accommodated in this yacht—and we had the royal oars! My friends all attended me, and they did not leave me till the ship was under weigh. This was about four o'clock in the afternoon; the wind favoured us till ten the same night, when it changed and a storm arose, which continued with great violence, and the captain thought it advisable to return to Spithead, as we had not cleared the land, and therefore might be wrecked. Thus we returned, fired a gun for a pilot, and got safe back again. The commissioner immediately ordered his yacht to fetch me ashore, but the sea rose so high that they would not venture out to the ship that day, Thursday. Friday, which was yesterday, he, with Mr. Stables and Joe,* came to

* Mr. Joseph Sage of Stanmore, mentioned p. 287. He was for upwards of forty years master of the mint.

me aboard, and carried me in a boat to the yacht in such a sea! You would have died to have seen it. But I arrived safe here, and met my two female friends, Mrs. Bund and Mrs. Stables, who would not leave the place, till they were sure I was safe away, which the wind would inform them of.

Now, my dearest sister, I know you will shudder at this account, which I would not give you, but that the papers may alarm you by saying the ship was drove back. Will you believe me, my dear sister, when I tell you that there was not a stouter heart aboard? I was neither frighted, sick, nor sorry. I know not how it was, but I felt myself amazingly supported. The two young ladies with me were sick to death, so were both my man and maid. I was well enough to nurse them, and was not only well, but in great spirits; for two hours before I left Portsmouth I received a letter from my beloved Sage. Think what a blessing! think what I could go through with cheerfulness after this cordial! The wind is now fair again, and the yacht is once more ordered. I go without a fear; fear not for me. God bless you, my dear, dear sister and brother. I scarcely know what I write, as you will see; I wish you may be able to read such a scrawl. My head is confused, as you may imagine, with such new and such variety of scenes.

I cannot write to my mother. Send her this account, and tell her that I had wrote a letter when I first went aboard, as I thought it would be a comfort to her to receive a letter from me dated from the ship. This letter I gave to Stables, but he did not send it, as he feared the wind was likely to change. I now burn it. Commend me to my dearest mother, brothers, and sisters. My love to dear Mr. Wickham and the children. If I do not go this evening, I shall write again to my mother, or some of my dear friends. Oh! my dear Fanny, send my blessing to her. I would not think of her.

God preserve you all. I shall never cease to think on you or love you. Adieu, my dear sister.

E. SAGE.

MRS. SAGE TO MRS. WICKHAM.

Island of Madeira.
Funchaul, February 6, 1776.

WHAT joy do I feel in addressing you, my dearest Madam! How happy does it make me to consider, that this letter is likely to reach you very soon, and remove a great part of the anxiety which I fear you have felt for me; and for some time to come, this is the only satisfaction I am to expect. The happiness of hearing from my dearest mother, is a hope removed at a great distance from me. Yet I trust that comfort is in store, and Heaven and my own heart only knows what joy it will give me; how ardently I shall long to receive a letter from the best of mothers, which I hope will convey an account of her health, and that of my dear brothers and sisters. Believe that my friends in Somersetshire are ever present to my mind, and that no time or distance can remove them thence.

Safely arrived at this port, we esteem the worst part of the voyage over. Though we were horribly tossed, owing to rough seas, yet we met with little bad weather, and have reason to think ourselves particularly fortunate, as several other ships on their passage here were greatly distressed. Captain Johnson, of the Granby, who sailed a month before us, did not make this land till a week after we arrived. I was so happy as to suffer nothing from sea-sickness during my passage, though the ship rolled so violently, that even those were affected who had been to sea for twenty years. So far from being indisposed myself, I have not known such health since the birth of my dear Fanny, and am really grown fat; for the sea air gave me such an amazing appetite, that I was eating continually, and with a degree of hunger as I never felt before. You will be surprised at this account. I am surprised at myself, when I look back and compare my late heroineship with my former fears. My two companions suffered a great deal, as did my maid and man-servant, who were ill the whole time; but they have nothing farther to dread on that score, as we shall get immediately into the trade winds after leaving this place, and have not even a probability of meeting with any bad weather, between Madeira and Bengal, at this season of the year. An angry sea, though a tremendous, is a fine sight. I used to sit in the balcony and look on it, when the waves rolled mountains high, and perhaps a large sea broke over the ship, and wet every one on the deck from head to foot; but when she goes nine or ten knots an hour on a smooth sea, with all her sails out, you can scarcely conceive anything more delightful; nor can anything surprise one more, than that so large a body should go so fast as ten miles an hour, and even without your feeling any motion.

We anchored here the 27th, and came ashore the same evening. I confess I did not expect to find myself received by such a family as this, as I had not been taught to expect anything here, beyond necessary convenience. On the contrary, we have passed our time most agreeably, and have so many schemes and engagements, that it is with difficulty I steal an hour to take up my pen; for as every amusement is studied on my account, I cannot well absent myself. You will expect some description of this place, and the style of the people. The island of Madeira is about seventy miles round, and appears, when first you approach the land, like a chain of barren rocks. Indeed, they are little more at this season, as the hills are covered with vines which have not yet put forth their leaves, so that there is no appearance of verdure, but a great number of houses scattered on the side of an immense high hill, have a very romantic look. These are houses belonging to families who reside here in the winter, and resort to the mountain in the hot season; this, which they call their winter, is as warm as a very fine day the latter end of May, or beginning of June, in England. Such has been the weather ever since we arrived, nor is it at any time cold enough to light a fire. Indeed, there are no chimneys in any of the houses here, except the kitchen. This is a large city; just at the bottom of the hills and close along the sea-shore; from this description you would form an idea of its being a pleasant place; on the contrary, you can have no conception of anything so vile.

The Portuguese are wretched architects, so that the houses have a very uncouth appearance, and are built so close together that there is scarcely room for a carriage to pass along the streets, which, from the extreme nastiness of the inhabitants, are offensive beyond measure. Every species of cleanliness seems an idea extinct among these people. All the lower rank, both men and women, go without shoes and stockings, and their houses are literally pig-sties, for they live together in common. You will see a number of women, children, and hogs, lying on the floor side by side, and it is difficult to determine which is the greatest beast. The Portuguese ladies are, I think, the most wretched of human beings, as they are brought up in the greatest ignorance and confined to their houses, unless when they go to mass, and then their heads and faces are covered. Thus, from education and custom they are wholly excluded from amusing themselves at home or receiving entertainment abroad. The houses of the genteeler kind of people have all iron grates before the windows, and the other houses are not glazed, but have lattices just open enough to admit the light, but not to give you a sight of the horrid brown faces behind them, unless they lift them up, which they are continually doing, as they seem to have no other employment but to peep at the people who are passing the streets. There is a small playhouse here, which was lately built, and is a tolerable one. They act twice a week and always on a Sunday night. This amusement was set afoot by the governor, who seldom fails being present. At this place I have had an opportunity of seeing the Portuguese ladies, some of whom have within this little while been permitted to appear there, but always in boxes by themselves, excepting their maids, who also attend them when they walk. Gentlemen are never of the party. Whether this custom arises from delicacy on the female side or contempt on the other, I will not pretend to determine.

The style of the Portuguese ladies' dresses is very singular; they always wear black silk, with a quantity of red or yellow ribbon. They never wear any caps, or indeed any ornament on their heads but what Nature has given them, except small tortoise-shell combs, which are stuck about as we would dispose our diamond pins. The hair is combed straight back and fastened up behind very loosely, and, as they are very fond of pomatum without the use of powder, you may imagine a head thus equipped cannot have the most delicate appearance. In general, the women have good hair and eyes; in other respects Nature has not been so lavish of her favours. Their complexions are swarthy, their persons short and fat—that kind of make which we vulgarly term squalid. The men have as few advantages of person to boast of; and, as they always walk with their hats in their hands, you may conceive the sun to have made great ravage among the roses and lilies in their faces. The priests (who look scarcely human) have all their heads shaved, except a small ring of hair round the head, which much resembles a black fringe that has been dipped in oil.

Churches, chapels, crosses and skulls present themselves

in every street. We need not be so frequently reminded of the misery of mortality or the fallen state of man while we view the Portuguese. The churches are very fine; I went to see one the other day which is more magnificent than you can well imagine. We were shown a chapel hung with crimson velvet, with the most superb gold ornaments, and the roof beautifully worked with gold, and large gates of solid silver. At the top of this chapel, raised on a throne, the Virgin Mary is placed in a gold chair; she is dressed in a sacque of rich brocade, with a large hoop, and her head and neck profusely adorned with jewels and ribbons. I was afraid to express my astonishment, not to say horror, at this sight.

Religion here wears the most farcical appearance; the churches look more like places of entertainment than those dedicated to devotion. You will see a priest sitting in his confessional chair, with two poor creatures kneeling one on each side, pouring out their sins to receive the balm of his forgiveness, while he is looking through his glass at those who are passing along. One of them surveyed me from head to foot in this manner. Here people walk in and out, and talk and laugh without giving offence. Sometimes you see a fellow with a dozen live turkeys hanging on a pole come in, drop down on his knees, and lift up his eyes in silent adoration, while the poor turkeys chant aloud, and devoutly pray for liberty, which petition I felt myself much disposed to listen to. The English gentlemen who reside here are all wine-merchants: the vineyards belong to the Portuguese, who make the wine and sell it to the English.

There is but a small society of ladies, but a great number of gentlemen. I was invited the other day to dinner where we sat down with more than twenty gentlemen and only six ladies; in the evening we had a very agreeable dance, and last night we had a very clever one at home, and such a number of beaux, for I assure you the gentlemen here are very smart, and as polite a set of men as I ever saw. Our party at home is a very large one; here are two gentlemen in partnership, and they are both married to genteel agreeable women. One has an unmarried sister, who lives with her, a very amiable sweet girl. There are also seven or eight gentlemen, some belonging to our ship and some to Captain Johnson's. It is the custom for the captains and what passengers they choose to introduce to continue at the houses where they deal for wine, and this is esteemed the genteelest, as one of the gentlemen is the English consul, which gives him some kind of consequence here.

Our evenings are generally passed in the musical way. Mrs. Many (who is the consul's lady) is a capital performer on the harpsichord, and has the finest instrument I ever heard, and a pianoforte also. Some of our gentlemen play the violin, others the flute, and your daughter Elizabeth is the vocal performer; and humble as her abilities are in the singing way, they have called the attention of all the beaux in Madeira. But a prophet, you know, has no honour in his own country. The governor, hearing of the second Mrs. Sheridan, expressed a wish to hear her, and accordingly a concert was prepared to which he was invited. The band consisted of two violins, a bass, the harpsichord, and a psalter, on which a gentleman here plays very well, and it is really a sweet instrument. We had likewise an Italian who sang pretty well. Could you have given a peep at me warbling Jackson's strains before thirty people! — but I did not want anyone to blush for me. The governor is very fond of music; he is a fine-looking man, and perfectly polite. We often talk of our friend Mrs. Hyde (who was much admired here), and my Lord Francis is my constant toast. There are great quantities of orange and lemon trees, but the fruit is not yet ripe enough to be very good. In the summer this island produces all kinds of fruits in great abundance.

The roads are so steep and rough that carriages are not made use of. When the ladies ascend the hills, they either go on horseback or are conveyed in a kind of palanquin; this method I chose. In the town they make use of sedan chairs. Could my brothers have seen me in this style, they would never have ceased laughing! The Portuguese are too proud to carry a chair, therefore the black men do it. Suppose me then in a chair, with one chairman six feet high, the other four feet five inches, each the same-sized great coat, which forms a train to one and a jacket for the other. Shoes and stockings are deemed unnecessary on these occasions, and often hair, as they are frequently shaved without calling on the friendship of hat or wig. Thus seated, with a footman on each side with flambeaux, a servant out of livery before with a sword on, and four or five gentlemen attending full-dressed (without a smile on their faces), moving to the play-house. Before I arrived there I was quite exhausted with laughing. Vanity, you see, exists in every climate, though the means of gratifying it is incomplete.

Here are roses, jessamine, and other flowers in great plenty, and I have generally half a dozen nosegays sent me in a morning by different gentlemen, which is thought here a great compliment. You will expect some account of my two companions, and it will give you pleasure to hear that I am much pleased with them. How can I be otherwise, when they are solicitous in every word and action to oblige and please me. They are both extremely sensible and good-natured. Miss Northall, Mr. Rumbold's niece, is very accomplished, but more of the school-girl than Miss Brooke, who is older, and has been educated under her father. She has a very good natural understanding much improved, and possesses a generous honest heart. I am almost angry with myself that I should neglect thus long to speak of Captain

Gore, whose kindness and attention calls for my acknowledgments. Indeed, he has seemed to study nothing but my convenience and comfort, and watches my very looks that he may fly to oblige.

MRS. SAGE TO MRS. WICKHAM.

Cape, April 28, 1776.

After so long a silence, what joy do I feel in addressing you, my dearest sister! And the affection which you have at all times and on all occasions shown me, affords my mind, at this moment, the flattering assurance that it will give you a very sincere pleasure to hear from me. We landed at the Cape the 21st of this month; but, being an uncertain season of the year, anchored at False Bay, which is a much safer harbour than this. False Bay is twenty miles from the Cape Town, which was a disagreeable circumstance, as the road hither is very bad. Indeed, it was the greatest inconvenience I had encountered, as our passage from Madeira to the Cape was so very favourable, that we were unacquainted with any kind of distress.

Thus far my undertaking has been attended with great success, and much beyond what I could expect, having enjoyed an uninterrupted state of health, which has wrought such a change in my looks, that I doubt whether my dear Sage will not think me a counterfeit, unless he remembers Miss E. W.; for I am really grown young again. The mill they talk of is certainly turned by salt water. Near the line we found it very hot; but the heat was more supportable than I expected to find it. Here we were entertained with catching sharks and other fish; and as we approached the Cape, a great number of birds flew about the ship, particularly a bird which they call an albatross; one of these we caught by a line and bait, which they dart down into the water and seize the moment they see it; this which we hooked measured three yards from the extent of the wings, which are very wide, for the body of the bird is not larger than a goose. This was a young bird; Captain Gore has seen them measure eighteen feet.

How do we magnify everything in prospect! So far from being alarmed, I enjoyed the voyage, and really assure you that, with a serene fine sky and smooth water, nothing can be so delightful. Nor was I ever better satisfied, or felt myself more at home, than aboard the Nassau. Indeed, I had every indulgence and comfort that a ship could afford; and my pleasure and convenience were alone consulted by Captain Gore, whose whole study was to please and amuse me. He kept a separate table for me, which is an unusual thing; but this and every other respect he paid me. Our table was well supplied with mutton, poultry of all kinds, roasting pigs, kid, salt fish, hams, pork remarkably fine, all kinds of pies, tarts, and puddings; and every day a dessert of oranges, almonds and raisins, and brandy fruits; hot rolls, and indeed everything except fresh butter.

Our passage was uncommonly favourable, having met with no bad weather from Madeira to the Cape, and, what is as extraordinary, out of two hundred and ten people, not to have one sick all the time!

Our journey from False Bay to this place was truly ridiculous! I can look on it in that light in retrospect, though at the time fear so fully possessed my mind, that no ludicrous idea could relieve me. We stayed at False Bay two days, till a coach could be procured to convey us hither. You are to conceive this vehicle an enormous tub, lined with red velvet, and adorned with yellow fringe; to this was harnessed four pair of rats. On a kind of box sat a black fellow, without shoes or stockings, to hold the reins; while another man ran by the side, never ceasing to make use of a whip five yards long at least; and, however severe this exercise may appear to you, it was often ineffectual; for when they chose to stop they would do so, and we waited till they chose to proceed — with how great a degree of patience I leave you to judge! Indeed, the road was chiefly through so deep a sand, that sometimes all the united efforts of eight horses was insufficient to move the carriage without the assistance of our men. For five miles we drove so near the sea, that I apprehended the carriage would be launched every moment! After this we drove over rocks; here my fears took a new turn, as being overset was the most palpable idea that could occur to our frightened imagination! Nor was it any comfort to reflect that we were passing through a country inhabited only by Hottentots, whose appearance is scarcely human, and would be totally disrobed were it not for the friendly aid of a sheep-skin thrown over their shoulders.

Our peregrination lasted from eleven o'clock in the morning till the setting of the sun. However, we had a good stout party, which supported our spirits. Captain Gore, Miss Brooke, myself and maid, occupied the coach; and Miss Northall, with a young gentleman (a relative of Mr. Stables, who is going out as writer, and put under my care), rode in a kind of two-wheeled chaise, drawn by four horses. We had another gent with us, and three servants. Thus we entered the Cape Town, which as we approached the scene changed to one very delightful, which was formed by a number of vineyards and pretty houses scattered about. Indeed, the face of the country round this place in general is very beautiful. The town is large and well-built, and the appearance of neatness is very pleasing. The house we are in is situated in a square, with turf, and rows of trees. The custom here is to board, and we have a very plentiful table, which is all I can say of it, for the Dutch are strangers to elegances. Our dinner and supper are much the same, only the joints are varied, except a boiled leg of mutton, which, did it not smoke, I should conceive was never removed from the table, as it appears there twice a day. Fruits and wine are set on with the other dishes. I find my friend Mrs. Hyde was at this house. We have a parlour twenty-one feet square, and two bed-rooms of the same size. Our stay here will only be a few days longer; we then sail for Madras, but stop for a few sheep (we take two hundred from hence) and fruit at Johana, which is just half-way between this and that.

I am much pleased with my companions, and have great reason to be so. They are not only extremely fond of me, and solicitous to oblige me in every instance, but they are both good-humoured and sensible, and have a great deal of knowledge. Miss Northall is the most accomplished girl I have met: indeed, she has had every advantage that the best masters and an expensive education can give, and really has a fine understanding. Miss Brooke is what you call 'a good creature;' she has been instructed chiefly by her father, and has read a great deal. Nothing can be more happy than our society. Captain Gore is a most amiable man; to give you an idea of his mind in one word, it is a counterpart of my dear Mr. Wickham's. How fortunate was I to sail with such a man! for, in general, these India captains are the greatest boors in the world! Captain Gore is the gentleman in every thought and action: he is the son of an Irishman of large fortune; his elder brother has now an estate of seven thousand a year. Captain Gore is the youngest of ten; and though of a family nearly related to the first noble families in Ireland, was placed in this style of life, which is a humiliating situation to a man of fashion, possessed of a liberal mind. For to acquire a fortune in these trading voyages, they must do many dirty things, and regard only self, which is the last object Captain Gore is attentive to.

I long to ask a thousand questions regarding yourself, Mr. W., and the dear children. How is dear little Mary, as good as ever? Give my kind love to all; and believe that they and you, my ever dear sister, have my warmest wishes for every kind of happiness. I often look on you with a mental eye, and with a heart full of affection.

Do not forget me, or cease to love me. Be assured no time or distance can make me less yours. Adieu, my dear sister. I shall neglect no opportunity of writing, and hope to address you from Madras.

E. Sage.

May 1.

Present my kind remembrance to Mr. and Mrs. Whitchurch. Give my love to Mrs. Edgell; tell her I have not forgot her, or ever shall.

MRS. SAGE TO MRS. WICKHAM.

The Cape, April 28, 1776.

I believe I have mentioned to none of my friends, in my letters, the no small fright I was in at leaving Madeira. You must know, before Captain Gore sailed from Portsmouth, he received by express an order to avoid steering the usual way, for fear of being taken by the Bostonian pirates, which were cruising about, and to prepare his guns and men for engagement. Think what I felt at the idea of going a prisoner to Boston—to lose my dear Sage—and be locked up! I said nothing of this in my letter to my mother from Madeira, as I would not give her fuel for fresh anxiety. Her imagination would have placed me in a dungeon immediately. However, we saw nothing of these rebels.

I have just received an invitation from the governor's lady to sup with her to-night. We have before exchanged a visit.

I hardly know what I have wrote; I have wrote so much to-day, and have not time to look it over, but I would wish to tell you that I am perfectly well, and am grown quite fat. Indeed, you must come to sea, Mary! I never ate with such an appetite in my life.

Present my compliments to Mr., Mrs., and Miss Horner, and Mrs. Bishop.

I left my guitar at Thorn Hill. I wish my Fanny had it. Don't forget to remember me to Mrs. W. Keate.*

MRS. SAGE TO MRS. WICKHAM.

Bankipore, Nov. 1, 1776.

My heart, in its present state of happiness, is open to no other, save that which arises from hearing of those dear connections it still retains the fondest remembrance of. This vacuum my friends have kindly filled. With what rapture do I break the seal which locks up the affectionate proofs of their continued regard, and an account of their health and welfare; which adds as much to my present stock of happiness as it is capable of receiving. Your kind letter, my dear sister, came to my hands on my passage hither; need I assure you of the satisfaction it gave me? Warmly affectionate as your heart is towards your friends, I must appeal to your own feelings to judge of mine on this occasion. Distance, variety, and a new acquaintance, which act as the waters of Lethe on minds void of constancy and sentiment, have an effect directly opposite on persons of a different disposition, and cause their bosoms to expand with an in-

* Mother of the late head-master of Eton.

crease of tenderness, on the recollection of those friends whom sea and land separate them from. The mind dwells with pleasure on every minute circumstance that awaits those, to whom they are connected by the ties of nature and affection!

At length, my dear sister, I am arrived at Bankside, after a voyage replete with happy circumstances, and continued health and spirits. This climate has had no other effect, than that of giving a kind of languor which violent heat must always occasion. Fever and bile, complaints that the inhabitants of this clime are most subject to, I have been entirely free from; and now the cold season is advancing, the prospect is invigorating to a mind oppressed and body fatigued on this Eastern shore, which is barren, in my opinion, of any real joys, nor allows any to those detained on it, which do not arise from self. You may, perhaps, be surprised when I tell you, that to me a life of parade and state, which Mr. Sage's consequence here gives me, is irksome. Yet so it is; nor do I derive any satisfaction but from his society and tenderness, which is, if possible, more than ever; nor do we feel a pleasure independent of each other.

An Indian life is chiefly divided betwixt dressing and sleeping. My style of passing my time is as follows:—We rise pretty early, when Mr. Sage mounts his horse, and I pursue the exercise of walking, during which I could wish you to see my attendants. One man walks by my side with an umbrella, also another kind of state servant (which are perfect shadows to their mistress), and behind him four others, with long canes. Thus in procession I take my ramble till breakfast, after which Mr. Sage pays me a visit, for we do not take this meal together, nor are we in the same house. I have apartments of my own, which consist of a bed chamber and three small rooms adjoining (one of them a bathing room), also a very good room which Mr. Sage built for me, when he first heard of my coming out. He has always company to breakfast, and the rest of his morning is engaged in business. I spend mine in reading, writing, and the grand study of dress, to prepare which I have always three tailors (who are men that work very neatly) employed. Mondays and Thursdays are council days, when Mr. Sage has a public table: on those days I eat in my own room; on other days I dine with him. After dinner we go to bed, rise again about five, dress for the evening, and take an airing in the carriage till tea. But as the day closes in this part of the world very early, our rides are somewhat singular. As it is generally pretty dark before we get home, on our return we are met by ten or a dozen servants with flambeaux, and, instead of horsemen attending the carriage, a man runs by the side of each horse, which they are so accustomed to, that they keep pace with them, and will go for ten miles without being out of breath or fatigued. On our public days I join the evening party, which is large enough to make five or six tables, and we play cards till supper.

There is but a small society of ladies immediately around me. At the distance of six miles are cantonments (barracks), where there are a good many ladies, who have all been to see me, but I intend only to visit them once, as it is farther than I like to go, and those near me are such as I like better. One of the council's wives is a very genteel pretty woman, and her husband is Mr. Sage's most intimate friend at this place. Our house is situated in the midst of a green, with walks and trees; my apartments at the distance of about twice the length of the garden, and close on the banks of the River Ganges, which renders it both pleasant and cool. We have also a small paddock stocked with deer, which brings very good venison to our table. The mutton here is pretty well, and kid supplies the place of lamb. We only kill beef in the cold season, and this is stall fed. The cattle here are small and very poor, insomuch that they are first bought for the value of 40*s.*, yet every pound costs more than 2*s.* by the time it comes to the table. But I assure you the meat is very fine, and there are now forty large oxen in our stalls as fine as any in Europe.

From the indolent style of life Mr. Sage led in England, you would not imagine him a man calculated for business, yet he is immersed in it, and goes through it with an ease that would astonish you. On council days there are from 800 to 1,000 people, with complaints, petitions, and other matters; emissaries from different parts of a province as large as England, which appeal to this council, and when there is any particular cause to be determined 1,500 people have been assembled together round the house. The council meet about nine o'clock, and sit at the board till three (which is an hour later than we dine on other days), but fatiguing as this may appear to you, it is the less arduous part of Mr. Sage's department, as the number of private letters and public addresses to the government and board below keep his head and pen constantly at work.

They have lately been re-letting all the farms, as the leases have expired. What say you to a man taking a farm of 12,000*l.* a year, and some of 20,000*l.*? Many such there are. Great as this will place such a renter in your idea, they are the most wretched of all human beings. Possessed of vast wealth, they are destitute of every joy in life. They live in mere hovels, eat nothing but rice, nor have any amusement whatever but that pleasure which arises from amassing one hoard upon another. Indeed, they have no idea or wish to spend money, but in the purchase of jewels, with which they load themselves, and women—of whom they keep a great number, immured between walls, which they are never suffered to go beyond the boundaries of. As to mental enjoyments these people are utterly deprived of them, from a total neglect of education. The only knowledge they possess is that of getting money, and this is so strongly inculcated in their earliest youth, that it makes a lasting impression, and absorbs every other idea. Do not you think it a virtue to dispossess these people (such as I have described them) of some of their trash, which they do not know how to use, and which would be the avenue of happiness to so many worthy people distressed from the want of this alone? However, this country has been tolerably pilfered; but in the present constitution of things, a rogue is obliged to play the character of an honest man; but as feigned characters must ever sit awkward on those who assume them, the man of real honour and integrity will still be distinguished.

If you wish to know the particulars of my arrival at Bengal, and of my reception there from Mrs. Hyde, I refer you to my mother; and to Frank or Dick for the account of my voyage from Calcutta hither, which was attended with such singular circumstances, that I repeated them to both, thinking it might be some entertainment, and as I did not suppose they would see each other's letter.

You may imagine us fixed here for some years, but that is far from our intention. Had I not taken this resolution of coming out, Mr. Sage would have set sail for Europe probably in the very ship which conveys this to you, unable, as he told me, to support a longer separation. He was settling his affairs to return when the account of my intention arrived, and he left it entirely to me to resolve whether I would go this season or the next; the latter I preferred both from a pecuniary motive, and as my mind rejected, however pleasant the voyage has been, a repetition of it so soon. One year, my dear sister, will soon elapse, and it will be no more after this reaches your hands (with the permission of that Being who has protected me till this time), ere I embrace my dear friends in England, and revisit my native land. I long to make a thousand enquiries after your whole self and dear children; and a something whispers me, that this will find an addition to the group of prattlers. Be that as it may, believe that you and the little circle of my acquaintance often engage my thoughts.

A very worthy woman, whom I shall recall to your remembrance by the name of Finetta Bathurst, is daily brought to mine by a Mr. Bathurst, who is of our family, and not only like her in face, but disposition, for he possesses the best of hearts. This young man is a near relation of Lord Apsley's, and was sent out by him to the care of Mr. Hastings, the Governor-General, who recommended him to Mr. Sage, in consequence of which he has lived with him ever since he came to Patna, and was a great comfort to Mr. Sage in his bachelor state, for he is a most excellent companion, and quite the gentleman. We have here beaux in plenty, insomuch that the old lady's proverb is reversed: many shoulder knots, as there is a military force of 7,000 men at Dinapore, only six miles off.

I was much pleased to hear that Thornhill was so well let, and extremely obliged to dear Mr. W. for the trouble he has taken on that account. I will farther beg the favour of him to select any five poor people that he shall judge in the greatest distress, and allow them weekly a shilling each till I return. I left orders for a trifle to be paid constantly by Clift to two or three poor creatures, which I hope he did not neglect to do, or since the place was let to acquaint you with to continue it.

Captain Gore has promised to smuggle ashore a few things for me; among them is a sacque for you, which I beg your acceptance of. Also in the parcel there are some shawls, from which I desire you will make first your choice, and present the other two, one to Mrs. Whitchurch, and the other to Mrs. Edgell, with my love and compliments. Tell Mrs. W. I thought it would keep her shoulders warm of a Sunday morning; and Mrs. E., when she walks from Frome Field in the snow; from these motives I am tempted to offer them such ugly things. My dear Molly will excuse a very indifferent piece of muslin for a frock; but there are no better worked in this neighbourhood. The very fine work is all done at Dacca, from which place I expect a cargo soon. Tell Molly I divided a piece between her and her cousin Fanny, and that I hope the same love subsists that was wont to do betwixt them. Tell her also, I shall hope to bring home some little birds called amadevats, and would send her now, but that it would be vain to commit anything of this kind to the care of a person during a long voyage, or this part of the world might supply me with the means of obliging her.

You will easily imagine, my dear sister, how happy it has made me to receive such good accounts of my darling child, the separation from whom would constantly corrode on my peace, did not hope borrow comfort from futurity. I am in this place interrupted by the arrival of seven gentlemen, clothed in yellow, some of our favourite acquaintance, as they have the most extensive influence. These are seven brothers, who go by the name of Salam. Frank will introduce you to their acquaintance more intimately, as I have given him a history of the family, which often visit Mr. W. in his office, in the European dress; and he has my earnest wish for their being on the most intimate footing. To enlighten your mind towards the solution of this enigma, I will further add that there are two attendants which tread close on the heels of the above-mentioned gentlemen, of very opposite characters, the one called Honour, the other Disgrace. Yet the latter never dared to put his foot on Mr. W.'s threshold, though he too often knocks very loud (insomuch that the world hears the report) at a lawyer's door.

I am loath to bid you adieu, my dearest sister, but the number of letters I have still to write obliges me to resign this employment, which I could, from inclination, pursue much longer. Farewell, then, my dear Mrs. Wickham, and believe me, with every wish for the happiness of you and yours, which, though a hackneyed conclusion, is offered with the warmest zeal,

By your sincerely affectionate

ELIZA SAGE.

P.S.—My kindest love awaits Mr. W. and your young folks.

I have sent by Captain Gore a bottle of ottar of roses, which I beg you will present to Mrs. Horner, with my most friendly compliments.

Remember me to poor Mary, to whom I have sent some muslin handkerchiefs, no otherwise valuable than as a proof that I do not forget her.

Miss Burney thus speaks of Mr. Anstey:

'Mr. Anstey, I cannot doubt, must sometimes be very agreeable. He could not else have written so excellent, so diverting, so original a satire. But he chooses to keep his talents to himself, or only to assert them upon very particular occasions. Yet what he can call particular I know not; for I have seen him with Mrs. Montagu, with Mrs. Thrale, with the Bishop of Peterborough, and with Lord Mulgrave; and four more celebrated folks can hardly be found. Yet, before them all he has been the same as when I have seen him without any of them. Shily important, and silently proud!'

CHRISTOPHER ANSTEY TO DR. WHALLEY.

Bath, August 3, 1779.

DEAR SIR,—I return you many thanks for your civilities to my son, whom you have made extremely happy, as appears from a letter we lately received from him, in which he tells us that his life is one continued round of pleasure and diversions. We begin, however, to be a little apprehensive that you may have had almost enough of his company, and would wish to know when it would be agreeable to yourself and Mrs. Whalley for us to send for him home. We are lately arrived here from Cheltenham, where Mrs. Anstey received much benefit from the waters. The rest of my family now with me, in number seven, are in good health; and all join in compliments to yourself and family, to which Mrs. Anstey and myself must add our particular thanks to yourself and Mrs. Whalley for your kind attention to our son; and if my old and much respected friend your mother, Mrs. Whalley, is now with you, I desire to be in the kindest manner remembered to her. I am, very sincerely,

Dear Sir,

Your obliged and most obedient humble servant,

CHR. ANSTEY.*

LADY MILLER TO DR. WHALLEY.

Bath-Easton Villa, October 30, 1779.

SIR,—I am sat down to a table furnished with pen, ink, and paper, with intention of answering your letter. But I tremble all over, and have actually a nervous complaint (which, I hope, is only temporary) at the very idea of writing to you again—conscious of my own deficiency.

* Mr. Anstey, the author of the well-known Bath Guide, lived in one of the first built houses in the Royal Crescent, and his gardens extended to the site of what is at present St. James's Square. Madame D'Arblay complains of his reserve in society, and that he always appeared to remember he was the author of the Bath Guide. This poem, then so celebrated, would not now be tolerated in a drawing-room, as whatever merit it may possess, on the score of wit and versification, is more than counterbalanced by its indecent portraiture of immorality.

The greatest service I could do the public would be to print your letter, concealing the person's name to whom it is addressed; for the elegance of the style, the purity of the language, the heavenly benevolence which beams throughout, render it worthy the author, and worthy the applause and imitation of all those who attempt letter-writing. It is the best paraphrase, or rather definition, of that glorious and brightest ornament of our faith— charity—in all its extent.

We are all exceedingly concerned at the dreadful accident that has befallen Mr. Melmoth. He has our most cordial and sincere wishes for his speedy recovery. I was so anxious to learn the result of Dr. De la Cour's profound skill, that I postponed writing to you to enquire after your sick friend till to-day, as I was to call upon Miss Gould, from whom I expected to hear, what I heartily wished, the decision of that learned leech. But this disciple of Celsus, it seems, could not visit Langford Court; so I returned just as wise as I came.

If it is possible, under such sufferings as Melmoth's, to feel comfort from the genial influence of friendship, surely he must feel alleviation under your hospitable roof from the sharpest afflictions of body or mind. I enclose the copy of the advertisement he sent me. Be so obliging as to tell him he has our most hearty wishes for his perfect restoration to health and happiness.

My mother and Sir John unite with me in best compliments to you and Mrs. Whalley. The children are much obliged to your amiable family for their kind notice; and I am perfectly sensible of your attention to the poetical business here, and flatter myself that under your auspices the 25th will be a brilliant day.* Bath fills very fast. There are several very genteel families arrived, and more expected every day. I cannot mention the news (the political); every

* For the Bath-Easton Vase, described p. 234.

moment is so replete with reports, that it would take a quire of paper to hint at one-half.

Addio, dear Sir, and believe me to be, with the greatest esteem,

Your much obliged humble servant,

ANNA MILLER.

LADY MILLER TO DR. WHALLEY.

Bath-Easton Villa, November 20.

DEAR SIR,—I have been very ill again, and had not sufficient spirits to answer your kind letter for some time past. I have been obliged to repair to the hot wells, where I remained some days, and happily have acquired the health I sought.

I beg you will let me know, as soon as possible, how you and Mrs. Whalley do? and tell me that our unfortunate friend is better, for whose recovery and welfare I am extremely interested.

I do not think I am naturally inclined to meddle in other people's affairs; it is an odious propensity; at the same time I cannot resist the asking you a very familiar question—Why do you think it necessary for Mr. M. to attempt to set up any sort of business, while you do not find him burthensome to your family? You have a friend in him, of that rare species that seems to me to be very difficult to meet with above once or twice in one's whole life. A man of such liberal qualifications is always fit to converse upon ingenious topics, which must be delightful to you; for I believe I may say without being the least censorious, that you must have met with many persons amongst your acquaintance whose glimmerings of reason have been so scantily bestowed, as not to have understood one word in twenty that you had proffered to them. For as you are neither a votary of Bacchus nor St. Hubert, nor a knowing one upon the turf, your fine feelings and sentiments they must have viewed through a glass darkly, and, to the utmost of their tenebrous spectacles, must have pronounced you incomprehensible. Now so learned and so ingenious a man as yourself can never feel tired in Mr. M.'s company; not to mention your character as an author; there is a great convenience in having a friend one may trust as an amanuensis, which would save you a vast deal of trouble. If you think me impertinent, burn this scrawl instantly; the fire is not far from you.

Accept all our united compliments and good wishes for all your healths. Tell Mrs. Whalley, Bath is become very pleasant, there is good music, good fires, good plays, cards, assemblies, &c. &c. The children send their love to Miss Sage and Miss Davie; the boy is going to Mr. Ireland's school in two or three days — the reason of his removal from Harrow you shall hear when we meet.

Adieu, and believe me to be, with the sincerest esteem, your much obliged and obedient servant,

ANNA MILLER.

LADY MILLER TO DR. WHALLEY.

Bath-Easton Villa, November 3, 1780.

A CONTINUANCE of your elegant poetical favours is earnestly entreated against the 21st of next month (December); the subject—'Delays are Dangerous.'

I give you the earliest notice possible, and beg you will not refuse the assistance of your charming muse, on the first day of opening the Vase for the winter season. We had hoped we should have seen you and Mrs. Whalley before now at Bath, but suppose you are planting clumps, &c., at that elegant retreat, Langford Court. Excuse the hurry I write in, for this is the fifteenth letter I have written this day, and dinner waits. I am, &c.,

A. MILLER.

CHAS. P. LAYARD* TO DR. WHALLEY.

(Probable date) May 12, 1781.

My dear Friend,—A month has elapsed since I received from you a letter, written in a style, as worthy of your abilities, as its sentiments are of your friendship. I thank you for every part of it, but especially for that which conveys your just and kind censure. I should degrade the regard that subsists between us to the level of a sentimental attachment between boarding-school Misses, if I could expect or bear an apology from you, for revealing to me the manifold thoughts of my heart. Give me your honour, I beseech you, that you will continue this sure token and proof of your interest in my welfare, that I may have the singular felicity, which millions want, of having a man in the world that will tell me all the truth.

Many men who are secure of their own respect and love of religion, and the dispensations of God's wise and good providence, want only affliction to convince them of their error. I profess to you that I have felt like a heathen that has not God in the world, and I profess it to you, my friend, because at the Last Judgement my enemies will all know it.

I am resolved to keep up my spirits as to this world. I know Lord Conyngham's kind dispositions towards me, and I know also that they have been cherished by you. Do not start at being detected in doing good; it has happened to you so often, that you should no more blush at reading this sentence than the paper it is written upon. Show it, I com-

* Mr. Layard, a name which has been rendered more distinguished in his grandson of Nineveh celebrity, was many years rector of Uffington, near Stamford. In January 1801 he was appointed to the deanery of Bristol, in which city he died two years later, aged 55. There is a monument in the cathedral to his memory, mentioning him as 'an eminent divine, accomplished scholar, and a good man.' In the *Gentleman's Magazine*, and *Watt's Bibliotheca Britannica*, he is also spoken of as 'a man of great learning and most amiable manners.' A list of his publications is there given.

mand you, to your lady, and she shall tell me at Langford, whether you behave as such a culprit—as a hardened culprit in benevolence ought to do.

I hope, by God's grace, before I wait on you, to become an humble, social, and conversable animal, and not so like a mad bull as I have been some months. I insist upon being treated according to my demerits, and sent out of the house, even in a storm, if I presume to be gloomy in your presence; so give directions to your groom to prepare the iron pincers to take me by the nose if I should be unruly.

That Mr. Pratt gains character and countenance at Bath, I wonder not on his part, but I wonder on the world's. I have been such a fool as to think that what I could say to Lord Conyngham of him would do him credit. It was well meant, however. The late Earl is gone.* Where is the eye that weeps or the heart that groans? God's mercy is as the ocean that he made. May the deceased find there a harbour. Say all that sincerest regard and esteem can dictate from my wife and self to your dear lady.

You know I am, because I ought to be,

Your obliged friend,

C. P. Layard.

MISS WESTON TO DR. WHALLEY.

Tetley House, May 20, 1781.

The encomiums my dear cousin Thomas has so agreeably bestowed on my last letter, by flattering my vanity, would alone have been sufficient to have secured him a speedy reply; but, alas! that was written under the happy influence of health and spirits; and the present clouds of

* Henry, first Earl of Conyngham, died April 3, 1781, and was succeeded by his nephew, Francis Pierpoint Burton, who died May, 1787. His eldest son, Henry, was created Marquis of Conyngham in 1816.

severe indisposition, while they exclude every idea of this sort, give me good reason to fear it will be very long ere my pen will again entitle me to the same incense, or afford either amusement or pleasure to my friends.

Far more powerful motives, however, induce me to take the first opportunity that leisure and a little mitigation of corporeal suffering allows, to thank you for the most entertaining packet that ever was written; and while friendship and gratitude dictate this plain and simple return, I know it will be as acceptable to your worthy heart, as if the genius of a Seward was exerted, in all the pomp of song, to pay the tribute.

That name reminds me of the monody on Major André, with which I am greatly charmed, as I am also with his letters annexed to it. I cannot, however, greatly honour his fair mistress, Honora, who, I think, discovered unpardonable levity, or very weak compliance, with the wishes of her family by entering into any other engagements; for if parental authority 'frowned on the maid and bade the youth despair,' in my opinion eternal constancy was the least tribute due to the merits of such a lover. If her feelings were at all what one must suppose them, from the enthusiastic attachment expressed both by Miss Seward and the unfortunate André, happy was it for her that she was removed from all sense of mortal pain before the news of his fate arrived — a fate that her instability most certainly precipitated him into.

I long to see Pratty's new poem, and hope our dear Amelia will have the goodness to send it me, with some things I expect by the return of a family from Ludlow, who are now at Bath. Poor Pratty! most heartily do I wish him all and every degree of prosperity, but I fear for him, from a thousand causes. Mrs. Provis is in town, and stays there till Whitsuntide, then goes down to Ayat

St. Lawrence. I heard from her a few days ago, and find her health is much in the same state as when she left Bath. The journey and change of scene gave a little fillip to her spirits, and she thought herself much better the first ten days she spent in the metropolis; but made a little trip into Hertfordshire, and was worse again for the sharp air of the country. She writes me that they propose being at Cheltenham the last week in July, or the first in August, and very kindly claims my promise of meeting her there, which I shall certainly do, as I sincerely love and greatly wish to see her, and because I am in hopes the waters may be of service to me; otherwise, between that automaton being, Miss A., and the folly and philanderings of the old Baronet (both of whom are to be of the party), I do not look forward to this scheme with any lively expectations of pleasure.

Indeed, I have long given up all thoughts of ever enjoying again the satisfaction I formerly experienced in Mrs. Provis's society; for she is now constantly environed by a set that, in my opinion, exclude every possibility of the agreeable, which I never can taste in any degree (even with the friend I love) amongst characters so totally uncongenial to my feelings, inclinations, and disposition. I cannot, therefore, think with much glee of the Crescent establishment, which, from its vicinity to you and Amelia, I should otherwise do; yet, I admit the propriety and truth of all you say on the subject, from which, however, I can only draw this conclusion, viz. that I find myself very unfit for the world I live in, and am clearly convinced shall never make my way through it with any sort of advantage.

The Cheltenham scheme will afford me an opportunity of profiting by your lecture; yet I will not flatter you, my dear friend; I know myself too well, and am quite sure I shall make nothing of the plan you so well recommend. Though, if anything could stimulate me to act so contrary to th bias of my nature, it would be the temptation of sometime passing a few weeks in the neighbourhood of you and my much-loved Mrs. Whalley. With such a reward in view I may not only appear, but actually in time come to esteem and adore old Tapestry, by considering him the means of procuring me so desirable a good. We will see what can be done; however, it is lucky I am not over sanguine in my expectations, and that I am sensible many alloys will mingle with this satisfaction, even if it should prove attainable, as it will secure me from the shafts of disappointment, which it is about ten to one I experienced on this ground, if I had set my heart warmly on the prospect it presents. For, as I understand, the old gentleman is to have an apartment appropriated to his use whenever he thinks proper to occupy it, and as I conceive it probable that between Bedford Square and the Crescent, they will be seldom asunder, I do not think it very likely Mrs. Provis will often (if ever) have an apartment at liberty to accommodate any other friend, Miss Atwood having now become a constant inmate.

I conclude you, my dear cousin Thomas, begin to cast a longing eye after the hawthorns, and a longing heart after all the tranquil pleasures of Langford Court.

I am infinitely obliged by your kind wishes to see me there, and hope I shall be able to look in upon you in the course of summer, or more likely in the autumn. If it is in my power to contrive matters so, I certainly will, for dearly do I love to dwell amongst your tents; it is the very holyday of my spirit to visit you, and Langford Court my Tempe, my terrestrial paradise. I am at present with Mr. and Mrs. Greenly, very old and very worthy friends of mine. You must formerly have heard of the family at Bath. It is a very amiable and agreeable one, abounding in cheerfulness and domestic harmony. The worthy pair, her mother (a sensible, pleasing middle-aged woman), and a sweet little girl, about ten years old, form the group.

This spot is next to Langford Court, one of the pleasantest I know, and everything in my present situation conspires to give me the most perfect enjoyment of this lovely, vernal, blooming season; but my ill health is such an alloy, it will not suffer me to taste satisfaction.

I see by the papers Miss Akerman is married. So Mr. Squire (who, I understood, had a little penchant in that quarter) was destined to feel a disappointment similar to his sister's about the same time; or, at least, in the general acceptation of the phrase, to wear the garland; for we cannot properly call Harriet's a disappointment, as she rejected the swain.

Poor Lady Miller! Upon the whole, she has been severely and hardly used. Don't you think it possible this poem might be in some way conveyed into the Vase by an enemy without her knowledge? for if she had ever perused it, it is impossible to think she would have suffered it to have been read. Mr. and Mrs. L. Rokeby are expected every day in the neighbourhood of Ludlow. I shall be very happy to find them there on my return, and long to see him; she becomes the character of a matron. I am now on the borders of Radnorshire, in full view of the Welsh mountains, about twenty miles distant from Ludlow, whither I shall return about the second week in next month. Let me find a packet from you, my dear cousin, I entreat. If you knew the joy and contentment they give me, or what a cordial it is to my spirits to receive the least instance of regard and attention, either from yourself or Amelia, I need make no appeal but to your benevolence, though I own I am better pleased to owe all favours of this sort to your mutual friendship.

Adieu! be assured I am, with every good wish, ever faithfully and affectionately yours,

P. S. Weston.

MISS SEWARD TO MR. PRATT OF BATH.

Lichfield, June 16, 1781.

Dear Sir,—Your injunction, 'write soon,' had my wish to be more immediately obeyed; but it was not in possibility. The reviewers have not done their duty by your poem; neither have they praised it half enough. They have no right to omit pointing out the varied excellence of a poem, which they acknowledge to be excellent. The episode quoted is indeed a very fine one, yet is still the least polished part of the poem. They ought to have shown the author's great powers in landscape, as well as history-painting, and to have given instances of the justness of his reasoning.

Conscious that the party-principles of the monthly reviewers would militate against my poem on André, I expected a less portion of praise than they have vouchsafed to bestow; but they can never persuade me that poetical advantages might have been obtained by acquitting the decree at Tappan of injustice. Suppose André to have suffered justly, the pathos, the spirit of the poem had been lost. They speak of the similitude between a passage in the exordium of this work, and the first stanza of Collins' 'Ode to Mercy,' as if such similitude lessened its merit. The same resemblance exists also between a passage in the conclusion of my Monody and that of Pope's 'Elegy to an Unfortunate Lady;' both were designed as imitations, and if such imitations are not inferior to what they resemble—if new images are thrown in, so as to leave only a general likeness, then is the author not only exempt from plagiarism, but happy in such resemblance. Collins and I have each placed Mercy by the side of Valour. In which is she most distinctly brought to the eye? Collins says:—

> Oh thou! that sitt'st a smiling bride
> By Valour's arm'd and awful side,
> Gentlest of sky-born forms, and best ador'd!
> Who oft with songs divine to hear,
> Win'st* from his fatal grasp the spear,
> And hid'st† in wreaths of flowers its bloodless head.

In André's Monody the injured and indignant genius of Britain,

> Bids steel-clad Valour chase his dove-like bride,
> Enfeebling Mercy! from his awful side;
> Where long she sat, and check'd the ardent rein,
> As whirl'd his chariot o'er th' embattled plain;
> Gilded with sunny smile her April tear,
> Raised her white arm, and stayed th' uplifted spear.

In Collins' Ode I don't like the idea of Mercy winning Valour with songs in such a moment. The instantaneous impulse, by which she stays the uplifted spear in my poem, is more natural, and, I will be vain enough to say, a better picture.

The reviewers object to the epithet enfeebling, but surely it is natural for the rage of Revenge to represent Mercy as contemptible. I do not, therefore, think the critique altogether just; but their characteristic distinction between the Elegy on Cook and the Monody on André is highly just. They quote the exordium, not cited by any other public critic, and it is the best part of the poem; they praise the letters, and cite the most beautiful. I have great reason to be satisfied.

Major Gordon has not answered my inquiry concerning the date of Mr. André's commission. Perhaps he might not

* Hard! † Hard again!

be in Shrewsbury when my letter arrived there. Yet I should suppose his letters would follow him. This silence vexes me. I hate suspense, and had rather be assured of an unpleasant circumstance than apprehend its possibility.

Introducing Mr. Saville and you to each other I knew I should open to both a new source of delight. Each speaks to me of the other's powers of pleasing with equal enthusiasm. Mr. Saville is all he appears to be, only much more ingenious. To his chaste and classic taste in poetic composition I am indebted for many an ingenious idea, and for the happy alteration and higher polish of many a couplet. His temper is impetuous, yet kind and gentle

> As zephyr blowing underneath the violet,
> Scarce wagging its sweet head; yet, being chaf'd,
> Rough as the wind, that takes the mountain pine,
> And stoops it to the vale.

But this indignation always subsides in a few minutes, and leaves no trace upon his mind. His truth is sacred. His honour was never doubted, even by those who abuse him for not living with an ignorant and shrewish wife. No vice ever tainted his youth or riper years. He denies himself every luxury, yet knows not how to deny others. He has a bleeding sensibility of every want and every woe, and it is too much for his peace. He pours, as you know, all the spirit of his virtues and his talents into his song. How then should such singing fail to charm every noble-minded listener?

Adieu! Adieu!

MISS SEWARD TO DR. WHALLEY.

Lichfield, August 20, 1781.

THERE can indeed be no music so sweet to the ear as the voice of friendship from those we have long admired, revered, and loved. The tribute, my dear Sir, which I had the pleasure of paying to your enchanting poem, was not less the result of my weighed and determined judgment, than of my warmest enthusiasm. I cannot express to you how much I was delighted to find in Mr. Pratt's most intimate friend the source of those sweet sensations which had so many times enraptured my hours of cheerfulness, and soothed those of care, anxiety, and concern. Being assured, upon the strongest internal evidence, that from the riches of the imagination alone the beauties of that poem could not have proceeded, my spirit perpetually apostrophised its then unknown author, and wished to hold acquaintance with a mind thus elegant and exalted, full of all those sweet affections, of that awakened sensibility, so precious, and so rarely found. When to the sacred memory of my loved Mr. André some passages flowed, which I hoped might draw from their readers a few such kind drops as had lavishly mingled with the ink which traced them, I said to myself, 'If the author of Edwy and Edilda should thus sympathise with me, the knowledge of being so honoured would repay all the fatigue and anxiety which attends publication, the reproofs of the critic, and the sneers of the ill-natured.'

Ah, Sir! if it is for you to apprehend a bias of partiality in the warmth of praise, how ought I to fortify my mind against the intoxicating effects of ardent encomium from one who holds the light of genius so much above me. And how shall I reply to a humility which covers me with blushes, and to kindness which warms the inmost recesses of my heart! You are too good to flattor, and for the candour which thus above all measure overrates my talents, and for the generosity which disposes you to love me, accept my glowing thanks; as also for the elegant tribute of praise paid to my elegies in the 'Bath Chronicle.' From a hint in your last, I conclude it was yours. A lady of Lichfield sent it me from thence, and a gentleman here, who amuses himself with a small printing press, hearing of these verses, asked for a copy, and the next day was so obliging to present me with a couple of dozen papers printed as you see to disperse amongst my friends. Mr. Pratt gave me no hint to whom I was indebted on this account. I suppose the subject did not happen to occur to him while he was writing. I have been a little distressed about the method in which he gave my hasty critique upon his poem to the world. You know, I dare say, that it was addressed to himself, without any view of publication. It is one thing to consent to have one's opinions made public at the request of a friend, who fancies they may be of use to him, and another to appear stepping forward with obtrusive effrontery uncalled and unsolicited as a decisive critic. I confess to you every feeling of my soul recoiled at the idea of seeing my name at the bottom of two long letters in the newspaper.

Though I had consented to Mr. Pratt's request of publishing this critique, I did not receive notice of the projected manner of doing it till it was too late to be prevented. Absent from Lichfield when Mr. Pratt's letter arrived, it waited my return a whole week, else I should have written instantly to entreat him to change the mode of displaying me to the world as a critic, that I might have appeared in a more amiable as well as in a more just point of view, as yielding to the request of one of the author of 'Sympathy's' friends, to whom I might have been shown as addressing these opinions, and who might have declared that he had prevailed upon me to consent to their being laid before the public. I wish it had been managed thus. I am blamed for an apparent arrogance, of which in fact I have not been guilty; but what is over cannot be helped. Mr. Pratt did not mean to give me pain or expose me to censure. Sad work is made, through misprints and false stops, with the sense and English of the first letter, but that is a trifling consideration in comparison of the other.

Mrs. Provis and I have long loved each other. She has indeed obliged me in conciliating for me Mr. Whalley's esteem. It grieves me to see her languishing under ill-health in the prime of her life. Alas! how few, even of the good, the gentle, and the generous, are happy! how few escape the envenomed darts which sickness, sorrow, and malice are perpetually aiming at human peace, and that generally fly sure as the shaft of Edbald!

I turn from these sad reflections, and invoke brighter ideas to dawn upon my pen. If I should ever be so happy to see and converse with you, to be presented to Mrs. Whalley, to receive her and your permission to style her friend, and to love her as my sister, it will recall the transports of those hours so long since fled, when I held between mine the plighted hands of André and Honora. I have many things that might be better in my disposition, but it is faithful and ardent, it can glow for the good of those I love, and make their blessings mine. Happy, thrice happy am I that you, who are so eminently worthy felicity, find an Eden in this vale of tears—

> And wear and taste, without its thorn,
> The never fading rose.

A friend of mine, and a kindred spirit of yours, whose eyes have shed unnumbered tears of generous joy and melting pity over the poem of our idolatry, has seen your picture by Mr. Beech. I would give much even for that imperfect satisfaction; judge then with what delight I should meet the original, and embrace his Eliza!

Something, say you, has interested Miss Seward in favour of Edwy and Edilda. Yes, indeed, there are many somethings. To find each wild woodland charm of luxuriant nature, whose reality had ever ravished my attention, toned in the softest, brightest colours; to find in Edilda the exact portrait of my lost Honora; in the effusions of Edwy's mind sentiments which, years ago, I had listened to with esteem, admiration, and tenderness; to perceive every moral reflection in exact unison with all the principles of my heart; to trace a genuine, rich, and inexhausted vein of poetic fire; numbers, whose flowing sweetness and careless ease snatch graces beyond the reach of art; the magic simplicity of elder times, with the distinct and accurate imagery of the present. These are the 'somethings' which call your poem from my shelves so often, when I am blest with the society of elegant spirits.

Yesterday evening I found three such within my dressing-room circle, the 'blue region,' of which Mr. André talks in his letters with so much partial enthusiasm. We were nine of us in all, and met for the express purpose of reading Edwy and Edilda; not that any of the chosen three were ignorant of its beauties; but some of the colder souls had expressed a wish to hear that poem, of which we had often given such warm description. Four of us took it by turns to read aloud, and of three of those readers it may be said, that 'poetry is poetry indeed from their lips.' This is the fifth time I have heard it read regularly through to different companies. No repetition can weaken its powers over my soul. I long to speak of some of my eminently favourite passages, but must not trust myself, lest I write a volume, and time presses on, my hours are besieged.

I wear a heart perpetually sick with anxiety for the drooping strength and fast-wasting life of my only parent. Growing worse within this week, I had no spirit, and indeed no power of returning that immediate acknowledgement to your thrice welcome letter which my heart panted to transmit; for I would not touch the string of so sweet a joy with fingers slackened by the languor of apprehension. My spirits are easily depressed and as easily elated; to day he is better, and they revive. Often when they sink fatigued by complicated attentions, by a load of solicitude, or by the regrets of deprivation, the love of Kirman comes full upon my imagination, and I long to retire for life in exactly such a cell. Heavens! what a beautiful scene; how calculated to steal the mourner from his woes, at least to soften all their asperities. Ah! I have lost many blessings, some dear ones yet remain of the original stock; and Mr. Whalley, and our new poetic luminary at Eartham, with each of their Elizas, and Mr. Pratt, all of these admit me into the circle of their amities. Dear Lady Miller! what remains to me from her are esteem for her virtues, and sighs for her loss—I mean to say for my own.

May you and Mrs. Whalley never know a grief, but what arises from your sympathy with the afflictions of those who love you. Such alloy your joys must have, and from such I know you would not wish to be exempt, except your power of bestowing felicity were equal to your desires of doing so, and besides the donation of positive good, could avert from the bosom of every friend the arrow of every misfortune.

Adieu, my dear Sir! you are become the rival of your muse, your kindness disputes with her the preeminence in charming my affections. The victory seems doubtful; but my attachment to you is indisputable.

I am, most faithfully,

Your obliged friend and servant,

ANNA SEWARD.

My father desires you to accept an old man's blessing for your goodness to the child he loves.

I enclose this letter in a frank to Mr. Pratt.

MISS SEWARD TO DR. WHALLEY.

Lichfield, October 1, 1781.

I AM too sensible, my dear Sir, of the blessing I shall possess in your friendship, not to seek it with the utmost eagerness, not to value you with the most sacred regard; nor am I like the base Judean, capable of flinging such a pearl away. What inducement could I have for so wanton a levity? instability was never among the number of my errors. Indeed its opposing firmness has been severely tried. There was a time, a long extent of time, when I had occasion to remember that generous maxim of Dr. Young's, to which I steadily adhered:

A friend is worth all hazards we can run;
How gallant, danger for earth's highest prize!
A world in purchase for a friend is gain.

The most diabolical machinations of spite and envy, the pleas of interest, and the interposition of misled authority were exerted in vain. The wishes of a noble heart, the affection of the most ingenuous sensibility, conscientious piety, with an awakened taste for every elegant science, these qualities constituted the counterpoising blessing. I preserved it at every hazard, and am rewarded with the entire approbation of my own mind on the subject, besides the delight I take in the virtues of my friend.

And shall I throw Mr. Whalley's amity away, so rich in the virtues which made me preserve another's, when interest and vanity pleaded strongly for its resignation? that good, of which I was ambitious ere I knew the name of him whom I wished to call friend; that good, of which it is not probable that any plotting mischief will attempt to deprive me? When I do neglect it, despise me as I shall deserve.

You say I may now draw back with honour; however that may be, I am sure I cannot do so with any portion of sensibility or gratitude; neither am I likely to commit so desperate a suicide upon my own comforts.

O you, who are of a class of beings almost extinct upon this vain, frivolous and sordid earth, receive the plighted friendship of a heart, in which guile, ingratitude, and fickleness have no place, which looks up to your wishes with the most affectionate veneration, and to your happiness with the most cordial sympathy.

One thing only have I to regret concerning you, that the rigidness of your modesty should thus repress that honest enthusiasm over your genius, which I have so much pleasure in indulging. Cannot you be contented with supposing me partial? Yet whence this groundless diffidence of talents, so greatly exalted above the level of common ability? surely to know the value of those talents committed by the God of nature to our care and cultivation, is a species of gratitude towards the Bounteous Giver, which is far removed from arrogance. But shining lights will border on their kindred shades; some sullying vein will be found in the brightest gem; and a virtue, carried to an excess, which borders upon error, is the spot in my new sun. See how early I claim the privilege of friendship and chide you! Indeed you shall not find me a flatterer. Permit me then to pour my undisguised and unrestrained spirit upon every paper which is to meet your eyes. If Mr. Pratt showed you my early comments upon his beautiful poem, 'Sympathy,' when in the dim dawn of its excellence, he sent it me in manuscript, surely you could not thus suspect me of overweening partiality towards the powers of those I esteem; of that pernicious and coward tenderness, which shrinks from the duty of pointing out imperfection in what it loves.

When you would exalt my talents above your own, how notoriously does this naughty diffidence lead you into that partial exaggeration which you would impute to me.

Accuse not nature, she has done her part!
And still remember, nothing profits more
Than self-esteem well managed; with thyself
Weigh me; and soon at least thou wilt perceive
That to realities yield all my shows.

Thus have I twisted the sensible admonition of Raphael to Adam to the purpose of our dispute. By changing some of the words, which were not applicable to us, the sentiment loses none of its force. But let us not, my excellent friend, ever again dispute this point. Each of us has received intellectual gifts above the common race of mortals; let us cultivate them to the honour of the Giver, rather than endeavour to think slightly of their powers. Is it not with these, as with every other of our blessings, that we ought to reflect upon them with gratitude and joy? How numerous are our treasures of enjoyment to which they are the key. 'Scarce a flower of the Spring passes unheeded by us;' while every feature of the beautiful, the sublime, or even the terrible in nature, absorbs us in delight. We must be sensible that they have no such effect upon ordinary minds: such minds console themselves for their conscious inferiority by sneering at our enthusiasm; but in point of real happiness theirs is the loss, and ours the vast and still accumulating gain.

Our senses, thus deliciously preoccupied, have no room for the uneasy solicitudes of sordid passions, of those frivolous ambitions which bring with them carking care, stinging envy, and bitter disappointment. Then let us not think it a small thing that we possess these clear and elevated perceptions, whatever preference we ought to give to the moral virtues of our hearts. If we cultivate upon principle that generosity which shall guard us against jealousy of rival abilities, we may surely be allowed to set their proper value on our own, and to remember that humility is wisdom only when it is in a just degree.

Believe me, thrice amiable friend, however highly I prize your genius, as the source of much real happiness to yourself, to those that love you, and to the world; yet are the virtues of your mind far more dear to your Anna. Without them the most splendid imagination boasts but the comet's blaze, knowing not to foster with any kindly heat the blossoms and the fruits of our heart-felt comforts.

For the peculiar temperament of your mind, it were perhaps vanity to say that it is congenial to my own; yet self-love will busily whisper something of that sort. Be this as it may, that I can love such a disposition is certain, and, to use your own words, 'worth all the powers of my soul.'

So you said of Mr. Pratt. I am happy to find he is so dear to you — you, who are the master-spring of his hopes and wishes. It was regret, which bore not the shadow of anger, that I felt about the manner in which my critique was published. I perceived that the intoxication of literary ardour had blinded his judgement, nor once suspected him of any unkind carelessness about my credit. If his generosity had not preserved him from such a want of sensibility, as I am sure it would, yet our interests, as the praiser and the praised, were too closely united not to have made him shrink, through very selfishness, from the idea of placing me in such a light as must infallibly lessen the value of my commendations; but he was not sober enough to be aware of this consequence.

It is indeed an interesting and charming portrait which you held up to me of him. Such were the graces with which he appeared to one of my most esteemed friends, who became intimate with him last spring, at Bath.

Accept my cordial thanks for the generous pains you took with the mind of Mrs. Hobart, in vindication of my injured Monody. Ah! my kind friend, other things have given me sharper and more lasting affliction, but the behaviour, the ungrateful, cruel behaviour of the André family on this subject, was much the greatest disappointment I ever felt. Every hope of poetic credit but weakly stimulated my industry, in comparison of the assured trust that this poem would soothe their sorrows, and convince them of my unchanged and energetic amity. I am curious to know whether the perusal of the work in question has produced any favourable change for me in the sentiments of Mrs. Hobart. Will you inform me? I shall not, from the information, be again disappointed. I know the baleful power of prejudice, and expect the continuation of its bad effects from all over whom the Andrés have any influence.

Another trust of mine solicits your attention, in which my poetic reputation is concerned. I have almost always been so limited in the space of time allotted me for the composition of everything I have written for the Vase, as to be obliged to send the first prompt copies, with all their errors on their heads. First thoughts, poured forth in the heat of poetic composition, will always have glaring defects in the requisite consistency of metaphor, and in the necessary excellence of perspicuity. I therefore always stipulated with poor Lady Miller that she should not print these impromptus, but exchange them for corrected copies before she sent them to the press. By some mistake, however, the rough draught of the Monody on Garrick is printed in the fourth volume of 'P. Amusements,' instead of the more accurate one. The sight of it sickens me a little, and I would wish to avoid another mortification of this sort. I was reduced to six hours for the entire composition of the 'Ode to Fancy,' and when I sat down to the task at ten o'clock in the morning, had not conceived a single idea upon the subject—was obliged to send it away at four that afternoon—not one night's rest to sober my imagination for the perception of absurdities. When the blotted transcript met my sight next morning, a fine number of them stared me in the face. I sent two subsequent editions of this ode to Bath-Easton, being very desirous that if it is printed at all, it may be after the last copy. Will you be so good to find out, when you next go to Bath, whether Sir John means to form another volume, which my sweet friend intended doing, from the present bank-stock? and if he does, to obtain from him the two first copies of this ode, taking care that if it is published it may be in its best state. I enclose a transcript as it is likely to remain, being the best I can do with it; pray indulge me with a copy of its sister ode.

Yes, my dear Mr. Whalley, the nobleness of your own heart enabled you to see Lady Miller's character in its true light. When my first emotions subsided, after hearing the sad intelligence, I felt that something of public tribute to her memory would be expected from me. But many restraining considerations arose in my mind. I imagined, amidst all Lady M.'s good qualities, notwithstanding the advantage the Muse of Elegy might receive from the singularity of the poetic institution, and its triumphs over the malignity of ridicule, that, however these circumstances might animate the death-song, there would still remain a marked inferiority of subject to those of my two former elegies; that such inferiority would produce, as I feared, an inevitable and pitied bathos in any attempt of this kind. In the fate of Cook and André the whole nation was previously interested, and perused with grateful prepossession their 'storied urns.' Lady Miller was surrounded by a hornet's nest, composed of those who were disappointed in their expectations of being summoned to her intellectual feast; and of others whose rhyming offerings could neither obtain the wreath, nor be admitted to a place in her Miscellany. Who knows not the active malice of wounded vanity 'to blot the fairest worth and blast the brightest fame?' From its venom, excellence cannot even find a repose in the grave; and it never fails to descend upon those who dare defend the claims of the deceased. Thus pondering, I resolved to sigh in secret, when a letter came to me from Mr. Hayley, powerfully stimulating to a different resolution. He has imbibed none of those prejudices which could prevent his esteem for her virtues. He tells me that she claims their celebration at my hands with angelic authority; that he shall not be contented, without the poem, which he makes himself sure of my writing, has all the magnitude as well as the excellence (so he soothingly says) of my former elegies. I am attempting the task, yet scarcely think it will ever pass the press. I have no time to write verses. The frivolous engagements and perpetual interruptions one is obliged to encounter in such a town as this—a continual succession of long letters from distant friends—how should I have time to support the profession of an author? The affections of my heart have a far dearer claim upon my exertion than the flattering hopes of Fame, and are continually outweighing them. The poem is flung aside, the letter is snatched up. My greatest regret for the pen is, that the extent of my correspondence often obliges me to delay replying to beloved individuals through many a day that fleets over my head. I have a number of enemies, but I am also blest with a large number of friends. Mr. Hayley, though, like yourself, he never beheld me, is beyond expression kind; he calls me sister, and addresses me with all the affectionate freedom of a real brother.

I am sorry sweet Mrs. Provis still continues so ill. Alas! it is a sad thing that disease should prey, with so little intermission, on the prime of her life. I hear from her sometimes, and nothing can be more glowingly affectionate than her letters. Yet one circumstance in our amity has often startled me. Amidst all the warm attachment she expresses, she never seems to remember any part of the contents of my letters; so that our writing to each other, though we mutually cover many pages, can scarce be called a correspondence.

My poor mother lingered painfully during a year and a quarter. I saw her danger, and was miserable in her sufferings. Mrs. Provis received from me, during that time, at least three or four letters, tinged with many a deep and strongly-expressed regret on my dearest mother's account. Yet, in her answers, she took no notice of the circumstance, generally saying at the conclusion, 'I hope both your dear parents are well.' And when this beloved mother had been dead two months, and Mrs. Provis's friends, the Baines, had written to us on the mournful occasion, and I should have thought must necessarily have mentioned the event to her, however she might have forgotten it, yet, so long a time after her decease, she expressed the same hope, that both my parents were well! Was not this a little unaccountable, a little inconsistent with that extreme sensibility which she possesses? The same thing happened about Honora. I had entered largely upon the particulars of her conduct and destiny early in our correspondence, yet I found the narration had not made the least impression upon her mind, from what she said to me about Mr. André's Monody.

The heart demands sympathy as well as affection in friendship; indeed, till Mrs. Provis corresponded with me, I had no idea that the latter could possibly exist without the former. I have gently complained of this inattention, but no notice was taken of the complaint in the next glowing letter with which she favoured me. That she sincerely loves me, I must believe; but, slightly perusing my letters, and never looking at them afterwards, every trace of their contents fades away before her ill-health and numerous engagements permit a reply. I shall not again hint my dissatisfaction to her gentle yet careless mind. We must take people as we find them; but is it not strange? Just after I had first read 'Edwy and Edilda,' I remember writing to her in raptures about it. Of this also she took no notice. How natural to have said 'the author is my friend.' But she never mentions books of any sort, nor can I extract from her any literary remarks, though her letters are very long, and though her language has an accuracy and flowing eloquence, that I should suppose must be the result of having read the best authors. Do not you, my dear Sir, speak upon the subject. We cannot essentially alter nature; and I should not like to have an appearance of sympathy studiously assumed through the fear of offending.

The young lady you mention is, I presume, Miss Weston, of whom my dear Mrs. Knowles speaks with much esteem, in regard both to her talents and her heart.

Do you know Mrs. Knowles? She has great genius and a masculine strength of understanding.

Adieu! Present my most affectionate amities to Mrs. Whalley. Do not think me vain that I send you another conspicuous proof of Mr. Hayley's partiality to me. It has so delighted my poor old father. The friendship I am honoured with from yourself and from him, are an invigorating cordial to his failing age.

I am, dear Sir, your most faithful and obliged,

A. Seward.

MRS. SIDDONS TO DR. WHALLEY, AT LANGFORD COURT.

Bath, October 31.

According to our friend's request, my dear Sir, I send you the cause of pleasure and of pain. I rejoice to find the piece so well calculated for the stage (which, indeed, I never doubted), and grieve that I shall not be able to avail myself of this golden opportunity. Mr. P. gives it out that he has had no application from Sheridan himself, though he knows the proposals made by Mr. Pratt must have been authorised by him. I cannot but think myself very unfortunate. Had Mrs. Crawford played the part I should have been happy; but Miss Farren's attempting a character of so much and so great action, will (in my humble opinion) be inevitable ruin to the piece. I hope I am mistaken, and that this and every other of his desires may be crowned with success is the sincere wish of, Sir,

Your much grieved and grateful servant,

S. SIDDONS.

My best affections attend dear Mrs. Whalley, and I will trouble you to present my respectful compliments to all your household. I hope my sweet little Sappho is well.

MRS. SIDDONS TO DR. WHALLEY.

Bath, November 8.

O, MY dear Sir, what strange vicissitudes are we subject to. I snatch a moment from extreme hurry to inform you poor Mr. Pratt is again disappointed. Mrs. Crawford will not play, it seems, after all; and Miss Farren is in possession of 'The Fair Circassian.' My heart aches for the anxieties he must have felt, and must still feel. He is, I am told, worn to a mere skeleton with vexation and fatigue. The play will come out in three weeks. I am in great hopes that the beauty and innocence of Miss Farren's person will dazzle the eyes of criticism; and her being so much the fashion is greatly in favour of my poor wearied friend. In about half a dozen lines, he begs me to tell you that you must shortly expect whole volumes. I am now at the rehearsal of

'Caractacus,' which is to be performed on Monday at Bristol. A thousand thanks for your kind letter and lovely nosegay! rendered more sweet, more fragrant, being bestowed by you. Be assured I feel all the greatness of Mr. Inman's character. My best compliments attend the household; and do you, dear Sir, accept the sincere regards of

Your obliged and grateful

S. SIDDONS.

Thanks, my dear Mrs. Whalley, for your kind remembrance of me. All I have time to say is, God bless you! I enclose Mr. Pratt's note, which will better speak the state of his mind than anything I can say. Adieu, dearest, best of friends!

I don't know whether my woman's vanity suffered me to make the delicacy of my presentation very clear, for I own I never felt it more strongly than at the moment when you entered the room. Mr. Piggot presented me with sixty guineas, in order, as he said, to secure tickets to that society of gentlemen, who supposed it proper to do it thus early, knowing the demand would be so great for them by and by. Was it not elegant? Adieu, and God bless you.

Copy of advertisement pinned at back of letter:

'In the press, and very speedily will be published,
Verses addressed to Mrs. Siddons,
On her being engaged at Drury Lane in 1781.
By the Rev. Mr. Whalley,
Author of "Edwy and Edilda," "Fatal Kiss," &c. &c. &c. &c.'

MISS SEWARD TO DR. WHALLEY.

Lichfield, November 22, 1781.

MY heart vibrates to every sentence of your last charming letter, and I have wished in vain to avoid this dull delay in the communication of its responsive ideas. Just as it arrived I had pledged myself for the immediate execution of two poems, which together make up 250 lines—one addressed to Romney, on his having drawn Mr. Hayley's picture for me; the other to Mr. Wright, on receiving an inimitable portrait of my father, precious to me beyond all expression. When I had written only one stanza of the latter, I received a fervent request from our friend Benignus * for a prologue, or some couplets towards one, for his 'Fair Circassian.' He traced the plan, which consists chiefly of Melpomene's complaint that her darling Sheridan, ungrateful for her happiest inspirations, had devoted himself to Thalia.

On Saturday last I sent him a prologue upon this idea, consisting of fifty-six lines; but I don't think it will do—that Mr. Sheridan will allow the fitness of such high, though just compliments to his genius, being spoken in his own house. Be this as it may, I have proved my disposition to serve Mr. Pratt, and that I retain not the slightest resentment for his late error in judgment respecting me. I do not allow myself to resent errors in judgment to any person, whatever unpleasant circumstances they may bring upon myself.

Above all other accounts, I wished to have written immediately to express my grateful joy at the idea of seeing you soon beneath our roof. My father, who wept over the sweetness of your last letter, longs scarcely less than myself to see you. We hope Mrs. Whalley will accompany you; for I impatiently desire to embrace and call her sister. How kind are those wishes which you express that I may, in future, become your guest! My spirit will participate in every comfort you enjoy. For myself, adventitious objects, beyond the beauties of nature, must, in such society, be wholly indifferent to me. Nor should I love, revere, or delight to

* Mr. Pratt.

be with you one atom the less, were your dwelling the little parsonage near you, which Mr. Pratt has so happily consecrated to poetic memory. You will easily believe me when I assure you, that my luxuries are of another nature than those which are supplied by what is called polished life. Even my ingenious friends laugh at me for my awkward simplicity. I wear no powder in my hair, and mind nothing of dress beyond the clean and decent; and I could live for ever upon mutton broth, thickened with oatmeal, fried pork, and potatoes. Prepare yourself, therefore, my dear, dear friend, that you may not be disgusted with the utter absence of elegance in me and about me.

Dr. Darwin* left Lichfield only about eight months since. When he lived here, we two were the poets of the place. If Darwin chose to appear under that character, he would be one of the first of our time. *He* looks like a butcher, and *I* like a fat cook maid.

Mr. Hayley travels out of Sussex on purpose to rivet our amity by personal consciousness. Yet do not think, fair spirit of excelling virtue, that I can love any person better than yourself, who has not to plead the privileges of ancient friendship. You possess all the sensibility so dear to me in the friend I mentioned to you in my last. That singleness of heart—a heart in which nothing selfish or cold can dwell; that zealous and active benevolence, which would gladly endure fatigue and trouble to serve even an enemy. Ah, Heaven! I did not flatter myself that the earth contained ten beings of this order, still less that I should ever be blest with the tender amity of four of them. I almost wish, for the honour of my sex, that some of you were women; for though I have many amiable female friends, and one of them of exalted abilities, with many virtues, yet I cannot say that

* Dr. Darwin, best known as the author of 'The Botanic Garden.' Miss Seward published his life in the year 1804.

she or any of the rest soar to so high a pitch of generous excellence and tender ingenuous feelings. Once, O once! virtues exalted as any of you possess, natural endowments great and comprehensive as yours, a considerable portion of knowledge, and taste refined and accurate to the utmost possibility — these graces was I wont to contemplate every day, and all the day, in my dearest Honora! I had, indeed, as her André told me, 'seen them expand and ripen from their early infant bud.' All were attained, in a perfection which scarce admitted of increase, at the blossoming period of sixteen. At twenty-one, pernicious principles, from the lips of a too much adored husband, undermined their foundations; and at twenty-seven the laborious and unnecessary domestic exertions, which he had the cruelty to exact from a frame that he knew to be consumptive, laid low her lovely head in the church porch of the little village of Weston.

In May last I passed close to the hallowed spot, as I journeyed into Shropshire. Amidst a flood of passionate tears I took out my pencil, to soothe my anguish into the softness of complaint, and my heart whispered, in the style of Isaiah, 'Honora, fairest among women! deep is thy slumber in the dark and narrow house. Thou has not heard the voice of the morning, though the lark warbled loud on its beam; and it is in vain that the sun at noon looks golden on the bed of thy rest. Its rays cannot unveil the eye-lids of my slumberer. The day is soft, and warm, and bright; beauteous in the valley, shining with every lucid hue of spring. Full is the foliage of its woods, and glassy is the lake in its bosom. The birds are choiring in every entangled brake; but beauty fades upon my sight, and music sickens on my ear. My spirit turns away from their graces, and perceives only the lost graces of my Honora!' Such were the ideas which flowed from my pencil as I travelled through the consecrated valley.

Mr. Hayley comes to us the second or third week in next month. I should have inexpressible pleasure from introducing you to each other. The desire of doing so has not in it the selfish economy of delight, for that might dictate a wish to see you separately. Its lavishness, however, would be recompensed by the transport of feeling myself instrumental in bringing into contact congenial minds, and linking them in the indissoluble bonds of intercourse and love.

During many halcyon years, Honora and I enjoyed this felicity, respecting the friend* I mentioned above. What joy did we not feel in convincing our wealthier friends that all the mental virtues and graces, with gentle and polished manners, might exist in a sphere of life considerably below their own! How do I recognise those luxuries of communication when my mind dwells on Galvan presenting Edwy to his nobles!—luxuries which I experienced for so long a time! At length, some nine years ago, the malice of our ceremonial beings, cooperating with the machinations of a shrewish, vulgar, and many ways unamiable wife, gained upon the easy nature of my father to estrange his heart from our friend, whose gentle disposition experienced the 'altered eye of hard unkindness' from him, and bled under the sense of it. No prospect of worldly disadvantage — and I was threatened with the highest — could induce me to renounce the blessing of a tried and faithful friend; but, by ill-advised and mistaken authority, most of its sweetest comforts were mercilessly lopt away. You will love and esteem an injured man, of whom this frivolous world is not worthy. Were he prosperous, his virtues would ensure him your esteem; and half

* All the following innuendo relates to Mr. Saville, the leader of the quire in Lichfield cathedral — her Giovanni, and is evidently written to prepare Dr. Whalley for his future acquaintance.

of them, when you shall come to know him, under the pressure of domestic sorrow, and of the neglect of the proud, would consecrate his claim to the amity of a heart like yours, and that within its dearest recesses.

I am charmed with your ode. The splendours of imagination pour along it in spring-tide fullness. How can you say it is not worth correcting! Naughty Edwy! It does, indeed, appear to me so beautiful as not to want correction; but hitherto I have only perused and reperused it with the eye of congenial enthusiasm. That is luxuriously satisfied. Were it to be given to the cold, fastidious public, I would, with your permission, endeavour to do by it, as by my own poems—divest myself as much as possible of feeling, and dissect it with the surgical coolness of a dispassionate and impartial critic. I know not if, even in that character, any lines could be lopt as luxuriant, or any eligible alteration suggested. This ode has the fire of Gray, and its numbers have magic sweetness; nothing can open more beautifully, and the third stanza is divine, except that its last line hurts the ear a little, from its not being a perfect Alexandrine. The powers of Milton and Shakespeare are finely contrasted. Such a poem ought not to conclude with a striking anti-climax, though my heart is charmed with the partiality which led you into the error of placing my name after that of the elevated Beattie, and the inventive Hayley. They might justly be offended; but they are well-natured spirits, and with the same complaisance with which they would wait at the door of a ball-room till I had passed them, would now step forward, conscious of the retrograde nature of poetic dignity, and say, 'O, by all means! pray let the lady go last!'

It will always delight me to perceive that our tastes, as well as our principles, accord; that my favourite authors have been your favourites. 'The mournful and angry Night

Thoughts' are, I see, engraven on your memory. I cannot look into them without gloomy rapture. The title I have borrowed for them from Johnson, who is tolerably civil to Young, brings that being, so heterogeneously constructed, to my imagination; at once the most liberal, and the most ungenerous; the most dark, and the most enlightened; the most compassionate, and the most merciless; the most friendly, and the least sincere; the best humoured, and the most acrimonious; the most soothing, and the most abusive; the most grateful, and the most ungrateful, of mankind.

I know him well. He was a native of Lichfield. His parents extremely poor. My mother's father, a clergyman, and an eminent schoolmaster,* gave him his education, and without the most distant idea of ever receiving a penny on his account, took equal pains with him as with the sons of the wealthiest gentlemen. He comes down for a month every two years, the guest of his daughter-in-law, an old friend of ours.

Dr. Johnson may be called the most liberal of men, because he has open-handed bounty for all who need it, and has been known to divide his last guinea with the distressed, when all he possessed was earned from day to day by his writings. Ungenerous, because he has no mercy upon reputation of any sort, and sickens with envy over literary fame; as his late work sufficiently evinces. The most dark,

* This was Mr. Hunter. In Boswell's Johnson we have this character of Mr. Hunter: 'According to Johnson's account, he was "very severe, and wrong-headedly severe. He used to beat us unmercifully, and he did not distinguish between ignorance and negligence, for he would beat a boy equally for not knowing a thing, as for neglecting to know it." It is, however, but justice to the memory of Mr. Hunter to mention, that though he might err in being too severe, the school of Lichfield was very respectable in his time.' Boswell makes no mention of Mr. Hunter teaching Dr. Johnson gratuitously. He went to the school in the year 1721, being about twelve years of age, and remained there two years.

for his bigotry and superstition pass credibility; they are malign and violent. The most enlightened, since his prodigious genius and immense knowledge can throw lustre even upon the gloom of his own malignance. Compassionate, because he will weep for the unfortunate, provided their miseries arise either from sickness or poverty, and he will exert himself to relieve them. Merciless, for that he exults over the anguish and disgrace of every person, whose party or religious principles have been different to his own. Friendly, because he will kindly commiserate and serve with activity those who seek his good offices. The least sincere, because he delights to sneer and render contemptible those very people whose society he seeks, whom he caresses with tenderness, and whose interests he promotes. Soothing, for no man's manners are more affectionate, as long as implicit assent is given to his declamations. Abusive, because, from the instant that the slightest opposition is made to his opinions, he exalts his voice into thunder, and 'don't talk nonsense,' and 'sir,' or 'madam, it is false,' and 'if you think so, you think like a fool,' becomes the language he uses, and with which he interlards his imperious dogmas; while to the pliability of yielding fear and unlettered simplicity he is ever easy, cheerful, kind, and indulgent. Grateful, because he dedicates his time to the society and exerts his good offices even to the most stupid people, from whom, or from whose family, he has received kindness in the days of his poverty. Ungrateful, because he would as soon expose the failings of his most liberal benefactors, as those of the most indifferent people; magnify them into faults, and lavish on them the epithets of blockhead, fool, and rascal. He has been in Lichfield some time.

I heard Johnson pronounce Beattie's charming 'Minstrel' a dull, heavy, uninteresting fragment, whose second book he could never prevail on himself to look into. Mason's 'English

Garden' he calls a very miserable piece of laboured insignificance. Mr. Hayley styles him 'the noble leviathan of criticism, who lashes the troubled waters into a sublime but mischievous storm of turbulence and mud;' yet allows that, with all his mighty powers, he is a very odd fish, though, he says, he reverences him as the lord of his element, but that he is welcome to tear his poems as the 'lion tears the kid.' From the publication of the 'Lives of the Poets,' I date the downfall of just poetic taste in this kingdom. The splendour of Johnson's literary fame, and of his *ignis fatuus* reasoning, co-operating with the natural envy of the ignorant, or rather half learned, will enlist a numerous army under his banners, overpowering by their numbers and by their clamour the generous few who have perceptions of excellence, and who dare think for themselves.

A disposition like yours, my dear friend, must have met with perpetual disappointment from human depravity. Yet, if you should ever be disappointed in me, I shall not owe the mortification of such a circumstance to the practice of falsehood, coldness, or insincerity. But my faults are many; I am impetuous, resentful, and without an atom of what the world calls discretion, except in matters of property, where I think it is dishonest to be neglectful. Your system of friendship accords with all my ideas of that refined affection. This heart, attached to your virtues, and charmed by your tenderness, embraces your creed, and fervently breathes its amen.

Alas! I have long feared that my fair friend, Mrs. Provis, better knew how to describe than to feel the holy ardours of affectionate amity; yet, as her good qualities are genuine, and her faults adventitious, we must continue to love, and be careful not to wound, by a too rigid sincerity, the frail but gentle being, stricken by disease in the prime of that life, whose early years had been reduced to find a shelter in dissipation from married insipidity! I should be most happy to see and know Miss Weston, of whom I have conceived a very high opinion. If she is still with you, I desire she will accept my unfeigned regards and good wishes. I wish Mrs. Hobard may conquer her prejudices against me; but for the Andrés — no, my dear friend, they will never forgive me for the injuries I have received from them; for with one spark of generosity they could not have treated me so cruelly. What possibility of conviction to the truth exists in hearts wound round with the impervious folds of conscious ingratitude!

I meant to have filled my paper, but an unwelcome interruption from insipid company has driven me to the verge of the post hour.

You see my pen can enter the lists with yours for the palm of slovenly writing; but epistolary niceties will never be matters of consequence between you and myself.

My father's affectionate respects unite with mine to you and to your Eliza. I trust we shall all meet soon. He is not so well as he was a month ago. The vital strength grows gradually less; my heart aches to perceive it.

Adieu! adieu! Your faithful friend,

ANNA SEWARD.

What you observe upon the subject, increases my desire that Mr. Hayley may permit my Elegy on Lady Miller to sleep till it appears in a miscellany, which I have thought of publishing; but he must govern the destiny of a poem written at his own instigation. Mrs. Hayley is at Bath. Do you know her personally? Perhaps you are, or may become, acquainted with her. I have an idea that she is an angelic creature, but pray speak to me on the subject. You will find a frank enclosed, for I have plenty; and if you have a little poetic manuscript by you to spare, indulge me with it.

MISS SEWARD TO DR. WHALLEY.

Lichfield: March 5, 1782.

My dear Friend,—Every portion of leisure is at present denied to my wishes, which might enable me to reply to the most charming letter in the world, so as in any degree to satisfy the feelings of my heart. A torpid indisposition has hung about me lately; it chains me to the pillow till late in the day, and incapacitates me for much writing. Leisure and brighter hours will, I trust, ere this month elapses, befriend my solicitudes to address you more copiously. Now it is only allowed me to say how delighted my father and myself are with the hope of seeing you at the time fixed, or as much sooner as you please. O that Mrs. Whalley and your sweet Fanny would yet be persuaded to join you on this excursion.

You quite frighten me by suggesting the possibility of our friendship ceasing upon personal acquaintance. Fine talking, indeed, of my superiorities! I declare to you solemnly, that I never felt myself superior to any person of common sense and tolerable education, unless they were either affected, proud, or envious. Is it therefore probable that I should feel this insolent consciousness towards you? You, to whom I look up with enthusiastic esteem and veneration.

You are just such another painter as Meirs, who has also drawn a picture of me, sweet, graceful, and interesting; it has but one defect — that is — *nobody knows it.* Yours, alas! resembles me as little. Trust me you deceive yourself, and would never discover me from this flattered portrait of your fancy. You dispute ideal grace for actual clumsiness, and easy for embarrassed manners. If yours have really that want of self-possession which you complain of, we shall certainly sputter at each other like two roasted apples, and it will be long ere a ray of perspicuity will dawn from either of us. I was in this way with Mr. Hayley till he began to be impatient and unreasonable about the delay of a post letter; to stuff his head with the painful illusions of groundless apprehension, and to tease one with repeated enquiries, which he might know one could not answer. This weakness in the dear exalted, gave me strength. I laughed at him, and rallied him without mercy. 'You are a fine person, truly,' said I, 'to give the world lectures upon serenity.' From that moment all restraining awe gave place in my bosom to easy familiarity and open confidence.

I have written to Mr. Pratt in behalf of a young couple who wish to join the Bath comedians. I wish they could be received. Will you have the goodness to talk with Mr. Pratt upon the subject. I have sent him an impartial description of their talents. Your interest joined with his, might do much; they are good young people. I hope that you and Mr. Hayley, Mr. Pratt, and Sir John Miller have received my new poem on the death of our amiable friend. It travelled to all of you in separate franks.

I have scribbled in the utmost haste, snatching up the first bit of paper I could find. My father joins me in affectionate respects to yourself and Mrs. Whalley. My love to sweet Fanny. Adieu! adieu!

A. S.

MISS SEWARD TO DR. WHALLEY.

Lichfield: March 22, 1782.

How much I have to thank you for, my excellent friend. Yet, amidst the large debts of my gratitude, there is some little in the commerce of our amity for which you are indebted to me, to my forgiveness—yes, to my forgiveness. Is it nothing to suspect me of so frigid a stupidity, as that I should yawn over some of the most animating pages that ever met my eye? Just as much should I be inclined to doze over the Eden of Milton, or the Temora of Ossian. Believe me, the sublimest flights of imagination in the science I best love awaken, not more effectually my attention, than the effusions of so beloved a spirit — a spirit, which meets me in those blossomed paths, unexplored by common minds, and in which I so much love to wander.

Let us, however, quit them for a few minutes, and talk a little more in the style of worldly folk. I wrote to Mr. Pratt just before I received your last, inclosing a letter for you, which spoke to you of the pleasure we had in expecting you at the time fixed. I solicited from Mr. Pratt the quickest possible reply, that the young people, in whose favour I applied to him for his interest with the managers of the Bath Theatre, might not suffer needless suspense. Not having yet received his answer, I apprehend he might be in London when my packet got to Bath, and that its pursuing him thither might occasion this delay. If so, possibly the one enclosed for you may not yet have reached you, and I am at this instant appearing most unworthy of the honour and happiness which you are so good to design for me. The apprehension seized my mind yesterday. It will oblige me to hasten through this letter with all possible rapidity.

The discriminating praise you kindly bestow on my last public work delights me excessively. I wish Sir John Miller may view it through kindred optics. I sent it to him by the post preceding that which conveyed your copy. As yet I have not heard from him on the subject. Without being at all acquainted with me, Mr. Jerningham has done this poem the honour of very politely acknowledging my tribute to his Muse.

It grieves me to hear you complain of want of health, to know that indisposition clouded the morning of your youth, and that its mists still hang about your noon-tide sun. Mr. Hayley, too, is an invalid. I had hoped that the congeniality of your destinies, for in many respects they are congenial, would not have extended to this circumstance. Alas! from your last letter I learn that this hope flattered me. You complain of your nerves. Their want of firmness and strength, however, alarms me less, than if you had complained of a cough or a pain in your side. Amongst violent diseases the word fever terrifies me most; and in the slower ones, I start at every complaint incident to consumption. To the first, my beloved and amiable sister fell a sacrifice, at the age of twenty, and amidst her bridal preparations; and the last was fatal to my still, if possible, more dear, though changed Honora. Your sister died of a consumption; that disorder is very apt to run in families, five of Honora's sisters died of it. I am glad you do not speak to me of a cough and pain in your right side.

The letter enclosed to Mr. Pratt complained that you had quite alarmed me by suggesting a possibility that our approaching interview might dissolve, instead of riveting our amity. The flattery of a vivid fancy, respecting its idea of me, inspires but too reasonable a dread of its happening, though never through the means which you point out.

There can be no danger that my esteem for you will be less affectionate than that which I feel for Mr. Hayley, except that, by appearing in my proper person, I should fall so immeasurably as that no sincerity of regard on my part might raise me up again, even to the lowest level of your amity. It is true Mr. Hayley is not less graceful and engaging than he is learned and ingenious; yet I think there is more resemblance in my turn of mind to yours than to his. He has not so much enthusiasm as either of us in sentiment, however his imagination may outglow us both — for ah! whose is so vivid?

I must persist in ardently wishing you and he might become acquainted. Believe me, there is about his manners no labour to keep up to an exalted character. Minds of equal genius, cultivation, and generosity to yours and his are scattered very thinly over the earth. Whenever their contact is possible it ought to be forwarded.

The want of self-possession, which you complain of, is indeed an evil; it rears many an icy barrier between souls, which would otherwise spring towards each other, by the magnetism of kindred excellence. This groundless diffidence, which spreads over your mind the sickly hue of distrust, is the point of insanity in Giovanni's disposition. He opposed my introducing him to Mr. Hayley with teasing violence. Aware of the ravages which time, ill health, and affliction have made upon his pleasing form, he fancies himself personally disgusting. Few are so well informed, or have so much natural genius, yet with tears in his eyes, and with the most pathetic earnestness, he is continually protesting that it is a disgrace to me to have so stupid, so unaccomplished a friend.

Mr. Hayley presses him to pass a month at Eartham this summer. I fear the not being able to persuade him to go thither at all, for though Mr. Hayley's affectionate attention to him has dispersed all groundless doubts of his approbation, yet now the provoking creature fancies Mrs. Hayley will not like him. He has a thousand of these fears about you; says my partial representations make him appear worse than he really is. So unfortunate a bias in his mind gives me much pain. It has largely increased of late, and makes him shun society; and well I know domestic affliction will intrude upon solitude. He was lately seized with an alarming deafness. Imperfection in the sense of hearing would descend upon him with a more than common weight of deprivation. I thank Heaven this malady is in a great measure gone off. I hope you will meet, though his modesty will not permit him to hope it. Much would you be delighted with the animated graces of his pathetic song; and you would perceive in his countenance and manners, however they might be embarrassed, many a melting sensibility, many a gentle virtue.

Music affects me not less keenly than yourself, especially when it unites its powers to those of poetry. Mr. Pratt, I find, can describe the enthusiasm of taste more glowingly than he can feel it. Beauties in retrospect often seize the poetic imagination much more strongly than present ones. But it is not so either with you, Giovanni, or myself. A hovel, gilded by the setting sun; the smoke of a cottage-chimney among trees; a little redbreast singing on a naked spray, while the winds of winter lift his ruffled plumage; with a thousand of such every-day graces, thrill our nerves, and make the tear of pleasure start into our eyes. Yet it is not always that the soul is attuned to impressions of delight. If lurking apprehension chills the veins, if suspense pulls at the heart-strings, one might wander—yes, Edwy, even you might wander among Hilda's fields to the steepy rock undelighted, or, in the first of all beautiful dells, might bend an unmoistened look upon the venerable yew, fast by the cave of Hermon,

> Tho' at its font the murm'ring brook
> With shining face appeared.

With what happy simplicity do those two lines bring the whole scene to the eye!

I care not for whatever cold criticisms you may have listened to and adopted concerning Edwy and Edilda, that poetic darling of mine. If it has defects, they are only those of careless versification, and carry about them a certain easy grace, which hardly allows us to wish for them a correcter polish.

I positively deny that the descriptions are too minute; their easy amplification makes the poem paint so well. If any creature breathing but yourself had told me it does not rise above mediocrity, I should be apt to conceive considerable contempt for their taste and sensibility. Yet must I still wish this poem had ended happily. It is true I would not lose the striking picture of the malignant Edbald behind the tree, bending with deadly aim the bow of Edilda; I would not lose the animated terror it inspires, nor the bitter taunt of the foe, which freezes the soul, and which is so much in the best manner of the ancient English poetry. I would have Edwy wounded, but not mortally. As to your pious apology for this mournful catastrophe, in truth, I listen to it with a cold ear. The argument you bring to justify these events represents all sorrow for the early death of the excellent as irrational; but my spirit holds no acquaintance with such, even Christian stoicism. I dare be sworn you possess it not, my very reverend pastor, though, in a fit of inexorability, foreign to your disposition, you drown us in tears over the fallen lovers. You have, it is true, sent the lovers to heaven. But, indeed, the dismission is cruelly premature. Remember, amidst all the joys of eternal life, the sweetest delights of finite existence are not to be found. Since in heaven "there is no marrying nor being given in marriage," you should not have denied this amiable, this charming pair, the roses of love, after having so severely pierced their tender bosoms with its thorns. But if I still dissent from you on this subject, you have converted me about the Italian poem — my judgment at least, though my ear, with the disease of modern refinement, rebels too obstinately against the claim of simplicity to the use of expletives.

Your sentiments over Ossian and over Dr. Johnson's late work charm me. I perceive in those sentiments the rectitude of justice, the warmth of benevolence, the indignation of generosity, and the graces of a poetic imagination. Well may you exclaim against the injury done by this illustrious scavenger to the memory of Addison. But his attempt to muddy that silver current is vain—at least in the instance so weakly produced. Supposing defects to have existed in high and splendid characters, I have ever strongly felt, with you, how injurious it is to the interests of morality to drag those defects back to public view, after they had been lost in the preponderating magnitude of contrasting virtues, or had disappeared amidst the blaze of mental endowments. Sacred be the veil which human gratitude has spread over the faults of such beings; and I am almost disposed to exclaim, with the Clara of Rousseau, 'accursed be the sacrilegious hand which shall presume to lift it up!'

How vain is the insolence of this colossal critic, in supposing his paradoxical assertions can wash white the stains of voluptuousness, or take the rose of public opinion from the 'fair forehead of an innocent love, and leave a blister there!' Yet he attempts it by vindicating the moral character of the luxurious Eloisa, and by asserting that the chaste, the tender Emma, who ingenuously asks, 'if e'er her eye betrayed one thought to which angels might not listen and virgins repeat,' by asserting that she can excite neither esteem nor pity. Yet he professes to admire the heroine of Pope, who despises wedded happiness, prefers the name of mistress to that of wife, and who exclaims 'that glowing guilt exalts the sense of pleasure.' For so rigid a moralist as Dr. Johnson, upon my life, this is a pleasant preference of Eloisa to Emma. Not but I allow that the voluptuous passion of Eloisa at length grew virtuous from its excess and constancy. The sacrifice she made was a noble one; but in the eye of reason, or in the soul of sensibility, she can never rise to the spotless excellence of Emma's character, whose purposed exertions were greater, and whose clear flame has no smoke of sensuality. I am aware that it is objected to Emma that she wished to follow the fortunes of an exile and a murderer; but be it remembered, that while she deplored her Henry as unfortunate, she did not believe him guilty. She had all that confidence in the nobleness of his mind which it is so natural that a young, amiable, unsuspecting woman should entertain towards an accomplished and ardent lover, on whose honour she had the most rational dependence, since, in their frequent private interviews, it appears that he had respected and preserved her innocence, while he adored her person. Surely it is consistent with angelic worth not to entertain a thought that such a man could be a villain; to resolve to fulfill her vows of sharing his destiny, with whatever dangers it might be surrounded. She never loses her esteem for his virtues or her trust in his love till he reproaches her unjustly with levity. Is it not also natural that the gentleness of such a heart, a female heart, should rather sink in despondency under this severe disappointment than rise into indignation? From that moment despair takes possession of her bosom, and even when she thinks him unfaithful, she prefers a lingering death by his barbarity to the shock of instant and everlasting separation. Whatever Dr. Johnson may do, surely no one that has a heart can refuse the most affectionate pity to such an amiable weakness, springing from an excess of tender and virtuous attachment. So much for hypercriticism. How comprehensive must be the powers of your charming friend, Mrs. Siddons, and how worthy of yourself is all you say concerning her!

If my last letter has reached you, it will show you how much my father and myself regret that you cannot prevail on Mrs. Whalley and sweet Fanny to be the companions of your journey hither. She, too, I find, like Giovanni, distrusts her powers of pleasing. The natural reserve of her temper makes such groundless apprehensions, though not less to be regretted, less wonderful than in him, who is an enthusiast, and naturally of a vivacious and gladdened spirit. Mrs. Hayley tells her husband that your Eliza (Mrs. Whalley) is a very engaging being. Who can doubt it, for was she not the choice of her Edwy's heart? Ah! how can she doubt her powers to conciliate affection?

I have had the pleasure of a charming letter from Mrs. Hayley. She has much wit, and infinite good qualities, but she professes herself to be wholly void of poetic taste. It is strange that she should not receive it by inspiration amidst the bowers of Eartham, made vocal by strains

> More tunable than reeds, or lute, or harp,
> To add more sweetness.

Giovanni could not sing as he does if his enthusiasm did not extend a little farther than to the air he warbles. You make me long to know my rival prologue-writer; but you draw your portraits with 'colours dipt in heaven.' It were well if we were really as angelic as you fancy us.

I am called down stairs to company; shall not be able to resume my pen before the post-hour arrives. Adieu, therefore, my dear friend. My father unites with me in every kind remembrance to yourself, Mrs. Whalley, and to the fair blossom of your own transplanting hand.

> May she long flourish,
> Grow sweet to sense, and lovely to the eye!

I thought I was concluding, but I must not leave you without saying that a young clergyman of our neighbourhood has published a few poems which bear the stamp of a rising genius. They are published for Portal, in the Strand, Faulder, New-Bond Street, and Kearsly, Fleet Street; their title, 'Poems by William Bagshaw Stevens.' I wish, should they fall in your way, that you would send them; if with approbation, 'raise the song of the young bard, and let him not pass away without his fame.'

Again, and yet again, adieu! Heaven grant us a prosperous and a happy meeting!

Your affectionate and faithful friend,

A. SEWARD.

Mrs. Pratt's charming letter was put into my hands ten minutes ago. I will answer it in the first hour of leisure.

MISS WESTON TO DR. WHALLEY.

Ludlow, March 27, 1782.

ACCEPT the best thanks of an obliged heart, my dear friend, for your last most delightful packet. Yet, believe me, you never need take the trouble of 'racking your brains,' on the score of sentiment, or entertainment, to ensure your epistles a glad and cordial welcome at my hands. Did the paper contain only the bare testimony of your remembrance and friendship, displayed by nothing more than marking a few characters upon it to that purpose, and accompanied with an assurance of your welfare, I should hail its arrival with joy, nor once feel that anything further was wanting to render it a *morceau* of complete eloquence. But your last favour was a treat of the superlative kind; it is not in my power to describe the pleasure and amusement it afforded me, therefore I shall not make the attempt; but am sure of this, that were it possible for you to know how happy and how proud one of your incomparable letters make me, you would, from the mere benevolence of your disposition, indulge me with them more frequently. I read them over and over, and really feel myself of some little consequence in the scale of beings while I am perusing your letters, and consider myself as your correspondent. My spirits are exhilarated for a week after the receipt of one of your packets, and I actually do not sink, in my own opinion, into a perfect nonentity again till I have replied to it; for, except when roused by the kind attention of yourself and a very few other far distant and congenial spirits, I really am not sensible to anything beyond a merely animal or vegetative existence in this place, which is at present so completely desolate and forlorn, that it seems as if the plague, or some other depopulating calamity, had carried off at least three parts of its inhabitants.

Of all melancholy and depressing spectacles, an empty town, with the windows of all the best houses shut up, is to me one of the most striking. Let me see the sun shine upon the sweet verdure; the fields stocked with their proper, though silent, tenants, and now and then the cheerful swain go 'whistling o'er the lea,' and I am content. Nay, as far as mere external objects go, I wish nothing more agreeable, or better suited to my taste; but dull, dirty streets — or, in dry weather, the grass growing most unnaturally out of them (a circumstance that, upon my honour, may often be seen in the most populous parts of this town), without one animating or amusing object through the day, is to me, of all situations in life, the least desirable.

My brother has returned to town above these six weeks. My mother is a very good woman, but our minds are, unfortunately, cast in such different moulds — our pursuits and ideas on every occasion and every subject are likewise so — that it is of very little moment our speaking the same language. Our *tète-à-tètes*, therefore, you may suppose, are not much enlivened by the arts of conversation. Indeed, I see very little of her, for she is either busied in domestic matters, praying, gardening, or gossiping most part of the day; while I sit moping over the fire, with a book or pen in my hand, without stirring (if the weather is unfavourable) for weeks together, without the cheerful face of a friend, and without a single creature or circumstance intervening to enliven my solitude, till my brains are perfectly addled, and my ideas so confused, that history, poetry, sentiment, morality, and politics, all swim in one incongruous and undistinguishable mass before me; and I am sometimes tempted to make an essay of my own voice, merely to satisfy myself that I am anything like the thing I was, and have not totally lost the power of articulation with my other faculties.

I have not laughed so much since the week I spent at dear Langford Court with your sweet laughter-loving and mirth-inspiring sister, Mrs. Wickham, as at your account of poor mother Mac's mortifications. I cannot conceive anything more ludicrous than the idea of that old beldame fretting over the demolition of her feast, and execrating the wicked spirits who caused it.

I return you Miss Seward's letter, with a thousand thanks for the high delight it has yielded me. Her correspondence is a treasure, of which almost you alone, my dear cousin Thomas, can be worthy. I am more and more in love with her heart the more I see its qualities expand, and in my poor judgment the traits she exhibits are so natural, and at the same time so strong and unstudied, that they cannot be counterfeits, they cannot deceive. Poor thing! how naturally does she endeavour to prejudice you in favour of that friend, and how assiduously, and at the same time ingenuously, does she seek to lay open the nature and progress of her connection with him, and to remove from your mind any prejudices you might have imbibed from rumour on that account. How heartily do I subscribe, from my own experience, to her sentiments on female friendship! I am afraid we are not, in general, capable of much disinterested or steady attachment towards each other. Remember me to your charming Mrs. Siddons. I should imagine her loss and Lord North's new tax, when they both fall, must inevitably ruin Palmer's theatre; which his own avarice, in imposing an additional shilling upon the public for box tickets, seemed likely enough to have accomplished without any other assistance. What a pity this man did not sooner become sensible to Mrs. Siddons' value and his own interest! The terms he has now offered, were she at liberty to accept them, would be such a security to her ease and happiness (which, with all her merit, I am afraid is not so certain in town), that one cannot help lamenting such perverse infatuation. I am quite captivated with the description of your French ladies, particularly your Marquise de Menar, who must be a most angelic creature. Pray tell me something more about them; you have quite interested me in the fate of the latter, &c. From

SOPHIA WESTON.

MISS SEWARD TO MRS. WHALLEY.

Lichfield, Wednesday, April 10, 1782.

WE do indeed, my dear friend, regret the delay of our wishes, and still more regret the cause of this delay. We trust, however, that a disease, brought on by this cold ungenial spring, will have all its dregs dispersed by the milder gales that now seem disposed to breathe, and by the warmer beams that begin to play upon the earth. But, my dear Mrs. Whalley, why will not you accompany the precious object of your tender care? His health so precarious, I know you cannot be happy in his absence. Let me then be indebted to your anxiety for the double pleasure of receiving with a friend so tenderly esteemed, the choice of his heart, his Eliza, so fondly and so deservedly beloved.

Business of consequence obliges Mr. Saville to be in the

Isle of Ely before April expires. He delayed his journey to the last hour to which it could be postponed, Thursday seven-night, for the sake of seeing you. I hope he will not be absent more than three weeks, and that he may have the pleasure of paying his respects to a gentleman whose genius and virtues have long possessed his love and veneration.

I am pleased that you approve Mr. Saville's little memoir of me. It was my wish, that if you had thought it improper for the press, you would have prevailed with Mr. Pratt not to give it up to public sarcasm.

It grieves me that Palmer will not receive my theatrical friends, because they had set their hearts on going to Bath, but I have received no notice of this rejection from Mr. Pratt. A letter of his once miscarried, and from that time I am apt to suspect the Bath post of being careless of my treasures. Pray, therefore, let him know that I have not heard from him since I wrote last.

A party of ladies prevailed upon me to set out this day at one o'clock with them for Birmingham, to see a play this evening, and return to-morrow morning, unless I had the pleasure of seeing you before that hour arrived. Your letter of yesterday cut off my hopes of being so delightfully absolved from my engagement, and they hold me to my promise. Mr. Penn, some few years ago of the Bath Theatre, has acted here all the winter, and is the best tragic performer we ever had in Lichfield. The poor man is modest and gentle in his behaviour. An extravagant termagant wife has plunged him in difficulties. He has a benefit this night at Birmingham, Thursday in Passion week. He earnestly requested a prologue from me on this occasion, and had persuaded himself that my name for an affair of this sort in his bills, would help to fill his house. Without one prologue idea in my brain, short as was the notice, I promised to make an effort to oblige him. A hurried composition of near sixty lines has been the result of my labours. It has no other merit than being calculated for stage effect and dramatic speaking — glancing over a number of those characters in which he appears to the best advantage. He will speak it to-night.

Have you seen the Archæological Epistle? It is the work of a master-hand, being undoubtedly Mason's. I enjoy that cutting irony which, both in the preface and poem, makes Dr. Johnson's high-fed consequence bleed under its stroke. This poem proves, that all those inimitable satires, under the signature of Macgregor, are Mason's. I long believed they were, and now I am sure of it. Pope's, Young's, and Johnson's satires, however excellent, are copies of Juvenal and Horace, these of Mason's are truly original, and blend with 'curious felicity' the sport of frolic, humour, and burlesque ideas, with the energetic pomp of elevated numbers.

My father is tolerably well; he talks every day of your visit to us, and always with delight. He begs me to assure you how kind he takes your remembrance of him, and how sorry he is that we do not see you this week. Disappointment, like the north-east wind, has a keen cold breath. We shudder, but try to console ourselves with the hope that 'warmer days will come.'

Much as we long to see you, we do not wish you to set out before your health has regained its usual degree of strength. Alas! that this degree should be so limited. No earthly joys come to us unalloyed. If you had health, Mrs. Whalley would be happier than a human creature is allowed to be. I have written to the last moment. I shall long to hear that you are quite recovered. Perhaps May would be, on all accounts, a better season for your journey than this wayward month. Adieu! adieu!

Yours most sincerely,

ANNA SEWARD.

MISS SEWARD TO DR. WHALLEY.

Lichfield, May 1, 1782.

MY DEAR FRIEND,—A letter to you of yesterday, set forward only a few hours before yours, written last week, were both at the same instant put into my hands. I am excessively concerned for the sad event which detains you from us, regret our disappointment, and mourn for the affliction which falls heavy on a mind gentle and kind as yours. I hope to God that long ere this time the violence of the poor lady's disease has subsided, and hope and cheerfulness been restored to yours and to amiable Mrs. Whalley's bosom; that, with those precious feelings, is returned the resolution so flattering to my wishes, and which of late was so unhappily impeded. Good God! what a scene you describe. I shuddered as I read, and the impression waned not from my mind scarce a minute through yesterday evening. The sad images presented themselves to my slumbers. Alas! how prone to misery is our mortal state! Not wisdom, health, and virtue, with the gifts of fortune superadded, can avert its piercing arrows from the feeling heart.

Two years ago mine bled at every vein during a long period of several weeks, in which my dearest mother struggled with a slow but mortal distemper; and this trial succeeded immediately to the shock of my beloved Honora's dissolution. Alas! the hour of six, yesterday morning, was the anniversary of that mournful event. I too well knew, at that period, she could not live: seven or eight days before I had heard her gay husband declare, in a public concert-room, that 'the arrow was in her breast;' yet, languishing in a little village in Shropshire, thirty miles from the friends who fondly loved her, I knew not that the fatal hour was so near. However, that whole night, which was the last of her existence, my spirit in slumber hovered round her bed; plain as I ever had seen her, was that dear dying face before my closed eyes. I saw her fondly stretch out her emaciated arms to the wretch who had destroyed her. I saw her gasp, and bend her head towards her lovely little children. 'What!' said I, 'Honora, and not one kind parting look to thy Nancy, who would yet die to save thee!' She heard me not. Her head fell back, and I beheld her cold and lifeless. Screaming with the shock, I awoke, bathed in tears, and my hands damp with chilling perspirations. The morning sun shone bright, and the clock struck six. The dreadful vision haunted me through the day, and at night the unhappy tidings came that Honora had died between five and six o'clock that morning. People may think me superstitious; but I shall ever believe this vision was too strongly coloured to be merely accidental. I am soothed that it was thus; that my spirit was not suffered to be insensible in these awful moments. I have probably, I think undoubtedly, mentioned this vision to you before, for it is perpetually on my mind: if so, excuse the fond repetition. Through the whole day, last Monday, I told myself, 'She was alive this time two years.' I had an anxious, unhappy night, and dreaded the approach of that hour which should rob me of this fanciful consolation. Impressions of this sort were yet stronger the preceding anniversary. In some degree I believe they will through life arise upon my mind, in mournful celebration of that day's calamity.

I had flattered myself that there were only a few shy scruples of diffidence to oppose my wish of seeing Mrs. Whalley with you at Lichfield, and that you and I together should have the power of subduing them. As it is, I can only sigh, and look forward to periods more propitious to my hopes.

I, too, have a patient at present, to whom I mean to devote every hour I can spare during a few ensuing days. On Monday, a lady and gentleman, on their road to London, were overturned in Lichfield streets. The lady dislocated her wrist, and broke her arm. She had all proper assistance, and is, thank God, in a fair way of doing well. Her husband is a clergyman. Both of them were strangers to me, only that I once received a civility from this gentleman's brother, the only time I ever saw him. I have visited this unfortunate lady, and obtained my father's leave to offer her an apartment in this house till she recovers. To this proposal I cannot persuade her to attend; but the gratitude they both express for my desire to alleviate their misfortune is unbounded, and far exceeds the trifling merit it may claim. I passed the afternoon with her yesterday, and grieve that previous engagements for three afternoons this week will prevent my passing them with one who tells me my society is a blessing to her, and speeds the weary hours of pain. She is very sensible and well informed; so is her husband. They have been much in the world. Mr. Bates is a very tender and cheerful nurse to his poor wife. I joy to see how fondly he loves her. She has an excellent surgeon, and will do very well.

I shall impatiently wait another letter from you. Oh! that it may bring me good tidings of your sweet unhappy patient; of your own and Mrs. Whalley's health; of your near approaching journey to Lichfield.

Amidst all the delight which I could not help feeling in the wit of the Archæological Epistle, and its glorious satire against Johnson, and in the sublimity of the five last stanzas, my heart revolted against any sportive profanation of poor Chatterton's to me ever sacred name. His fate has cost me a thousand sighs, and many a tear. It is an everlasting blot upon English humanity. If Chatterton wrote those famous poems, his wonderful talents ought to have secured him patronage. The deceit, excused by poverty, should have been pardoned. At any rate, the contempt he met was base and inhuman; and I can seriously exclaim, '*enstroted* Walpool! Mason is a charming poet, but I have reason to think his disposition unamiable.

I must lay down my pen. I am summoned to make my father's breakfast, after which Mr. Bates will come up to conduct me to his wife. I have promised to read her your 'Edwy and Edilda,' at least part of it, this morning.

Heaven bless, protect, and send comfort to you all! My father is excessively sorry for the event which disappoints us both.

It is fine to hear you talk with so much insane modesty over our first interview. Believe me it is you, not I, to whom disappointment is inevitable.

Your affectionate and faithful,
But clumsy, unengaging Friend,
A. S.

I may as well send you a frank, for I have plenty, with the hope of tempting you into a long letter, some time or other.

MRS. SIDDONS TO DR. WHALLEY.

Dear Sir,—Let me thank you a thousand times for your kind concern, and request that you will cease to reproach yourself on my account. I am very much overpaid for what inconvenience I felt in many instances, and if you were pleased, I am happy in my suffering; for, to be sure, I was studying from the time of my return from Bristol, Monday night, twelve o'clock, till three. But this was partly my own fault, for could I have resisted my inclination for seeing the Crescent Sunday night, I might have, perhaps, perfected myself then; but however, so much pleasure for much less pain, were it to do again, I should gladly accept them on the same terms. Is not this rather an unkind reproach from

Miss Hervey which I found here on my return from Bristol? when I declare I would not have done for anybody what I did for Mr. Brunton, and she, too, knows with what pain and labour. I enclose my brother's letter for yours and Mrs. Whalley's perusal; when you read, you will wonder how I could be so absent to give it Mr. Pratt: it was very fortunate I had recollection to demand it back before he had read it. Do not, my dear sir and madam, set this young man down for a vain coxcomb in so speaking of himself, but consider him writing to one whose affection is unlimited, and to whom he is as dear as brother can be to a sister. I shall do myself the pleasure to attend you on Sunday, and am

Your most obliged servant,

S. SIDDONS.

My best regards to dear Mrs. Whalley, and compliments to Miss Squire. I owe my Saturday night's powers to the Tent and egg, for I tasted not a morsel or drop the whole day besides. Mr. Siddons' best compliments attend you all. I am in a monstrous hurry, as you may perceive.

MRS. SIDDONS TO DR. WHALLEY.

Bristol, July 16.

DEAR SIR,—I cannot express how much I am honoured by your friendship, therefore you must not expect words, but as much gratitude as can inhabit the bosom of a human being. I hope, with a fervency unusual upon such occasions, that you will not be disappointed in your expectations of me to-night, but sorry am I to say I have often observed, that I have performed worst when I most ardently wished to do better than ever. Strange perverseness! And this leads me to observe (as I believe I may have done before), that those who act mechanically are sure to be in some sort right, while we who trust to nature (if we do not happen to be in the humour, which, however, Heaven be praised, seldom happens) are dull as anything can be imagined, because we cannot feign. But I hope Mrs. Whalley will remember that it was your commendations which she heard, and judge of your praises by the benevolent heart from which they proceed, more than as standards of my deserving. Luckily I have been able to procure places in the front row of the next to the stage box, on the left hand of you as you go in. These I hope will please you. I am afraid Mr. Keasbury will have a very so-so house. Our most respectful compliments attend Mrs. Whalley, who I hope is well.

I have the honour to be, dear Sir,

Your most obliged and grateful servant,

S. SIDDONS.

P.S.—Many thanks for the grapes.

MISS SEWARD TO DR. WHALLEY.

Between June and September 1782.

MY DEAR SIR,—That famous old lyric ballad, *the Battle of La Hogue*, made on the naval victory by Admiral Russell, when the great French ship, the 'Rising Sun,' was sunk, I altered and rendered applicable to the late victory by Rodney. The tune is spirited and sublime—nor less the energy, the fire with which Giovanni sings it. The old ballad has some fine poetic strokes amidst many vulgarisms. I strove to retain the former, while I discarded the latter. A wretched attempt of this sort appeared in the newspapers a few weeks since, and suggested the idea to me of managing it a little more happily. He made full accompaniments and took it to Cambridge. He speaks thus of its effect on the audience:—'I have only a moment, in which to tell you that I received such applause for your charming song, as I believe never before rang through the Senate House. Its effect was sublime, from the glorious accompaniments, the full chorus, and the thunder of the kettle-drums. It was encored twice. Having put forth all my powers, I believe I should have dropt down in a third effort; therefore, to the second encore I bowed with my head upon my breast, as entreating to be spared, upon which the words "no, no!" and "cruel," were heard on all sides, and after them another thunder of applause, as evincing a cheerful acquiescence in my involuntary incapacity of going through it a third time. My voice was never, I think, so loud and clear: the subject inspired me, and if you had heard the compliments I received from people of the highest rank crowding around me, after the song was over, you would have been inclined to fancy me almost as great as the glorious fellow you have so nobly celebrated. The intoxication of the *amor patriæ* seemed to dispose the folk to deify me, instead of the Admiral; but well do I know that I am indebted to the beauty of the composition that my poor vocal powers were thus empowered to awaken one of the most generous feelings which can delight the human soul.'

My dear Mr. Whalley, I do not send you this ballad, because I would wish you should first hear it with the splendid advantages of his voice and expression.

Your faithful and obliged,

A. Seward.

MRS. SIDDONS TO MRS. WHALLEY.

Weymouth, August 20.

Dear Madam,—I hope the travellers returned safe before you had suffered much anxiety on their account. I anticipated all the pleasures of the Cottage on Friday; we had frequent showers and one very heavy storm, but I hope most sincerely that neither the weather prevented your intended visit to your favourite habitation, and that no circumstance the most trifling alloyed your happiness when there. You will be pleased to hear that Mrs. Carr was very civil to me, gave me a comfortable bed, and I slept very well. We were five of us in the machine, all females but one, a youth of about sixteen, and the most civilised being you can conceive, a native of Bristol, too.

One of the ladies was, I believe, verily a little insane, her dress was the most peculiar, and manner the most offensive, I ever remember to have met with; her person was taller and more thin than you can imagine, her hair raven black, drawn as tight as possible over her cushion before and behind, and at the top of her head was placed a solitary fly-cap of the last century, composed of materials of about twenty sorts, and as dirty as the ground; her neck, which was a thin scrag of a quarter of a yard long, and the colour of a walnut, she wore uncovered for the solace of all beholders, her Circassian was an olive-coloured cotton of three several sorts, about two breadths wide in the skirt, and tied up exactly in the middle in one place only. She had a black petticoat, spotted with red, and over that a very thin white muslin one, with a long black gauze apron, and without the least hoop. I never in my life saw so odd an appearance, and my opinion was not singular, for wherever we stopped, she inspired either mirth or amazement, but was quite innocent of it herself. On taking her seat amongst us at Bristol, she flew into a violent passion on seeing one of the windows down; I said I would put it up if she pleased; 'To be sure,' said she, 'I have no ambition to catch my death.' No sooner had she done with me, but she began to scold the woman who sat opposite to her for touching her foot: 'You have not been used to riding in a *coach*, I fancy, good woman.' She met in this lady a little more spirit than she had found in me, and we were obliged to her for keeping this unhappy woman in tolerable order the remainder of the day. Bless me! I had almost forgot to tell you that I was desired to make tea at breakfast. Vain were my endeavours to please this strange creature; she had desired to have her tea in a basin, and I followed her directions as near as it was possible in the making her tea, but she had no sooner tasted it than she bounced to the window and threw it out, declaring she had never met with a set of such awkward, ill-bred people; what could be expected in a stage-coach, indeed? She snatched the canister from me, poured a great quantity into the basin, with sugar, cream, and water, and drank it altogether.

Did you ever hear of anything so strange? When we sat down to dinner, she seemed terrified to death lest anybody should eat but herself. The remaining part of our journey was made almost intolerable by her fretfulness; one minute she was screaming out lest the coachman should overturn us; she was sure he would, because she would not give him anything for neglecting to keep her trunk dry; and, though it was immoderately hot, we were obliged very often to sit with the windows up, for she had been told that the air was pestilential after sunset, and that however other people liked it, she did not choose to hazard her life by sitting with the windows open. All were disposed, for the sake of peace, to let her have her own way, except the person whom we were really obliged to for quieting her every now and then. She had been handsome, but was now, I suppose, sixty years old. I pity her temper, and am sorry for her situation, which I have set down a disappointed old maid.

At about seven o'clock we arrived at Dorchester; on my stepping out of the coach a gentleman very civilly gave me his hand—who should it be but Mr. Siddons, who was come on purpose to meet me? He was very well, and the same night I had the pleasure of seeing my dear boy more benefited by the sea than can be conceived. He desires me to thank Mr.

Whalley for the fruit, which he enjoyed very much. We have got a most deplorable lodging, and the water and the bread are intolerable, 'but travellers must be content.' Mr. Whalley was so good as to be interested about my bathing—is there anything I could refuse to do at his or your request? I intend to bathe to-morrow morning, cost what pain it will. I expected to have found more company here.

I went to Dorchester yesterday to dine with Mr. Beach, who is on a visit to a relation, and has been laid up with the gout, but is recovering very fast. He longs to see Langford, and I am as anxious to have him see it. I suppose Mr. Whalley has heard when Mr. Pratt comes; pray present the kindest wishes of Mr. Siddons, little Harry, and myself; his little girl has returned to school. I hope Mr. Whalley will do me the favour to choose the ribbon for my watch-string. I should like it as near the colour of little dear Paphy's ear as possible. I did not very well comprehend what Lady Mary (Knollis) said about the buckles. Will you please to give her my respectful compliments, and say I beg her pardon for having deferred speaking to her on that subject to so awkward a time, but hope my illness the last day I had the honour of seeing her ladyship will be my excuse. I hope I shall be favoured with a line from you, and that her ladyship will explain herself more fully then. Harry has just puzzled me very much. When going to eat some filberts after dinner, I told him you desired I would not eat them; 'but,' says he, 'what would you have done if Mr. Whalley had desired you would?' I was at a stand for a little while, and at last he found a means to save me from my embarrassment, by saying: 'but you know Mr. Whalley would not desire you to eat them, if he thought they would hurt you.' 'Very true, Harry,' says I; so it ended there.

I look forward with inexpressible delight to our snug

parties, and I have the pleasure to inform you that I shall not go to London this winter. Mr. Linley thinks my making a partial appearance will neither benefit myself nor the proprietors. Mrs. Crawford threatens to leave them very often, he says, but supposes she knows her own interests better. I should suppose she has a very good fortune, and I should be vastly obliged to her if she would go and live very comfortably upon it. I'll give her leave to stay and be of as much service to my good and dear friend's tragedy as she possibly can, and then let her retire as soon as she pleases. I hope I shall not tire you; Mr. Siddons is afraid I shall, and in compliance to him (who, with me, returns his grateful acknowledgments for all your kindnesses), I conclude with, I hope, an unnecessary assurance, that I am ever your grateful and Affectionate servant,

S. SIDDONS.

P.S.—Please to present our joint compliments to Mr. Whalley, Mrs. Whalley, and Miss Squire, and, in short, the whole circle, not forgetting Mrs. Reeves, to whom I am much obliged. In an especial manner, I beg to be remembered to the cruel beauty, Sappho. She knows her power, and therefore treats me like a little tyrant. Adieu! God for ever bless you and yours. The beach here is the most beautiful I ever saw.

C. P. LAYARD TO DR. WHALLEY.

October 24, 1782.

MY DEAR FRIEND,—I believe I have already expressed to you the satisfaction I propose to myself in seeing you in London next spring, though that satisfaction would be more complete if I did not know that it was to precede a separation for some years from a man whose heart always affords me an exception when I lament the unfeeling iniquity of the world. When I consider how many you have obliged and how many you have made happy, I tremble at the variety of ingratitude that you must, by your own complaints, have experienced; nay, I almost hesitate to ask you whether a lady who is now removed from the applause of Bath to acquire more and more money here, has shown herself not unworthy of the encouragement with which you distinguished her merit in her profession, and her very proper conduct. If you think still well of her, it will be my duty to encourage in a certain person, who has power to serve her, a disposition to do it; but if you do not, justice will demand of me the very contrary.

To grow hard and callous is a dreadful charge against any who have been happy in indulging amiable affections; but men who are benevolent on principle seek retribution from Heaven, and endure ingratitude as the martyrs did persecution, with complacency, because it enhances their reward.

Indeed, constancy of mind is the greatest happiness attainable on earth, because it comprehends a complete power over the desires, affections, sentiments, and expressions, the ability of resisting adversity, of enjoying pleasure without intoxication, and beholding an end of it without dismay. One of the best methods to acquire it is, to give many hours to oneself, to shut out the world often, to look on it like a prospect through a window, and to examine and try one's own strength, in order to prepare the mind for future events, a certain number of which, of a very grievous sort, await every man, and death in the last place.

This is preaching; but I fancy I talk past experience; for since the misfortunes of my family I have abandoned everything that did not stand the test of adversity. Accordingly, I live privately, work hard, and double my affection to those I have reason to love. You and your good lady are of these few. My wife joins in respects to you both. Farewell!

Yours sincerely,

C. P. Layard.

MRS. SIDDONS TO DR. WHALLEY.*

Friday.

My dear, dear Friend,—The trying moment is past, and I am crowned with a success which far exceeds even my hopes. God be praised! I am extremely hurried, being obliged to dine at Linley's, have been at the rehearsal of a new tragedy in prose, a most affecting play, in which I have a part I like very much. I believe my next character will be 'Zara,' in the 'Mourning Bride.' My friend Pratt was, I believe in my soul, as much agitated, and is as much rejoiced as myself. As I know it will give you pleasure, I venture to assure you I never in my life heard such peals of applause. I thought they would not have suffered Mr. Packer to end the play. Oh, how I wished for you last night, to share a joy which was too much for me to bear alone! My poor husband was so agitated, that he durst not venture near the house.

I enclose an epilogue which my good friend wrote for me, but which I could not, from excessive fatigue of mind and body, speak. Never, never let me forget his goodness to me. I have suffered tortures for the unblest these three days and nights past, and believe I am not in perfect possession of myself at present; therefore excuse, my dear Mr. Whalley, the incorrectness of this scrawl, and accept it as the first tribute of love (after the decisive moment) from

Yours ever grateful and truly affectionate,

S. Siddons.

* This letter evidently alludes to her début at Drury Lane, Oct. 10, 1782, in Southern's tragedy of 'Isabella.' Her biographer Campbell says, from that moment she 'mounted with but few steps to unrivalled possession of the tragic throne.'

MRS. SIDDONS TO DR. WHALLEY.

149 Strand, November 20.

Just at this moment are you, my dear sir, sitting down to supper, and 'every guest's a friend.' Oh! that I were with you but for one half hour. 'Oh! God forbid!' says my dear Mrs. Whalley; 'for he would talk so loud and so fast, that he would throw himself into a fever, and die of unsatisfied curiosity into the bargain.' Do I flatter myself, my dear sir? Oh! no; you have both done me the honour to assure me that you love me, and I would not forego the blessed idea for the world. Your letter to poor Pratty is lying on the table by me, and I am selfish enough to grudge it him from the bottom of my heart, and yet I will not; for just now, poor soul, he wants much comfort, therefore let him take it, and God bless him with it! You have heard of the laurel which the gentlemen of the bar have adorned my brows with, no doubt. It is, indeed, an honour I could not have hoped to arrive at; but (in the sincerity of truth I speak it) not half so grateful to my soul as that sweet wreath, with which your friendly hand encircled my humble head. I wish, for your honour more than my own, the subject was more worthy of your commendations; but, indeed, your esteem confers a value wherever it is placed. I hope you don't forget, my dear sir, that you are to give me your picture.

I did receive all your letters, and thank you for them a thousand times; one line of them is worth all the acclamations of ten thousand shouting theatres. The 'Fatal Interview' has been played three times, and is quite done with: it was the dullest of all representations. Pratty's Epilogue was vastly applauded, indeed. I shall take care how I get into such another play; but I fancy the managers will take care of that, too. They won't let me play in

Pratty's comedy. How cruel! I am sadly grieved about it. I have yours and my dear Mrs. Whalley's hair in a ring, set round with small gold beads; it looks neat and quiet. Pray remember me in the kindest manner to all my friends. I thank Miss Weston for the kind concern she takes in my success. Give my love to my dear, dear Mrs. Whalley, and believe me, dear sir,

Your ever-affectionate and grateful,

S. SIDDONS.

Oh, for a piece of Langford brown bread!

Pray kiss Paphy Piddy* for me. I hope you have told all the good news about me.

Mr. Siddons and Harry desire their best wishes.

I am hurried and fatigued to death. 'Isabella' to-morrow, 'Jane Shore' Saturday.

MISS SEWARD TO DR. WHALLEY.

December 4, 1782.

THE fertility of your invention, the rapidness of your execution, my beloved Edwy, excite in me wonder, that keeps equal pace with my affection. I shrink under the consciousness of my own inferiority, when I reflect how many hours of sequestration and labour must have preceded such a poetical resurrection in my brain, as started up from yours instantaneously, and in vivid beauty, after the fatigues of a three hours' darkling journey, and amidst the gloom and torpors of midnight. What charming verses, too, in the title-page! Your facility even outstrips Mr. Hayley's. I thought to have passed the evening in talking with Giovanni over the virtues and graces of the dear departed guest, and thus to have broken, sweetly broken, the asperities of a sorrow so recent; but fate had decreed it otherwise.

* The favourite spaniel Sappho, represented in Dr. Whalley's portrait.

Who do you think tapped at the dressing-room door, in about half an hour after you left it, and entered with a smiling countenance?—who but Dr. Darwin, verily and indeed? He told me it was an age since he had seen me. I replied that I was happy to see him then, and did not even look a reproach for an absence so long and so unfriendly. But where my affections are tenderly interested, I must reproach before I can forgive. This is being, I own, very sadly under the dominion of the passions; and greatly does it prove me unworthy of the lavish, the partial light you have thrown around me, through which these dark spots of pride and anger will thrust themselves.

I know well enough that Mr. Romney's art was the loadstone which drew hither that large mass of genius and sarcasm; that he had heard of the picture, and wished to see it. He saw it with seeming pleasure and very warm praise. Without affection enough to express, or to feel resentment (ah! we must at some time at least have believed ourselves beloved ere we can feel personal tenderness), I have yet that sort of regard for Dr. Darwin, as will always make me see him with pleasure when he looks willing to please; but I wish he had made his visit the preceding day, because I know you would have liked to have conversed with him. He stayed till the 9 o'clock bell summoned us to go down and pass the remainder of the evening with my father. The Doctor went, but Giovanni stayed. As poor André says in his letters—'Ah, need I name the subject of our conversation?' He set out for Coventry this morn, and does not return till Thursday. It was fortunate that the business of his profession, which takes him so often out of Lichfield, did not once snatch him away during the too swiftly flying hours of your residence here.

Adieu! adieu!

A. Seward.

MISS SEWARD TO DR. WHALLEY.

Friday, December 13, 1782.

Ah, Edwy, your presents, your too elegant, too costly presents! Indeed, dearest friend, I must chide you. The ribbon for myself I would have accepted gladly, but the bracelets; ah! I wanted no costly tokens of my Edwy's love. You are too generous ever to be rich; and, like Mr. Hayley, you are swelling to a countless number the obligations I owe you. Your visit, however, your exquisitely kind visit, that was indeed an obligation, compared to which the gift of gems would be poor. It is perhaps well that the amount of business I have upon my hands, indispensable, though perhaps immaterial, leaves me so little leisure to indulge the regrets of deprivation; else, my dear Edwy, could I sit listening to the winds that howl over the lawn, and through many a pensive hour pay the tribute of a frequent sigh and tear to the distance which already divides us, and to the idea that, yet a little while, and we shall no longer be in the same kingdom. But let me not cloud, with the present vapourish tendency of my spirits, that gaiety of your heart, in the light of which I have so loved to bask; rather will I try to assimilate my feelings to your happiness, than hold out the magnet of melancholy. Last night, I trust, restored you to the faithful and now happy arms of the dear and excellent Amelia. My mind's eye perceives her at this moment sitting by you, and looking unutterable things of tenderness and delight; while the squirrel frisks over your shoulder, and the faithful Sappho is fawning upon your hand. I see also your venerable parent complete the interesting group, her eye beaming with complacent sweetness and tender sympathy.

My little muses are extremely beautiful; yet do not think me ungrateful, if I acknowledge that I had rather the golden counters they cost were in your purse than that they should have ornamented as they did my arm to-day, or take their station, as they have now done, in the box with Honora's bust and portrait, Giovanni's picture, and the locket formed of poor André's hair. The keepsake of my Edwy has an indisputable right to be deposited in that tender and consecrated place. Mrs. Inge, confined with a cold, our reading party is postponed till she is well enough to venture out. So I passed the hours, between 6 and 11, *tête-à-tête* with Mrs. Newton. From dinner-time till I went to her, Miss More's Sacred Dramas, which till then I had not had time scarcely to look at, fascinated my attention. Many a tear of delight flowed upon their pages, while my spirit eagerly drank their varied beauties.

Mrs. Porter's first words to me on Wednesday were: 'You may keep your folk at home for the future—you had best a-done exhibiting—you 'll ne'er again have anything to show that will be worth either seeing or hearing after Mr. Whalley;' and so she went on for half an hour, exalting you above anything, either male or female, which she had ever seen, which she was assured she ever should see. M. Cobb was in Romney's levée this morning. She allowed you elegant and pleasing; but she has not a heart to feel your superiorities, like old honest Lucy Porter, or feeling, would not be forward to express her sense of them.

Adieu! adieu!

A. S——.

MISS WESTON TO DR. WHALLEY.

Rhode Hill, January 26, 1783.

Your kind letter, my ever dear and amiable friend, was most welcome to me, and I greatly rejoice to find you have got through all the fatigues of your business, and that so entirely to your satisfaction; yet, as these matters are preparatory to a moment I cannot look forward to without the most painful sensations, a few weak tears would fall in spite of my better judgment, and blister even the paper which informed me all the trouble and perplexity I left you involved in was come to a period so desirable, and had put you once more in possession of that ease and tranquillity to which you have been so long a stranger, and which no one can more ardently or more devoutly wish you uninterrupted enjoyment of, than does your poor cousin Sophy. But while we carry this clog of mortality about us, self, vile self, will interpose, and mingle its interests and regrets with our most generous feelings and affections. Your departure from this country for a length of time so alarming, is one of the severest blows that could have fallen upon me; and, though reason whispers a thousand consolatory arguments to soften the stroke, sensibility is at present too powerfully affected by the prospect of its near approach to draw all the comfort which it may some time hence experience from this source.

I have likewise great joy in the prospects of immediate peace* upon your account, for it will not only relieve you from much trouble on the journey, but certainly contribute to make your residence in France more pleasant and agreeable. In short, my dear friend, I flatter myself Fortune has pushed aside her bandage, and made a turn in your favour. You seem likely to set out under every sort of good auspice, and the happiest circumstances will, I trust, attend you throughout the whole of your undertaking, and render your return to the land of your nativity a day of joy without alloy. I love the Leeves, for their attentions and sensibility. Ah! what a loss they will have, and how easily can I conceive their regrets! They are worthy estimable people, and I hope will find all possible recompense in their new neighbours;

* Jan. 20, 1783:—Preliminary articles of Peace were signed at Versailles, between England, France, and Spain; but the war continued for some months longer, and the Peace was not ratified till September 3rd, when America was included in it.

but though the Gunnings are also very worthy estimable people, I am not clear that the Leeves and they are altogether calculated for each other; and certain I am, however well disposed, they can never make up to our Wrington friends the loss they must sustain in the late inhabitants of Langford Court.

The dejected and discontented strain of Mrs. Provis's letter, convinces me all is at an end with the old baronet; besides, she tells me, 'they intend spending some weeks in town this spring, and are to be in a lodging in St. James's Street.' For various good reasons I am not sorry this absurd connexion is broken off, but confess it does not tend to raise Mrs. Provis in my esteem and good opinion, as I do not suppose the circumstances which brought it to a period, were more commendable than the motives which drew it on, and carried it to so reprehensible an extreme. And I do think she must have acted with infinite ingratitude towards Sir L. L., who, however vain, ostentatious, and foolish in his conduct, was, I do believe, sincerely her friend; and as she suffered herself to receive so many obligations from him, he was entitled to a better return than that of being sacrificed to a woman he knew so little of. Mrs. Provis will miss his attentions, his society and conversation; nay, I am sure she does, and is wretched. Poor woman! she is always drawing herself into some scrape or other.

I should think Mr. Pennington* and Coz. Somers would

* Mr. Pennington was an American Royalist, who retired with broken fortune to this country, after the Act of Independence. He was many years Master of the Ceremonies at Clifton, where, though his foibles created diversion to the gay, his kindness of heart and upright conduct gained him general esteem. His probity was strikingly evinced on his voyage from America. A fellow-passenger, a voluntary exile from the land of his birth, like himself, but who had amassed a considerable fortune, which he took with him, conceived a strong attachment to Mr. Pennington, and opened his mind on various subjects, and, among others, upon the little prospect of satisfaction he felt in tracing out his distant relatives in the land of his forefathers. The

feel themselves very comfortable in the same habitation. Our dear little nursery thrives and comes on charmingly; but poor Mrs. Williams's complaints, which are chiefly nervous and rheumatic, will, I am afraid, prove very tedious. The weather is dreadful at present; such storms and tempests I never saw or heard, and such as will not incline me in future to plan a visit upon the coast in winter, if I can avoid it. I have received my cousin Thomas's delightful letter, and return him a thousand thanks for it. He shall hear from me during his visit at Frome. Say all that is kind for me to him, and make all proper compliments for me where you are. How I rejoice in our divine Melpomene's * amazing popularity! It is feared she will hurt herself by introducing a sister who is not at all approved. Poor Benignus,† what a hard fate! His play, with all its merit, will be lost in the blaze of his friend's popularity, I am sadly afraid, if they will not let her appear in it. I cannot help thinking she might and ought to insist on doing him this service.

Adieu! my very dear friend. I find my style wretchedly embarrassed and languid; but my heart feels perfectly animated and warm towards you; and I am, and ever must be, with every cordial wish and sentiment,

Faithfully and affectionately yours,

P. S. Weston.

voyage was long, and after a time this gentleman became ill, and was assiduously nursed by his new friend. He grew worse, and feeling he should not survive, made a will, in which he left everything to Mr. Pennington, saying that he had received great kindness from him, and wished him to inherit his property in preference to his unknown relations. He died on the voyage, and on arriving in England, Mr. Pennington destroyed the will, found out the relations, and put them in possession of all the property of the deceased.

This was the gentleman whom, not long after the date of this letter, Miss Weston married, a union which produced her much happiness for more than thirty years.

* Mrs. Siddons, on her second engagement in London.

† Benignus, Mr. Pratt of Bath, author and publisher for many years.

MISS SEWARD TO DR. WHALLEY.

March 19, 1783.

Now let me express gratitude to you from another source, and the joy I feel in the success of your kind and generous endeavours for the establishment of the ingenious and amiable Cizos in the fair city of his wishes. Here he was lost. Few in Lichfield are the patrons of dependent genius, though sustained and adorned with the most gentle virtues. But for the ties of my long friendship for the noble-minded and unfortunate Giovanni (to whom that friendship is the sole counterpoise for the ills of his fate), and for the insanity of that local dotage upon scenes and objects which so strongly bear the stamp and image of the everlastingly absent—my dear sister, my lost Honora, and all the joys of my youth—were it not for these ties, I should not think of continuing here after the decease of my father, when so many hours in every day are necessarily sacrificed in societies where I am obliged to suppress my sensibilities, and keep my talents dormant, through the fear of exciting the stare and the contempt of every-day minds. Yet it sometimes surprises, and, on looking into the motives, diverts me, to observe that when a literary being descends amongst us, whose fame is gone forth in the world, especially if they are of independent fortune, how lavish these good folk are of their encomiums—with what smiling attention they listen, and how they speak to me of the delight they feel in listening to such conversation! Their enthusiasms appear to glow so fervently whenever they talk to me of yourself, Mr. Hayley, and Mrs. Knowles, that I have been more than once taken in to fancy I had mistaken their minds, and that I should perhaps be more pleasing to them if I put forth a faint emanation of that sort of spirit, in whose radiance they seemed so charmed to bask, when issuing from the orbs of my friends. But no such thing: before the coldness of wandering attention, and the repelling power of a sarcastic smile, my imagination has shrunk back, and sought shelter for its delicacy in the veil of common conversation, the bald disjointed chat, to which they listen with pleasure, and reply to with intelligence. I have often heard Mrs. Knowles say, such was the reception which the powers of her mind met amongst the gentry in the little town of Rugeley and its environs, during all the prime of her life. Settling in London, and her fame reaching from thence the home of her youth, those very people who, when she lived amongst them, affected to despise her as a romantic chatter-brain, now pay every homage to the recollection of her, and seem to take pride and consequence to themselves that she was born and educated at Rugeley. Nay, I even found the gentry of Chichester stare, amazed and incredulous, when I said Mr. Hayley was the first poet of the age. 'Really! they were glad to hear me say so. They knew the reviewers had complimented him highly, but they were so partial, their praise was no great honour; they should be pleased to hear Mr. Hayley was really so highly thought of, for he was a mighty worthy good sort of man.'

TO MISS WESTON AND DR. WHALLEY, GREETING.

Brick Hill, Monday night, March 24, 1783.

My dear Friends,—I am on my road to town. My eyelid feels easy. I have an hour's leisure; in London I shall not have a moment's. My heart dictates, and my hand will not be restrained from obeying this same triangular varletess, who, 'betide me weal, betide me woe,' ever must be, as she ever was, the arbitrary decider of my conduct and of my fate. Oh, pardon this disobedience to the kind solicitude that charms me! To qualify it as much as I feel myself able, instead of two letters, I mean only to write one, addressing myself equally to my Sophia and my Edwy. That same 'my' is a proud little word, is it not?

Sophia, I am rejoiced that you will shortly leave Mrs. Provis: she is not a being of your class. The congeniality of our sentiments assures me you have discovered that souls are created in classes—that it is vain to hope for permanency, either in friendship or love, for beings of separate ones, even though each may be virtuous, and in essentials perhaps equally so. How doubly impossible, then, that the wreaths of amity should not fade, where there is so wide a disparity in virtue, as well in intellect, as in sensibility! Mrs. Provis has no heart, my dear creature, and is not worth our contemplation; but we will be very civil to her, for she is not worth even an air of resentment. Her beauty, tottering on the autumnal verge, whose graces are the *summum bonum* of her peace, with what ill-humour is not the consciousness of its fast-approaching devastation necessarily pregnant! When its dominion is perfectly laid waste she is likely enough to commence devotee, and to pray outrageously, under the idea that, when she gets to heaven, her angelship's countenance will be more glorious and her wings of finer plumage, for the frequency and fervour of devotional adulation.

I am afraid I shall not be able to go to Cheltenham this spring. My father is convinced that Harrowgate is of superior efficacy in scorbutic complaints, and seems to have set his mind on carrying me thither about June or July; but I trust you and I shall meet at Lichfield long before that period.

Percy Street, Tuesday night.

My dear friends, I arrived here at five. Think of my mortification! Mrs. Siddons in 'Belvidera' to-night, as is supposed for the last time before she lies in. I asked Mrs. Barrow if it would be impossible to get into the pit. 'O heaven!' said she, 'impossible in any part of the house!' Mrs. B. is, I find, in the *petit-souper* circle; so the dear plays, oratorios, &c., will be a little too much, for my wishes, out of question. Adieu! adieu! O that Sophia were to be of our party in the pleasant week to which I look forward!

My dear friends, yours entirely,

A. Seward.

MISS SEWARD TO DR. WHALLEY.

Monday, April 10, 1783.

From the midst of hurries, which even surpass my formidable dread of their excess, let me snatch a few minutes to send my beloved and excelling friend a few hasty and grateful lines by the most glorious of her sex. Powers, which surpass every idea I had formed of their possibility, press so forcibly upon my recollection, that my pen has more than once stood still upon my paper, transfixed by the consciousness how poor and inadequate are all words to paint my Siddonian idolatry. Every attempt fruitless to procure boxes, I saw her for the first time, at the hazard of my life, by struggling through the terrible, fierce, maddening crowd into the pit. She only could have recompensed the terrors and dangers of the attempt; and the recompense was full! She far outstrips that ideal perfection which, through life, I have vainly searched for in the theatre. Her energy, her pathos, her majestic scorn, is inspired by the same sensibility and nobleness of soul, which produces all the varied expressions of these passions in Giovanni's singing, and casts the Yates, the Crawfords, and the Youngs at the same immeasurable distance, at which he throws every other singer in the world. I have seen her in 'Jane Shore' and in 'Calista,'—conceive with what rapture, for it is impossible to describe it. I am as devoted to her as yourself, and my affection keeps pace with my astonishment and delight; for I have conversed with her, hung upon every word which fell from that charming lip; but I never felt myself so awed in my life. The most awkward embarrassment was the consequence.

Mrs. Siddons in the theatre, and Giovanni in the orchestra, have made all amusements, dramatic and musical, so insipid where they are not, that I hate to go to the opera, the oratorio, the concerts; and to a play I will not be dragged when the sun of excellence withdraws her beams, or where they are not accustomed to shine. We are going to the Pantheon to-night. I expect to be finely haunted by the demon *ennui* in that brilliant dome. My eyelid is almost well; scarce a vestige of the disease remains. My health is also better than I have known it for many weeks.

You received a letter from me, addressed to you and to our dear Sophia jointly, and written on the journey to town.

Oh! my beloved friend! your raillery upon my scruples is too severe — it made me weep. Your wit has thrown them into a false light. Did your fortune exceed the limits of those demands which habituated elegance and open-handed bounty make upon it, thy Julia had accepted thy generosity frankly and pleasurably as it was offered.

Edwy, my dear Edwy, teach thy Amelia and thy Siddons to love me! Sophia's heart, that mine of mental wealth, is affianced to me already, if my horrid figure and embarrassed dialect do not blot the fair compact.

Thursday, the 10th.

What a beautiful letter is your last! I took the liberty of reading it to my loved Miss Powys — a charming woman of polished manners and highly cultivated mind, to whom I must introduce you. She has been my warm and kind friend since we were back. She is charmed with your imagination and with your heart. Her attachment to Honora while living, and now to her memory, is scarce less passionate than my own. I enclose her last letter to me, received six weeks ago, because it speaks what you will like to read of our solar divinity, whom I worship with more than a Brahmin's devotion.

Fortune favours the spirited. No box to be procured for 'Venice Preserved.' I prevailed with my little Jessica to whirl down to the play-house, and, under the protection of her brother, to wait in the lobby for the chance of given-up places. The romance of the hope was finely scouted by Mr. Barugh and others; but I persisted, and we ventured. A gentleman of Mrs. B.'s train accidentally popped us, before the play began, into places a man was keeping in the fifth row of the front boxes, on our promise of retiring if they were claimed before the first act was over, after which we should, by the rule of the house, have a right to keep them. Oh! even when the siren spoke, with all her graces and melting tones, I wished to have the speech over, so ardently did I long for the moment when possession for the night might become secure. Our stars fought for us, the act was over, the box-keeper retired with a shilling reward for not bustling us, and in a second the people who had taken the places claimed them! Vain was their claim; our beaux asserted our right to keep them, and keep them we did. But time flies, and words could but feebly shadow forth the yearnings of my soul that night; my tears flowed in full and ceaseless streams. Her superhuman powers have been so strictly just to every character she has represented, that I find it impossible to pronounce in which she is greatest; yet if some friend was to say to me, I am only to see Mrs. Siddons in one character, and if this friend was a being capable of discerning and strongly feeling all her excellences, and was to leave to me the choice of the character, I should say 'Calista,' because, though less soul-harrowing than 'Belvidera,' it exhibits such a conflicting and sublime variety of passions.

Oh! I must leave you. Heaven grant we may soon meet in peace and joy beneath these proud towers!

My best love to Sophia. There is so much of awe blended with the affection I bear to your Amelia, that I hardly dare send her so familiar a remembrance, yet let it not be less kind.

Heaven preserve you, and all you love, my generous Edwy! Tell Benignus I will write to him in the first hour of leisure — alas! I must find that in Staffordshire. It gratifies me that our tastes are sympathetic over the faults of his style in his prose works. How infinitely true is all you say on that subject! My affectionate, felicitous good wishes will ever attend him.

MRS. SIDDONS TO DR. WHALLEY.

Dublin, July 14, 1783.

I THANK you a thousand and a thousand times for your dear letter; but you don't mention having heard from me since you left England. I wrote a few hasty lines in a letter of Mr. Pratt's, a great while ago. We rejoice most sincerely that you are arrived without any material accident, without any dangerous ones I mean, for to be sure some of them were very *materially* entertaining. Oh, how I laugh whenever the drowsy adventure comes across my imagination, for 'more was meant than met the ear.' I am sure I would have given the world to have seen my dear Mrs. Whalley upon the little old tub. How happy you are in your descriptions! So she was very well; then very jocular she must be. I think her conversation, thus enthroned and thus surrounded, must have been the highest treat in all the world. Some parts of your tour must have been enchanting. How good it was of you to wish me a partaker of your pastoral dinner! Be assured, my dear, dear friends, no one can thank you more sincerely, or be more sensible of the honour of your regard, though many may deserve it better. What a comfortable thing to meet with such agreeable people! But society and converse like yours and my dear Mrs. Whalley's must very soon make savages agreeable. How did poor little Paphy bear it? Did she remonstrate in her usual melting tones? I am sure she was very glad to be at rest, which does not happen in a carriage, I remember, for any length of time. I can conceive nothing so provoking or ridiculous as the Frenchman's politeness, and poor Vincent's perplexity. You will have heard, long ere this reaches you, that our sweet D—— is safely delivered of a very fine girl, which I know will give you no small pleasure. Now for myself. Our journey was delightful; the roads through Wales present you with mountains unsurmountable, the grandest and the most beautiful prospects to be conceived; but I want your pen to describe them.

We got very safe to Holyhead, and then I felt as if some great event was going to take place, having never been on sea. I was awed, but not terrified; feeling myself in the hands of a great and powerful God, 'whose mercy is over all His works.' The sea was particularly rough; we were lifted mountains high, and sank again as low in an instant. Good God! how tremendous, how wonderful! A pleasing terror took hold on me, which it is impossible to describe, and I never felt the majesty of the Divine Creator so fully before. I was dreadfully sick, and so were my poor sister and Mr. Brereton. Mr. Siddons was pretty well; and here, my dear friend, let me give you a little wholesome advice; allways (you see I have forgot to spell) go to bed the instant you go on board, for by lying horizontally, and keeping very quiet, you cheat the sea of half its influence. We arrived in Dublin the 16th of June, half-past twelve at night. There is not a tavern or a house of any kind in this capital city of a rising kingdom, as they call themselves, that will take a woman in; and do you know I was obliged, after being shut up in the Custom-house officer's room, to have the things examined, which room was more like a dungeon than anything else,—after staying here above an hour and a half, I tell you I was obliged, sick and weary as I was, to wander about the streets on foot (for the coaches and chairs were all gone off the stands) till almost two o'clock in the morning, raining, too, as if heaven and earth were coming together. A pretty beginning! thought I; but these people are a thousand years behind us in every respect. At length Mr. Brereton, whose father had provided a bed for him on his arrival, ventured to say he would insist on having a bed for us at the house where he was to sleep. Well, we got to this place, and the lady of the house vouchsafed, after many times telling us that she never took in ladies, to say we should sleep there that night. I never was so weary and so disgusted in my life.

The city of Dublin is a sink of filthiness; the noisome smells, and the multitudes of shocking and most miserable objects, made me resolve never to stir out but to my business. I like not the people either; they are all ostentation and insincerity, and in their ideas of finery very like the French, but not so cleanly; and they not only speak but think coarsely. This is in confidence; therefore, your fingers on your lips, I pray. They are tenacious of their country to a degree of folly that is very laughable, and would call me the blackest of ingrates were they to know my sentiments of them. I have got a thousand pounds among them this summer. I always acknowledge myself obliged to them, but I cannot love them. I know but one among them that can in any degree atone for the barbarism of the rest, who thinks there are other means of expressing esteem besides forcing people to eat and to drink, the doing which to a most offensive degree they call Irish hospitality. I long to be at home, sitting quietly in the little snug parlour, where I had last the pleasure, or rather the pain, of seeing you that night. For the first time in my life I wished not to see you. I dreaded it, and with reason. I knew (which was the case) I should not recover that cruel farewell for several days. Oh! my dear friend, do the pleasures of life compensate for the pangs? I think not. Some people place the whole happiness of life in the pleasures of imagination, in building castles; for my part, I am not one that builds very magnificent ones, nay, I don't build any castles, but cottages without end. May the great Disposer of all events but permit me to spend the evening of my toilsome bustling day in a cottage, where I may sometimes have the converse and society, which will make me more worthy those imperishable habitations which are prepared for the spirits of just men made perfect! Yes, let me take up my rest in this world near my beloved Langford. You know this has been my castle any time these four years, and I am making a little snug party. Mr. Nott and my dear sister I have secured, and make no doubt of gaining a few others. Is not this a delightful scheme?

I have played for one charity since I have been here (I am now at Cork, I should tell you), and am to play for another to-morrow—your favourite Zara, in the 'Mourning Bride.' I am extremely happy that you like your little companion so well.* I have sat to a young man in this place, who has made a small full-length of me in 'Isabella,' upon the first entrance of Biron. You will think this an arduous undertaking, but he has succeeded to admiration. I think it more like me than any I have ever yet seen. I am sure you would be delighted with it. I never was so well in my life as I have been in Ireland; but, God be praised, I shall set out for dear England next Tuesday.

* Mrs. Siddons refers here to the miniature of herself, the engraving of which is given.

This letter has been begun this month, and finished by a line or two at a time, so you 'll find it a fine scrawl; and I am still so mere a matter-of-fact body, as to despair of giving you the least entertainment. I can boast no other claim to the honour and happiness of your correspondence than a very sincere affection for you both, joined with the most perfect esteem for your most amiable qualities, and great talents. Say all that 's kind for us to my dear Mrs. W., and believe me ever

Your most affectionate

S. SIDDONS.

Cork: August 29.

I hope you will give me the pleasure of hearing from you soon.

Written by Mrs. Siddons,
Supposed to have gone to London.*

October 7, 1783.

For God's sake, my dear friends, pray for my memory. I had forgot to pay the postage, as you kindly desired, and this poor letter has been wandering about the world ever since I left Cork. It was opened in Ireland, you see, so I must never show my face there again. The king commands 'Isabella' to-morrow, and I play 'Jane Shore' on Saturday. I have affronted Mrs. Jackson by not being able to procure her places. I am extremely sorry for it, as I had the highest esteem for herself, and her friendship for you had tied her close to my heart. I have done all I could to reinstate myself in her favour, but in vain. Poor Mr. Nott has been in great trouble; he has lost a brother lately that was more nearly allied than by blood, and for whose loss he is inconsolable. He is not in town, but I hope soon to see him.

* This letter, not being prepaid, must have been returned by the General Post Office, to Mrs. Siddons, and was forwarded by her in another cover.—*Ed.*

Adieu! Mr. Siddons, &c., desire kindest wishes. The last letter I wrote to you I was very near serving in the same manner. Is it not a little alarming? I fear I shall be superannuated in a few years.

MISS SEWARD TO DR. WHALLEY.

February 14, 1784.

Oh, my beloved friend, through what magnificent and beautiful scenery do you lead me! Were Claude, Poussin, and Salvator now living, and were they also my partial friends; for my amusement were they to employ their magic pencil, and throw the scenes through which you have passed on their breathing canvas, transmitting them to me, my imagination could not more forcibly receive the distinct ideas of their glowing beauty and astonishing sublimity, than it now does from the unmatched pages now before me. Your letter to Sophia lies on the table with mine. They form a priceless volume. How tame, how cold, how indistinct are all other descriptions of the Alpine scenery that I have read, compared to yours! Their light must not be hid under the bushel of private friendship; they must not pass away with the short term of your existence and mine. We—I mean our mortal part—must perish, but they should endure. I deny myself the pleasure of commenting upon their particular features, or many sheets would not bound the traces of a pen goaded on by the delight of such varied gratification. I indulge a chosen few of your warm admirers with a participation of this mental luxury. Many tears have been shed over the interesting portrait of the young Bernardine and his unhappy story. I cannot, however, help being sorry that he chose that order, and had rather have found him within the bleak, the lone, and windy walls of the Chartreux. The severest corporal mortification cannot be equally oppressive to a mind so tempered, as the constant intrusion of convivial and unfeeling mirth. Infinite is the reluctance with which I oblige myself to pass over in silence those descriptions to which my imagination recurs perpetually. Were you an entire stranger to my heart, I should yet feel that my darling Ossian contains no passage which more strongly seizes the imagination, than when you transport us within the desolate walls of the castle of Chatillon, and when the spirits of the lake seem to howl amongst the midnight winds.

Giovanni thanks you a thousand times for your kind remembrance of him. He says the friendship of minds like yours, is a sweet compensation for all he may suffer through the malice of beings, who have nothing but their outward form in common with Mr. Whalley's nature. He says your last letter is one of the first pieces of fine writing in our language. We both long to be seated by you on one of those magnificent Alps, to contemplate with you the aerial solitude, and all its great and varied sublimities; and we all rejoice that you and your Amelia's constitution shrink not beneath the Alpine blasts. The English ones are amazingly keen this winter: nothing like it has been felt, they tell me, since the year '40. Our ladies are learning to skate. Hitherto I have escaped my winter cough, but my spirits have not recovered the shock of my poor Nanny's death. I warmly congratulate you on the health of your beloved mother.

Mr. Hayley meant to have published again as last month; but business of a less abstract nature has retarded the Muse's progress. I do not exactly know the subject and style of the expected publication, but believe it will consist chiefly of plays. I think I mentioned to you those little comedies of his upon a new plan, which appeared to me of such exquisite happiness. His last letter but one alarmed me exceedingly, by mentioning a weakness which he began to perceive in the left half of his frame, whose use was, together with his intellects, entirely taken away during two years by that cruel fever, which attacked him in his eleventh year, and whose description has an effect so beautifully pathetic in his last noble poem. It was in vain that he spoke gaily and wittily over the startling mementoes of this dread disease, and, though he found the left side full ten years older than the right, conjured me not to suspect any decay of warmth and vigour in his affection for my person, or zeal for my fame, though their seat was found in the superannuated division. After the first perusal of his last letter I cast it upon the table in a pet, since it takes no notice of my anxious inquiries upon this important subject, only that these words are crowded into a diminutive corner of the paper: 'My weak side sends you its grateful devoirs for your solicitude. My comfort is, that everybody has a weak side.' His friend Mr. Sarjent, and he, publish at the same time.

Sarjent is a new poetic luminary. 'The Mine,' his first publication—I must have spoken to you of it—is a dramatic poem of extreme beauty. The story, an Italian nobleman banished to the gold and diamond mines, and followed thither by his wife, who attends upon him disguised. This poem has supernatural agency—the gnomes, who sing mineralogic odes. Sarjent restores them to the benevolence with which Rosicrucius invested them, and of which Pope deprived them to serve a beautiful purpose in his 'Rape of the Lock.' Mr. Sarjent, like Brooke Boothby, is a man of fortune and the *bon-ton.* His intimacy with the Bard of Britain has drawn forth the latent fires of genius, like lightning from the summer cloud, whose gay silken form seems little likely to contain any.

You surprise me in thinking Mason's pride will be hurt by the comparison of himself to David, and Johnson to Goliath, since surely the former is the more glorious hero. Surely Philistine Critic is not a title of honour to excite the jealousy of Mason. The obligations of his muse to Gray are acknowledged in many parts of his works:—

ENGLISH GARDEN.

Clos'd is that curious ear, by death's cold hand,
That mark'd each error of my careless strain
With kind severity; to whom my muse
Still lov'd to whisper what she meant to sing
In louder accent.

I am much mistaken if the idea of Mr. Gray leading her up poetic heights, as the eagle leads his young to the sun, is not somewhere expressed in Mason's works. But you are probably right in supposing that he will not like to see that superiority glanced at by others, though he voluntarily himself confesses it. I have often smiled to think what a catalogue of direful sins we all confess in the church, yet complain of injury, forsooth! if the slightest foible is attributed to us by our fellow-creature. I forgot to observe, when I was on the painful subject of Mr. Pratt's duplicity, that in the paper in which I traced his writings, I never once, upon any occasion, saw a paragraph of scandal.

My 'Louisa' is in the press here: I chose it for the sake of correcting my own press. In point of orthography I know I shall do it ill, from my natural heedlessness; but the close revisal will probably show the errors in the composition, for whose correction the work may be the better. The Lichfield printer is very dilatory, so it may be long ere the poem comes out. My cat and lark are well, and are honoured in your and your Amelia's remembrance. I rejoice in Sappho's health and improvements. It is almost three months since I heard from or of the sweet Helena Williams. Mr. and Mrs. Hayley, Miss Powys, Mr. Newton, Miss Notts, and Mrs. Porter, all desire to be kindly remembered to you. My dear Edwy, I shall never, I am afraid, teach you to be an economist. Since you pay for the letters you send, as well as those you receive, by weight, why write upon such thick small paper? A large sheet of this size and thickness would contain as much as two of those you use, and not weigh a fifth as much. Do not learn of Sophia to send me little bits of paper; they are liable to be lost, and we pay the price of a whole sheet for them. We pay half-a-crown here for every separate paper which comes to us from abroad, let the scrap be ever so small. I do not consider the King as an object of charity, and I always reflect upon the use which the sums we lavish upon useless epistolary extravagance might be to many a poor family. In vain have I endeavoured to impress these considerations on the mind of Sophia, whose narrow fortune renders her insensibility to them a very serious evil.

Will the charming Chatillon accept my amitiés? — my fruitless longings to share with you the delights of his society? Say all that is affectionate for me to the dear and excellent Amelia. My father sends his kindest regards to you both. I think I have already transmitted to you the glowing testimonies of Giovanni's attachment. Let me not forget poor Cizos, who is well, and as enthusiastically devoted to your idea as ever.

My dear Miss Rogers passed five days with me the week before last, on her road to Sophia, with whom she means to stay six weeks, and then reside some time with me on her return.

Ever yours,

A. SEWARD.

MRS. THRALE TO DR. WHALLEY.

Bath, March 6, 1784.

YOUR kind letter, dear sir, should not have lain so long unanswered, or at least unacknowledged, but having no other direction to you except the date, I durst not send a long scrawl to Chambery for fear of its being lost, as I did not dream of your spending such a winter within the mountains of

Savoy. Miss Gould, however, quickened my almost blunted purpose by showing me this morning the partial passage in your letter to her, relating to me. How little should I deserve your obliging desire of my friendship were I insensible to such proofs of your good opinion! continue it to me, my dear sir, and obtain for me that of Mrs. Whalley. If I thought your pen excelled in portrait as in landscape painting, one need only be selfish to cultivate your kindness; but the pictures you draw of the scenes in France and Savoy make one impatient of confinement, and eager to climb those Alps you are contented to view from the French side.

Mr. Chatillon's character, among the general group you had been surrounded with, refreshed one's spirits, as the little elegant valley refreshed your eyes; it is not, however, like that, I find, made less pleasing by closer inspection. It was a happy circumstance to meet with such a friend, and I should have thought it an odd one, if you had not been the finder; but elegant and gentle manners are attractive in all nations, and you have not drawn iron to you but gold.

The description of monastic life would, I was confident, be agreeable to Dr. Johnson, who is very ill in London, so I sent it to amuse him, for which I make you no apology.

Our mode of existence at Bath has, as you know, little variety, but much placid quiet; and with a society one liked, your intent of ending your days here might prove the wisest possible. Every accommodation for sickness, every provision against sorrow, every indulgence to retreat, and every inducement to gaiety may be found at Bath.

Have you interested yourself about the air balloons? and do the French people tire each other with talking about them as much as we do? Not a country town in England that has not subscribed towards the general desire of subduing a new element to the government of all-expecting man. What have I else to tell you? You are happily secluded from the noise and nonsense of political disputants, who tear their own country and their own throats to pieces, only to show that useless eloquence which might be more innocently and pleasingly employed. But you enquire for my family, and encourage me to tell you something of my health. It is not good, nor has been for some time: a warmer climate might, perhaps, restore it, but Bath is the best succedaneum for a southern latitude, and with that I must be contented for the present. One of my daughters, the youngest, has been ill, too, but Dr. Dobson's care has set her out of danger—so far as that is a phrase for mortals. Adieu! dear sir, and assure yourself of my true esteem, and doubt not of the pleasure I shall one day feel at seeing you again, and of assuring you how sincerely I have the honour to be yours and Mrs. Whalley's

Obliged and faithful servant,

H. L. THRALE.

Let me hear from you soon again.

MRS. WHALLEY TO FANNY SAGE.

Chamberry, July 27, 1784.

YOUR letter, my dearest Fanny, relieved your uncle and me from a great deal of anxiety. Why, my love, will you ever neglect to pay the postage of the letters you send me? I cautioned you, too, on that head but in my last letter. As Avignon (where I must beg you to direct your next *à la poste restante*) is not in the territory of the French king, you must take care to pay the postage through France, and have it marked on the back of your letter. I am rejoiced to find you are so well and happy, and enjoy yourself with your friends this summer, and that you are to pass the next winter under the protection of Mrs. Blair; and should Mr. Sage think it eligible to bring you on the Continent next summer, I need not say what infinite pleasure it will give me and your uncle, who hopes your dear father has received the letter which he wrote him a considerable time since; but we conclude the employment of his office must occupy a great part of his time. I am very glad your little cousin is so much better; you do not tell me whether she has any brother or sister. If the weather is as fine in proportion with you as with us, you must enjoy the country vastly.

The heats are so intense here at this season, that there is no stirring but very late or early, and indeed my walks have been much abridged lately by my having had a most miserable toothache and swelled face; but I have regretted nothing more than that my legs had not strength enough to carry me three leagues from the town, where the roads are impassable for a carriage, but where, between the mountains covered with snow, there are numberless little plots where the ground is entirely covered like a carpet with flowers of various hues, placed there by the hand of Nature, but in beauty far surpassing all the works of art. You there find auriculas, pinks, anemones, and almost all the common flowers cultivated in our gardens, with numberless other sorts to which we are strangers, springing spontaneously, and wafting their perfumes to a considerable distance. Your uncle ate a cold dinner in one of these delightful spots; and while he gathered flowers with one hand to ornament his hat, with the other he reached snow to cool his wine.

Mr. Whalley has made excursions over the greater part of Savoy, and has made a very entertaining journal on the subject, which I hope you, my love, will one day read. As these expeditions are only calculated for men, and even very *pénible* to them, I have contented myself with the amusements which Chamberry and its environs afforded me. There are an infinity of silkworms kept in this country; hardly a gentleman's villa is without a building allotted to their use, and a grove of white mulberry trees for their sustenance.

Many families make a hundred pounds a year from these industrious little creatures, whose various progressions and curious labours have afforded me an infinite deal of entertainment. I make no doubt but you will find a very particular account of them in Goldsmith's Animated Nature.

I very lately saw a nun take the veil. It is a sight that well merits a stranger's observation. At my entrance into the chapel of the convent, I was placed on the bishop's right hand, close to a thick grate which separated the inhabitants of the convent from the rest of the congregation. It enclosed a large choir, at each side of which were stalls, where the nuns sat with their veils up, and each with a large wax flambeau lighted in her hand. Behind were all the *pensionnaires* full dressed. In the centre of the choir was a large figure of our Saviour on the cross; on each side a nun.

The poor victim knelt near the grate, and opposite the bishop. On each side of her were two of the *pensionnaires*, girls about your age, who represented bridesmaids, were gaily dressed, and each held a torch. There was a full band of music in the church. The ceremony began with the bishop performing mass; then a young, eager-looking priest, gave us a very dull, and, to say the truth, I thought in some respects an offensive sermon; that ended, the new nun advanced to a little door which was opened in the grate opposite the bishop, who administered the sacrament to her. He then asked her several questions, which amount only to the enquiry whether she is willing to quit the world and be married to Christ. After answering in the affirmative, she read aloud her vows of perpetual poverty, chastity, and obedience. The abbess then advances, takes off her novitiate veil, and puts on that of her order; after which she lays down, four nuns spread a pall over her, as an emblem of her being dead to the world, the organ swells forth the most solemn tones, and all the bells toll. After five minutes she gets up, the bishop presents her with a small gold crucifix, her bridesmaids pin a nuptial garland on her head, and the music strikes up the gayest airs. She then prostrates herself before the bishop and the abbess, embraces and is embraced by all the sisterhood, and the ceremony ends with chanting and music. As it was quite novel to me, and I love to inform myself of everything I have hitherto been a stranger to, I did not regret being detained three hours from my breakfast. I wish the long detail may not have tired you.

The Duke and Duchess of Chablais (the king's brother) passed through here lately, on their way to a water-drinking place in the neighbourhood of Geneva. There was great rejoicings and illuminations here on the occasion. On their arrival at the place of their destination, they found the Duke and Duchess of Gloucester there; but the latter moved off immediately, on being informed by the Duchess of Chablais that she could not be received by her as the sister of a king, as she was not received in that light at our court, on account of her obscure birth. I am not sorry her pride has met with such a repulse.*

There are several medicinal springs in this neighbourhood. At one about seven miles off, the name of which is Aix, there is a great resort of company. The waters are hot, and, in their nature and property nearly resemble those of Bath. There is a most singular circumstance attends that situation, which naturalists are at a loss to account for: creatures venomous in every other place are harmless at Aix, and for two miles round. Children play with vipers in the streets; and I, from my window the other day, saw a man with a cap,

* William Henry, third son of Frederick, Prince of Wales, and brother of George III., was born in 1743, and created Duke of Gloucester, &c. He married, 1766, Maria, relict of James, second Earl of Waldegrave, and daughter of Sir Edward Walpole, second son of the first Earl of Orford. The expression of 'obscure birth,' must therefore be taken with limitation, and in comparison with royal blood. She died 1807, surviving the duke two years. William Frederick, Duke of Gloucester, sprang from this marriage, being born at Rome in 1776.

doublet, collar, girdle, garters, and bracelets of living serpents of Aix, which did not do him the least injury.

We propose leaving this place next Tuesday, and, after a few weeks spent in Switzerland, from which I expect infinite entertainment, shall pass on to Avignon, where I shall depend on finding a letter from you. As soon as we are set down there, you may expect to hear from me.

Pray present our kindest regards to Mr. Sage, accept our united love, and believe me ever, my dearest niece,

Most tenderly yours,

ELIZA WHALLEY.

DR. WHALLEY TO FANNY SAGE.

Avignon, October 6, 1784.

THOUGH I consider you as your aunt's correspondent, yet, my dearest Fanny, I cannot deny myself the pleasure of now and then encroaching upon her rights, and assuring you, with my own pen, that absence only serves to increase my affection for you. It is impossible, my darling niece, to describe the satisfaction that the account of your merits gives me from all quarters. To see you grow up amiable and accomplished has always been my chief ambition, and I cannot hear that you equal my fondest hopes, without the most sensible joy and pride. How delightful, also, must it be to you, my sweet girl, to see yourself the blessing of your dear father's life; and that you find it in your power, by your talents and your tenderness, to recompense him for all his cares, and almost to restore to him all the domestic delights and comforts that he lost, in losing your charming and excellent mother. What a happiness to myself, as well as him, to see her living again in you; to see all her graces and all her virtues blooming and ripening with your years! But I must no longer trust my pen with so interesting a subject, otherwise it will lead me too far. You have probably heard from Molly Wickham* of our motions to the time of our quitting Savoy.

Geneva was our next station. It appeared to the utmost advantage in our eyes, after the dirt, beggary, and ill odours of Chamberry, which is a disgrace to the beautiful country of which it is the capital. Geneva, on the contrary, is well built, neat, rich, and flourishing—advantages which it derives as much from its government, as from the majestic lake and the rapid Rhone, which renders its situation so favourable for commerce. We stayed in all ten days there, and you would have thought your dear aunt grown a glutton (a vice you would never have suspected her of), had you seen the delight with which she rather devoured than ate the only good roast beef that we have ever met with since our leaving England. Good tea and toast and butter were also two other delicacies that she rioted in, and of which she had long been deprived. Add to this, the neatness of the people, and beds free from bugs, and you will suppose her triumph complete. The situation of Geneva we thought a very fine one, but that of Lausanne still more beautiful. The little hills above it covered with wood and vineyards; the green lake stretched out in noble mirror before it; the picturesque villages on either hand; and the bold rocks and fertile plains of Opablais on the other side, with a sublime pile of Alps to close the scene, renders its situation as striking as it is renowned.

In our way back to Geneva, we stayed two days at the Château de Prangeans, belonging to the Baron of that title. His wife is our countrywoman, and as your sweet friends, Flora and Julia,† who are possibly at your elbow, could inform

* Dr. Whalley's sister, wife of James Wickham, of Frome. He died 1791; she died 1817.

† Miss Julia Davies married the late John Beadon, Rector of Christian Malford, Wilts. She survived him, and died a few years since in Bath, without issue. Her father was Mrs. Sedgwick Whalley's first cousin.

you,—sister to Mr. Cleveland of the Admiralty, Mr. Davies old neighbour, and particular friend. We were received with the greatest politeness, and treated with an ease, as well as hospitality, that did honour to Rousseau's description of the manners in the charming Pays de Vaud. You can imagine nothing so enchantingly beautiful as the situation of this noble château. It stands on a verdant rising above the lake, and the prospect it commands is as much more various and picturesque, tell your amiable young friends, than the celebrated one from Tapely, as that is more charming than a common point of view.

At Geneva I had luckily fallen into company, and formed an intimacy with two highly informed and amiable young Danes, one of whom (my favourite) is Gentleman of the Bed-chamber to the Prince of Denmark, and as agreeable in his manners and lively in his temper, as he is improved in a naturally fine understanding. We went to the glaciers together, and their society rendered it one of the most charming excursions I ever took. The whole road from Geneva to Chamouni, the village near which those marvels of all people are situated, is abundant in noble and picturesque points of view; and as you approach the glaciers, nature seems to dilate her features, and every successive object to grow more grand and imposing. The glaciers* themselves fell far short of

* No less than thirty-four considerable glaciers are counted upon the region of Mont Blanc, and the most important of them is the Mer de Glâce, near Chamouni, which Dr. Whalley here describes. It is estimated that the whole contiguous surface of ice and snow, connected with this glacier, covers a space of seventeen square miles. The lowest part of it, called Glacier des Bois, and which is the source of the river Arveiron, two miles beyond Chamouni, descends with a rapid inclination into the valley. At the châlet of Montanivert, no great distance up the mountain, the glacier is found to be of a very gentle inclination, and so continues for many miles towards the centre of the chain. It is there about half a mile broad.

A little reflection on the nature of the glacier would dispel the idea of its possessing the beauty of transparent ice. Its formation has been compared, 'parvis componere magna,' to that of an icicle hanging from a roof, which has my expectation, though certainly vast and wonderful objects; and, from their singularity, amply worth all the pains that curiosity takes to visit them, yet not deserving of all the praises that the overheated imaginations of some authors have bestowed on their sublimity and splendour. Conceive narrow arms of a tempestuous sea, rushing down in the hollow between stupendous rocks, and suddenly arrested in its fury by a mighty frost, and you have them before your eyes.

But I fondly expected that the congealed billows would present all the *éclat* to the sight of pure ice, and imagined them sparkling in the sunbeams with the most radiant lustre. No such thing, my dear girl! They everywhere offer to you a surface of dirty snow, except in the vast cracks, or rather gulfs, that yawn, to the depth of an hundred feet, at every step, and the inside edges of which appear of a clear and dark blue ice. But this has little effect as to the general *coup d'œil*; and it was from that *coup d'œil* that I expected so much beauty and splendour, and in which I was so much disappointed. The august scene of rocks, and woods, and mountains round, eclipsed the glaciers in my eye, crowned by the imperial Mont Blanc, the sublimest of all sublime objects, who lifted up his head high above them all, resplendent with eternal snows, in which the glaciers

been formed by the gradual melting of the snow above. Thus the glacier commences on the mountain's side, at an elevation little below the freezing point, where it is formed of partially-melted snow, and as it descends lower, this substance becomes ice; and though sufficiently firm, not only to hold together but also to resist indentation, still it is in a partially fluid state. The pressure from behind continually urges it forward with a motion differing in rapidity according to the season of the year. In the summer, a glacier will sometimes advance four feet in twenty-four hours. This movement causes the great fissures with which it is intersected, and enables it to bring into the valleys a mass of fragmentary rocks and sand, either fallen upon it from the heights above, or collected by attrition in its passage along the sides of the mountains. Far, then, from possessing that transparent beauty of ice, the glacier has a generally dull white and dirty appearance.

found their source, and from which they derive their support. Mont Blanc is now, by accurate observation, determined to be the highest mountain in the known world*; and is, beyond all comparison, the most glorious object, when viewed to proper advantage, that I ever beheld.

At Geneva I parted with my two Danish friends, but not without regret, nor without a promise to keep a correspondence in French with my favourite, who forced me to accept a fine ruby ring, set round with brilliants, as a mark of his regard. From Geneva we went to Lyons, and from the latter passed to Avignon by the Rhone. The *trajet* was delightful, as the banks of that river are thick set with the most picturesque villages, and the greatest number and variety of grand ruins that I ever saw. Yet, upon the whole, the banks of the Saone, from Macon to Lyons, pleased me more, as the landscapes are more rich, pastoral, and varied. We like this city much, and purpose spending the winter, at least, in it. Provisions of all kinds are good and reasonable, and the fruit exquisite beyond expression. Tell your dear father that I have at last received the things his brother was so kind to purchase for me in town, that they are just what I could have wished, and that I will write immediately to Mr. Jenkyns to remit the money for them to Mr. Sage. We had left Chamberry before the Marquis de la Pierre's return into Savoy, which occasioned the long delay in our receiving our various packets from

* Subsequent investigation, as is well known, has entirely destroyed this assertion. The mountain systems, both in Asia and America, present elevations far exceeding that of Mont Blanc. The highest elevation of this mountain is 15,810 feet above the level of the sea, which is exceeded in America by the rocky mountains, and the Mexican table land in the northern continent, and still more so by the great Cordillera of the Andes in the south, one peak of which in Chili rises to the height of 24,000 feet. In Asia, the Caucasian mountains are more lofty than the Alps, whilst the greatest ascertained elevation is to be found among the Himalayas; the Kinchinginga being, according to Keith Johnson, 28,176 feet high.

him. We are happy to find you are to return to Mrs. Blair this winter, and doubt not that you will make it a means of perfecting yourself still further in all those accomplishments which will be so great a resource, and a subject of such laudable self-satisfaction to yourself, as well as the delight and boast of your friends, not one of whom can love you more tenderly than

Your ever affectionate uncle,
THOMAS S. WHALLEY.

Sappho* is very well, very gay, understands French perfectly, and begins to talk it. She sends her love to her cousin Fanny. Adieu.

You and your dear father will rejoice to hear that we have had a considerable and very unexpected addition to our income and estate, which fell to your aunt by old Mrs. Sherwood's death, and which let in her time for 180*l.* per annum, which our steward in the west has now raised to 600*l.* per annum.

MISS SEWARD TO DR. WHALLEY.

Lichfield, January 3, 1785.

MR. HAYLEY is still ardent in his studies, beneath the now leafless bowers of Eartham; soon, I suppose, to flash upon the public in a new flood of learned and imaginative brightness. My health impaired, my muse banished, my quiet ravaged by continual letter-writing, and by the solicitude occasioned by involuntary long delays, to many whom I love, from the perplexing number of my correspondents, Mr. Hayley excuses my writing to him very often, the rather as his own time is so precious to him; but when I do write, I always mention my dear travellers, of whose welfare he expresses himself right glad to hear. Charming as his letters are, they

* The Blenheim spaniel represented in the portrait of Dr. Whalley.

very seldom are replies to mine, which somewhat abates the pleasure I have in receiving them. I ask him a thousand questions about books and people, whose answers are of importance to me, but I seldom get these queries noticed. He expresses affectionate partiality for me in brilliant and flashing terms of wit. They flash through three sides of a half sheet, covered with tall and widely-written words. He then tells me that the unfortunate disease in his eyes forbids him to say more, and adds a kind but abrupt farewell.

How provoking it is that you never got Hayley's 'Plays,' nor my 'Louisa!' What does Lady Langham say about them? —did she receive them from Robinson? Miss Langham does 'Louisa' great honour in forming drawings from her story.

Mrs. Smith's* musical improvements keep on their rapid pace. Her benefit concert room was crowded beyond every idea. Miss Hammond, and Mrs. Gell of Hopton, sent her five guineas each, though they could not attend. By the generosity of her friends, it was, after all expenses were paid, worth sixty pounds to her. She sings with her father at the Worcester concerts this winter, and is infinitely approved and admired; but poor Giovanni is hurried almost out of his life. Engaged at the Shrewsbury concerts, and solicited to go every fortnight to concerts at Wakefield in Yorkshire, which are to be six in number; but he cannot undertake them, the distance is too great. It is flattering, however, to be thus sought and celebrated. Miss Hammond and the Jaunceys complain of the comparative unpleasantness of the Bath singers to Giovanni and his siren daughter. They say Miss Cantelo's lower notes are froggish.

Sophia tells me she shall write to her beloved friends at Avignon very soon—had found her health and spirits hitherto unequal to entering upon the sad theme of your and your

* A married daughter of Mr. Saville.

Amelia's loss, with which she had mournfully sympathised, and which she could not pass over in silence. I thank God that neither of your healths have fallen a sacrifice to fruitless regret and unavailing tears.

The public papers have informed you that the literary Colossus bestrides this narrow world no longer. The incense they offer up to his manes, of extravagant and unqualified praise, is ridiculous; yet had not I attempted to dispel its truth-involving smoke, but that I feared its fumes might give more force to the venom of his envious strictures upon our deceased bards. Therefore was it that I sent the following character of him to the 'General Evening Post.' It appeared on Monday sevennight's paper, but without a name. On Mrs. Porter's* account, I do not choose to be known here as its author. I care not where else I own the composition, conscious that it proceeded from a sense of justice to others, not from ill-will to him:—

'THE LATE DR. JOHNSON.

'Speak of him as he was;
Nothing extenuate, nor set down aught in malice.

'It is right that mankind should form a just, rather than a partial and dazzled, estimate of exalted genius. Such exclusive and hyperbolic praise is now poured on the public ear, concerning an illustrious, but a very mixed character, as seems likely to produce ideas of a judgment which could not err, and of a virtue which could not falter. In believing thus partially of one great man, injury is done to others whose worth he has depreciated, and to whose talents he has been unjust.

'Dr. Johnson's learning and knowledge were deep and universal. His conception was so clear, and his intellectual stores were marshalled with such precision, that his style in common conversation equalled that of his moral Essays.

* Mrs. Lucy Porter, Dr. Johnson's daughter-in-law.

Whatever charge of pedantic stiffness may have been brought against those Essays by prejudice or personal resentment they are certainly not less superior to all other English compositions of that species, in the fertility and efflorescence of imagination, harmony of period, and luminous arrangement of ideas, than they are in strength of expression and force of argument. His Latinisms, for which he has been much censured, have extended the limits of our native dialect, besides enriching its sounds with that sonorous sweetness, which the intermixture of words from a more harmonious language must necessarily produce; I mean in general,—for it cannot be denied that they sometimes deform the Johnsonian page, though they much oftener adorn it. His "London" is a very nervous and brilliant satiric poem, and his "Vanity of Human Wishes" appears to me a much finer satire than the best of Pope's. Its poetic beauty is not exceeded by any composition in heroic rhyme which our country can boast, rich as she is in that species of writing.

'As a moralist, Dr. Johnson was respectable, splendid, sublime; but as a critic, the faults of his disposition have disgraced much of his fine compositions with frequent paradox, unprincipled misrepresentation, mean and needless exposure of bodily infirmities—as in the "Life of Pope"—with irreconcilable contradictions, and with decisions of the last absurdity. Dr. Johnson had strong affections when literary envy did not interfere; but that envy was of "such deadly potency" as to deform his conversation, as it has deformed his biographic works, with the rancour of party violence, with national aversion, unjust and unchristianlike invective. It is in vain to descant upon the improbability that Dr. Johnson, under the consciousness of abilities so great, and of a fame so extensive, should envy any man; since it is more than improbable—it is wholly impossible—that an imagination so sublime, and a judgment so correct, could decide sincerely, as he has decided, upon the works of some who were at least his equals, and upon one who was yet greater than himself. Dr. Johnson was a furious Jacobite while one hope for the Stuart line remained; and his politics, always leaning towards despotism, were inimical to liberty and the natural rights of mankind. He was fervent and practical in his devotions; but his religious faith had more of bigoted fierceness, than of that gentleness which the Gospel inculcates. To those who had never entered the literary confines, or, entering them, had paid him the tribute of boundless praise and total subjection, he was an affectionate and generous friend—soothing in his behaviour to them, and active in promoting their domestic comforts; though, in some spleenful moments, he could not help speaking slightingly both of their worth and abilities. His pride was infinite; yet, amidst all the overbearing arrogance it produced, his heart melted at the sight and the representation of disease and poverty; and, in the hours of affluence, his purse was ever open to relieve them. In many instances his affections seemed engaged by people of whose talents and disposition he scrupled not to speak disrespectfully, at all times and in all humours. To such he often devoted, and especially of later years, a large portion of that time which might naturally have been supposed precious to him, who so well knew how to employ it. When his attention was called to modern writings, particularly if they were celebrated, and not written by any of "his little senate," he generally listened with angry impatience. "No, Sir, I shall not read that book," was his common reply. He turned from the compositions of rising genius with a visible horror, which too plainly proved that envy was the bosom-serpent of this literary despot, whose life had been unpolluted by licentious crimes, and who had some great and noble qualities accompanying a stupendous reach of understanding.'

So much for the vanished but immortal Johnson. I hav the pleasure to tell you that my father endures the rigour o this inclement weather more tolerably than I could expect— that Cizos is well, and that we often pass a literary evening together, in which your idea always mingles with our con-verse. He sends you, and dear Mrs. Whalley, his gratefu amities. You have my father's, Giovanni's, his daughter's Mrs. Porter's, Miss Nott's, Mr. Newton's, &c.

Cumberland's 'Carmelite,' written for Mrs. Siddons, and supported by her through many nights with *éclat,* pleases me exceedingly. It is not without faults, but the beauties greatly overbalance. I know few of our late modern plays that I like so much, except my darling 'Naronne.' Adieu!

> Omnia nox tenebris, tacitâque involverat umbra,
> Et fessos homines vinxerat alta quies,

when I wrote most part of this long letter, though my wearied eyes ached to share the general repose. Good night, there-fore, my dear and excellent friends. I have not said half enough of the gratitude I feel for your charming verses, but they warm my inmost heart.

Giovanni flatters himself with the hopes that you will bring him some seeds of Alpine plants. He longs for some seed of the Campanula Pyramidalis, which may be had in the south of France: it does not ripen its seed here.

Ever yours,

A. SEWARD.

MRS. SIDDONS TO DR. WHALLEY.

January 12, 1786.

ALL is well over, my dear Mr. Whalley. I have another son, healthy and lovely as an angel, born the 26th of Decem-ber; so you see I take the earliest opportunity of relieving the anxiety, which I know you and my dear Mrs. Whalley will feel till you hear of me. My sweet boy is so like a person of the Royal Family, that I am rather afraid he'll bring me to disgrace; my sister jokingly tells him she's sure 'my lady, his mother, has played false with the Prince,' and I must own he's more like him than anybody else. I will just hint to you that my father was at one time very like the King, which a little saves my credit. I rejoice that you are well, and have such pleasant society, but I wish to God you would return!

I have no news for you, except that the Prince is going to devote himself entirely to a Mrs. Fitzherbert,* and the whole world is in an uproar about it. I know very little of her history, more than that it is agreed on all hands that she is a very ambitious and clever woman, and that 'all good seeming by her revolt will be thought put on for villany,' for she was thought an example of propriety. I hear, too, that the Duchess of Devonshire is to take her by the hand, and to give her the first dinner when the preliminaries are settled; for it seems everything goes on with the utmost formality; provision made for children, and so on. Some people rejoice and some mourn at this event. I have not heard what his mother says to it. The Royal Family

* The Prince had become deeply enamoured of Mrs. Fitzherbert, a widow lady, who held the Roman Catholic faith. She was of gentle birth, and of great beauty; and both in her widowhood and in her two former marriages had borne an irreproachable character. To avoid the Prince's importunities, she had gone abroad in 1784, but on her return at the close of the ensuing year, those importunities were renewed. Any legal alliance between them was impossible, from the terms of the Royal Marriage Act; but to quiet her scruples, the Prince offered to go through the religious ceremony. A rumour to that effect was quickly noised abroad; and Fox, in the true spirit of an honourable friend, wrote at once to his Royal Highness, remonstrating in the strongest manner against 'this very desperate step.' The intention was denied, but it was persevered in. On the 21st of December, 1785, the ceremony was performed in private, by a clergyman of the Church of England, and in the form prescribed by the Book of Common Prayer, and the certificate, bearing the same date, was attested by two witnesses. Thus it might be said, did the heir apparent attempt to take to wife a private gentlewoman in the teeth of the Royal Marriage Act, and a Roman Catholic in the teeth of the Act of Settlement: a breach of the law in the one alternative, or a forfeiture of the crown in the other. —*Earl Stanhope's Life of Pitt*, vol. i. pp. 331-2.

have been nearly all ill, but are now recovering, and they graciously intend to command me to play in 'The Way to Keep Him,' the first night I perform. They are gracious to me beyond measure on all occasions, and take all opportunities to show the world that they are so. How good and considerate is this: they know what a sanction their countenance is, and they are amiable beyond description. Since my confinement, I have received the kindest messages from them; they make me of consequence enough to desire I won't think of playing till I feel quite strong, and a thousand more kind things. I perceive a little shooting in my temples, that tells me I have written enough. I don't take leave of you, however, without telling you that I am very much disappointed in Sherriffe's picture of me, and am afraid to employ him about your snuff-box. I don't know what to do about it, for that promised to be so well that I almost engaged him in the fullness of my heart to do it. I have not been in face these last four months, but now that I am growing as amiable as ever, I shall sit for it as soon as possible. God Almighty bless you both!

Yours,

S. SIDDONS.

MRS. WHALLEY TO FANNY SAGE.

Avignon, February 20, 1785.

I KNOW the goodness of your heart too well, my beloved Fanny, ever to suspect that your silence proceeds from want of affection towards an uncle and aunt who love you with all the tenderness of parents, and who are removed near a thousand miles distant from you; but I cannot say I so entirely acquit you of negligence, for as you are so amply possessed of a talent for which your dear mother was so justly celebrated, I cannot help wishing you would cultivate it more, and never shall think a variety of engagements a sufficient excuse for depriving me for six long months together of the pleasure of hearing from you.

We are both well, and just returned from a most agreeable jaunt to the Pont de Garde and Nismes, about thirty miles off. The aqueduct at the Pont de Garde merits going far to see, and Nismes abounds with the antiquities of Roman grandeur. The Amphitheatre is a beautiful piece of architecture: the outside of one front remains entire, and in the inside many of the stone benches, from which the Romans viewed the sports, though it makes humanity shudder to think of what nature those sports were. The Rotunda is about the size of the Circus at Bath; the whole building was large enough to contain forty thousand spectators, but the centre in the interior is now filled up with shabby houses. The Maison Quarrée is a most perfect piece of ancient architecture; it was built ten years after the birth of our Saviour, and is kept in high preservation by a community of monks, to whom Louis XIV. gave it, and who have converted it into a chapel. There are also the remains of a Temple of Diana, and the ancient Roman Baths are converted into a magnificent fountain, in the midst of a garden as large as, and much resembling, the Tuileries at Paris, but infinitely better kept. As it was Shrove Tuesday, there were nearly two thousand people assembled round this fountain, some dancing, some playing on different instruments, others singing, while others again were in masquerade, or exhibiting puppet-shows. All this gaiety ended with the carnival; and at twelve o'clock they all retired to spend the next forty days in penitence and fasting. The outskirts of the town of Nismes are most beautiful, and ornamented with a canal of great length, planted on each side with trees; but within the walls it is, like most of the French towns, ill built and dirty. It carries on a great manufacture of silk and stockings, and contains seventy thousand inhabitants, of which half are Protestants.

The residence of the Duke and Duchess of Cumberland has rendered Avignon very gay this carnival — suppers, balls, or masquerades every night; but we have partaken sparingly of the amusements, one pic-nic (which is the name of public ball and supper), one masquerade, two suppers at the Duke's, one at General Morris's, and one at Mr. Fitzhugh's, make the sum total of our carnival diversions. We have found our chief pleasure where only true pleasure is to be found, by our own fireside, and in the society of our agreeable friend Mrs. Wapshawe, the bearer of this, whom I part from with great regret. We propose setting off the beginning of next month for a very pleasant country-house, which we have taken in the neighbourhood of the famous fountain of Vaucluse; there we hope to receive your dear father and you, and there we shall stay till we set out for Italy.

I find you have had a very severe winter in England, and you doubtless envy us our serene sky and May-like weather, which we enjoy at least three parts of our time; but when the *vent de Bise* blows, you can have no conception how penetrated we are. At this moment our thin-built mansion rocks, and though sitting by a good fire, my fingers are so cold I can hardly hold my pen, which, together with having many letters to write, makes me obliged to shorten this. Adieu, then, my dearest. Remember us in the kindest manner to your dear father, your friends at Stanmore, and your uncles and aunts, and be assured that your uncle and I are ever tenderly and affectionately yours,

T. E. WHALLEY.

Pray make our compliments to Mrs. Blair. I am very glad your little cousin is so much better. Direct to Avignon, as usual.

MRS. SIDDONS TO DR. AND MRS. WHALLEY.

Gower Street, Bedford Square, March 13, 1785.

MY DEAREST FRIENDS,—I hardly dare hope that you will remember me: I know I don't deserve that you should, but I know also that you are too steadfast and too good to cast me off for a seeming negligence, to which my heart and soul are averse, and the appearance of which I have incessantly regretted. What can I say in my defence? I have been very unhappy; now 'tis over I will venture to tell you so, that you may not 'lose the dues of rejoicing.' Envy, malice, detraction, all the fiends of hell have compassed me round about to destroy me; 'but blessed be God who hath given me the victory,' &c. I have been charged with almost everything bad, except incontinence; and it is attributed to me as thinking a woman may be guilty of every crime in the catalogue of crimes, provided she retain her chastity. God help them and forgive them; they know but little of me. I dare say you will wonder that a favourite should stand her ground so long; and in truth so do I. I have been degraded; I am now again the favourite servant of the public, and I have kept the noiseless tenour of my temper in these extremes: my spirit has been grieved, but my victorious faith upholds me. I look forward to a better world for happiness, and am placed in this in mercy, to be a candidate for that. But what makes the wound rankle deeper is, that ingratitude, hypocrisy, and perfidy have barbed the darts. But it is over, and I am happy. Good God! what would I give to see you both, but for an hour! how many thousand thousand times do I wish myself with you, and long to unburthen my heart to you. I can't bear the idea of your being so long absent. I know you will expect to hear what I have been doing; and I wish I could do this to your satisfaction. Suffice it to say, that I have acted Lady

Macbeth, Desdemona, and several other things this season, with the most unbounded approbation; and you have no idea how the innocence and playful simplicity of the latter have laid hold on the hearts of people. I am very much flattered by this, as nobody ever has done anything with that character before. My brother is charming in Othello; indeed, I must do the public the justice to say that they have been extremely indulgent, if not partial, to every character I have performed.

I have never seen Mr. Pratt since I heard from you, but he discovers his unworthiness to my own family; he abuses me, it seems, to one of my sisters in the most complete manner. How distressing is it to be so deceived! Our old Mary, too, whom you must remember, has proved a very viper. She has lately taken to drinking, has defrauded us of a great deal of money given her to pay the tradespeople, and in her cups has abused Mr. Siddons and me beyond all bounds; and I believe in my soul that all the scandalous reports of Mr. Siddons' ill-treatment of me originated entirely in her. One must pay for one's experience, and the consciousness of acting rightly is a comfort that hell-born malice cannot rob us of. Lady Langham has done me the honour to call with her daughter; her drawings are very wonderful things for such a girl. In the compositions she has drawn me in 'Macbeth' asleep and awake; but I think she has been unsuccessful in this effort. Next week I shall see your daughter* and the rest. Sarah is an elegant creature, and Maria is as beautiful as a seraphim. Harry grows very awkward, sensible, and well-disposed; and thank God we are all well. I can stay no longer than to hope that you are both so, and happy (see how disinterested I am); that Reeves and the dear Paphy are so too; and

* Dr. Whalley stood godfather to Mrs. Siddons's daughter Cecilia.

that you will love me, and believe me, with the warmest and truest affection, unalterably and gratefully yours,

S. SIDDONS.

My whole family desire the kindest remembrances. We have bought a house in Gower Street, Bedford Square; the back of it is most effectually in the country, and delightfully pleasant.

God bless you, my dear Mrs. Whalley! How perfectly do I see you at this moment; and you, too, my dear friend, for it is impossible to separate your images in my mind. Pray write to me soon, and give me another instance of your unwearied kindness. Adieu!

MRS. SIDDONS TO DR. AND MRS. WHALLEY.

March 15, 1785.

I CERTAINLY did write the letter I promised to write; you have not received it, and were you not the very soul of benevolence you would not treat me as you do. Mrs. Wapshawe has been so good as to bestow half an hour upon me. She speaks of you as I should speak of you —as if she could not find words, and as if her sentiments could not enough honour you both. If you could look into the hearts of people, trust me, my beloved and ever-lamented friends, you would be convinced that mine yearns after you with increasing and unalterable affection. See there now—how have I expressed myself? That is always the way with me: when I speak or write to you, it is always so inadequately, that I don't do justice to myself; for I thank God that I have a soul capable of loving you, and trust I shall find an advocate in your bosoms to assist my inability and simpleness. You know me of old for a matter-of-fact woman. Mrs. Wapshawe has revived my hopes; she tells me that you will return sooner than I hoped. Now, I'll begin my cottage again: it has been lying in heaps a great while, and I have shed many tears over the ruins; but we will build it up again in joy. You know the spot that I have fixed upon, and I trust have not forgotten the plan! Oh! what a reward for all that I have suffered, to retire to the blessings of your society; for, indeed, my dear friends, I have paid severely for my eminence, and have smarted with the undeserved pain that should attend the guilty only; but it is the fate of office, and the rough brake that virtue must go through; and sweet, 'sweet are the uses of adversity.' I kiss the rod. I shall get Sherriffe's print of Tancred and Sigismunda, and hope to find an opportunity of sending it to you; it is not published yet. The picture is charming. You once thought Cosway, no doubt, would paint me well in a character; but I have been waiting to see this fore-named picture finished, that I might with more certainty assure you that Sherriffe has been more successful than any miniature painter that I have sat to, and if you have faith enough in my judgment to believe this is true, we will put your picture in hand directly. Mrs. Wapshawe was quite delighted with Mr. Beach's picture of you; but she tells me that you wear coloured clothes and lace ruffles; and I valued my picture more, if possible, for standing the test of such a change as these (to me unusual) ornaments must necessarily make in you. I think I should long to strip you of these trappings. I am so attached to the garments I have been used to see you wear, and think they harmonise so well with your face and person, that I should wish them like their dear wearer, who is without change. Don't tell me that your dear Marquess is no more; you leave it doubtful, and I will hope the best. I am proud of your chiding, though God knows how unwillingly I would give you a moment's pain; nay, more, He knows that I neither go to bed, nor offer prayers for blessings at His hands, in which your welfare does not make an ardent petition. But why should I wound your friendly bosoms with the relation of my vexations? I knew you too well to suppose you could hear of my distresses without feeling them too poignantly. I resolved to write when I had overcome my enemies: you shall always share my joys, but suffer me to keep my griefs from your knowledge. Now I am triumphant, the favourite of the public again; and now you hear from me.

A strange capricious master is the public; however, one consolation greater than any other, except one's own approbation, has been, that those whose suffrages I esteemed most have, through all my troubles, clasped me closer to their hearts; they have been the touchstone to prove who were really my friends. You will believe me when I affirm, that your friendship and my dear Mrs. Whalley's is an honour and a happiness, I would not forego for any earthly consideration. Tell my dearest Mrs. Whalley that neither avocations nor indolence would have prevented your hearing from me long ago, but for the reasons already mentioned. I wrote to you last Sunday, when I had not received your dear letters; so you will do me the justice to remember that I was not reminded of you but by my own heart, which, while it beats, will ever love you both with the warmest and truest affection; however, as she is so seldom mistaken, we shall have the honour and glory of laughing at her. Would to God I could laugh with, or cry with, or anything with you, but for half an hour! To say the truth though, your tender reproaches gave me a melancholy which I could not (and I don't know if I wished it) shake off. Pray let me hear from you very soon and very often. I shall be a better woman, and more worthy of your invaluable friendship, the more I converse with you. The only column (or at least almost the only one) to keep one's steps in the straight path through this winding labyrinth of life, is that whose base is virtue, whereon friendship is indelibly engraved in characters too clear and true to be mistaken, though many may appear in the journey to come pretty near that sacred tablet whose top reaches to heaven (I hope I have made myself understood). Surely the converse of good and gentle spirits is the nearest approach to heaven that we can know; therefore once more I beg that I may often hear from you; and if you do love me, do not think so unworthily of me as to suppose my affection can, in the nature of things, ever know the least abatement. I conjure you both to promise me this! for I cannot bear it—indeed I can't.

I must beg you will not mention (I believe I am giving an unnecessary caution) anything I have told you concerning Mr. Pratt.* I would not wish him to know, by any means, that I have been informed of his last unkindness, because it might prevent his asking me to do him a favour, which I shall at all times be ready to grant, when in my power. I must tell you that after the very unkind letter he sent me, in answer to mine requesting the ten pounds, I never wrote to or heard from him till about three months ago, when he wrote to me as if he had never offered such an indignity, recommending a work which he had just finished to my attention. He did not tell me what this work was, but I had heard it was a tragedy. To be made a convenient acquaintance only, did not much gratify me; but, however, I wrote to say he knew the resolution I had been obliged to make (having made many enemies by reading some, and not being able to give time to read all tragedies), to read nobody's tragedy, and then no one could take offence; but that if it was accepted by

* So often mentioned by Dr. Whalley's various correspondents, and so rarely with approbation; but Dr. Whalley would not give him up, and still continued to befriend him at Bath.

the managers, and there was anything that I could be of service to him in (doing justice to myself), that I should be very happy to serve him. I have heard nothing of him since that time till within these few days, when he wrote to my sister Fanny, accusing me of ingratitude, and calling himself the ladder upon which I have mounted to fame, and which I am kicking down.

What he means by ingratitude I am at a loss to guess, and I fancy he would be puzzled to explain; our obligations were always, I believe, pretty mutual. However, in this letter to Fanny, he says he is going to publish a poem called 'Gratitude,' in which he means to show my avarice and meanness, and all the rest of my amiable qualities, to the world, for having dropped him, as he calls it, so injuriously, and banishing him my house. Now, as I hope for mercy, I permitted his visits at my house, after having discovered that he was taking every possible method to attach my sister to him, which you may be sure he took pains to conceal from us, and I had him to my parties long after I made this discovery. In short, till he chose to write this letter, which I disdained to reply to, he called as usual. He had the modesty to desist from calling on us from that time, and now has the goodness to throw this unmerited obloquy on me. I am so well convinced that a very plain tale will put him down, that his intention gives me very little concern. I am only grieved to see such daily instances of folly and wickedness in human nature. It is worth observing, too, that at the very time he chose to write this agreeable letter, I was using my best influence with Mr. Siddons to lend him the money I told you of before. I find he thinks it is not very prudent to quarrel with me, but has the effrontery to think that I should make advances toward our reconcilement; but I will die first. 'My tow'ring virtue, from the assurance of my merit, scorns to stoop so low.' If he should come round of himself (for I have learnt that best of knowledge, to forgive), I will, out of respect of what I believe he once was, be of what service I can to him; for I believe he meant well at one time, when I knew him first, and the noblest vengeance is the most complete. Once more, your fingers on your lips, I pray!

My sister Frances is not married, and I believe there is very little reason to suppose that she will be very soon. In point of circumstance I believe the gentleman you mention would be a desirable husband; but I hear so much of his ill-temper, and know so much of his caprice, that though my sister, I believe, likes him, I cannot wish her gentle spirit linked with his. I had the pleasure of hearing Mrs. J. Jackson is well, last night, by her husband's brother. I must bid you adieu. I am now going to act in 'The Carmelite,' a tragedy of Cumberland's, and to-morrow I set out for Ashton to see my lovely girls. Don't laugh at my partiality; what all the world says must be true, you know. I must be gone. 'With thee conversing, I forget,' &c. &c. God bless you, my dear Mr. Whalley! I am ever your truly affectionate and grateful

S. SIDDONS.

Mr. S. and my sister return a thousand thanks for your kind remembrances, and return your good wishes a thousand fold. Pray write to me very soon. The prints from Sir Joshua and Hamilton are not come out.

Kiss pretty Sappho for me. I rejoice to hear she is well.

MRS. WHALLEY TO FANNY SAGE.

May 30, 1785.

YOUR affectionate letter, my dearest Fanny, gave your uncle and me inexpressible pleasure; and I esteem, as a strong instance of your unabating love towards me, your entering so minutely into the particulars of your present situation, as you well know everything that relates to you cannot fail to be interesting to me. It gives me infinite satisfaction that you are so happily placed with Mrs. Gordon, in whose favour I hear great things. Do you know I have the honour to be distantly related to that lady, and a great intimacy formerly subsisted between the late Lord Portsmouth, her grandfather, and my father, who was well acquainted too with her father, Lord Lymington, and her uncle, Captain Wallop? but all the parties dying when I was very young, I never was acquainted with the present family, and I dare say Mrs. Gordon is ignorant she has such a relation in the world.

I cannot quit the subject of your present establishment, without repeating, my dearest girl, the jôy it gives me that the Almighty has blessed you with a parent whose every wish seems to centre in your happiness, nor does he think any expense too great that may contribute to your advantage. I am sure your heart must expand with filial love and gratitude towards him, and I make no doubt but you will in return be everything, both in conduct and accomplishment, that he can wish—that you will gild his days with joy in the meridian of life, and crown his latter years with peace.

It is now three months that we have left Avignon, and find, upon the whole, no great reason to repent the exchange of a pure air, instead of an assemblage of every offensive smell, and the amusements of reading, writing, working, and walking, for that of remaining up half the night to see people with battered constitutions and haggard countenances sitting round a gaming-table and trembling for the event of every card; indeed, upon the whole, though I have often felt myself much entertained with the foreign assemblies and suppers, yet those of Avignon never afforded me any pleasure; the general character of the people is to me offensive to a degree.

I wish it was possible for you to look in upon us at our country retreat; you would be in raptures with the situation. The house is neat, roomy, and comfortable; it is placed in the midst of meadows and corn-fields, which, from not being enclosed, and thickly planted with mulberry-trees, give it all the appearance of a park. In front, about half a mile off, appears the town of Lisle, which, though a poor dirty hole when you come into it, is beautiful in prospect. On the left hand you see Vaucluse at a little league distance; the hill behind it may truly be said to flow with wine and oil, as it is entirely planted with vines and olive-trees. But what pleases me most, and I am sure would charm you, is the room where I am now writing; it is fitted up with neat simplicity, by an English gentleman who lived here before us. A thick grove, which is a great resource in these hot countries, extends its branches quite to the windows, which are open, and I am as if in a bower, while innumerable nightingales* and other birds are serenading me, the river Sorgue tumbling in cascades through the grove. Nothing can be pleasanter than the appearance of the water between the trees on a hot day. I have a pretty little garden, in which I amuse many a vacant hour; it produces us peas and beans, salads, melons, &c. I have made it gay with common flowers, and it is said to produce the finest figs and grapes in the whole country. Our country folks at Avignon took it in their head to adopt your uncle's taste, and three other families have taken houses in this

* We may presume that Petrarch penned the following lines on the song of the nightingale, from his favourite retreat at Vaucluse:—

Quel Rossignuol, che si soave piagne
Forse i suoi figli, o sua cara consorte,
Con tante note si pietose, e scorte;
E tutta notte par, che m' accompagne,
E mi rammente la mia dura sorte;
Seconda parte.

neighbourhood, and more would if they could get them: as we had the first choice, we are the best off. Three weeks ago, the Duke and Duchess of Cumberland,* with Lady Ferriers and the Portuguese Ambassador to the Court of Vienna, visited Vaucluse, and on their return did us the honour to dine with us. We invited all our English neighbours to meet them, and all the company were, or had the politeness to seem to be, pleased.

We were a few days since at Carpentras, a town about three leagues off, which was formerly the capital of the Comtat † and the residence of the Popes. It is only remark-

* The Duke of Cumberland was second brother to George III., and was born 1745. He married, 1771, Anne, daughter of the first Earl of Carhampton, and widow of C. Horton, Esq. He died without issue, September 1790; the Duchess in 1803.

† The Comtat (unde derivatur? not Provençal), or Comté of Avignon, was known by old geographers as the county of Venascine; in Latin, 'Comitatus Veniessimus,' from Ávenio, now Avignon, the chief city. This little territory formed one of the seigneuries of Provence, the name given to it by the Romans. Another seigneury in Provence was Orange, the hereditary principality of the noble William of Nassau, so well known as 'the Silent,' whose history has been ably told by Motley, in his 'Revolt of the Netherlands.' The Venascine was ceded by Philip III. of France to the Popes in 1273, as their share of the spoil of the territories of Raymond, Earl of Provence, against whom they had proclaimed their diabolical crusade; and further confirmed, for a sum of money, to Clement V., by Jane, Queen of Naples, who also styled herself Countess of Provence. At the present time, when so much importance is attached by many to the temporal sovereignty of the Pope, and his continued residence at Rome, it is well to mark how little these considerations really affected the vitality of Roman Catholicism in the fourteenth century. The turbulence of Rome had often driven the Popes from their capital, before Clement, Archbishop of Bordeaux, was raised to the Papal chair, under the title of fifth of his name, and summoned his cardinals to meet him beyond the Alps. He resided for a time both in Poitou and Gascogny, where he had no shadow of authority, before he fixed his abode at Avignon, a city over which he possessed but an imperfect claim, as is evident by his paying down a round sum for it to the Queen of Naples. In this city, separated by the Alps from Italy, did eight Popes in succession, from the year 1300 to 1377, continue to exercise the power of the keys. In spite of the lamentation of Popish historians, who compare this time to the Babylonish Captivity, in spite of the canzoni of the tender Petrarch, exposing and bewailing the vices of the Papal Court, and in spite of the eloquence of Rienzi, directing the new-born liberties of the Eternal City, did the Papal chair here evince its accustomed

able for its fine situation in the midst of a most luxuriant vale, a noble hospital, and an aqueduct of a great length; but to us, who had seen that Pont-du-Garde, this appeared very inferior, and in comparison a mere modern structure, having been built not more than two hundred years since, whereas that was the work of the ancient Romans.

You will expect me to say something of the celebrated fountain of Vaucluse, but no description I could give of it could create an adequate idea in your mind of its singularity and beauty. Imagine to yourself a chain of rocks of an immense height, covered to the top with vines and olives, the centre of which forms a vast gulf; from the further end of which issues, with amazing force, tumbling down the rock in cascades, the water, which, after filling the gulf below, divides itself into numberless little rivers and rivulets, watering the adjacent country for many miles round. Under the title of the Sorgue, I do not wonder Petrarch celebrated this fountain so much; you can conceive nothing more picturesque than its appearance. The little village of Vaucluse at its entrance, as well as the curate's house, peeping out from between two cypresses, have an admirable effect. They show you the ruins of an old castle which they call Petrarch's, upon a rock which overhangs Vaucluse; there are likewise two original pictures of that celebrated poet and his Laura, preserved in the village, but they are miserable daubs. Charming as this spot is, I never desire to see it more; for in walking thither, some little time since, we had the misfortune to lose our dear little favourite Sappho;

power and weakness. It was unable to preserve its patron, the King of France, from the defeats of Crecy and Poitiers, and from captivity; while it was so powerful, that under the weight of a spiritual anathema, an Emperor of Germany, Louis IV., offered, as the condition of its removal, to perform public penance, or even to resign his crown.—*Dictionnaire Provençal et François.* Avignon, 1723. *Heylyn's Cosmography*: London, 1669. *Gibbon*, ch. lxix. *Menzel's Hist. of Germany*, ch. clxxvii.

she was seized with a fit while she was playing before us, and died before we could render her the least assistance.

I have taken the opportunity of sending you this by a family returning to England; I cannot therefore lengthen it, as I hope to send others by the same conveyance. I will therefore bid you adieu, my beloved child. Do not let the term give you umbrage, for I know we are very delicate on certain points at fifteen; but I shall always consider myself as your mother, if I live to see you thirty, since I never can yield myself second in affection towards you to any human being but your father, as, believe me, every maternal feeling, every tender solicitude for your welfare, expands the breast of your ever affectionate

ELIZA WHALLEY.

P.S.—If Mr. Sage has not left town, remember us in the kindest manner to him, as well as to all your other friends.

Theodore Luders desires his compliments to you; he has been with us all the summer. We are endeavouring to nurse him up; but I doubt he is in a very bad way. Pray let me hear from you soon. I know the goodness of your heart, but I cannot bear even the semblance of neglect in one I love so well.

MRS. SIDDONS TO DR. WHALLEY.

Dublin, June 21, 1784.

MY love for you, my ever honoured and valued friends, is —though I have been, and still am, prevented telling you as I could wish—without change or shadow of turning; and let me be believed when I assure you, that your dear letter by the Marquis was more welcome to me than all the treasures of the earth. What is so precious as the affection of those we love? You desire me to write that I am well merely, which is all I can do at present. I pant for retirement and leisure, but am doomed to inexpressible and almost insupportable hurry. You guessed, as you generally do of me, rightly, generously, like yourself. You suppose I should have written in answer to you and my beloved Mrs. W., could I have given a tolerable account of myself. To say the truth, I have been more and longer ill this last winter than I ever was in my life. Let it suffice to say, that I am at present well, and as happy as possible. I have been wretched to know where to address you, my dear Mr. W., and fear you will have left Savoy ere this can reach you. I have a vast deal to say to you, but have not time at present. If you can, do let me know particularly where I can address you in August, as I hope I shall then be able to call a few hours my own. I wish to God I had seen the Marquis, but I was unfortunately gone to Scotland. They treated me most nobly. How happy should I have been to choose your buckles. I am enquiring how I may convey a pair to you, but despair of success.

You cannot be more pleased with my picture than I am, strange to say, with yours, for it is the only one of a friend I ever was satisfied with; perhaps it owes its excellence to your lamented absence. How you chill all the hopes I cherished with so much pleasure by making a doubt of your return. Oh! do not so soon pull down the peaceful cottage you yourself so lately assisted me in raising. Mr. Pratt, Mr. Nott and family, were well when I saw them. The former I see but seldom. I have offended him, and I am sorry he should see cause for offence. I fear he thinks unworthily of me. All I can say is, that I do not deserve it; that I should be most happy to render him any service; though I cannot stoop to a vindication of myself to one, who ought to know me better than to accuse me of a vice which is of all others the least excusable, and I hope the least likely to find a place in my bosom. The matter is this. He asked for a little money, which I was so happy as to be able to furnish him with, some time ago; and he very civilly tells me he knows that I am getting a vast deal of money, and wonders I can be so unfeeling as ask him for the trifling sum he owes me. In short, he says as plainly as possible, that not necessity but avarice prompts me to this request. Mr. Siddons was very happy to be able to lend him five hundred pounds last winter, and I thought my little modicum, lent a year before, and which I was to be paid in a few weeks after it was lent, might be spared from that. I have said thus much, that you may not think it strange in future to find no exact account of him from me, for I never see him now. Poor man! I respect his talents and pity his imprudence.

We all unite in love to you and my dearest Mrs. Whalley. Tell her I hope she will not cease to love me, and that this letter is as much her property as yours. Remember me to Reeves and dear Paphy Piddy. I suppose she is bullying from morn till night. I am now in Dublin, where your letter was sent me from London. You know how I dote on this country; I am as fond of it as ever.* Be satisfied, my dearest friends, that I am not yet forsaken by the public; they are very, very kind to me. I stay here till the end of July, and then return to London. God Almighty bless you both! and I only desire you to love me as I do you. Direct to London thus—Gower Street, Bedford Square; here—the Theatre.

P.S.—If you should meet a Mr. Seton, who lived in Leicester Square, you must not be surprised to hear him boast of being very well with my sister and myself; for

* Her letter from Dublin, of the date of July 14, 1783, which, owing to her omission of prepaying it, was opened and redirected in Ireland, explains her real meaning in this passage.

since I have been here I have heard the old fright has been giving it out in town. You will find him rather an unlikely person to be so great a favourite with women.

DR. WHALLEY TO MISS SAGE.

Vaucluse, August 21, 1785.

THE wind has heard your whisper, my dear Fanny, and whistles back to you this reply; which, if the wings of the 'Bise'* conveyed, would presently reach Park Lane, though you would find my courier rather boisterous, and all unfit to salute the soft ears of a delicate damsel with his rude breath. You have been at Thornhill, and I have been at La Grande Chartreuse. I grant that there is no similarity in the places, but we alike reaped pleasure and amusement from our different excursions.

But did you ever hear of La Grande Chartreuse? As this is doubtful, I will hasten to inform you that it is a celebrated convent, founded by St. Bruno seven hundred years ago, and in the most romantic solitude you can imagine. Its distance from Grenoble, the capital of Dauphiné, is about fourteen miles; and you climb to it by steep and rugged paths up mountains, the summits of which have been cultivated, through the wise and benevolent care of the Chartreux, with such laborious industry and so much success, that the desert smiles, and a paradise appears opened in the wild. The most picturesque cottages, the most fertile and pastoral landscapes smile with humble tranquillity; and the most attractive, though unostentatious graces are seen, amidst stupendous rocks and cloud-capped heights, where you would not expect a trace of cultivation or population. The convent itself is farther on, in a gloomy hollow, and shut out, as it were, from the cheerful haunts of men by a surrounding chain of stupendous mountains, piled

* 'Bise' is the name given to the North wind.

one upon another, thrown into every possible direction, and offering different angles to the wondering eye; though in general cast of features similar, and of similar grandeur and beauty. I never saw such a world of wood; such a deep mass of various shade! All the savage and solitary graces seem to be assembled there, to sit pensive upon the rocks, moan through the sombre woods, and hang over the foaming torrents, that rush on every side down the shady steeps to the gulf below.

You have remarked the expression '*belles horreurs*' in some of your French books. The French people, prodigal of swelling words, apply it on every trifling occasion; but its emphatic force is well adapted to scenery like this, where nature is beautifully awful, and terribly sublime. My Italian friend, the young Count Galaté, met me at Grenoble, and accompanied me to the convent. As his uncle is Grand Visitor of the Order, we were received there with particular distinction; though I should have needed no recommendation to the good monks' hospitality, which is extended with grace and bounty to all who knock at their gate. The retirement of these *religieux* from the gay world and the busier scenes of life, seems by no means to have rendered their hearts cold, or their manners rustic. But is not true piety the genuine source of glowing affections? and can any courtesy equal that of a benevolent heart, purified from worldly pride, and unknowing of false shows? Mistaken as their principles of retirement may be, and more useful as their lives might become by a right exertion of their talents in the world, it is impossible not to be pleased with their meekness, their humility, and their brotherly love; and possessors as they are of princely revenues, there is a something that excites deep respect in their austerity and their privations. The convent is a little world within itself; and so it had need be, almost inaccessible as the world is to it. The Chartreux amount to about sixty; but a long range of buildings, at a little distance, is destined to their various workmen, where reside their carpenters, masons, joiners, sawyers, blacksmiths, &c., and where the hats, shoes, stockings, and even religious habits of the society are fabricated. The Grand Prieur told me that above four hundred people were fed at the convent daily, and that the annual concourse of strangers, drawn thither by curiosity, amounted to ten thousand. He said there were thirty guests besides ourselves on that day—Swiss, Germans, Italians, and French.

As we descended the next morning, we met an English party ascending, one of whom I am certain, though disguised *en cavalier*, was a female. You know, I suppose, that female foot is never suffered, knowingly, to enter the walls of a Carthusian convent. I hope the good monks knew nothing of this strange profanation, for the peace of their spirits and of their flesh; nor am I apt to think that St. Bruno would imagine it worth his while to descend from heaven on purpose to warn them against the approaching evil. But you will say I have been rambling long enough from home, and wish me to return thither.

It is impossible to tell you how much delighted your excellent aunt was with your letter. Not only the tender regard glowing so artlessly throughout its pages, but the style also in which it was expressed, charmed her. Indeed, my dear, it was a convincing proof to us that Mrs. Gordon's letters are full of graces, and that you have profited by them. It is truly kind in her to correspond with you, and shows not only her attention to your improvement, but that she knows also how to appreciate your understanding, and draw out those emulations which are the spur to excellence, and which excite and enable us to go on from strength to strength. While you are emulating the charms of Mrs. Gordon's style, think also, my sweet girl, that you are imitating that of your dear and incomparable mother, who eminently excelled in letter-writing, and whose example in every respect it should be your pride, as it will be your advantage, to follow. You lost her, indeed, but too soon to be deeply impressed with a sense of her merits; but your dear father has exerted his utmost endeavours to supply to you that loss on every side; and I cannot tell you how happy it makes me to see your lively gratitude for his tenderness and cares, and the prospect that you give him of recompensing them fully by restoring to him, in your person, the talents and the virtues which he was deprived of by the untimely death of a beloved wife.

You have heard that we are in a country house, delightfully situated near the justly-celebrated fountain of Vaucluse. Our days glided on very pleasantly till the death of our dear little dog; since which we have had continual trouble. Vincent was soon after seized with a bilious fever, in which he lay dangerously ill for several weeks.

Poor Luders* relapsed from a state of rather promising health, into all the distressing symptoms of consumption. He now lies in an almost hopeless state; still he entertains himself with a prospect of returning strength, and talks of future schemes whilst the lamp of life is already half extinguished. It is a comfort to us to render assistance to a friend in a foreign land, to cheer his drooping spirits, and soothe his last sufferings. Poor Reeves, also, has been very ill. Such is our present situation, my dear Fanny; but hope still sheds its balm on our hearts, and a deep conviction of being under the eye and governance of an almighty and all-merciful God, enables, and will enable us to support everything that comes from His hand with patience. We purposed setting out for Italy the end of this month, but all our schemes are now at a stand, and must be till the issues

* Mr. Luders was a friend often mentioned, who died at Leghorn soon after. Vincent and Reeves were Dr. and Mrs. Whalley's man and maid-servants.

of life and death are determined by Him who alone holds them in His hand. Luders will either soon be restored to a short span of tottering existence, or close his eyes for ever to this world. But the latter is much more probable than the former; and did I not see his extreme repugnance to part with the glimmering of painful being that is left him, I should think it much more desirable.

But I will turn my thoughts and your attention to a more cheerful, though perhaps, my love, not more useful theme. As you assure me your father was pleased with my last letter, I trust he approved my plan of joining us in France the ensuing year. It is natural that you should have no objection to such a trip; and though our affections would cry aloud to invite you to us, I think we should have resolution enough to silence their clamours, did we not believe that pleasure and improvement would go hand in hand with you for some months on the Continent. But it will be time enough to treat this subject some time hence; only that man loves to glance over the present hour, and fix his eyes on those to come. Let us hope, however, that this pleasing scheme will be realised. The enjoyment of such hopes is at least something, though but the shadow of promised pleasures.

Convince me that you have conquered your former dislike to writing, and continue to be emulous of writing with elegance and ease, by returning a long answer to this soon, and in a style as full of grace and spirit as your last. Your aunt says nothing to you, because she cares not about you, and never had your health, happiness, and accomplishments at heart; and as husband and wife ought to think alike, so I leave you to suppose how perfectly I agree with her in her sentiments towards you! Tell your dear father that Mrs. Whalley would have answered his letter ere this, but for her many cares. She is sorry to send, as he will be sorry to receive, such an excuse.

If you had ever seen me write a letter without blots, or in a hand decently legible, I would pretend to blush and apologise for this scrawl; but as this is out of the question, I must talk of the fairness of my affections, and making them atone for all the foul sins of my pen, pray you to love me as well as if I wrote like a great man's secretary. A scurvy simile; so I wish you brighter ideas, and hasten to leave you to them.

Love to dearest Fanny,

Most affectionately yours,
T. S. WHALLEY.

When you write to your dear grandmother, do not mention our melancholy situation, as it may pain her tender heart.

MRS. SIDDONS TO DR. WHALLEY.

September 28, 1785.

MY DEAR FRIEND,—I feel at this moment in the most painful situation I ever experienced. I tremble to offend you, to disappoint your expectations. But have you not conjured me to be sincere? and shall I not obey you? Yet, was that conjuration necessary? No; for to you I ever have, and always will, lay open my whole heart. I am aware what danger I should incur in the present instance with any living creature but yourself; but you are noble-minded, and will not love me less for my honesty, and the agonising proof I now give you of my at present torturing affection for you. It is impossible for you to conceive, though you may a little guess, by the length of this (to me) dreadful preface, how difficult it is to say—how shall I say it?—'Astarte' will not do as you and I would have it do! Thank God! 'tis over. This has been so bitter a sentence for me to pronounce, that it has wrung drops of sorrow from the very bottom of my heart. This has been one of the severest trials that friendship and affection ever experienced.

You have already rejected all praise, but such as should follow every effort of yours, therefore I am silent. Yet, let me entreat, if you have an idea that I am too tenacious of your honour, that you will suffer me to ask the opinions of others, which may be done without naming the author. I must however premise, that what is charming in the closet often ceases to be so when it comes into consideration for the stage. Surely, surely, my ever dear Mr. Whalley will not be angry with me. I shall be the most miserable of women till I hear from you. You have not an idea of what I have suffered for these three days past, and the very painful struggles I have sustained between my affection and my delicacy. Let me dismiss the grievous subject with conjuring you to speak your wishes, and to rely on my performing them with all the powers of my soul and body.

I received a letter from you yesterday, and hope by this time you are convinced that I did not deserve the reproaches it contained. How sorry am I to hear of your distresses! Yet what are the inconveniences to you, my dear and beloved friends, of being strangers? Are not all that have the blessing of knowing you your friends? If not, I pity them even more than you.

Your letter has been a great while coming, and I began to think you had forgotten me. Let me therefore hope that Affliction has long taken her flight, and that health and gladness have succeeded to her possession. I am very sorry to hear my good friend Mrs. Reeves has been so ill, as well for her sake as yours, for a person of that description is an invaluable treasure. How very terrible must it be to you to see your relation, cherishing with such avidity such vain hopes without a thought of settling accounts for the tremendous moment that is so near. He is determined to stop his ears against the voice of the charmer, charm he never so wisely, or how could he resist the energetic eloquence with which I see and hear you endeavouring to open them? This, indeed, must be a great affliction to you.

I shall execute all your commissions in the first moments I can call my own. At present, I am very busy. I played, the first night the theatre opened this season, Desdemona. My second night was Douglas, by command of their Majesties, who are gracious to me beyond all expression. The Queen has been graciously pleased to admit me to her presence twice, at her house in town; and the other day, when I was on a visit to Lady Harcourt, they came there and stayed all night. They saw me twice in the course of the day, and the whole of the family who were present overpowered me with their condescension and goodness. It is impossible for words to express their goodness. I have read to them three times, and the other day her Majesty very graciously sent me a box of powders, which she thought might be of use to me, and which she said I need not be afraid of, as she always took them herself when in my situation. These very superior honours, as you may suppose, create me many enemies; but it always was so, and I must bear their malignity with the best grace I can, though I am sometimes weak enough to wish any one else invested with them, so I might but enjoy my life in peace, which never can be, till I cease to offend one part of the world by doing my duty, and succeed to my utmost wish in pleasing the other part.

My sister Elizabeth is married very well to a Mr. Whitlock, a very worthy actor. Mr. Pratt and I are much on the same terms. I know not what he is doing; he has made some advances towards renewing our friendship, but it is too plain, from his own words, that he has thought, written, and spoken of me in a manner which has convinced me that esteem and confidence are vanished as they had never been, and without these there is no foundation whereon to renew the structure. I am sorry for him, and if ever I have an opportunity of being of use to him, shall be most happy to embrace it. I hope he had no hand in the abuse you saw: he swears he had not. Your little Eliza is as fair as wax, with very blue eyes, and the sweetest tuneful little voice you ever heard. Mr. and Miss Beach return you many thanks for your kind remembrances of them. I fear he will not do much here, and I am heartily sorry for it, for he is a most respectable, worthy man. He has made a picture of the dagger-scene in 'Macbeth,' my brother and myself. My brother's is the likest, and the finest head I ever saw. 'I am afraid to think on what I have done.' God Almighty bless you both, my dearest friends, and pray let me hear from you with all speed. I am now going to dress for Margaret of Anjou.

Ever yours,

S. SIDDONS.

Mr. S. and Miss R. desire kindest wishes.

Miss Young is married to a Mr. Pope, a very boy, and the only child she will have by her marriage. I am going to undertake your adored Hermione this winter. You know I was always afraid of her, and I am not a bit more bold than I was. Once more adieu! and remember I am wretched till I hear from you.

MISS SEWARD TO DR. WHALLEY.

Lichfield, September 30, 1785.

YOUR last letter enchanted me by the lonely grandeur of desolate scenery. It places me amidst the wild, rocky, and trackless heights of Vaucluse. I see the birds of prey sit on the pointed cliffs—hear their harsh screams, and drink the aerial solitude; yet, amidst these solemn delights of my imagination, my heart sickened at the rashness of the adventure. I begin to feel a dread of that exploring spirit, which has hitherto been an inexhaustible source of delight to me, to Sophia, and to all our friends, whose internal sight has strength to perceive the perfect features of the beautiful and stupendous scenery it delineates. Oh! for your Amelia's, for all our sakes, never again encounter such hazards. Ah! I felt assured, obscure as was the hint you gave, that you had reason to believe Chatillon yet lived! My imagination unfolded the interesting enigma thus. You had mentioned the depression upon the spirits of your noble friend after the death of his mother. Resolutions of quitting the world, and devoting, even in the prime of life, the remainder of its duration to the religious duties of a cloister, often seize the minds of Roman Catholics. I concluded they had possessed the soul of your Chatillon during his severe sickness, — that on his recovery, to avoid the trial of combating the remonstrances of one so fondly loved, he had desired you might be made to believe that he was no more, till the year of his probation had passed, and his vows were become irrevocable. I congratulate you, from the bottom of my heart, that the precious fact of his existence is built on a far more joyous basis. May I soon learn that his recovery is perfect! and then the joy of your reunion will compensate the bitter pains you have felt.

The dear and brilliant Sophia left me yesterday, after having enlivened these walls during the space of ten weeks. Her able reasonings and counsels strengthened my mind to the better endurance of many trials in the course of that period. The feeble flame of my father's existence she has repeatedly seen sink in its socket, past recovery, as we thought; yet he struggled through all those attacks, and is now as well as he has been known to be these many months. You have heard of the prodigious *éclat* of our Handelian commemorations, when the musical strength of this whole kingdom, and perhaps the flower of the science through Europe, were assembled together by the royal wish, hinted, yet not amounting to either command or desire; so that the assistance of every individual was voluntary, and met no golden fee of reward. The King having expressed some chagrin to several of his musical nobility, that Mr. Saville was not in the orchestra the first commemoration, and Mr. Bates, the conductor, observing that his absence was taken amiss, he conquered his diffidence, and offered himself at the last. He performed the chief of the contra-tenor songs with much applause. He considers the tenor songs as more his forte, but of that fort Mr. Harrison had got possession, whose vocal powers, energies, and sensibilities are far inferior, though he is confessedly a very elegant singer. I had refused a kind invitation to the Barrows each time from the dread of going so far from my father, in the precarious state of his health.

A great musical festival was appointed at Manchester this month. Cramer, Crosdill, the celebrated Madam Mara, with all the finest English singers; the double drums from the Abbey,—a band, noble and complete in all its parts, under the conduct of Mr. Saville, who was to sing all the principal tenor and contra-tenor songs, exhibited a temptation past my strength to resist, as my poor father was not, at the time we went to Manchester, at all more likely to die than he had been for near a twelvemonth past. Sophia, therefore, her brother, and myself passed last week at Manchester, in a full revel of harmonic delights, and had the satisfaction of finding my father tolerably well on our return last Sunday eve. The first morning, 'Samson,' with 'Pious orgies' and 'Ye sacred priests' between the acts, by Mara. In the eve, 'L'Allegro' and 'Il Penseroso;' with two bravura Italian songs between the acts, by Mara. Next morn, the same selection of songs, anthems, and choruses as were performed at the Abbey. At night, a ball. Next morn, the 'Messiah,' opened by Giovanni with inimitable pathos, energy, and grace. Mara paid him the highest compliments upon it. At night, a miscellaneous concert, with two more Italian bravuras from Mara. Next morn, a public breakfast, with catches and glees.

You have doubtless heard of this new-risen star in the harmonic world, who seems to have turned the brains of the whole kingdom. Her voice certainly does what never human voice did before; yet it is not of faultless perfection. All her notes below the first B in the treble cleff are harsh; but the instant she soars above that pitch, her voice is of the richest, fullest, and most sonorous sweetness, — it warbles through mazes of melody, in altitudes which no other vocal organs can explore. At the price, however, of excessive bodily contortions, when perfectly in tune, however muscularly strained, she reaches F in alt; but when, sliding from those supernatural heights a few notes, she closes with a shake, free and brilliant as the light, we may apply to her the line in Milton, —

> She takes the imprison'd soul, and wraps it in Elysium.

Handel's songs, being often set for low female voices, are apt to expose the defective tones of this miraculous woman, and she is, besides, a little inclined, spite of all her great skill, to put too much gold fringe upon the sublime mourning robes of his pathetic airs. She is particularly guilty of this error in 'I know that my Redeemer.' However, her energies are very noble, and possess all the force and spirit with which the mighty Handel composed. She had a hundred and fifty guineas for her assistance. She is a fine woman in her person —has an open and intelligent countenance, with a sweet smile; but her temper is capricious, haughty, and avaricious. The choruses! — but language is weak to express their astonishing majesty. Mara led off one of them, from 'Israel in Egypt.' Giovanni preceded it with a recitative, to this effect, 'And Miriam the prophetess arose and sung;' then Mara, with high clear sounds, and all the majesty of energetic expression, sung the air, 'For the Lord hath triumphed gloriously; the horse and his rider hath he thrown into the sea; the Lord hath triumphed gloriously.' Here the choruses, instantly pouring in, displayed the wonders of complex harmony, till we absolutely saw through the ears the whole Egyptian army thrown into the ocean. Nor less stupendous was the chorus, 'He gave them hailstones, and coals of fire; fire ran along the ground.' And so, indeed, it seemed to do, through the power of skilful dissonance; the brazen trumpets, the notes of terror from the voices, and the volleying thunder of the drums. The crowds of company were immense. A mob of several hundred well-dressed people, of both sexes, besieged the door half an hour before it was opened, on the morning the 'Messiah' was performed. Most people quitted their coaches, we amongst the rest, and struggled for admission through columns of fine people, fierce and violent as the *canaille* when the Siddons plays. My friends, Mr. and Mrs. Gell, their brother, Captain Gell, and their friend and your warm admirer, Miss Swymmer, received us into their party. She desires affectionate compliments may be presented from her to yourself, and dear Mrs. Whalley. The accommodation of Mr. Gell's coach and servant was a vast affair to us in point of comfort. The music-room was large and elegant. The orchestra and gallery opposite each other, in light and graceful semicircles, were adorned with balustrades of pale blue and gold.

I am most truly sorry that you have lost the dear little Sappho. I delighted to hear you speak of her engaging little habits, and it gratifies me to learn that a long-established conviction of mine, concerning the imperishable nature of the brute as well as the human spirit, has your sanction, and that of other able reasoners. Your verses on this benevolent theme are beautiful; yet I am loth that they should pass over in silence the strongest argument for this uncommon but not irrational belief. Were brutes as exempt from suffering as they are incapable of sin, the fatality of their actions might not unreasonably be supposed to exclude them hereafter from claims upon the divine justice. But since their blameless natures are often the victims of cruel pains and deprivations, from famine, disease and human tyranny, the Creator seems bound by those laws of benevolence and justice, which form a part of His essence, to reward, in some future state, the pangs of suffering innocence, whose infliction and endurance He thought good to permit. Has any person travelled post, and seen the ineffectual efforts of tired horses to obey the barbarous stimulations of the whip and spur, and can he believe that this state is the 'be-all' and 'end-all' of such suffering patience? You have a copy of your stanzas on Sappho. Inweave in them, I conjure you, this powerful argument, and impress it on the heart with all your usual energy. I wish that every essay of yours which meets the public eye, might convince the reason while it charms the imagination and melts the heart. I shall wait for a transcript of these stanzas thus strengthened, ere I indulge the editors of the 'Gentleman's Magazine' with a copy.

Our dear and estimable Miss Hammond is by this time married to a Major Velly. He bears a very good character, and is thought an agreeable man. His age about thirty-three, his fortune moderate, with good expectations. The attachment, though concealed, is said to have been of some years' duration, and, combated in her bosom by the dread of disobliging Mr. and Mrs. Jauncey, who thought the affection interested on his part, and it produced that ill-health under which she has laboured the two past years. He met her at Bath last winter, and love prevailed over every scruple. I pray Heaven that increase of felicity may be the consequence of this change in her state; but if the love of show, parade, and selfish expenses, on the part of her husband, should limit the long-accustomed expansion of her liberality, I am sure she will be far less happy than in her peaceful state of gentle celibacy. I feel for the Jaunceys in the irreparable loss they will sustain, and I regret the deprivation to myself of such pleasant and social neighbours. I do not correspond with her, nor have the Jaunceys written to me lately; but Giovanni and his daughter supped with Miss H. and her lover in London last spring, and G. tells me that her esteem for you seems not to have lost any of its enthusiasm. It is a year and a half since the Jaunceys or Miss H. were here: they have resigned their house.

A Mr. Boyd, a scholar and no mean poet, has just given to the world an English translation of the gloomiest of all poets, Dante, in the Spenseric stanza. Comparing with it Mr. Hayley's far sublimer translation of the three first cantos, we can have no strong reliance on the competence of Mr. Boyd's powers for so arduous a task. Great, indeed, is the inferiority in perspicuity, spirit, and picturesque grace. Yet if Hayley himself had led us through all the long succession of fiery furnaces, we must have turned with sickening horror from the general sameness of the penal flames, in spite of all the strength and grandeur of Dante's terrible graces. The powers of vengeance are insatiable through this poem, and the sum total of their inflictions amount but to this,—

> Immerse him in that boiling tide,
> Then on yon gridiron burn him!
> And, broil'd for ages on one side,
> I prithee, Devil, turn him!

You had a divine retreat for the summer in the precincts of Vaucluse. I seemed to gaze on the whole lawny scene through the windows of the dear green parlour, and catch the sparkling gleams of the Sorgue beneath the branches of those spreading oaks. Your portraits in the epistles dated from that valley are no less striking than your scenery. The account your last to Sophia contained of your poor friend Luders gave us much concern. Giovanni unites with me in all that is affectionate which language can express for the welfare and happiness of yourself and Mrs. Whalley. Excuse, as usual, this hasty and inaccurate testimony of that tender and grateful regard with which I am her and your

Devoted friend,

A. SEWARD.

The idea of Major Taylor rapidly recedes from the recollection of Sophia. I think I can assure you the peace of her heart on his account is quite restored. She left with me her tender love to you and Mrs. W.; but she means not to write at present, since, leaving me so lately, hearing from one of us is much the same as hearing from both. My father sends kind compliments.

MRS. SIDDONS TO DR. WHALLEY.

Gower Street, Bedford Square, Nov. 11, 1785.

MY hand ceases to tremble, and my heart to sink and palpitate, but your goodness still blinds my eyes with tears. My happiness at this moment overpays me for long, long sufferings, and the most agonising suspense. In short, I am in such a tumult of joy, that I shall almost literally obey your injunction, my best, my noblest friend; for these appellations can belong to no one so properly as to your glorious self. My heart is so full, I cannot give vent to my feelings in anything like coherent language; but may the happiness you have given to it be returned a thousand and ten thousand-fold to your own breast! My dearest Mrs. Whalley, why did you not write a word of comfort to your unhappy friend?

Oh, tell her she must set my heart entirely at rest,—yet are you not one soul? You are, and I will be happy. Did you, or did you not, my most honoured, receive two letters from me when I was in Edinburgh this summer? for you have never mentioned them, and I cannot bear that you should think me guilty of the wretched indolence that I know you do a little suspect me of.

Mr. Nott is not the man we took him for; that history cannot be developed till we meet — when will that blessed hour arrive? With what transport do I look forward to the time when we three meet again in the dear, dear cottage! I have three winters' servitude, and then, with the blessing of God, I hope to sit down tolerably easy, for you know I am not ambitious in my desires. I think I would not wish to know the time of your return, having a touch of your condition, impatience. I hope to deliver the set of prints to your sweet Fanny next Sunday. I have been a martyr to a cold for these three weeks, or she would have had them long ago. God Almighty bless you and my dearest Mrs. Whalley! I would fill up my paper, but I know your friendly heart will yearn to know that you have made me more happy than words can express, and, therefore, I hasten to assure you that you are, if it be possible, ten times more dear, more precious, than ever, to the faithful heart of your

S. SIDDONS.

Again and again may the blessing of the Almighty be with you. The hour of terror will arrive before I can hear from you again, if I ever do. Oh, God! what a tremendous idea! but if not here, we shall surely meet in a better world. Adieu! adieu!

Pray make our compliments to Mrs. Lescure.

My poor husband is relieved. He knew I was wretched to hear from you, but did not suspect the cause. He begs, with my sister, to offer you the best wishes.

DR. WHALLEY TO HIS MOTHER.

Leghorn, November, 1785.

You will rejoice to know, my dear mother, that we landed safe and well at Leghorn, about two hours ago. Our little voyage ended as propitiously as it began unfavourably. The two first days we were obliged to put back to Nice and Monaco, after contending some time with a contrary wind and an angry sea; but from the latter place hither all the elements have conspired to make our watery way delightful. My last was written from Marseilles, from thence we proceeded to Toulon, where we passed three days to rest poor Reeves, whose bowels had been sadly shaken by a rough and steep road, but we did not think our time lost, as that celebrated seaport was well worth attention, and as we made an excursion from it one day to the beautiful little town of Hières, the situation of which may vie with that of the Fortunate Islands, and where spring and autumn seem to reign together in endless amity and endless luxuriance. To the north and north-east it is defended from every cutting blast by a majestic curtain of mountains drawn closely round; but to the south and south-east, it commands a noble and picturesque view of the sea, finely broken by several islands, and animated by the numberless vessels that pass and repass to and from the ports of Italy and France. A rich vale, and hills clothed with olives and vineyards, form the intermediate and more distant landscape, and its own orange groves incense the air for miles round. These trees are loaded at once with fruit and flowers, which charm the eye with their beauty, and the smell with their fragrance, at the same time that they enrich their possessors, a considerable part of France being supplied from them with essences and fruit. The common hedges stand thick with pomegranates and myrtles, and these, if not equal in value, are at least equal in beauty, to the precious gardens whose golden fruit fills the purse with real gold.

You may imagine my dear wife's raptures in this delicious spot. Had we known of it sooner, we certainly should not have passed our last winter on the boisterous banks of the Rhone. We found the road from Toulon to Antibes bad, tedious and unentertaining. Our last day's route lay up and amongst tremendous precipices, which we were four hours mounting and descending; but the weariness of our way was somewhat beguiled by the beautiful plants that formed the whole tufted carpet of the vast wild. I formed from them an immense bouquet for my wife, of the rarest and most lovely heaths, arbutus in fruit, myrtle in blossom, and various other pretty flowers and shrubs unknown to us.

At Antibes we were pleased with the fine view of the sea and adjacent country from a noble paved, but unshaded, walk round the ramparts. Here we engaged a felucca to carry us quite to Leghorn, and never were people luckier in their haphazard choice of a captain and sailors. Unremitting in care of the vessel, and in ready and respectful attention to us, not one dispute, not one oath, not the sound of grumbling discontent, nor the troublesome clamour of boisterous mirth, was once heard amongst them the whole way. Yet they were all Genoese; and how have the poor Genoese been becalled and blackened for the most troublesome, imposing, disorderly, insolent, and rascally people upon earth? But this was not the first instance wherein we found things diametrically opposite, to the representations we had heard and read of them. At Nice we stayed, perforce, one night. It by no means answered the descriptions I had heard, and the idea I had conceived of it. The country houses, built thick about it, are doubtless pleasantly situated, have a fine view, though nothing singularly so, of the sea; but the town itself is a dismal, dirty hole, and fuming with every outlandish stink.

I had depended either on seeing or hearing from my

dear Chatillon at Nice, but was cruelly disappointed, and am uneasy lest a sad relapse should have retarded his purposed journey thither. The weather seeming more propitious, we groped our way safely to the felucca at half-past three in the morning, but had not proceeded above four leagues before the wind changed, the skies threatened, and the sea began to roll in a manner that set all our stomachs in an uproar. Still, hoping better things, we laboured on, by dint of rowing, three leagues more; but appearances then became so formidable, that, by our captain's advice, we turned our ship's prow and hurried back to Monaco as soon as possible, where we were all rejoiced to find shelter, and especially your son Thomas, whose mouth had been acting the part of a pump for eight hours. However, we did not regret this delay, as it gave us an opportunity of seeing Monaco perched highly on its rock, and pertly defying the angry waves that dash and foam against its solid foundation. You know that it gives his title to a sovereign, though a petty one. Two other little towns, picturesquely situated on the banks of the Mediterranean, with an extent of territory about eleven miles long by three wide, stolen from rocks, and producing nothing but olives, form the whole principality. However, the Prince's palace is by no means a despicable one, though it wears the marks of better days, and might lodge, not unseemly, a greater potentate. The people have an air of great poverty. How should it be otherwise, in a country productive of none of the necessaries of life but water and air, and paying a heavy tax to support its petty sovereign's petty state, who comes in the summer to wring the hard-earned tribute from their hard hands, and goes to drop it into the insatiable gulf of Parisian luxury in the winter?

The Genoese territories join those of Monaco, and lie in lovely prospect along the borders of the sea. Nature, it is true, had raised up a haughty mound of frowning mountains and rocks that seemed to say to barrenness, This shall be thy seat for ever; but human perseverance, joined to human industry and human art, have fertilised the wild, and animated it with the busy hum of men, wherever man could set his foot. The vast and continued woods of olives form a very considerable branch of commerce, but not the only one for these adroit and diligent republicans, who find another source of riches in the sea that lashes their shore, and which they make, proud and rebellious as it is, the handmaid to their prosperity. The immediate bank of the sea is almost a continued line of towns, which have all a neat and thriving air, and numberless villages and scattered cottages enliven the heights above. Genoa herself stands in the centre of them, with imperial state. The approach to it is strikingly fine, built as it is on the undulating sides of several hills, or rather mountains, and crowding as it were from thence into a mass to the plainer borders of the Mediterranean. You have heard and read much of its riches and its splendour, and it merits all that can be said of them. Well might she be called Genova la Superba. Her nobles, indeed, live in palaces, and whole streets are formed of them; but sumptuous as they are, and they abound in the rarest paintings, gilding, carvings, and ornaments of every kind, where magnificence and taste go hand-in-hand, they cannot vie with the temples of her God, which exceed in sumptuousness not only everything I have ever seen, but almost what I could have imagined. The insides of many are entirely encrusted with the most beautiful and precious marbles, formed into the most delicate mosaic work, with infinite ingenuity, labour, and cost. The roofs are finely painted and profusely gilded. In short, they are too magnificent, as the noble simplicity of the architecture is adulterated and spoilt by a load of ornaments that alike distract and dazzle the eye. Our inn at Genoa was the best in all respects that we have yet met with, and our apartments commanded a charming view of the port, sea, and adjacent hills, covered with the country palaces of the nobles. In short, had our purses been better furnished, we should have spent a fortnight there with pleasure; but prudence bounded our wishes, and after two days' pause we crowded sail, and going on day and night with glorious weather and smooth sea, and a light and favourable wind, reached this celebrated port in about thirty hours.

Our first concern was to make enquiries about poor Luders; we soon heard with more sorrow than surprise, that he survived his arrival at Leghorn but a few days. He had every possible help and attention paid him by some good English people with whom he lodged, as well as by our consul, Mr. Sidney, and an English merchant, a Mr. Partridge, who had been his particular friend from his boyish days. Knowing this, I cannot but be glad that he did not die under our roof, as it would have shocked us greatly, and been a large addition to our cares. Vincent is quite recovered, and Reeves* gains ground daily; you see I have hardly left a corner for our united prayers, loves, &c., to yourself and our dear brother and sister, and the signature of, my beloved mother, your ever tenderly affectionate son,

THOMAS S. WHALLEY.

I long to hear from you, and hope to do so by the next post. Remembrances to all friends. My dear wife will address you next, and would have done so now, had she not been very busy settling all matters on our arrival.

* His two servants.

MRS. WHALLEY TO MISS SAGE.

Pisa, December 7, 1785.

If your uncle, my dearest niece, who is so much more capable of entertaining you than I am, had not taken the pen from me, I should not have remained so long without giving myself the indulgence of an hour's conversation with you, whom I so tenderly love. I shall, however, now repay him in his own coin, and as he answered your letter to me, I now acknowledge the receipt of the one you wrote to him; and I am the more inclined to do so, as a variety of employments and studies might possibly prevent your hearing from him for some time, especially as he intends very soon writing to Mr. Sage.

You are no stranger to the melancholy scenes we experienced during the latter part of our stay at St. Jean, which made us really glad to quit that place, though it was in itself a little earthly paradise; I shall therefore say no more on the subject, than that our servants are at length restored to health. I suppose you know that poor Mr. Luders died a very few days after his arrival at Leghorn.

Our journey to this place, both by land and sea, had many *agrémens*, and some unpleasant circumstances attending it. On our way from St. Jean to Antibes, we spent a week at Aix, another at Marseilles, and a third at Toulon. The first is a very neat well-situated town, in a very fine air; we passed our time very agreeably there; the second is a city of immense commerce, and reckoned to be the best built in France; the third is celebrated for its fort, which is esteemed the most impregnable in Europe. As we had a very fine season, and passed through Provence in the height of the vintage, which was the most plentiful ever known, it added greatly to our pleasure; and wherever we passed the peasants were running to the side of the carriage, offering us grapes, and while we allayed our thirst, a few sous in return made them very happy.

During our stay at Toulon, we made an excursion to the little town of Hières, a few miles distant from it. I suppose it may vie in singularity and beauty with any spot in Europe. It is situated in a rich amphitheatre of orange and citron trees, which cover a circuit of many acres. We walked in one grove which brings in £1,400 yearly to its owner, in fruit and essences, with which they furnish the greater part of France and Savoy. These groves, where the trees are all in the open ground, are guarded on the north, east, and west, by a chain of mountains, richly bespangled with houses *de plaisance* for the inhabitants, or to accommodate strangers; and only open to the south, where a range of beautiful meadows, the hedges being all of pomegranate and flowering myrtle, extend to the Mediterranean Sea, on which the eye is perpetually amused with seeing vessels of all sizes and countries.

The country from Toulon to Antibes presents everywhere the most grand and picturesque views that can be imagined; but the roads are so dangerous and so infested with banditti, who, in this country, are but too apt to add assassination to robbery, that between my fears of having my neck broke on the one hand, or my throat cut on the other, I could not admire, as I should otherwise have done, the noble prospects which everywhere surrounded me, or the myrtles, heaths, and all the other plants with which we decorate our greenhouses, and which there cover the ground for miles together. Upon the whole, however, it is a route by which I would counsel no woman to go into Italy, though we were fortunate enough to arrive at Antibes without any accidents. From thence we took a felucca for Leghorn, which is about three hundred miles distant. The first part of our voyage did not prove very prosperous, as we were twice driven by contrary winds, and a storm, into the ports of Nice and Monaco. However, the delay gave us an opportunity of seeing those places, which we did not at all regret, especially as nothing could be more agreeable than the remainder of our voyage. We had not one cross accident from Monaco, and were highly entertained with viewing the numerous towns and villages which border the coast, through all the Genoese territories: we counted no less than eighty-three, in one of which Christopher Columbus was born, and in which some of his descendants still live. We arrived on the eighth day at Leghorn, after spending two at Genoa, where the magnificence of the palaces and churches far exceeded all I had eyer conceived of them. Well, indeed, does it merit its title of *superb*.

We stayed but a few days at Leghorn, and then came here for two months, which are now nearly expired. We shall then return thither for the Carnival, which is very gay there, and shall come back here in Lent, as the Grand Duchess has then assemblies four times a week; and as we have had the honour of being presented at her court, we shall attend them, as well as an elegant concert given once a week by the Grand Prieur. We have very agreeable society here, both of English and Italian; and I am very happy in having for my near neighbour the late Miss Crawford, whom you must remember to have seen at our house in Bath, and who is lately married to General Lockhart, the father of the young lady who is at Mrs. Gordon's. We have a very pleasant burletta opera here every evening; the music is delightful, and the first buffo man and female dancer are as excellent in their several styles as my dear Mrs. Siddons is in hers: but the plots of these pieces are too *outré*. Imagine to yourself a man who fancies he sees the spectre of his departed wife, and after showing all the horrors that such an appearance must naturally produce, he suddenly sets himself in order to dance a minuet with Madame le Revenant!

I never regretted anything more than my inability to draw, as it would not only enable me to impress on my mind more strongly the objects which strike me most in the different countries I pass through, but I would likewise sketch the dresses of the different peasants. They are all singular, and some of them very pretty, and if the limits of my paper would admit, I would give you a description of them.

This town is very ancient, and has been very populous, though it is no longer so. It is large, neat, and well built; the three bridges over the Arno afford a striking *coup d'œil*; our apartments are opposite the centre one. The climate here is as mild as in the month of May in England, but the rains, which at this time of the year are very frequent, often prevent me from enjoying the beautiful walks that everywhere surround the town. The Cathedral, Baptistery, Campo Santo, and famous Leaning Tower, are, in their style, wonderfully beautiful, and, in the lightness and elegance of their architecture, exceed even those of Genoa.

Your uncle is playing cards by my side with another gentleman, and they make such a noise, and jog the table so, that I know not what I write; accept, therefore, our tenderest wishes, my beloved Fanny; write to us soon, and believe me ever most affectionately yours,

ELIZA WHALLEY.

Pray present our respectful compliments to Mrs. Gordon.* Convey the enclosed to Mr. Sage, and direct to me at Leghorn.

MRS. WHALLEY TO MISS SAGE.

Pisa, March 13, 1786.

YOUR letter, my dearest Fanny, as everything that comes from you does, gave your uncle and me the most heartfelt

* An Honourable Mrs. Gordon. She received a few young ladies into her house, who wished to profit by London masters.

satisfaction. It found us at Leghorn, partaking of the amusements of the carnival, which are very brilliant in that town, where we spent two months, and, besides the operas and masked balls, were invited to many very handsome entertainments at the houses of the governor and many of the principal English merchants; besides being much entertained with the innumerable masks which most evenings patrol the streets, and introduce themselves at the opera, where they are permitted to enter all the boxes; and the infinite variety of their dresses and characters is extremely amusing, especially in the eye of strangers. But all these diversions are now ceased; Lent is come in, and riot and dissipation give place to penitence, fasting, and prayer.

We have been returned hither a month, and your uncle proposes staying another here. The only amusements at present are a music and card assembly, once a week, at the Grand Prieur's, and the assemblies, four times a week, at the court; and of these my dear Mr. Whalley has not yet been able to partake, having been confined to the house, ever since our return hither, by a very severe cold,—and, though better, he does not yet venture out in an evening. He charges me to tell you that it is the only reason that has prevented him from writing to you. I have been three times at court, where the goodness and affability of the Grand Duchess make ample amends for the dullness * of her assemblies. How, indeed, can they be otherwise, when the number is bounded to about ten of the principal ladies of Pisa, as many gentlemen, and the few strangers that have been introduced. It commences at seven, and, after the first

* As Pisa had been an independent state, and was little inferior to Florence in population or wealth, it was customary for the Grand Dukes of Tuscany to pass a portion of every year at that city. Leopold, who was afterwards called to the imperial crown under the title of the Third of that name, reigned at this time in Tuscany. Menzel says of him, that 'his government offered a model to princes.'—*History of Germany*, ch. 238.

formalities are over, everybody forms parties either at *ombre* or at *menquiaté*, an Italian game, in which all the cards are figures, and the pack consists of double the ordinary number. It is a most intricate game; the principal cards are the world, the sun, the moon, the twelve signs of the zodiac, popes, kings, queens, cavaliers, devils, &c. What an assemblage! you will say. Indeed, they are much more numerous than her Royal Highness' assembly, who play till her party breaks up, which generally happens about half after nine, refreshments having been brought in at eight. The ladies then stand in circle, and her Royal Highness passes round, addressing some little compliment to each, and then the evening concludes with an infinity of bows and curtseys.

We have lost the pleasure of Mrs. and Miss Lockhart's society; they are set out for Rome, and the General is gone to the Island of Sardinia. Many English families remain here, all of whom we visit; but none are equal, in my estimation, to those we have lost. We profit by every fine day, which is not very common at this season of the year (continual deluges of rain succeeding each other), to ride out to the different agreeable drives round the town, such as the Baths, which are at three miles distance, the Duke's Dairy, the village of Chalci, &c. Pisa lies in a flat plain, of large extent, but very fruitful; and the mulberry and other trees, which are everywhere united by festoons of vines, must have a beautiful effect in the summer.

When we go from hence, we propose seeing the Republic of Lucca on our way, and staying some time at Florence, and from thence to Bologna, Padua, Venice, Verona, and through the Tyrol into Switzerland, from whence I shall write to you again, if your uncle does not; and hope you will be entertained by our next letter, in proportion to the dullness of this. But my impatience to address my dearest niece was such, that

I would not suffer a dearth of subjects to be an impediment. Direct your next to Florence; and do, pray, let me hear from you soon. I am not yet certain what town in Flanders we shall make our winter quarters.

I have sent two boxes, filled with books, papers, and clothes, which I did not want, in the ship 'Thames,' from Leghorn to London, directed for Mr. Sage, to be left at the Custom-house till called for.

We are in daily expectation of the promised letter from Mr. Sage; and with our best wishes to him and you, I am my beloved Fanny's most tenderly affectionate,

ELIZA WHALLEY.

Pray make our best compliments acceptable to the family at Stanmore, and your uncles and aunts in town.

DR. WHALLEY TO MISS SAGE.

Zurich, June 15, 1786.

THOUGH your aunt is very and justly jealous of her right to your correspondence, my dear Fanny, yet she must allow me now and then to break in upon it, and assure you, with my own pen, of my tender affection, and the unspeakable satisfaction I receive from your kind and charming letters, and the tidings that flow in upon me from all hands of your accomplishments and virtues. Your last, of the 20th of April, reached us only yesterday, owing to its arrival at Florence after our departure; and it is well that a friend happened to cast his eye upon it at the post-office, otherwise it, and all its grateful and animated contents, might have dozed there unvalued as unseen. I wished often that you could have partaken with us of all the beauties and rarities of that celebrated city. We had heard and read enough of the famous gallery to enter it with very exalted ideas, but it surpassed them all. The eye scarcely knows where to fix its attention amongst so many *chefs-d'œuvre* of painting and sculpture, and, amidst its sweet intoxication, is restless and jealous lest some precious effort of art should escape its regards. The collection, also, of gems, medals, ancient Etruscan vases, and bronzes, is vast, curious, and inestimable. The Great Duke's palaces, both in Florence and its environs, are very sumptuous, and adorned with choice paintings. But there would be no end, if my letter were to mention, even cursorily, the variety of treasures we saw in Florence. Those in the churches alone are immense.

But one thing struck me, as I am sure it would have done you, as the greatest inconsistency, and at once offended my reason and my principles, and wounded my feelings. How could it be otherwise, when, after having had one's eyes dazzled by a profusion of riches uselessly dedicated to the service of a God, who declares that He only delights in the humble offerings of a pure and contrite heart, and that mercy and charity are far more acceptable in His sight than all the parade of sacrifice—how could one endure with patience, at issuing out of His temples, to find oneself surrounded by a mixed multitude of the most squalid and miserable objects, importunate in their cravings for wherewithal to sustain a wretched existence, when one's sight had, the moment before, been wearied by masses of gold and silver, proudly displayed on the altars of various real or supposed saints, and all in honour of a Saviour who was Himself all simplicity and humility, who decried all ostentation and show, and who continually preached up deeds of benevolence as the most acceptable offerings to God! I confess that I never could reflect on these things and not turn with a kind of horror from the priests, sinking under the weight of their golden robes, and fuming the ignorant people round them with huge incense pots, finely wrought, and of massy silver. But the Great Duke, who in a thousand instances has proved himself an enemy to bigotry, superstition, priestcraft, and ambition, has begun to exert his power against these mummeries and abuses. He has already suppressed above a hundred convents in Florence and its neighbourhood; and, just before we left it, had ordered mass to be said in the vulgar tongue. These innovations will doubtless be followed by others equally wise and salutary.

Our journey from Florence hither was long, but far from tedious, as we made several interesting pauses by the way in Italy, and found our route so beautiful and varied beyond its confines, as almost to regret its termination. At Bologna we spent two days, and found it a much larger and finer city than we had expected. I prefer its situation to that of Florence, as the cultivation is richer about it, and the hills more picturesque and less loaded with houses. The nobles' palaces at Bologna are very grand, many of them of beautiful architecture, and all adorned with fine paintings. In a church, finely situated on the point of a shady hill, is preserved with sacred care a picture of the Virgin, said to have been painted by St. Luke. Be sure the priests cherish to their utmost this belief; and the concourse of devotees who offer up their adorations to so precious a performance, is in proportion to the priestly sway and blind superstition in a great papal city. The church itself is a fine one, and three miles distant from Bologna. Would you have supposed that a noble colonnade was built from the latter to the former, on purpose for the convenience of the zealots who toil up to the daub of a Madonna? For a daub she is, though painted by the inspired hand of an apostle. The colonnade is of handsome and regular architecture, well paved, and built with white stone. Its appearance, as it runs up the hill, is strikingly beautiful, and it must have been erected at an immense expense.

Before I carry you with me to Venice, let me vent my spleen against the infamous road by the way. Never was there seen so diabolical a quagmire in a Christian country! Your poor aunt's screams, as we jolted and floundered on, were carried far and near upon the wings of the wind; and perhaps we might have stuck there to this time, had we not called in the timely aid of two oxen, and two poor cows, to drag us out of the deep and perilous mud holes. Yet this is the great highway from Bologna to Venice. What a scandal to the *santissimo padre* and the *serenissimo doge!* Of all the cities I ever beheld, Venice would be the very last I should choose for my residence, as I had not the honour to be born an amphibious animal. How should you like, my beloved Fanny, to paddle about in a black, unsteady canoe, entitled gondola, from one narrow, dark, and stinking ditch to another, stopt here and jostling there, in quest of amusements, or to visit your friends? Yet such is the out-of-door life of the noblest he or she in Venice; and from within, one sees water, water, and nothing but water; which one knows, indeed, to come from the sea, but which, in its appearance, no more resembles the azure deep, than Fleet Ditch does the Thames. However, there are streets without water, and so spacious, that, with some contrivance, I could squeeze by the persons I met in them.

St. Mark's place, indeed, is very grand, and the new quay still more so, with an arm of the sea running between it and the opposite suburbs, which are formed by several little islands covered with stately buildings. The great canal, which forms the principal street, I had almost forgot to honour. It is broad, above a mile long, and bordered by many noble palaces; but they are unluckily intermingled with beggarly houses, which hurts the eye, and takes off greatly from the effect. Across this canal is thrown the famous arch of the Rialto, which one has so long heard of as a wonder, that one forgets to wonder at it when seen. Of the fine paintings at Venice there is no end. The vast and sumptuous palace of the Doge is quite covered with them, and they are by the best masters. But, in the midst of all this royal magnificence, your eye and nose are disgusted with loathsome filth, which, even in the great and superb council-room, lies about in heaps upon the beautiful inlaid marble pavement. What pollution! what people! I turned my back on them with pleasure, and, sailing back to the large, but old and gloomy, city of Padua, went on from thence to Vicenza, and from Vicenza to Verona. The latter is a fine city, and beautifully situated on the Adige, with a rich and extensive plain on one side, and cultivated hills on the other. The ancient Roman amphitheatre is still in good preservation, and large enough to contain between twenty and thirty thousand spectators; but in the days of their national glory could not have pretended to vie, either in size or architecture, with that we saw in ruins at Nismes.

The day we left Verona we entered the Tyrol, throughout which delicious country nature is equally beautiful, pastoral, and sublime. I never saw such picturesque and captivating scenery, such various cultivation, or such an universal appearance of cheerful industry; and the people so civil, so simple, so honest! How different from the lazy, crafty, sulky, proud and insolent, yet servile, Italians whom we had just quitted! The variety of dresses, also manners and cookery, as we went on, amused us highly. What think you of a roasted fowl with stewed prunes; fried liver, stewed with brown sugar; and veal swimming in aniseed sauce? Our six days' journey through this charming country seemed very short. In four more we reached this town, which is the leading one in Switzerland, and most delightfully situated on its own lake, the banks of which offer a succession of the most captivating pictures to the eye. We have been here three weeks, and purpose staying but one more, as our host (and we are obliged to live at this inn for want of private lodgings) is as greedy of gain as any rapacious Jew, and fleeces us without mercy. From hence we shall go to Strasbourg, where we purpose staying till the end of August, when we shall move forward to the Low Countries. May we flatter ourselves with the hopes that your dear father will join us in the latter? I answered his letter from Florence, and wait his final determination with great and natural impatience.

I shall direct this to Thornhill, where a joint letter from your amiable friends the Misses Davies has informed us you are to be this summer. They express themselves with the warmest sense of your kind attention to them. Our compliments and good wishes await your Uncle and Aunt Joseph. Your aunt will write you from Strasbourg. Direct to me, at that place, *à la poste restante.* I suppose you will be often this summer with your favourite, Mrs. Burland, from whom you cannot fail to learn candour, and improve yourself in sweet tones.

Vincent and Reeves beg me to add their respects. Should Mr. Sage resolve to join us in Flanders, and wish to do so sooner than the period I have mentioned, let him hint only his wishes, and we shall be happy to fulfil them to our utmost. I am rejoiced that drawing and instrumental music are not neglected.

No, my beloved Fanny, we do not expect to find you the first singer in the world, nor shall we attribute your not being so to disinclination; but we are convinced that you possess sufficient excellence in the most engaging of all accomplishments to charm all that hear you. My ears (to say nothing of my heart) long for the treat. Remember us in the most affectionate manner to your dear father, love us as we love you, and write speedily to your fond uncle and faithful friend,

T. S. WHALLEY.

DR. WHALLEY TO MISS SAGE.

Strasbourg, July 15, 1786.

THE resolution is fixed then, my beloved Fanny, and we shall have the happiness to embrace you on the Continent. We shall owe your kind father an endless gratitude for so unequivocal a mark of his affection, and so powerful a one of his confidence. He will never have cause to be dissatisfied with our return to either. We purpose being at Brussels the 12th of August, and nothing, we hope, will prevent your meeting us there the 13th, or 14th at farthest. Your preparations will be soon made for such a journey; however, I wait your father's answer to this point, and wait it with anxious impatience. After so long an absence from my friends, what a joy to embrace the one who, after my mother, is the most dear to me! Desire your dear father to buy me a pair of buckles in London, fashionable, but not *outrée*. The choice of them I leave entirely to his and your taste. You may suppose my present ones are not too modish, as they are the same I brought with me from England—three years are an age in fashion. Buy me also a guinea pocket-book, furnished with knife, scissors, &c. How delightful to charge you with such commissions, as the idea of their completion and seeing you go hand in hand! Say everything that is kind, in our names, to Mr. Sage, and remember us affectionately to your uncle Joe and family, not forgetting our particular respects to your excellent grandfather, and best wishes to your aunt Peggy.

Answer me by word of mouth—the most grateful one I can receive from you, though fully sensible of all the merits of your pen. Adieu! my beloved Fanny. Would you could read in my heart how very very dear you are to your fond uncle,

THOS. SEDGWICK WHALLEY.

Your aunt bids me add that you may bring any kind of

gowns to France, new or old, without fear of their being seized by the Custom-house myrmidons.

MRS. WHALLEY TO MISS SAGE.

Strasbourg, July 6, 1786.

As your uncle addressed you from Zurich, and Mr. Sage but a post or two since, I should have deferred giving myself the pleasure of thanking you, my beloved Fanny, for your last very charming letter a little longer, had not Mr. Whalley forgot to mention in his letter to your dear father that I am under some concern for the fate of my two boxes, sent some months since to England from Leghorn, and addressed to Mr. Sage. The keys were put up in a separate parcel and directed for him, and to be left at Mrs. Gordon's. The boxes were to be left at the Custom-house till called for. I inclose the bill of lading, together with the inventory of the contents of the boxes, and I entreat the favour of Mr. Sage to take the proper methods to secure the boxes, and leave them in the care of his brother till my return to England. Any expense he is at I will thankfully repay.

It is with infinite pleasure I reflect on the probability that I shall soon, my dearest, embrace you on the Continent. May nothing interfere to blast these hopes, is my ardent wish.

After travelling more than a thousand miles in the last two months, we are glad to repose a little; and with that view have taken a very pleasantly-situated lodging here for one month. This is one of the largest and best fortified towns in France, and seems to be a very good one; but I have as yet seen very little of it. The steeple of the cathedral is much celebrated, and said to be the highest in Europe; one sees it at fourteen miles distance from the town. Its architecture is beautiful, being built of stone, and so curiously hollowed, that it appears like the finest filagree, which has a striking effect.

I conclude that your uncle gave you an account of the different towns we saw in Italy, and the various curiosities they contained, as well as a description of the delightful route we took through the Tyrol. I will therefore avoid a repetition of what would appear very dull from my pen, after being the subject of his; and shall only say that Italy on the side of art, and the passage of the Tyrol on that of nature, far exceed anything I could have conceived. Switzerland, too, abounds in picturesque beauties; and we have purchased some prints, which will give you a very lively idea of some of the lovely views with which our eyes have been feasted during our tour through that delightful country. Zurich is, I think, upon the whole, the finest situated town I have ever seen; though it was our head quarters, we made excursions to all the other principal towns of Switzerland we had not before seen.

I think Mr. Whalley wrote you after our return from Lucerne, and the Convent of Nôtre Dame d'Hermite. I was highly entertained at the latter, from its extreme singularity. Berne we found a very well-built pretty town, with sweet walks, kept in the highest order, on the ramparts. The colonnades on each side the streets, to which Mr. Cox * attributes its greatest beauty, was in our eyes its only defect, as they are built sloping, and have a very heavy air. The situation of Berne is extremely *riant* and pleasing, though it wants the strong features that characterise that of Zurich. The cathedral is a fine building and perfectly neat, but being a Lutheran church, is without ornament. From Berne we went to Soleure, where we spent a day very agreeably. The town has less to boast of than many others, but its cathedral, which has been built within the last twenty years, is a noble piece of architecture, and the inside is singularly elegant. We visited a hermitage, about half a mile from the town,

* Archdeacon Cox's 'Switzerland,' so often criticised in the journals.

with which we were much pleased; and of that too I shall be able to give you an idea, from some very exact prints we purchased of it. From Soleure to Basle our way lay between Mount Jura, where the magnificence of the objects reminded us of the Tyrol. Your uncle went a little out of the way to see a fall of water, which pleased him much; but I was not tempted, as we had from Zurich visited the falls of the Rhine at Schaffhausen, and after that everything of the same kind must appear trifling. Since I have been abroad, I have never seen anything that struck me so much. In contemplating it, the mind is at once impressed with surprise, terror, and delight. In the print, I shall be able to trace out to you the various spots from whence we viewed this glorious object, of which I cannot say enough.

We spent two days at Basle, which, as it is the last, so it is the largest town in Switzerland. There we met Mr. Weldon and his lady,* with whom I was acquainted. She is a daughter of Lord Conyngham. Their society was an additional pleasure to us. We were one morning much entertained with the sight of some walks cut among the woods and mountains, about six miles from the town, and tastefully ornamented with buildings, by some *chanoines,* who have given them the name of the English Gardens; and, indeed, I have seen nothing so much in the taste of my country since I left it.

I received a letter from Mrs. Lockhart by the last post. She seems to think they shall be in England this autumn, but they are always undecided.

Will you be so good, my dear, to desire Mr. Sage, before he leaves England, to call at Messrs. Ransom & Co., bankers, in Pall Mall, for some writings which they have of ours. If he lodges any sum of money with them, they will

* Ellen, daughter of second Viscount Conyngham, married, December 1777, Stewart Weldon, Esq., of Kilmorony, Queen's County, Ireland, and died without issue.

give him their circular notes, which are negotiable in every principal town in Europe. Your uncle unites with me in kindest love to you both; and I am, my sweet Fanny,

Ever tenderly and affectionately yours,

ELIZA WHALLEY.

I make no doubt but Wicky and Molly were delighted with their late jaunt.

Do you know, I am a convert to your dancing-master's opinions, for I've seen so many *danse des morts* in Switzerland that I think it must be hard if there are no angels among them.

MRS. WHALLEY TO MISS SAGE.

Strasbourg, July 23, 1786.

I AM set down, my beloved niece, to address a few lines to you, though it is unnecessary to write a long letter, as Mr. Whalley's and my last is a full answer to Mr. Sage's letter, which we received duly from Florence, and your last, which reached us a few days since. We have great pleasure in indulging the hope of soon meeting your dear father and you on the Continent. The only purport of this is to beg you would not omit bringing all your very best pieces of vocal and instrumental music. An instrument is very easily to be hired.

I hope you will not be later than the 12th or 14th of next month in being at Brussels, because it is absolutely necessary to set out for Holland as soon as possible afterwards, or the season will be too far advanced to take the tour, which would be very mortifying. Direct your answer to this, *à la poste restante, Malines, Flandre,* where we shall wait till we know what day we shall meet you at Brussels, which is only fourteen miles from it. Mr. Whalley desired Mr. Sage to come to the Hotel d'Angleterre; but we have since been told that the Bellevue is a better house, and much more agreeably situated. We shall, therefore, expect you there.

This is a very pleasant, large, and handsome city, and, for a French town, very clean. Eight thousand military render it perfectly gay. The principal public walk is a very noble one indeed. In the centre of it is what they call the Arbre Vert a foolish name, for who ever saw a tree of any other colour? It is a very singular thing: the head forms quite a house, with staircase, windows, &c. The side branches are plied down on stakes, so as to form a complete berceau round the tree, of extent large enough to place fourteen tables, or to admit of a numerous company dancing under its shade. There is nothing remarkable here but the steeple of the cathedral, which, I believe I told you, is one of the most elegant pieces of architecture I ever beheld. The inside of the cathedral is not worth seeing; but the clock is reckoned the most curious piece of mechanism in Europe—it has fourteen different movements. There is likewise a fine monument to Marshal Saxe in one of the Protestant churches here; and I think these are the sum total of the curiosities of Strasbourg. The environs are by no means equal to the town itself, as it is situated in a flat, marshy plain, which, to us who have been accustomed to such rich scenes, appears dull; but the climate seems delightful to us, after having broiled two summers under a Provence sun.

I direct this at your uncle Joe's, as I hope you will be in London by the time it arrives. Adieu, my dearest Fanny; accept our most affectionate wishes, present them to your valuable father, and believe me always

Most tenderly yours,

ELIZA WHALLEY.

Bring, especially, your best Italian songs, and forget not your drawing apparatus. I shall pride myself, as I always have done, in your accomplishments, and be anxious for their still higher perfection. Adieu, ma très chère; aimez-moi comme je vous aime.

T. S. W.

MRS. SIDDONS TO DR. WHALLEY.

August 11, 1786.

I SEE, my beloved friend, if I wait for a time when I can sit down and turn my eyes inward on my memory, to collect the thousand occurrences which, at the time they happen, I think I will store for your amusement, that I shall never write. Mine, you know, is a sieve-like memory, and, beside, 'Sufficient for the day is the evil thereof,' and I think I am as much, if not more, employed than ever. I am still gathering laurels to plant round the sweet cottage you and I have planned together, and you will be glad to hear they are variegated with gold; but, as I am not ambitious of finery, I shall be glad at a proper time (upon recollection) to exchange them for more modest plants.

How I rejoice to hear your precious health is so much restored you can guess, though I cannot express: but why don't you tell me you are coming back to us? Your niece is grown a very elegant young woman. You know she was always remarkably handsome, and always had more manner than any child I ever saw, and she has lost nothing of either, I assure you. I have thought myself very unfortunate in being unable to see her so often as I wished; but the constant succession of business, and the nonsensical though necessary round of etiquette, visiting, &c. &c., leaves one in London very, very little to use for one's real gratification.

Yes, my sister is married, and I have lost one of the sweetest companions in the world. However, I am not so selfish as to wish it otherwise. She has married a most respectable man, though of but small fortune, and I thank God that she is off the stage; this is a younger brother of the traveller, and as unlike him in every particular as it is possible. Your last was indeed a very scrambling letter, and I hope you will make amends in your next. I beseech you not to give me descriptions of the country, for I am totally uninterested in such accounts, and I grudge the room they take up in some of your letters, which might be so much more satisfactorily filled up with the most trifling accounts of your dear selves: all that relates to you is interesting, but I don't care sixpence about situation, vegetation, or any of the ations.

Pray, as you so politely give up your idea of the picture to Sir Joshua and your humble servant, may I venture to propose a large half-length miniature, or will you let me know what sized picture you would like? It is impossible to have anything done well so very small, or that can convey any idea of the manner and air of the person.

My paper wears apace. I leave this place for York next Tuesday, where I shall be about a month. In September, I shall be as usual at Nuneham, near Oxford, a seat of Lord Harcourt's. It has been impossible to get a place in the boxes for these six months past at York; they were all taken on the supposition of my playing there long before the affair was settled. Give a thousand thousand loves to my dearest Mrs. Whalley, and tell her I love her with the truest affection. My children are all well, clever, and lovely. I hope they will be worthy, too! I want sadly to find a genteel, accomplished woman to superintend my three girls under my own roof, and under my own eye; but I am afraid I shall find this a very difficult thing to accomplish. May God Almighty bless you both, my beloved friends, with health and all happiness!

MRS. WHALLEY TO MISS SAGE.

Malines, August 26, 1786.

I DID not think, my dearest Fanny, to have written to you again before I had the pleasure of embracing you on the

Continent; but since our arrival here we have informed ourselves of the direct and nearest route you are to pursue to Bruxelles. It will be considerably out of your way to go to Lille. After staying the day of your arrival at Calais, and amusing yourselves with walking about the town, seeing the cathedral and town-hall, you may set out the next morning, dine at Dunkirk, and sleep at Ypres. The second day you may, if you set out early, get to Ghent by dinner. You will put up at the St. Sebastian; and as Ghent is a very fine town, and the Abbaye de St. Pierre and the cathedral (in one of the chapels of which is a fine picture of Rubens) are well worth seeing, we would advise you to sleep there that night, and come on to Bruxelles the next morning.

I beg you will write me a line, to fix the day when (wind and tide permitting) you will be at Ghent. Your uncle forgot to mention that, on your things being examined at Calais, you must take a certificate, or passport, as it is called, to secure them from further examination while you continue in the French territories. When you enter the Emperor's, you will be stopped; the custom-house officer will ask your name, your quality, and whether you have anything contraband. You must tell him that your father is an Englishman, a gentleman, and no *marchand* (that is essential), and assure him, on your word of honour, that you have nothing contraband, accompany the whole with a douceur of half-a-crown, and he will wish *bon voyage* to monsieur and mademoiselle, and you will have no further trouble.

I cannot express to you the pleasure with which we anticipate your dear father's and your arrival; we talk of hardly anything else. It is such a step from hence, and I am so doatingly fond of the water, that if it was not for the expense I should be tempted to go to Dover, for the pleasure of accompanying you back; but that cannot be, therefore I must wait in patience here.

We unite in best wishes to you both, as well as to my brother Whalley and the Wickhams, who, I imagine, are with you. We hope Molly has received Mr. Whalley's letter, and am, my dear, with the warmest affection,

Yours,

ELIZA WHALLEY.

I hope Mr. Sage will find pheasants and partridges enough to afford him amusement, but not enough to make him regret his quitting them.

The Archduchess is this moment arrived; they are wetting the wheels to prevent their firing, while the horses are changed. All this haste is occasioned by a tour of six weeks to England. On her return we will pay her our devoirs. I wish I could peep at Mr. Sage and you on your first setting out from Calais; how you will laugh at the cavalry, the old ropes, &c.!

DR. WHALLEY TO FANNY SAGE.

August 18, 1786.

C'en est fait donc, my beloved Fanny: and we shall have the happiness to embrace you and your dear father at Brussels. My last told Mr. Sage that our visit to Nick Frog* and all his croaking kindred was laid aside. Indeed, your sparkling eyes and melodious voice too fully occupy my thoughts for the phlegmatic, sallow, and squabby Hollanders to thrust in the end of one of their pipes amongst them.

We shall take care to be at Brussels two or three days before your arrival, in order to have an apartment swept and garnished, and everything *comme il faut* for your reception. Load yourself with music, and fear not. Should the Cerberus at Calais begin to growl, warble a few notes of an Italian

* He had intended to make a tour in Holland.

air to him, or quaver through your Roman nose (for I find it is Roman) some tender passage from a French song, and the sop will be full as effectual as ever was Orpheus's to assuage his wrath. Remember, however, that you must bring over no article of clothes unmade, for after all the clemency of brutes is not to be wholly relied on. Your music books should not appear to be quite new—*voilà tout!* We cannot express our gratitude to Mr. Sage for the pledge of confidence that he is about to repose in our hands; but I will say that our principles and attachment both to him and yourself deserve it. Let us know the very day you are to set off for Dover. May the gentlest breezes waft you to the Continent! Poor old Neptune and his trident are out of fashion, or I would burn a whole pot of incense to him on your behalf. But a greater God than Neptune shall be invoked to bless and speed you to our arms. May the bugs have mercy upon you in your way through the French towns! I shall tremble for you the night you sleep at Lisle, or elsewhere, in your road from Calais. Stinking as the odious reptiles are themselves, with the *bon goût* of the Hottentots, fragrant odours are offensive to them, and the washing the hands and face with lavender water immediately on going to bed will keep them at an awful distance, if they are not *tout-à-fait affamés.*

I had almost forgotten an important commission of your dear aunt's — for what more important to a lady than her trimmings? Your aunt has, in the care of our banker at Leghorn, two of the *plumes des grèbes* which arrived there after our departure, and which she wishes to have sent to England, but stands in bodily fear of their being confiscated at the Custom-house. One is her own, one for a friend: they are beautiful, rare, and valuable, and she wishes to know whether they come under the article of prohibited goods, or whether they can be secured by paying a certain duty for them. A pretty commission this, is it not, for a *belle demoiselle*? But cast your eyes about you, and you will find some one, on your arrival in town, to fulfil it according to your behests. Now, is it not a terrible thing that a man who writes hardly legibly with the best pen, should be obliged to scrawl through a whole letter with the very worst that ever grew in goose's wing? However, you are used to decipher me, and, in the midst of all my foul blots, will distinguish and value the true affection of

Your ever-fond uncle,
THOS. SEDGWICK WHALLEY.

Do not forget to pack up some of your drawings with your drawing apparatus. Pick out all your best Italian songs. Italian music is my passion—the vocal, I mean.

I shall count the lagging hours till we meet. Your aunt says not a word to you. How unkind! Come and reproach her for it. *Carissima, addio!*

A dress cap for your aunt, as a present from me, and chosen after your own judgment and taste. I would have it elegant.

Remember that the *ton* of London is, in dress and everything, the rage of the continent.

MISS SEWARD TO DR. WHALLEY.

Lichfield, August 31, 1786.

INDEED, my dearest friend, nothing could be more involuntary than the silence of which you complain. I have accounted for it in a voluminous letter, which set out from hence the 12th of this month, directed to you in French—*Gent. Anglois, à Strasbourg, à la poste restante.* If you do not receive it before this reaches you, which must perforce be short, do write, and enquire after it at the Strasbourg office. My commission went yesterday to a bookseller in town to send, according to your directions, Hayley's Plays, and 'Old Maids;' 'The Mine;' Yearsley's Poems; Cowper's

'Task,' and 'Louisa.' Your letter did not reach me till Sunday last. I wonder what became of Hayley's Plays and 'Louisa,' sent for you to Lady Langham's house. Did you never hear anything of the parcel from them? I should have thought, in her large acquaintance, she might have found a safe conveyance for it to you. You enquire if I am about any poetic work. Ah, no! It is not likely that I should court the effusions of the muse, when the never-ending obtrusions of uninteresting yet indispensable employments oblige me to go on from day to day 'champing the iron bit' of restraint, while the most precious and animating pages from yourself and Sophia, and other beloved friends, lie unanswered in my desk through seven or eight weeks.

Several poetic tasks, and some prose ones, whose execution is important to my wishes, lie before me as water before the thirsty Tantalus. One Horatian Ode every month, for the 'Gentleman's Magazine,' is the sum total of my poetry for the last two months. I promised to supply it for a twelvemonth. I am assured that nothing I have written is more approved than these Odes; and I am excessively exhorted by several of my literary friends to go through the whole number, and see it flatteringly asserted in the public prints that a paraphrase of Horace's Odes, by Miss Seward, would be an important acquisition to English poetry. But how can I hope to get through 123, when I find difficulty in doing one in a month, though that one is never more than a six hours' business. No! I dare say the Ode to Apollo, for next month, which fulfils my twelvemonth's promise, will be the last attempt I shall have leisure to make upon the spirited poetic hints of the Roman Bard; for really these Odes are, in general, so obscure, that unless the ideas are drawn into daylight, they cannot please at this period in an English dress.

Sophia sent me your delicious letter from Strasbourg last week, rich, as all your letters are, in the most beautiful and interesting descriptions, in the clear lights of moral reflection, and in the warm glow of benevolence. Dear is it to my spirit above every one of its glowing rivals. Yes, above them all is it dear; forasmuch as it breathes an homeward spirit, and comes the precious pledge that the return of my much-loved wanderers to their native land is not far distant. But what it says of your health is not all I wish. I pray of heaven to banish those cruel vestiges of disease, and give you back to us with a strengthened constitution, as well as with a mind and memory stored with inexhaustible treasures of varied information.

In a very few days, if my father continues as tolerable as he seems now, I have promised to set my face towards Derbyshire, and reside about twelve days in the mansion of my interesting friends, the Granvilles.* Its situation is very singular; standing as it does on the extremest verge of a large and very lucid sheet of water, through which the river Dove comes winding down from Dovedale and Eyam. Gentle hills, the nurselings of the Peak mountains, circle round the lake at about half a mile's distance. It is a sweet crystal scene. The same party assembled there as met at the house of Mr. D'Ewes* in January, upon the then frozen banks of the Avon. My father's weak, though not diseased state, clouds with apprehension the approach of any meditated excursion; but they will not excuse me at Callige.

Adieu! my beloved friend. The dear old man and Giovanni join me in the kindest remembrances, and in a thousand good wishes for yours and Mrs. Whalley's welfare, to whom I am, not less than to yourself,

A truly affectionate, as well as obliged friend,

A. Seward.

* The families of Granville and D'Ewes, relatives of Mrs. Delany, and so often mentioned in her correspondence.

I am tempted to send you my last Horatian Ode, as it will just occupy the little opposite blank in my paper.

ODE TO HIS ATTENDANT.

From Horace, b. i. c. 38.

Boy, not in these autumnal bowers
Do thou the Persian vest dispose,
Of artful gold, and rich brocade,
Nor tie, in gaudy knots, the sprays and flowers!
Ah! search not where the latest rose
Yet lingers in the sunny glade!
Free be the vest, and simple be the braid!
I charge thee, with the myrtle wreath
Not one resplendent bloom entwine.
We both become that modest band,
As, stretch'd my vineyard's ample shade beneath,
I jocund quaff the rosy wine;
While near me thou shalt smiling stand,
And fill the sparkling cup with ready hand.

MRS. SIDDONS TO DR. WHALLEY.

London, October 1, 1786.

I WOULD it were in my power, my dear friend, to be of use in the business you hint at; but surely your connexions and intimacies are such as might warrant success, could you only be prevailed upon to speak your wishes. I will not think so injuriously of the great world as to suppose you might not enjoy them. Who would not be proud to execute your wishes, having the power? If such a creature lives, how do I pity him! Do not talk of this detestable reverse at Langford. I can't bear it. I beg we may drop the subject entirely; and, rather than recall such an idea, let my lovely cottage melt into air, as many a castle has done heretofore. If I can be of use in any shape, you know you may command me, and make me happy in so doing. You say you are but two days' journey from us. If I could speak French enough to bring me to you, be assured I would not wait many days for the happiness, which has been withdrawn from me so many years. What a thing a balloon would be! but, the deuce take them, I do not find that they are likely to be brought to any good. Good heaven! what delight it would be to see you for a few days only! I have a nice house, and I could contrive to make up a bed. I know you and my dear Mrs. Whalley would accept my sincere endeavours to accommodate you; but don't let me be taken by surprise, my dear friend, for were I to see you first at the theatre, I can't answer for what might be the consequence. I stand some knocks with tolerable firmness, I suppose from habit; but those of joy being so infinitely less frequent, I conceive must be more difficultly sustained. You will find I have been a niggard of my praise, when you see your Fanny. Oh! my beloved friend, you could not speak to one who understands those anxieties you mention better than I do. Surely it is needless to say to one who more ardently prays that God Almighty, in His mercy, will avert the calamity; and surely, surely there is everything to hope for from such dispositions, improved by such an education.

My family is well, God be praised! My two sisters are married and happy. Mrs. Twiss will present us with a new relation towards February. At Christmas I bring my dear girls from Miss Eames, or rather, she brings them to me. Eliza is the most entertaining creature in the world; Sally is vastly clever; Maria and George are beautiful; and Harry a boy with very good parts, but not disposed to learning. My husband is well; and I have at last, my friend, attained the *ten thousand pounds* which I set my heart upon, and am now perfectly at ease with respect to fortune. I thank God, who has enabled me to procure to myself so comfortable an income. I am sure, my dear Mrs. Whalley and you will be pleased to hear this from myself. I always remember you both to every one that knows you, who are extremely delighted to find themselves not forgotten by you. Mr. Siddons joins me in all possible good wishes to you, my best loved and dearest friends, and

I remain, with the truest affection,
Unalterably yours,
S. SIDDONS.

Pray let me hear from you very soon, and tell me that I shall see you before Christmas. I forgot to tell you that my brother is very deservedly a great favourite with the public. We have a great comic actress now, called Mrs. Jordan; she has a vast deal of merit, but in my mind is not perfection.

I assure you Lady Harcourt* is a very superior and a very charming woman, and her *lord* is a very ODD, respectable man.

MISS SEWARD TO DR. WHALLEY, AT MALINES.

Lichfield, August 13, 1786.

MY DEAR FRIEND,—That animated welcome which my affection, your virtues, and the full tides of wit, fancy, and information which flow through your letters, must always secure for them, my late anxiety for your health increased to an infinite degree. That you were, with truth, able to send me so favourable an account of it, first I bless God, and next congratulate dear Mrs. Whalley with all a sister's tender sympathy and fervour. How teased have I been that an engrossing number of engagements, uninteresting and yet indispensable, have kept me five weeks silent to the most entertaining, as well as the most interesting letter that ever fell even from your magic pen.

In a world so veering, and where many circumstances in my situation, which are of precious import to my happiness,

* Elizabeth, daughter of Lord Vernon. She married Viscount Harcourt, 1765. He was born 1736.

have long hung by such a cobweb thread as the life of an aged and unpersuadable paralytic, you would hardly expect, though I know you will rejoice that I have still a parent living, not wholly uncomfortably, though with intellects impaired daily more and more, and with limbs reduced to infant weakness; that I still range through the spacious apartments, and their green environs, of whose summer pleasantness you can conceive no adequate idea, from a recollection of them in their state of pallid barrenness.

Giovanni is well, but so devoted to Flora and her more scientific twin-sister the nymph of botany, that we seldom see him through these warm long days, except to take a hasty dinner, a dish of tea, or to make us wait supper for him till ten. His collection of rare and beautiful flowers and of curious plants attracts the attention of strangers, and almost rivals his friend Green's museum.

The Abbey Festival, whose magnetism was for me twice foiled by filial apprehension, this year drew me within its sphere. There is universal testimony that the world never produced anything of equal harmonic excellence. My imagination seemed, at the close of the last day's performance, to see the forms of awful nature and energetic art address the triumphant Cecilia, saying to her, while the spirit of Handel hovered exultingly over the trio, 'Thou hast reached the utmost bounds of thy reign—thy exertions have been to our honour as well as to thy own; but beyond these limits we do not allow thee to pass.'

The single airs have perhaps been heard to greater advantage in smaller rooms, but the sublimity of the harmonies in overture, concerto, symphony and chorus, exhibiting all those splendid effects which their great author conceived, but which the then but emerging state of general musical knowledge made it impossible he should hear with his mortal ears, —the exclusion of everything harsh and disagreeably noisy, by the care taken that, in an orchestra consisting of 750 performers, no order of instruments or voices should preponderate: the exquisite softness with which the single songs, duets and trios, were accompanied by a few selected instruments of perfect skill — the picturesque effect of several of the choruses, which caused the ear to perform the office of all the other senses—the brilliant appearance of an audience, consisting of more than 3,000 well-dressed ladies and gentlemen—the presence of the Monarch, surrounded by his lovely family, while 'at his left hand stood the Queen in a vesture of needlework'—the grave bishops in their black robes, extending in a sable line on each side the royal pair, and encircled by the flower of the English nobility,—these things combined equalled all the demands of my imagination, which had been busy and bold with the subject. The recollection of them will be gathered into my little storehouse of the past, where great things are capable of contracting themselves, to expand again at pleasure, like the legions in the state room of Pandemonium.

When Mara's songs allowed her to keep above the croaking notes in her voice, and when she restrained the luxuriance of her extraordinaries, her brilliant shake, her energies (for she has no softness), and matchless sostenuto, produced a degree of excellence far superior to anything I heard from the lip of Rubinelli, whom it is the fashion to idolise above her, above everything. His tones are nasal, and he is apt to sing too flat, but even through the disadvantage of singing in a language he did not understand, I could perceive that he is a very feeling performer. Giovanni was the principal contralto. He sang divinely: everybody I heard speak on the subject said, by far the best of any English singer there; and I am sure Mara had not his pathos, nor Rubinelli his energy. The King expressed himself more than once highly pleased with his performance. Mara, in order to prove to us, in the celebrated song in the 'Messiah,' that her Redeemer was alive, made him skip up and down the octaves in a most ungodly manner, producing the death of just expression, while she sung about resurrection. My overwhelming engagements would not permit me to go to the serious opera. The only night I could go to the Opera-house it was the burletta, and I have seldom heard worse singing; the voices were so overpowered by their brilliant accompaniments that they came to my ear only at intervals, as the sound of the organ to my dressing-room window in a high wind. That the singers at an oratorio are so much better heard than at an opera, must be in a great degree owing to the band being placed behind, instead of before them, as at the Opera.

Solicitous to return to my father, I confined my stay in town to seventeen days, and thought the London hurries would have killed me; yet I escaped that fierce cough which always, when it seizes, drags me out of London, like the wolf the bleating and reluctant sheep out of its fold. Every moment was so taken up with the much, and the many, I had to see and hear, and the shoals of penny-post notes I had to answer, that though seldom in bed before two, I was obliged to be up at six every morning. It was not given me to taste the luxury of Siddonian sorrow, but I saw the glorious creature in 'Rosalind.' In spite of the disadvantage of a very vilely chosen dress, I entirely think with you, against the clamour of the multitude, that her smiles are as fascinating as her frowns are magnificent, as her tears are irresistible. I was with the Barrows, and, considering my short stay, saw a great deal of the mirthful Helen Williams, with whom and with whose friends, we formed literary parties that were very interesting. I received from several of the literati very flattering encomiums, both in prose and verse, upon my Horatian paraphrases, and got a peep, but it was only a peep, at Mr. Layard.

I am sorry to disobey you, yet, notwithstanding your prohibition, I cannot help telling you, that Pratt had got introduced to the Barrows a little before I went up,—that he tried every possible art, by other people's interference, and various methods, to obtain civil notice from me, and to get permission to be of our parties into public; but I remembered what I owed to my own credit, to my avowed resolutions, and was steady. To his perpetual notes of remonstrance I always coolly replied that Mr. and Mrs. Barrow had a right to ask who they pleased to their house, but pleaded my own right of being allowed to consider Mr. Pratt as an unintroduced stranger beneath the roof where I was a guest, and to maintain my resolve of never being seen with him in public. He wanted to have established himself in the Barrow parties by a pretended passion for their little mistress. This was before I was expected in Percy Street. He had played upon her vanity the artillery of sighs, languishments, and amorous innuendos, but I put a spoke in his wheel of gallantry there. The day before I left town came the fifth note from him:—'Mr. Pratt's compliments to Miss Seward—has unfortunately mislaid a letter he very lately received from Mr. Whalley, and desires she will favour with his direction.' A boasting wretch! I knew he had not lately received a letter from you, since you told me you had totally renounced him, and so I ventured to assure some of the people who I knew would tell him again.

During my stay in town, that desperately-facetious Drawcansir, Peter Pindar, was introduced to me. I was glad to have an opportunity of deprecating for my little works the power of that burlesque vein, which has thrown the blight of contempt upon compositions of more ingenuity and value. How large is the majority of those, who are incapable of perceiving that it is in the power of humorous and especially of *vulgar* satire, to place real literary excellence in a ridiculous point of view, a truth of which Cotton's burlesque of 'Virgil' remains a glaring proof. Pratt has crept up Pindar's sleeve; and he set that engine to work with me, for the purpose of relaxing my resolves; but when I explained to him their motive he approved their stability. Peter Pindar's real name is Wolcot, a physician without practice, who for a maintenance commenced burlesque poet.

An anonymous work, in three volumes, entitled an 'Essay on Old Maids,' universally believed to be Mr. Hayley's, has attracted the attention of all sorts of readers: a vein of spirited, arch, and insidious sarcasm pervades almost every page, and has wounded the pride, the delicacy, and the sensibility of the whole female world. I confess I thought Mr. Hayley too much the friend of our sex, to have written such a work. It certainly casts a shade over that glorious benevolence which glows through his former writings. O! why was the great moral poet seized with an ambition unworthy his exalted genius, of rivalling Voltaire in 'the sparkling explosions of irritating wit' (partly to use his own words), after having stretched so far beyond him on the poetic line?

What a mine of intellectual wealth, and that of every sort, is your last letter! I have read it aloud to a number of my friends, who agree with me in pronouncing it one of the brightest, if not the very brightest gem in my Whalleyan casket; but alas! there are at least thirty lines, on the subject of Lavater, wholly illegible. In vain have I called assistance to decipher them—they are wrapped in impervious obscurity. Ah! never again suffer an atom of eloquence so precious to become evanescent by the diminution of its characters and the closeness of their compression. Alas! how unequal is our epistolary commerce respecting the value of the goods exchanged! You send me the most animated descriptions of countries, cities, and people, the varieties of nature and the exertions of art—and you receive from me in return, sketches of flowers, of music meetings, and their performers, with my opinion of books, which, till you read them, can but little interest, and when you read them you will form much more clearly for yourself.

I knew not that Lactilla* had abused Miss More with Billingsgate coarseness: such conduct is certainly indefensible. All I contended for, and of which I am still assured, was, that could Johnson have been precisely in Lactilla's circumstances, he would have spurned such a proposal from any patron, as Miss More made to the milkwoman, and would probably not have been behind her in the coarseness, any more than in the violence, of his fury. Mrs. Piozzi, a week after her marriage, showed Doctor Dobson a letter from Johnson, filled with the most brutal invectives. Few obligations could be of more binding force to demand the returns of indulgent kindness, than his to Mrs. Thrale; lifted up, then unpensioned, by her hand from a situation penurious and comfortless, to opulence and the luxury he loved so well. How highly was he indebted for the solicitous attention of so many years, every taste gratified, every troublesome whim indulged, every arrogant brutality passed over! To remonstrate against the indiscretion of her choice was the duty of friendship, before that choice was ratified at the altar; but subsequent upbraiding, was neither consistent with gratitude nor Christianity. Mrs. Thrale had violated no law of God, no

* Lactilla, the poetical name by which a certain Ann Yearsley was known. She is now only worth mentioning as exhibiting, through her own baseness, the beautiful Christian forbearance of her patroness. She was a poor milkwoman, near Bristol, who wrote a poem, which was shown to Mrs. H. More, in which the latter considered there were traces of genius, and in consequence raised a subscription to enable Lactilla to publish her composition. The sum subscribed finally amounted to more than 500*l.*, which she invested in the funds, in the name of trustees, for the woman's benefit: 10*l.*, which remained uninvested, Mrs. More put into her hand, when the ungrateful woman accused her of jealousy and fraud, and threw the money at her head. The Christian lady's only reply was —'May we never meet again, till we meet in heaven.'

institution of man. It was Johnson's part to have alleviated, not increased, the inevitable mortifications of so imprudent a marriage. Johnson ought to have spread that mighty shield, which he could have formed by his notice and his eloquence, between his fair patroness and the contempt of the world, especially since that shield had been tempered into a great accession of strength, by the respectability and consequence with which he appeared at Streatham, through the course of more than twenty years. I think his ingratitude to Mrs. Piozzi dark and indefensible, as Lactilla's to Miss More. I do not approve of either, but I think it unfair that one should be considered a saint, the other a demon.

I am in love with the Duke of Tuscany. If all potentates were like him, monarchy would cease to be, what it so generally is, 'the plague of nations, and the scourge of God.' Surely the abolition of so many convents, of the processional mummeries, and the order against saying mass in Latin, are great efforts towards shaking off the papal power. What says his holiness? Does he not thunder against the heresy of such edicts?

The account of the perpetual fire at Pietra Mala is quite new to me. It is interesting to hear of and to reflect upon these sports of nature, that puzzle philosophers, and reproach the arrogance of incredulity.

Bologna must be a noble city. It seems to deserve the honour conferred upon it by our immortal Richardson, in making it the birth-place of his glorious Clementina, where she rises in greatness of soul so far above the equally impassioned, but less generous Florentine, her violent rival. I should like to have bent with you the delighted but tearful eye of attention over the lovely banished Hagar, her dear little lad, and the serenely inflexible Abraham, and to have joined you in execrating the malice of Sarah, and to have pressed your hand in holy solemnity over the tombs of

Tasso and Ariosto, at Ferrara; but I felt no desire to flounder with you and your ludicrous equipage through the quagmires of the Venetian way, to try the strength of my screaming powers with those of dear Mrs. Whalley. I absolutely did not thank you for muddying the lucid streams of the Arno, as they flowed sparkling through my fancy; and I should perhaps have been as much dissatisfied with your staining the crystal mirrors of the marine city, and changing into bàts those fancied butterflies, the gondolas, if the just and sublime idea so finely made out of their being emblems of the grave had not softened my chagrin into pleasing melancholy. But what is it you tell me of the filth of the Italians? What but the dread of punishment could restrain them within any bounds of morality, or hinder them from violating every social tie? Such instances almost excuse Swiftean misanthropy. I fancy old Palma was an admirer of Dante, and loved to send folk to hell.

I see your dear long legs dragging your wearied body at the heels of your testy valet, whose patriotic vanity gave wings to those heels. Often have I been in the same situation, when the love of art has sickened beneath the fatigue of budging, loitering, standing still, and of gazing upwards. Fast is growing upon me the love of rest above that of gratifying my curiosity.

I should think the frequent encountering all the annual vicissitudes of spring, summer, and winter, in the course of a few days' travelling, would be dangerously trying to the natives of a climate which, however veering, is, on the whole, so temperate as ours. I see the Alps, the Savoy, and Swiss scenery maintain their empire in your preference, in spite of the gayer graces of the Tuscan vales. So I am sure they would with me. What matchless scenery do you show me from the inn window, a few leagues from Bolzano, and how I love to trace with you the Adige to its source in 'that picturesque cascade, which fell down the black rock in long floats to the valley, preceded by many a kindred stream, roaring and frothing amid sloping groves of fir and pines.' I am diverted with the grotesque piety that so ludicrously aims at once to sanctify and adorn the cottages in the neighbourhood of Innspruck. The industry, simplicity, and hospitality of the Tyrol inhabitants rival beneath your description the Valais mountaineers, whom St. Preaux' letters render so interesting; nor does the 'Sentimental Journey' contain more touching little scenes than we find in the conversation between Mrs. Whalley, her sweet resigned mourner, who bestowed the cherished nosegay, and the warm-hearted host, who received the snuff she gave him with so much honest grateful benevolence. I admire her generosity in thus losing the distinctions of rank in the glow of human kindness; but she could not have been the woman of my dear Edwy's choice, had any cold impeding pride hung about her heart, to close its passes against humble virtue.

The lake and tower of Constance you have finely described, and I am enchanted with the vivacity of your witty suppositions concerning the different views with which Huss and his persecutors, would survey the projected triumph of commerce over superstition, in the scenes once embroiled by their dissensions. The description of the Dance of the Dead is truly comic.

Knowing that Zurich was your destined home for some time, my heart congratulated your safe arrival. How you would both enjoy the scene, when, after a good night's rest, you saw the morning sun, for the first time, from your own windows, darting his beams into the ample lake, while the more rapid river Limma broke them into a thousand glittering fragments!

What an acquisition is the friendship and society of

Lavater! When I was at Wellsburn, last winter, Mr. D'Ewes often translated passages to me from his celebrated work. I cannot help considering the excesses to which he pushes his system as proofs that his brain has caught the fire of insanity, as kindles the chariot wheel beneath the rapidity of its motion. I have often seen genius inhabit those skulls whose formation, he tells us, must preclude its entrance; and others, in which, according to his rules, there is room for it to grow and expand, full of nothing but the most low and trivial ideas. It is remarkable that this city has in the same period given birth to a painter and physiognomist, whose talents resemble each other so much in sublime extravagance and delirious greatness—Fuseli's pictures are in general as mad as Lavater's philosophy. However, if I am not a convert to Lavater's system, I am a warm admirer of his virtues. But I will not send him my profile, for my head is flat and broad, the space between my forehead and the back part of my head consequently very contracted; he would set me down for an absolute idiot.

Cizos is settled at Manchester. I wish he may prosper better there than with us; but I fear the instability of his disposition. The ingenious and highly-benevolent Doctor Percival, of that town, warmly patronises him. At present, however, he has a strange scheme in his head—that of reading public lectures on the science of music. Doctor P. encourages him, who, not knowing music himself, has no idea, I suppose, how limited and incompetent must be any man's knowledge of that abstruse art, who took it up only at leisure hours, between twenty and twenty-five. Music has ever been the will-o'-the-wisp in Cizos' brain: besides, however wonderfully well he speaks English for a Frenchman, it will never do for public oratory on any subject; and had he the knowledge of a Handel, and the eloquence of a Rousseau, what could he rationally hope from such talents, exerted amidst a set of Manchester tradesmen, some of whom play tolerably well on the flute and the fiddle?

And now, dear Edwy, my worthless letter must have an end. I hope and trust it will reach you safely. You will value it as a memorial of my true and lively amity—so much yours and Mrs. Whalley's,—yes, with all the fervour with which it is capable!

A. SEWARD.

P.S.—My father and Giovanni send their affectionate compliments.

I forgot to observe, that your history of the poor old cottager, pining and half-starved amidst his little fruitful domain, through the tyranny of taxation, is excessively pathetic. It must, indeed, have a melancholy tendency to repress the glow of benevolent hope for the continental cottagers. It is not yet quite so bad with us.

END OF THE FIRST VOLUME.

CPSIA information can be obtained
at www.ICGtesting.com
Printed in the USA
LVHW110759120522
718525LV00003B/21

9 783375 000974